PRAISE FOR *The Radiant City*

Finalist for the Rogers Writers Trust of Canada Fiction Prize

"With extraordinary compassion, insight, and intelligence, Davis illuminates the human aftershocks of senseless violence and in that cold light, somehow, astonishingly, rekindles hope."
—Merilyn Simonds, author of *The Convict Lover* and *The Holding*

"I cannot imagine a more timely and relevant novel." — Robert Adams

THE RADIANT CITY IS A STARRED REVIEW IN *QUILL & QUIRE*: "Superb... [*The Radiant City*] is engrossing and convincing... packed with smells and sounds and street argot, the minutiae and contradictions of Paris life. Davis's question here is how can human beings look into a heart of darkness... and crawl back to the light again?"

THE GLOBE AND MAIL SAYS: "*The Radiant City* shines. [A]thoughtful, complex, meditative...brilliant novel."

THE MONTREAL GAZETTE SAYS: "*The Radiant City* is a compelling read, sociologically informed, dark in its subject matter yet illuminating in its insight... first rate ... left us craving more."

THE PARIS VOICE SAYS: "Lauren B. Davis evokes a Paris that is decidedly on the edge ... a cohesive, beautiful, and stunningly realistic portrait of life on the fringes of the City of Light, far away from the haute couture and tourist destinations that fiction about Paris is known for. ... While the book certainly delves deeply into the trauma of war - and Davis should be commended on her excellent research on the subject - *The Radiant City* is at the heart a novel about recapturing a sense of wonder and belonging.

BOOKS IN CANADA SAYS: "It's difficult to put the book down.... gripping cinematic progression . . . the fragmentation and bareness of the prose slices past the wafer-thin charm of surfaces to reveal a deeper reality: the truth of lives undone by violence. The writing communicates with precision and mediacy, and has a cumulative impact. Mer recipe to evoke a sureness of place and time that doesn't flinch from the rawness that fo neutral and indifferent." We can't afford to l tant revelation of all. "

THE WINNIPEG FREE PRESS SAYS: ". . . a starkly realistic story of friendship, courage and the effects of violence on the human spirit. Davis's taut, unadorned narrative breathes life into the characters... poignant ...this novel will resonate in the minds of many readers."

THE VANCOUVER SUN SAYS: "In this moody, exciting, clever novel, people hit the streets of the real [Paris] city neighborhoods . There are new things under the sun... For those who still think life in Paris happens on the Left Bank, *The Radiant City* is quite an update... Paris as a microcosm for the international movements of people who have been expelled from, or have chosen to leave, their homes..."

THE TORONTO SUN SAYS: ". . . a startlingly good novel about suffering and redemption. . . . memorable characters . . . A powerful and well-written story."

PRAISE FOR *The Stubborn Season*

"A gleaming debut ... a terrific first novel ... compelling social history ... This is a wonderful novel ... every character is sincerely drawn; these sentences just gleam. *The Stubborn Season* is one of those rare novels I look forward to reading again." — *The Toronto Star*

"Davis' portrayal of her [Margaret's] descent into madness is particularly moving. It's a tall order for one novel, a very ambitious undertaking for Davis. The story stays tight, with all of the subplots fully played out without detracting from the novel's main focus." —*http://womenwriters.about.com*

"*The Stubborn Season* raises the bar for first novels." — *The Gazette* (Montreal)

"Lauren B. Davis's *The Stubborn Season* ranges through a wide landscape of history and intimacy, thwarted private dreams and public oppression ... a skilful weaving of emotion and event ... poignant and well-crafted. [*The Stubborn Season* is] an epiphanic hourglass for the harsh dust that trickled through one of the worst of times." — *The Globe and Mail*

"Lauren Davis's debut novel, *The Stubborn Season*, is as close as you'd want to get to the Depression without being there ... meticulous research informs everything ... The writing is clean, direct, and efficient ... " — *Quill & Quire*

OUR DAILY BREAD

BREAD

A NOVEL

BY

LAUREN B. DAVIS

PRE-PUBLICATION GALLEY PROOF
RELEASE DATE: OCTOBER 1, 2011

There are only two kinds of people in the world; those who believe there are two kinds of people in the world, and those who don't.
— Robert Benchley's Law of Distinction

Hain't we got all the fools in town on our side?
And hain't that a big enough majority in any town?
— Mark Twain, *Huckleberry Finn*

La Grande, OR • 2011

ISBN: 978-1-877655-72-2
Library of Congress Number: 2011928120

First Trade Paperback Edition: October 1,2011
Cover Design: Kristin Summers, redbat design
Cover Art: iStockPhoto.com
Photo of Boy Scout Whistle: Ron Davis
Author Photo: Helen Tansey

Published by
Wordcraft of Oregon, LLC
David Memmott, Editor
PO Box 3235
La Grande, OR 97850
http://www.wordcraftoforegon.com

For media and event inquiries,
pleast contact Jocelyn Kelly
jocelyn@kelleyandhall.com

Wordcraft of Oregon, LLC, is a member
of the Council of Literary Magazines and Presses (CLMP)

Text set in Adobe Garamond Premier Pro
with titles in Trajan Pro

Printed in the U.S.A.

This book is dedicated to the children, like those of the Goler Clan, whose pleas fall on deaf ears.

CHAPTER ONE

"Satan draws the soul to sin by choosing wicked company.
'Do not be deceived; evil company corrupts good habits.'
*Corinthians 15, verse 33. I say to you you shall not suffer
yourself to dwell among the wicked, nor shall you permit
them to dwell among you, lest you become one of them.
You shall cast them out, as you would a wolf among the
sheep. Send them out, I say, to live in the wild places of their
wickedness, like wolves in the barren mountains. Suffer not
the sinners to taint the peaceful valley, where the righteous
dwell."* — **Reverend Edward Johns, Gideon, Church of
Christ Returning, 1794**

Near the top of North Mountain a tumbledown shed leaned against
an old lightning-struck oak at the edge of a raggedy field. Inside,
Albert Erskine bent over a sprouting box and gently, methodically,
planted the marijuana seeds he'd soaked last night. He placed each one
half an inch deep in the soil-filled paper cups, pushing the seed down
with his index finger, the nail black-rimmed. The air, hazy with dust
motes, smelled of warm moldy earth mixed with the fertilizer he used in
the sprouting mix. The seeds had been perfect, virile, and had given off
a good solid crack when he'd tested them on a hot frying pan. Once the
seeds were settled in their nest of humus, soil, sand and fertilizer, he'd
water them and leave them in the locked shed under a grow-light fueled
by a small generator. Later, in a couple of weeks, he'd plant the seedlings
out in the field. In the meantime he'd prepare the field with hydrated lime
and a little water soluble nitrogen fertilizer.

Growing a good cash crop of marijuana took smarts and Albert was
well aware of how smart he was. He knew, too, the potwer of his physical
prescence. He would have been called handsome in another place, with
the cleft of his chin, and the furious shine in his brown eyes. Even as a
whip-thin, lock-jawed boy there had been something about Albert, some
flash of sinewy grace.

Albert finished up, locked the shed with a bicycle chain and combination lock and headed back to the compound. It was a couple of miles through the woods, up and down and slipping sometimes on the spring-mucky ground, but he didn't mind. It was quiet out here, except for the song of the cat-bird and the early robin.

Halfway to the compound he skirted around the slope, coming up on an old trailer from the low side so he wouldn't be as easy to spot. He paused at the edge of a clearing. The uncles, Dan, Lloyd and Ray, were paranoid bastards at the best of times. Albert knew he should just keep clear of whatever they were up to in there, but yesterday his little brother, Jack, told him the uncles had started a cooking operation. Albert couldn't believe even they would be that stupid; he had to see for himself.

The rusty, partly-yellow trailer tilted on its blocks. The windows were covered with tin foil. The breeze shifted and the scent of something sickly sweet wafted toward him. And something else...ammonia? Jesus. Albert crept to a stand of trees closer to the trailer to get a better look. A small pile of rubbish lay half-hidden under some branches. Used coffee filters. Part of an old car battery. Drain cleaner. Dozens of empty cold remedy packets. If things had been bad on the mountain before, Albert suspected they were about to get worse. Much worse. Meth made everything worse.

"What you doing up here, Bert?"

Albert swung round. At the edge of the tree line, Ray, a shriveled, short man smiled at him over the barrel of a rifle. His teeth were brown stubs, and his close-set eyes glittered with malice. Uncle Ray might not be a big man, but even among the Erskines his temper was legendary. He'd beat his wife, Meg, so bad she had convulsions, and when his son, Billy, didn't have a black eye, he had a split lip or another missing tooth.

"Just getting my seeds ready for planting." Albert made sure he kept his voice steady. "Good day for it."

"Field's nowhere near here, now is it?" Ray shrugged the rifle closer in on his shoulder.

Behind Albert, the trailer door opened. "What's this then?" It was Lloyd's voice. "Ray, now, put that rifle down. Ain't nothing but Bert."

Ray did not lower the rifle. "He's spying on us."

Although Albert didn't like the idea of turning his back on Ray, he glanced over his shoulder. Lloyd, his dark hair and beard bleeding together in a shaggy mass, wore a plaid lumber jacket. His jeans drooped below his boulder of a belly. He stretched as though he'd been hunched over something and his back was cramped.

"Hey, Lloyd."

"That right, Bert?" said Lloyd. "You spying?"

"Just rambling."

Lloyd spat and stepped down from the trailer's cinderblock step. "Bullshit."

Albert stepped to the side so he could keep both men in his sights.

"Don't take another step," said Ray.

Lloyd was now within arm's reach. He scratched his beard. "You know, Bert, you are a mystery. You don't act like family at all now, do you? Don't come visiting. Live in your little shack. Course maybe you have your own parties. That it? You have the kids come see you? That's not hardly sociable, now is it? You got your own little weed-growing business going and we leave you alone with that don't we? We let you have your way there, ain't that true?"

"I think I'm generous," said Albert. "You get your taste."

Ray laughed. "You're generous? That's rich. This is Harold's fucking mountain, Albert. You breathe because Harold says you breathe."

"The point is," said Lloyd," you live like you don't want to be an Erskine, and that ain't right. Makes us think, especially when we find you snaking around like this. Nope. I don't think Harold's gonna like this at all."

"You do what you gotta do, Lloyd, but I'm telling you, nothing good's gonna come from—"

Lloyd's fist shot out. Albert crumpled to his knees, gasping for breath. It felt like he'd been hit with a pile driver. He struggled to keep his eyes open and watched Ray's boot travel in slow motion to his head. He rolled and the kick landed on his shoulder, another landed on his kidney.

Lloyd bent down, put his meaty hand under Albert's chin and twisted it so they were eye to eye. "Albert, you need to watch yourself, boy. You're Erskine. You're family. We take care of family, don't we, Ray?"

"We sure do."

Albert heard a zipper and felt something wet and warm spray on his legs. He wrenched his face away from Lloyd, kicked out and squirmed away from the urine stream.

"That's enough, Ray, put yer pecker away. Now, you get on back to that little shack of yours, Bert, and remember who you are. All right now, say it with me. Erskines don't . . ."

"Talk," he croaked.

"And Erskines don't . . ."

"Leave."

"Good boy," said Lloyd, and he pulled Albert to his feet. "Now, get on back where you belong."

It took half an hour to reach the compound. Albert made his way past the old outhouse. Bastards. One of these days he'd show them. His shoulder and back ached. He smelled Ray's piss. He slapped at a cloud of gnats. That's what the Erskines were: a cloud of biting gnats. No matter how you swatted at them, they reformed and came at you again.

A few minutes later he came on the cabin his mother Gloria lived in with whatever man she was shacking up with, and Albert's brother and sister, Jack and Jill, and Kenny, Jill's son. Smoke slithered out of the rusty chimney, so somebody was probably inside, but he kept going. Gloria had never been a source of comfort.

He veered toward the back of Harold and Fat Felicity's tin-roofed gray-sided three-room main house on which the compound centered. Harold and Felicity's grown children, simple-minded Sonny, Carrie and Carrie's son, Little Joe, lived there, too, as did an ever-revolving stream of uncles and cousins and other assorted Erskine flotsam. A pair of shutters hung on one of the windows. The shutters and the door had once been painted red, but all were faded and peeled now, as much gray as red. The top half of the door held three panes of glass and one of plywood. There were no curtains on the windows, and under the porch canopy rested a spring-sprung couch. Next to the house sprawled a pile of garbage: disposable diapers; plastic bags which rose up in the wind and festooned the trees, hanging on the branches like pale shredded skin; empty bottles of various kinds, some soda, but mostly beer, wine and bourbon; used sanitary napkins; a stained and swollen mattress; the twisted wheel of a bicycle, the spokes sharp and defensive-looking; a small refrigerator Uncle Dan had dragged home from the dump thinking he could fix, but with which he'd become bored after a day and there it lay on its side, its door gaping; various household objects—a bent spoon, a broken cup and three plates, an old brown-stained pillow where mice now nested; two shoes, not matching.

Scanning the house for signs of life, Albert caught a glimpse of

Sonny in the front window, waving. He waved back and Sonny smiled and picked his nose. Albert crossed the dirt and ignored Grunter III, the huge brown and tan mongrel who crawled out from under the house and sidestepped over to him, wanting a scratch behind the ears, but fearing a kick. A sympathetic desire, perhaps, but Albert was in no mood.

Six-year old club-footed Brenda, one of Lloyd's kids, stood on an old bucket and looked in a back window. She wore a boy's jacket over a filthy pink nightgown, and a pair of rubber boots several sizes too large, to accommodate her twisted left foot. She'd been in need of a bath several weeks ago. Albert knew what she was probably seeing in there, and he knew if she got caught she'd get a worse beating than he just got. If he called out he'd just scare her and she'd make a noise and then they'd both be in for it. He should just walk away and let whatever was going to happen go right on and happen. Erskine's don't talk, and Erskine's don't leave, and Erskine's better mind their own fucking business. She turned then, and looked at him, tears pouring down her face.

Brenda watched him come near, wiped her nose with her palm and then turned back to the window. Albert put his hand on her shoulder, and his head next to hers. The window was smoky with grime. Inside, a bare bulb hung from the ceiling. Dan sat on the side of the bed, wearing only a stained undershirt. His head was tilted back, his eyes were closed and his mouth was open and slack. Between his legs knelt Brenda's little brother, Frank. Dan cupped the boy's head and moved it back and forth. The child's hands flailed weakly.

Time peeled away, fled backwards and Albert was six years old again, his mouth full, gagging, the stench and the sound of moans, his own flesh tearing . . . bile rushed acidly into his mouth. His hands shook. His knees shook. He turned away. Spit. Spit again. One of these days, he was going to do it. He'd get his rifle and put an end to the Erskines, all of them.

"Down," Brenda said.

Albert lifted her off the bucket and watched her hobble off into the woods. He stomped across the yard, passing the plywood-covered well, and as he did he looked back at the front of the house. Old Harold stood on the tilting porch. He wore the same stained and smudged grey overalls he always wore, and the same John Deere cap. He was a big man, with a barrel chest, and if his arms were oddly short, they were thick with muscle, even though Old Harold had to be in his seventies. White stubble showed on his sagging features and his bulbous red nose was an explosion of broken blood vessels. His small, deep-set eyes—wolfish and keen—tracked Albert across the dirt.

"You come visiting, Bert?"

"Just heading back to mine," said Albert.

"That's not very sociable. Not right for relations to keep so distant. Come on in."

"Not today," said Albert.

"Be seeing you then. I'm watching you, boy."

Albert felt Old Harold's eyes on him until he ducked into the tree line and walked the short, but crucial, distance to his own place.

Three years ago, Albert had built a sparsely insulated, one-door, two-window cabin from materials liberated from building sites and scrounged from junk yards. The roof was lower by a good foot and a half on one side, no running water and no electricity, but it kept the rain off and mostly it kept out the cold. He pulled the string with the key on it from around his neck and unlocked the padlock. Inside, he tossed a log into the black potbelly and jostled the log to make sure it caught on the embers. When he was sure it blazed, he flopped down on the mouse-chewed brown corduroy couch that folded out into a bed. Photos of naked women, some astride motorcycles, papered the walls. On the floor were boxes of books and a stack of tattered paperbacks – *Lord of the Rings, Catcher in the Rye, Tom Sawyer, Lord of the Flies*. A sink drained through a pipe directly into a pile of gravel a few feet from the cabin, and over the sink was a shelf with a few canned goods, crackers and a box of corn flakes.

Albert reached under the couch for a half-full bottle of Jack Daniels, and drank. Good liquor from Wilton's Groceries and enough in the locked trunk under the window to last a man for weeks if he wanted it to last that long. No, it might not be much of a place, but it was his—a place where he was his own man. Albert drank again, wincing as the fiery liquor seared into a canker on the side of his tongue. He ran his hand down his stomach. Hard as a washboard. His arms were cut, baby, cut. He wasn't going to be another of the fat fucks up here. Two hundred push-ups every morning. One hundred chin-ups on a tree branch out back, rain or shine, winter or summer. Bring it on. Just bring it on.

He smelled the piss on his pants. "Shit," he said. He crossed the room and lifted the lid on a steel bucket in the sink. It was three-quarters full of water. It would do. He used his knife to shave slivers off the bar of soap on the counter, stripped off his pants and dumped them in the bucket.

Half an hour later there was a knock on the door. Not loud. A small, safe knock.

"Come on," he said.

Ten-year-old Toots shuffled in wearing a too-big duffle coat, her sullen, sharp-featured little face hidden behind a curtain of greasy hair, her skinny legs bare and scratched above the rubber boots.

"Put some pants on, will ya," she said, not moving too far from the door.

"Just washing mine out, don't worry." From where he sat on the couch Albert leaned over and pulled a pair of sweat pants from a small pile of clothes on the floor. As he was putting them on he said, "Dan's got hold of Frank."

"Yeah, I know. I won the mailbox race today. Felicity said I could run for Brenda, too."

The mailbox race—first kid to the mailbox and back won a day without having to be "nice." Kids learned to run awful fast. Albert could have won a fucking gold medal for sprinting.

"You run fast," said Albert. He sat back down on the fold-out bed and took a long draw from the bottle.

"Harold says you got any booze?"

"That what you're here for?"

"Harold said I had to come ask you."

"They drinking down there?"

"You're drinking, too."

"So?"

"I'm just saying." Toots folded her arms with her hands up the sleeves of her coat, scratching her elbows. "What you got to eat?" she said.

He took another swig from the Jack and guilt wriggled into his bloodstream with the booze. He was the oldest of his generation. He should have stolen cans of beans or something—soup or crackers. The younger kids looked to him: Little Joe, Toots, Frank, Griff, Brenda, Cathy, and Kenny. What was less clear was the nature of that responsibility, up here where the view was like heaven and the living was like hell.

He looked at the calendar on the wall, the one with the picture of the earth taken from space. Six days to go until the first of the month and the welfare checks. They'd be down to ketchup soup at the house.

13

"I got a couple jars of peanut butter." "Where?" Toots said, scanning his shelves. "You got any bread?"

Albert got up and went to a wooden box by the back window. He pulled out two jars of extra crunchy peanut butter and turned to the little girl. "No bread, sorry."

She grabbed the jars and stuffed them under her coat.

"You got no manners? You don't say 'thank you'?"

"Yeah, right. Thanks." She glared at him from beneath her dirty hair. "What about the bottle for The Others?" She used the kids' name for the adults.

He regarded her, skinny and defiant, practically feral, and so smart. What would she be like, if she'd been raised in some other place? It was a question he asked too often, this great *what if?* And it was always prodded along by the desire to get the hell out—the great lurching, gut-squalling impulse to grab a couple of kids and run for the city. But a *couple?* Toots and . . . who? How the fuck could you take a couple and leave the rest? How did you choose? He had no money, no schooling, and no skills. How would they live in the world beyond? Besides, Erskines don't leave. They were probably all fucking damned anyway. Erskines, for better or worse, stuck together. They'd drilled the code into his head since before he could remember. Nobody talks. Nobody leaves. Seems it didn't matter how big Albert got, how grown he was, Harold would always be bigger, and meaner.

"Where are the kids?"

"Gone to the woods. Kenny and Frank are inside."

"Kenny, too, huh? You going to the woods?"

"Can I stay here?"

"I'm drinking, too, aren't I?"

"You're not much good then, are ya?" She looked at him for the first time and her eyes were razors. "Not when you're drinking."

"Smart kid." He raised the bottle, turned away from her eyes. "Tell Harold to go fuck himself."

"You tell him," she said. "I'm going into the woods."

And she was gone then, like some scrawny forest sprite. She was fast, that one.

"Shit," he said to the pictures on the walls. Albert considered ignoring the demand, but they might come up and take what they wanted. They'd

14

clean him out if they found his stash, and God only knows what Ray and Lloyd were saying. He took a couple of bottles out of the trunk.

Albert stood in the middle of his cabin. He sure as shit didn't want to go up to the house, but what choice did he have? He ground his teeth and his knuckles whitened around the bottle necks. Wasn't there anybody on his side? Surrounded as he was by kin—practically drowning in them—there wasn't a single person Albert could call 'friend'.

CHAPTER TWO

When Tom Evans finally pulled into his driveway, the clouds had cleared and high noon did the yard no favours. There hadn't been much snow this year, and what came went again in odd thaws. The patchy grass looked as though it had mange and the big maple had lost two limbs in thunderstorms the previous summer, leaving jagged, angry-looking amputations. He'd probably have to cut it down next year. Shame. It had been there since he was seven. He remembered planting the sapling with his father, the way the earth had smelled that day, rich and loamy and entirely unlike the slightly rotting mixture of leaves and dog shit the yard gave off this morning. He remembered the way his father's biceps had bulged as he wrestled the root ball into the ground. If the old maple finally gave up the ghost, maybe Tom could plant something with Bobby, make it a new memory. The house looked a bit the worse for wear as well; could use a new coat of paint. His father would have been horrified. Robert Evans had built this house for his bride, with no help from anyone, neither plumber nor electrician nor roofer, which was the way he was. It was a sturdy, no-nonsense house, with a small attic and a wide porch, which was also the way Robert Evans was. No storm could damage a house like that, or so it had seemed to Tom growing up. The screen on the living room window was torn. Well, he thought as he jogged up the steps, this weekend for sure.

He entered the house and stepped over a mound of shoes and boots inside the front door. In the living room, unfolded laundry overflowed a tattered wicker basket on the couch. Rascal, the black and white mongrel, rose up from his bed atop a scatter of loose CDs and their plastic cases. The dog stretched, extending his claws into the discs. The resultant scrape set Tom's teeth on edge. A cartoon of the roadrunner and the coyote flickered on the television, but the sound was turned down. He walked toward the sound of running water and clattering plates coming from the kitchen.

Patty stood at the sink rinsing off dishes. She had her jacket on, the blue and white striped smock Wilton's Groceries made all their cashiers wear hanging below it. Tom picked up a piece of toast that had fallen to the floor in the morning's mayhem. He bent down to kiss the back of his wife's neck. She smelled of patchouli and lemony soap. A reddish-gold curl escaped from where she had gathered it, messily, enticingly, atop her head. He aimed for a tiny brown mole.

She shrieked and jumped back, a wooden spoon in her hand, ready to clout him. "Shit, Tom. You scared me!"

His lips were frozen in mid-pucker. Her face was a mix of rage and shock that seemed excessive. "Sorry. I thought you heard me," he said. Tom Evans had a voice so deep Patty said it was a well in need of an echo. It fit his size, for he was all shoulders and arms, kept strong from the flats of bread he slung around as if they were no heavier than paper and meringue. Patty was forever telling him to be careful of things he might break without realizing it. When Ivy and Bobby were small and he'd held their wrists and swung them round in circles, she said, "You'll dislocate their shoulders. You'll bash their brains out against a wall." But the children just laughed and laughed and asked for more. When Ivy was nothing more than a diaper with a big pair of brown eyes he'd bounced her on his palm, like a quarter he was flipping, and even though Patty had said nothing, he caught her looking at him now and then, her pale brows drawn in disapprovingly. Whether from a fear he'd drop the baby or from a dislike of roughhousing in general, he never could decide. Of course, at ten and fifteen respectively, Ivy and Bobby were too big for that now. But even when they were babies, Tom had never understood why Patty didn't know how careful he was with them. He would never do anything to put his children in harm's way. They were everything to him. They were the miracles of his life, as was Patty. The miracles that changed everything, forever.

Now, she stared at him with that look of irritation he was, sadly, becoming accustomed to. She wiped her bangs off her forehead with the hand still holding the wooden spoon. A dribble of water fell from the cuff of the pink rubber gloves she wore, staining the front of her suede jacket. She looked down at it and then up at him. "You're late."

"Yeah, The Indian Head said I got the order wrong and Dave wanted to have an argument."

"I thought the motel cancelled delivery."

"They started up again." He leaned in to kiss her, but it was a clumsy move and he mostly kissed her nose. "Maybe things are going better over there."

"Who eats at a motel?"

"I don't know. People who stay there."

She turned back to the sink. "Who stays at a cheap motel in a pissy little town like this in March?"

"I don't know. It's on the highway. Truckers. Salesmen, I guess." Tom was unsure why they were having this conversation. He put his arms around her, kissed that place on her neck. "Kids all right this morning?"

"As alright as they ever are. Sniping at each other. Bickering. Bobby hardly speaks. I don't know any of his friends. There's something wrong with that boy."

"He's fifteen, that's what's wrong with him." Tom chuckled. Bobby was a little surly, but what teenage boy wasn't?

"I don't see what's funny about it. And Ivy's so prissy." Patty frowned. "They're so different."

"Why don't you leave that? I'll do it."

Patty peeled off the gloves and draped them over the faucet. She turned in his arms and kissed him. She tasted pleasantly of coffee and toast. "I hate you working these hours. We're all out of kilter. We never do anything together."

"What can I do? Work's work."

"You leave in the middle of the night. It always feels like you're sneaking out. And I hate waking up to an empty bed. You know that. I get lonely."

"It's work, Patty."

"So you said. Isn't there anything else?"

"We've been through this. When the warm weather comes I can try and get logging work, or maybe landscaping, but if I do we lose the benefits I get with Pollack's."

"Logging's no good. You'd be off in a camp. Why do you say logging?"

"I'm just laying out the options. There's Kroeler's, they might be hiring, I heard."

"A paint factory? All those chemicals? Oh, that's a *fine* idea. I don't want you logging, Tom. It's too dangerous. Look at Greg Keane." Greg Keane's right arm was crushed and had to be amputated after a steel bind-wire snapped on one of the trucks and he got caught when the load shifted.

"Accidents happen everywhere, Patty. You grew up on a farm. You know that." Forklifts, highway accidents, machinery—an endless possibility of industrial accidents. He often wondered how the world looked to white collar workers, who had board room barracudas to fear, rather than tractors and folding cultivators and chain saws.

Patty pulled away and shuffled through a pile of unopened bills on the counter. "That fucking commune could hardly be called a farm. Where are my keys?"

"On the hook by the door."

"I'm going to be late."

He walked her to the door and grabbed her elbow as she stepped out, pulling her back to him. "Don't worry so much, babe. We're doing fine."

"Are we?" Her face searched his. "At least you like your job. I hate mine."

"Since when? I thought you wanted to work."

"I wanted to get out of this house. But Wilton's? Jesus, what a bore."

"Well, I don't know . . . quit then." He ran his hands through his hair. "We got by before you worked. We'll get by again."

"Getting by. What a life."

"I'm doing the best I can."

She put her small hand up to the side of his face. "You need a shave," she said, and kissed him good-bye.

He stood on the porch, with his hands deep in his pants pockets, watching her drive off. The old Chevy pickup, bought second hand six years ago, rattled and shook, then settled. Patty waved and he waved back. He kept his eyes on the truck as it moved down the street. In all the years since he'd first seen her, there was this one constant thing: he loved her so much it scared him, for the world was harsh and jagged. Rascal came out onto the porch and stood there wagging his long tail. The dog whined and cocked his head. Barked sharply, inquiringly. Tom bent down and scratched his ear. The dog leaned into his leg and whined again.

"They forgot to feed you, huh? Well, I can fix that, I guess." He went back into the house and closed the door behind him. On the silent television, the roadrunner had just tricked the coyote into stepping off a high mesa and his legs spun frantically for a few seconds before he looked balefully at the viewer and then plunged to his death, which was never quite a death after all.

CHAPTER THREE

The Church of Christ Returning was a cavernous room and, even festooned with white banners adorned with gold crosses, it still looked like the warehouse it used to be. Two, perhaps three hundred, shiny-faced, well-groomed worshippers filled row upon row of white folding chairs set up on the concrete floor. Outside, the day was raw and sleety, gray as dirty wool. The air inside was slightly too warm, and heavily scented with a mixture of flowery-sweet perfume, hairspray and coffee-breath. A large podium accommodated Reverend Ken Hickland and his wife, Stella, as well as the visiting pastor Bobby Dash, Reverend Dash's wife, Carolyn, and an enthusiastic, if not entirely tuneful, choir. Dorothy Carlisle looked around at the people holding hands, swaying, their eyes closed. She wondered if there was a required uniform women were supposed to wear at The Church of Christ Returning these days. Certainly, she seemed to be the only woman not wearing a pastel pantsuit over a frilly blouse. Well, to be fair there were several frilly blouse-skirt combinations and a couple of frilly dresses. Still, it seemed an inordinate amount of frill, and a quite unnecessary quantity of pastel, particularly for this time of year. Dorothy herself was dressed in black pants, a copper blouse, and a taupe wrap, which she felt was the appropriate attire not only for March, but for a woman of sixty-two. Certainly far more appropriate than the garden-party attire of Mabel McQuaid, to her left, who was in fact slightly older than Dorothy, although she wouldn't admit it. Mabel squeezed her hand, as if aware of Dorothy's unchristian thoughts.

Reverend Hickland's voice boomed over the PA system. "When I see these terrorists, I know Satan is at work. He has made himself manifest in the false prophets of the world. But I tell you, Satan is in a mess. He's frightened, frightened because so many Muslims are turning to Jesus." Reverend Hickland wore his trademark white suit and shoes and belt. He stomped his foot and looked heavenward. "Yes, praise the Lord!"

"Praise the Lord," came the congregation's respondent cry.

"Oh, yes! Satan is stirring up the Muslims, but we are winning. How do I know we're winning? I know because that's what the back of the Book says!"

"Praise the Lord!"

The band and the choir kicked up a notch, the drum beat steady and penetrating, and the voices rhythmic. Dorothy gently released her hand from Mabel's fleshy, overly-firm grip. "Arthritis," she said, rubbing her fingers, when Mabel looked questioningly at her. Although mortifying to admit, possibly simple curiosity had made Dorothy agree to attend this morning's service at the all new and improved Church of Christ Returning. What did people see in all this emotion and hysteria?

Dorothy Carlisle had a deep faith that an ineffable God existed, but believed there was no need for so much, well, thrashing about. All this praising, weeping, and squeezing of hands was not only a little embarrassing, but felt inauthentic. As though these people, swaying now, some of them rocking back and forth, tears on their cheeks, hands reaching heavenward, were looking not for the solace of Christ, but for some sort of slightly questionable ecstatic experience. The expression on some of her neighbors' faces was vaguely sexual.

The Church of Christ Returning, whether in this new building, or in the old clapboard in town, had always been at the center of Gideon, the heart of its beliefs and behavior. Members of other faiths would surely be locked out of heaven due to their lack of a true, intimate, personal relationship with Jesus—a Jesus who apparently had gone before them to build a house of very limited capacity, since there was much talk of the chosen few. A Jesus who, although he had been known to spend much quality time with prostitutes and lepers, would now, at the dawn of the millennium, damn all but the most rigidly perfect to the flames of eternal hell. A Jesus who, according to Reverend Hickland, manifested his love through the bestowing of material goods.

Dorothy supposed Mabel had wanted to show off this big new church building, all modern and vast enough for what Mabel was convinced was an oncoming tidal wave of conversions. Mabel had a bumper sticker on her car which read, *When the Rapture comes, this car will be empty.* It had taken some will power on Dorothy's part not to stick a note on Mabel's windshield saying, *If you're not using it, do you mind if I have it?*

Pastor Dash was speaking now. "When I started going to Africa over thirty years ago, I saw people living in desperation, in mud huts in abject poverty, and I told them they were not the Third World. No sir. They were the seeds of Abraham! Seeds of the Lord! Jesus is exploding all over the world! Praise the Lord!"

"Praise the Lord!"

"And now these people are driving cars, living in good houses, going to school. That's what Jesus promises—it's there in Ephesians, verse 3... *hath blessed us with every spiritual blessing in the heavenly places. . .* 'hath' people, that's the way of saying he already has. It's a done deal. We are empowered with all there is in heaven, already. It's waiting for us."

"Praise Him! Praise the Lord."

"And look now at Genesis 1." The Reverend had the book open in his hand and stalked from one end of the stage to the other. "God tells us man is made in His image, and he says 'let them rule over the fish of the sea and over the birds of the sky'. He says man has dominion over all the earth, and he tells man to subdue it, rule over it, over all the things on the earth, over every seed. It's all there for us, my brothers, my sisters. Praise the Lord."

"Praise the Lord!"

"We are the blessed. It wasn't given to the sinners! It was given to those who are in His image! A great fire will come to wipe out the sinners. It says so, my friends. It says so. Where does it say so? Tell me where!"

"In the back of the Book!" the room answered as one.

"Shout out for the Lord. Shout it out!" Reverend Hickland jumped up and down, yelling at the top of his lungs now. "Shout it out! I tell you! Shout it out!"

And much to Dorothy's alarm, the congregation did.

The next day was again miserable as a cold wet stray, Dorothy Carlisle knew there wouldn't be a single customer popping into Farmhouse Antiques and, in that regard, it was a day similar to many others. The lack of commerce did not bother Dorothy in the least. Commerce was not the point. Having a shop gave her a purpose, a place to go, and a framework for her days. She owned the old farmhouse at the corner of Quaker and Main outright, and had done so for years. Oh, there were a few sales—bridal gifts, or tokens for aunts, or the odd chair or tea table; and sometimes antiquing tourists wandered through. She even had a couple of contacts from the city who visited her once every six months or so to see if she had anything interesting they might pick up for themselves and sell at engorged prices to the urban rich. Once a year she took a drive for a few days, poking around attics and barns for interesting bits and bobs, but other than that, and regular dusting, very little upkeep was required.

It was just gone noon and although she would have to think about lunch soon, Dorothy poured herself a cup of coffee. It was decaffeinated coffee with a hint of cinnamon, which she thickened with half-and-half and sweetened with two teaspoons of sugar. On the side of the mug was a line drawing of Virginia Woolf and a quote: *You cannot gain peace by avoiding life.* Dorothy stood for a moment, holding the mug with both hands, inhaling the fragrance, which was at once both comforting and stimulating. She made a point of paying attention to such small details of life. Noticing, being grateful for, acknowledging beauty, these things gave meaning to life, did they not? She agreed with Virginia's quote. An elegant life was lived by immersion in the quotidian, by honoring creation with awareness.

As she crossed the creaky wooden floor to her desk, she flipped the door sign. The Farm House Antiques was officially open. One of the great benefits of being your own boss was that you got to keep your own hours. Dorothy adjusted the position of a cobalt blue glass bottle, placing it closer to the sweet little milk-glass vase on the Shaker ministry table. They set each other off so nicely, they were a pleasure just to look at. She particularly loved the lines of Shaker furniture. So simple. So uncluttered by unnecessary ornamentation – a thing reduced to its essence.

Dorothy settled into her old Boston rocker, dialed the radio to the public classical station, and opened Silas Marner to chapter sixteen, in which Aaron will offer to dig a garden for Eppie. She sipped her coffee and turned in happy anticipation to the page. However, the door rattled and she looked up, frowning. It was Mabel. Mabel owned Mabel's Gifts, around the corner on Main Street and sold what Dorothy judged were trinkets of dubious value: bean soup gift sets, blank-page books with embossed leather covers—so fancy one would be terrified to scar them with a single unworthy musing—chemically scented candles of sneeze-inducing intensity, papier-mâché parrot earrings, Tee shirts with sayings on them such as, *Give me the chocolate and nobody gets hurt.*

"Hello, Mabel." Dorothy did not rise. Oh, Lord, she prayed, please don't start her talking about church. Dorothy was still not quite over the unsettling image of Mabel McQuaid calling out to the Lord and babbling in a rhythmic jibber-jabber she referred to as speaking-in-tongues. Mabel, in fact, had not been at all pleased yesterday when, after the service, Dorothy asked her why angels didn't just speak in a language one could understand?

"Hideous weather," said Mabel, by way of greeting. She was a large woman who walked with a swaying side-to-side gait that bespoke bad knees and hips.

"How are you?" Dorothy regretted the question as soon as it was out of her mouth.

"Are you kidding?" Mabel rubbed her right hand. "With this weather? I couldn't even get the jar of coffee open this morning the rheumatism in my hands was so bad. And since I don't sleep anymore, I need my coffee in the morning." Mabel flapped her umbrella, scattering water droplets all around her.

Dorothy considered offering her a cup, but then didn't.

"So, did you hear?" said Mabel. "There's been a break-in at Wilton's."

"Really? How dreadful. A robbery?"

"Not during store hours. It was last night after closing sometime. I told Bob he should put in an alarm system. They got a few thousand I heard and took a bunch of liquor and cigarettes and junk food, which means only one thing as far as I'm concerned and you know what that is."

"Do I?"

"It means North Mountain people. Come on, Dot, those hill goats will be drunk for a week and then they'll come in to buy more and that's all I need to know. Erskines, most likely. They're nothing but white trash. I don't know why Carl just doesn't go up there and arrest the bunch of them."

"I'm sure Carl's doing his job. You can't arrest people on speculation." On *prejudice* she wanted to say. "If he finds proof he'll do what needs to be done."

"I guess you're right. What can you do? That's the mountain. Can't do anything with that bunch. But you lock your doors. You're a woman in here alone and you need to be careful." Mabel folded her arms over her substantial bosom. "I don't know why you even keep this place. You sure don't need the money."

"I appreciate your concern, Mabel. I'll be sure to be vigilant." She sighed. "Remember when we used to leave all our doors unlocked?"

"Times change. You just can't be too careful. It's dangerous times before the end."

"I refuse to live my life in a prison of fear," said Dorothy.

"Fine. Don't say I didn't warn you. Just lock your doors, will you?" She flapped her umbrella again and as she left, said over her shoulder, "It's going to get worse before it gets better. You heard what Reverend Hickland said at church, Dot. You can't ignore the signs."

"You and I will just have to differ on this point, I'm afraid."

"I was so happy when you came to church." Her voice was petulant now, disappointed as a child. "I'm very fond of you. I don't want to see you left behind."

"It was lovely of you to ask me. Really it was. And I do appreciate it. You've all done wonders with the new church."

"I hope you'll come back this Sunday."

"Hope springs eternal, but I fear I must insist on being left behind." Dorothy couldn't entirely repress a grin.

"I don't know why I bother. I really don't."

"Neither do I, dear."

"I'll pray for you," said Mabel as she left.

"We can all use more prayers," said Dorothy to the closed door.

Dorothy's coffee was cold now. She might as well make herself a grilled cheese sandwich, she thought, and headed back to the little kitchen, grumbling under her breath. Mabel McQuaid. Surely people should be made to understand that most everything was none of their business.

She wished William was still with her. He had always listened so well. But William was gone, wasn't he? When he died, she'd felt the grief and loss of her companion, her confidant—indeed her very heart—fiercely and fully, and for the first six months she couldn't bear being in the store, and so she kept it closed. Then she began to go in three days a week, and sometime around month eight she found herself humming along to a song on the radio, which made her cry a little, but she knew she would be all right. She also knew she would live the rest of her life alone, and the thought, rather than being disturbing, was deeply comforting. She still felt William was with her, in some way, as though he were simply in the next room. A stack of good books, good coffee, and her little store were all she needed. Dorothy would be snug and content in her shop, surrounded by bits of people's history, the discarded things she had rescued and restored. Burnished wood, sparkling glass, gleaming porcelain, the smell of polish and beeswax candles.

And so this afternoon passed—grilled cheese and coffee and *Silas Marner*. Around four, the wind rattled the door and she looked up again, frowning, but it was no one. Just the little Evans girl, Ivy, walking in the determined way she had, head down into the wind, gait longer than seemed possible given the length of her legs. She looked over her shoulder once, quickly, and Dorothy was struck by her unhappy expression. The voices of other children skittered on the wind, but Dorothy couldn't make out the words. Ah well, none of her business.

CHAPTER FOUR

Do you then expect that your mother would be glad to see you—that she would spread her mantle over you and take you up to heaven? Oh, if she were told that you were at the gate, she would hasten down to say, "O my sinning child, you cannot enter heaven. Into this holy place, nothing can by any means enter that **'worketh abomination or maketh a lie.'** *You cannot—no, you cannot come! If it were left to your own mother to decide the question of your admission, you could not come in. She would not open heaven's gate for your admission. She knows you would disturb the bliss of heaven. She knows you would mar its purity and be an element of discord in its sympathies and in its songs. The justice of God will not allow you to participate in the joys of the saints. His relations to the universe make it indispensable that He should protect his saints from such society as you. They have had their discipline of trial in such society long enough: the scenes of their eternal reward will bring everlasting relief from this torture of their holy sympathies. His sense of propriety forbids that He should give you a place among his pure and trustful children. It would be so unfitting—so unsuitable! It would throw such discord into the sweet songs and sympathies of the holy.* **— Reverend Charles G. Finney, President, Oberlin College, visiting preacher, Church of Christ Returning, September 29, 1852**

Albert woke with his heart already pounding. He didn't remember his dream, exactly. But it had been one of the bad ones. Some people tried to grab their dreams as they slipped under the surface of consciousness, but Albert pushed the spectres as far from his day-mind as he could. A smell remained, like gunpowder residue—acrid, but sweaty-dirty, like the breath of a man who has consumed sardines and creamed corn and beer—a familiar smell. He shook his head, blew out his lips so his breath sucked nothing of the terror back into him. The instant of waking was the only moment when one might consider Albert superstitious, when some remnant of his child-self lingered, before he stuffed it back down into The Hole, the solitary confinement of his unconscious.

Awareness of his queasy stomach and sawdust mouth slid in on the sunlight nudging through the hole in the sheet pegged over the window, even as the flickering horrors of his dream dissipated. The pillow smelled of mildew. Something crusty had dried on the blanket. He blindly reached around on the floor next to the foldout bed and found a bottle, empty.

Albert had been drunk last night. But not drunk enough. Yesterday was a shitty day. It had started off all right. Just another day with not much on his schedule except for chopping wood for the stove. He'd been using the ancient splitter near the main house when Dr. Hawthorne arrived around noon, his shiny target-red Volvo moving through the trees up the winding road to the compound. The kids appeared like tame squirrels from their various nooks and crannies, and flocked around his car. They looked like Third World beggars with their dirty hands out. Dr. Hawthorne, small and trim in his gray wool coat, stepped out of the car, his trousers tucked into rubber boots to protect them from the mud.

"Hey, now, you kids," the doctor said, smiling a white smile under his thin, carefully trimmed moustache. "You're not looking for candy, are you? You don't want to rot your teeth, do you?"

"I'm loosing a tooth," said Frank. "See?" He waggled his tongue against the wobbling incisor.

Brenda sucked on her fingers and looked up at the doctor with wide eyes. He bent down and lifted her chin with his long-fingered, girlish hands. "What's this? What's that around your mouth? Are you a dirty girl?"

"No," said Brenda. She wriggled and turned.

"Impetigo. Look at those oozy blisters." He let go of her face and looked at the rest of the children. "You'll probably all get it now." He sighed and looked long-suffering. "Such a shame. Lucky I've got antibiotic cream. I'm not sure whether I should give you treats."

"Yes, please," the children said. "Please, please, please."

"Oh, all right then." Hawthorne opened the trunk of his car and pulled out a box of granola bars. The children grabbed, ripped off the wrappers and stuffed their mouths, not caring if they consumed bits of paper with the nuts and raisins and oats.

"Greedy guts," said the doctor, pulling his black bag out of the back seat. He glanced at Albert. "Albert. How are you?"

"Good enough I don't need your treats." Albert spat through his front teeth.

"Glad to hear it. A man should be able to feed himself."

Fat Felicity opened the door of the house, her hair in greasy hanks, her housecoat stained. "What's up, doc?" she laughed.

"That never gets old, Felicity," said Hawthorne. "Thought I'd stop in and see how Carrie's getting along." Carrie had had bronchitis and couldn't stop coughing. "Are you using the cough medicine?"

"Yeah, but we don't have much left."

"You can't have gone through that already, Felicity. It's not recreational, you know." Hawthorne climbed the steps.

"Tell that to Dan. You coming in?"

"I thought I might, for a few minutes."

Griff climbed up the stairs behind him, smiling, gnawing on the last inch of his granola bar. The little boy plucked at the doctor's coat.

"You got more?" he said.

The doctor laughed and picked the little boy up, so that he straddled the man's hip. Albert watched him. *Carries the kid like a goddamn woman.* They disappeared into the house and the rest of the kids, looking for more handouts, followed them in. Albert finished chopping kindling and carried it back to his cabin. Cindy came through the woods wearing her nightgown, a hunting jacket and rubber boots. Her coat was open and her breasts swung braless. She was just a couple of years older than Albert and even though she'd had Ruby when she was seventeen, her breasts were still good. She had her hair up in a high ponytail.

"You seen Ruby?"

Albert jerked his chin in the direction of the house. "The doctor's in."

"Huh. He bring any food?"

"Says Brenda's got impetigo."

"Fuck. Again? Lloyd don't keep those kids clean."

"What do you want Ruby for?"

"Give me a break, Albert. Ray's pissed she wet the bed again." Ray was Cindy's dad. Cindy stomped off in the direction of the house to get Ruby.

An hour later she ran back, Ruby screaming in her arms. Dislocated shoulder. Thank God the good doctor was still around.

And now, this morning, with the memory of Ruby's cries in his head and the awful pop her shoulder made when the doctor yanked it back in its socket, Albert moved gingerly, cautiously, with full awareness that sudden movements could bring on vomiting. He made his way to the shelf where a gallon-sized plastic bottle of water stood. He raised it to his mouth, spilled some of it down his bare chest, corrected his aim and drank as though there was a leak in his stomach. The cold water made his belly cramp and he gagged, thought he would throw up, but didn't. Albert hung his head.

"It's not fair," he said. Although, had anyone asked him what, precisely, was not fair, he would not have been able to say. Life, he supposed, although he knew better than to expect that. But there was a greater injustice. How hard he tried. All the effort he put in to being not like *them*. The Others. He did what he could. What more was expected of him? Why did he wake up in the morning feeling like the best thing ahead of him was a long jump and a short rope? Life asked too much. It ground a man down like sausage meat. He was doing his best. And he had dreams, just like anybody. And if his dream sometimes slipped into fantasy, of having a big house with a pool in the back yard—blue as sapphire, twinkling in the sun like silver and diamonds—with a room for each of the kids and a pretty little nanny, someone halfway between Mary Poppins and Jenna Jameson, then why not? It could happen. Look at all those hip-hop millionaires. They weren't educated. They didn't get breaks. They took what they wanted, constructed and bent the world to suit them. It took guts. It took will, was all. And Albert had guts. He had will. It took a lot of will power not to do the things it was possible to do in a place like this, coming from the people he came from.

He should be fucking proud of himself.

But he wasn't.

He pushed the sheet away from the window, slowly. There was a break in the weather, one of those lovely not-quite-spring-yet days when the streams running down the hillside made a sort of tinkling music and the birds sang loudly, revelling in the possibility of avian romance and the smell of thawing earth was muddy and fecund. Albert put his hand against the glass. Warm, even. Hard to believe it was the same world as last night, when the wind had whipped the voices around the tree trunks as though lashing them to the bark, when the rain had banged on the doors like tiny fists, when the wet had dripped through the roof like tears and the chill had crept in through the chinks like an orphan.

Albert thought he'd sleep for another hour or two and then get the hell away from the compound for a few hours. Just give himself a mini-holiday. Movement in the clearing caught his eye. Eight-year-old Frank, Lloyd and Joanie's kid, was near the outhouse. He was still wearing his pajamas. Blue ones, with flowers on them, hand-me-downs from one of the girls probably. He hit something on the ground with a stick; hit it hard, repeatedly, as if he was trying to kill it, whatever it was.

Albert let the sheet fall over the glass and fell back into bed with an arm flung over his eyes.

By two in the afternoon, the temperature spiked, and Albert flung open the cabin door to air out the musty mixture of bacon fat, cigarette smoke, stale beer and his own cooped-up body. He decided to vacate the mountain for the afternoon. No work. No field. No deals. A holiday.

As he drove through town he hung his arm out the truck window. The air smelled of mucky water and earth and the faint sweet twinge of decay from the clumps of slimy leaves cluttering the storm drains. It was the ideal day to hang out by the river, one of his favourite places—deep in the woods, beneath the old stone bridge, long closed to anything except foot traffic.

He parked by the road and walked in, boots squelching in the soggy earth. When he reached the river he lay in the sun on a great slab of jutting rock, and watched the swirl and suck of the deep eddies. The sun relaxed Albert's neck muscles and made his feet tingle and legs twitch and inspired daydreams. It wouldn't last. Flocks of small sheep-shaped clouds dotted the sky, prophesying more rain on the way tomorrow, but today, who cared about tomorrow?

Albert rolled his jacket up under his head as a pillow. The dark rock acted as a heat magnet and even in just a T-shirt and sweater, he was warm. He smoked a cigarette. He watched the clouds. He listened to the gurgle and rush of water around the stones. Soon the world would be a humid stinking soup, and the garbage piles on the mountain would fester and swell. Tempers would flare in the stew of summer just as they did the locked-in freeze of winter. And with meth around, with The Uncles branching out into an entirely new product-line, things at the compound were even more dangerous, even more unpredictable. He'd told the kids to stay the fuck away from the trailer. Meth cooks blew themselves up all the time and they often blew up their kids as well. He hated the over-crowded isolation of the mountain, all of them living like rats in a cage, eating their own young. *Don't think about it.* He flicked his cigarette butt into the river, closed his eyes and tried to let the day be the day, tried to keep the future out.

He was slipping into a delicious doze when a loud **gloop-plop!** in the water startled him. Not a fish. Heavy. Threatening. Instantly he was awake and crouching, looking for the source of the sound.

"Sorry," said a voice. "I didn't see you."

A kid stood on the top of the bridge. Skinny. Pale. With funny, heavy eyebrows. Hands in the pockets of baggy jeans. Too-big windbreaker.

"What the fuck are you doing?" said Albert.

"Nothing."

Albert watched the kid. He looked familiar. Someone he'd seen around town.

"I just dropped a rock in," the kid said, and he looked embarrassed.

"Big fucking rock," said Albert. The kid had seen him start; did he think he'd scared him? He lay back against the rock.

"Bridge is coming apart."

"You gonna tear it down single handed?" No answer. "What's your name, kid?"

"Bobby. Bobby Evans."

"Come here, Bobby Evans."

The kid hesitated for only a moment and then scuffled down the bank. Once he made the rocks he was agile, sure footed even with the untied sneakers. Albert thought he probably wasn't as frail as he looked. He rolled over onto one elbow and watched the kid approach. He could tell by the way he kept taking quick peeks at Albert, and chewing on his lower lip, that the scrutiny made him nervous. This relaxed Albert. When Bobby neared him the boy didn't sit, but stood, as though waiting for an invitation. Albert squinted up at him. "Aren't you supposed to be in school?"

"Yeah, well," said the boy.

"You want a smoke?" said Albert, shaking a cigarette from his pack of Camel's. He gestured the boy should sit.

"Okay, thanks," said Bobby.

When he'd lit his own cigarette, Albert held his lighter out to the boy. Bobby puffed inexpertly, holding the butt tightly between his thumb and index finger. He coughed, and glanced at Albert.

"So, Bobby Evans, what are you doing out here?"

Bobby shrugged.

"Yeah, me too," said Albert. "My name's Albert."

"Nice to meet you," said Bobby.

"Albert Erskine."

"I know who you are."

"Oh, you do, huh?"

"Sure. I seen you in town."

Albert took another drag off the cigarette and Bobby did the same, inhaling this time, and managing not to cough. Albert sat up, pitched a small stone into the water, making it skip five times before it sank. Bobby pitched a stone as well but it sank after three skips and he tried another but it merely plonked dully into the water. Albert considered the boy, who was now picking moss off the side of the rock and rolling the bits between his fingers. Big hands, but narrow wrists. Growing into his bones yet, with a ways to go. Could be thirteen, but was probably older. He was a nice-looking kid, even if he was too pale. Nervous, though. There was an air of vulnerability about him. Something about the way he fidgeted, the way he kept changing his hold on the cigarette until at last he held it as Albert did, between his middle and ring finger. It made Albert smile.

"So, Bobby, what do you do when you're not in school?"

"Not much. I don't know."

"Choir practice? Altar boy?"

Bobby snorted. "No."

"Not a church-goer, huh? Well, that lets out a bit of the town. Uh, let's see. You're studying to be a brain surgeon."

"No." Bobby pouted a bit at that, as though he could be a brain surgeon if he wanted to be.

"Stamp collector? Birdhouse builder? Mitten knitter?"

Bobby laughed. "I don't do anything, I guess. What the fuck's there to do in this town anyway?"

"An excellent question, young Bobby. An excellent question." It was good, sitting here with this kid. It was friendly. "I can see you and I are of like mind."

"What about you?"

"What about me?"

"You work somewhere?"

"When I have to."

"Like where?"

Albert twisted around and unwrapped his jacket. He reached in the pocket and brought out a battered tin flask. "Like wherever the fuck I want to." He unscrewed the cap and raised his arm in a toast. "To Gideon. You want some? Old enough?"

"Okay."

Albert kept the flask next to his chest. "Hey, you don't have to, Bobby. I mean, you're welcome to a drink, but if you're not supposed to, then maybe you shouldn't. Doesn't make any difference to me, you know."

"No. I'd like one. Please." He held out his hand and Albert passed him the flask. He took a big swig. "I drink sometimes."

"All right then," said Albert.

"You make this?" said Bobbie, taking another quick sip before handing it back to Albert.

"Whatever have you heard about the Erskines?" He glared at Bobby until the boy dropped his eyes. Then he laughed a short *heh-heh-heh*. "Hey, kidding. No, I didn't make this. Good old Wild Turkey, straight from Wilton's. And more where that came from." Albert looked over at Bobby, waiting to see what his reaction was, waiting to see if he'd heard about the recent break-in at Wilton's. The boy said nothing, which Albert took as a good sign. Discretion was such a useful quality. "Who's your Daddy? Is it Tom Evans? Drives a bread truck, right?"

"Yeah."

Ah, the benefits of small-town life. Knowing whose son he was told Albert a great deal about Bobby. "Seems like an all right guy," he said. And Bobby nodded. Albert did not ask about his mother. Patty Evans was well known in town, pretty as she was, and so much younger than her husband. And then there was her reputation, built in the mysterious glimmer of New York City where Tom Evans had found her. Too much for old Tom to handle was the way the talk went. Patty Evans was held

34

at arm's length as not-one-of-us; a reputation not even the oak-solid respectability of Tom Evans could quite shake. Not a North Mountain reputation, of course, but still, young Bobby and Albert had a few things in common, maybe, the difference being only a matter of degree. Albert wondered what it would be like to be raised by a woman like that, with a figure like that. Did she parade around in her bra and panties? What did she smell like when she bent over to kiss Bobby good night? How hard would it be to get a flash of her in the shower? "Any other kids in the family?"

"Ivy, my sister. She's ten."

"Just the one, huh? I got a bunch up by us. That's why I come out here. To get away from the fucking noise."

The two spent the next hour passing the flask back and forth and watching the water. Bobby's tongue loosened with the alcohol. Albert learned he did not like school. Did not fit in at school. The other boys were always ragging on him. And he'd been beaten up a time or two. "That's tough," said Albert. "Who beat you up?"

"Some guys." Bobby blushed.

"Why?"

"I don't know."

"Listen, you don't have to tell me anything you don't want to, you know?" Albert slapped Bobby lightly on the leg to show it was all light-hearted and safe.

"They just talk a bunch of shit. Stuff they don't know crap about."

"Tell you what," said Albert. "Next time somebody hassles you, you tell me, all right? You remind me of my little brother, Jack."

"Okay, I guess. Thanks."

"Not a problem." Albert punched Bobby in the shoulder. "You're all right, for a kid, you know that?"

"I'm fifteen."

"Good for you. Listen, do you play pool?"

"Not really."

"I think we should head down to the Italian Garden, grab a pizza, play some pinball."

"Maybe. Sure, why not?"

As they walked through the woods to the truck, Albert rambled on about the art of pool and as he talked he liked the sound of his own voice more and more, liked the way Bobby looked at him—like he was, well, important. And why not? Why shouldn't he be? Maybe this was the key to his own pride. Like one of those Big Brother social workers. This kid probably had trouble at home. This kid could use an older brother type guy to show him the ropes. He could be a guy like that and could prove to the whole fucking world he wasn't like the rest of the Erskines. It would be a clean thing. A good thing. Albert Erskine had just made a friend.

CHAPTER FIVE

Dorothy was burnishing a silver tea set, rubbing in the noxious gray cleaner, and then buffing to a high shine, when the bell over the door rang. She turned, polishing rag in her rubber-glove clad hand and was surprised to see little Ivy Evans step in, bringing with her the scents of mud and rain. The girl's eyes met hers for only a moment. They were red-rimmed, teary. Her nose was also red and, good lord, dripping slightly. As though reading Dorothy's thoughts, she reached into the pocket of her navy wool jacket and pulled out a tissue, swiping angrily at her nose. The girl's coat was open, and revealed a pair of blue jeans and a green sweater, in a shade that was not at all flattering. Her shoes, Dorothy couldn't help but notice, were covered in muck.

"Would you mind wiping your shoes, dear? Just there on the mat."

"Sorry."

"Ivy, yes? It is an awful lot of mud, isn't it? Do you need a rag, perhaps? And are those your friends?" Two other girls had stepped up to the window and were looking in, their faces framed between upheld hands. Dorothy did not like the idea of a shop full of schoolgirls. Who were these girls? Cathy Watson and the Oliver girl, what was her name? Oh yes, Gelsey. *Gelsey*. It sounded like a sort of cow. Whereas Gelsey did bear an unfortunate resemblance to a dull-eyed ruminant, Cathy Watson was a startlingly pretty girl, in the puffy-lipped and pert-nosed ideal of contemporary fashion models. Cathy took after her mother, who never allowed you to forget her prettiness for an instant. The girls ignored Dorothy, but tapped on the window, gesturing at Ivy who, kneeling by a blue and white porcelain umbrella stand, kept her eyes firmly on her tan shoes. She spit on the tissue and rubbed at the leather.

"They seem to want you to go back outside," said Dorothy.

"I know."

Cathy whispered something in Gelsey's ear and Gelsey laughed. Dorothy thought Cathy's eyes had taken on a sly look, flattened at the corners and suspiciously conniving.

"I take it you do not wish to join them."

Ivy hesitated for a moment. "No," she said, in a voice that sounded as though she had just admitted something shameful. "If it's okay." There was the catch of tears in her throat.

Dorothy did not wish to become involved in any schoolyard feud, for she knew these things were unlikely to be resolved in an afternoon. Children and their war games were far more complex than adults cared to admit, and it never ceased to amaze Dorothy that adults, who had presumably once been children themselves, could so easily forget the brutalities of their youth. Campaigns of terror had been waged for years in locker rooms, assembly halls and home rooms. Memories of her own childhood surfaced, scattered vignettes of being ostracized, teased and betrayed. She was tempted to shush Ivy out, tell her to stand up for herself and be done with it. She looked at Cathy Watson and locked eyes with her, thinking the girl would crumple and back off under the clear disapproval of an adult. However, Cathy Watson merely cocked an eyebrow and—there was no other word for it—she smirked. It was something very close to a dare. If it had been a different era, and Dorothy was quite sorry it was not, she would have paddled her backside with one of the antique canes from the umbrella stand. The impudent little miss.

"Yes, I suppose it's all right if you stay for a few moments. It's not as though I'm up to my ears in customers, is it?" She peeled off her rubber gloves and walked to the window. Ivy stood up, glanced at Cathy and Gelsey, and then back to Dorothy. Dorothy smiled at her and flapped her hands at the girls outside. "Go on, away with you both." She opened the door. "Ivy has shopping to do; you'll have to go on without her. Bye-bye." She waved her hands again and closed the door.

Gelsey stuck her tongue against the glass, pulled a dreadful face, and then both girls shrieked with laughter and ran down the street.

"I can see why you might wish to avoid them," said Dorothy. "How revolting."

"Thanks, Mrs. Carlisle."

Dorothy looked out the door. The girls, as suspected, waited at the corner. "How are you at polishing silver?" she said.

"I can do that." The girl looked so keen to please it was slightly embarrassing. It was easy to see how a bully would turn that eagerness to her advantage.

"How old are you?"

"Ten."

"Is that, in your house, old enough to drink tea?"

"I've never had tea."

"Well then, it's about time you did. Follow me."

Dorothy set the kettle to boil. It all felt rather silly, as though she was some eccentric aunt in a Dickens novel. Ivy stood at the doorway to the kitchen, looking about her, taking in everything.

"Where does all this stuff come from?" she said.

"All over. People bring me things. And I go scrounging around in attics and basements and barns."

"Is everything old?"

"Yes. Some more than others. That plate over there," she pointed to a delicate blue and white platter with a pattern of flowers on it, "that's over two hundred years old."

"Wow."

"Indeed," said Dorothy. She handed Ivy two cups and saucers, fairly good ones, painted with green vines and gold rims. "Take those over to the table." She put several ginger cookies on a plate and carried the tray.

"Milk?" she said when she had poured the tea.

Ivy hesitated.

"I always take milk in my tea, but some people don't, and others prefer it with lemon," said Dorothy. "You strike me as a milk person."

"Okay," said Ivy.

Dorothy sipped her tea, holding the saucer in her left hand and lifting the teacup to her lips with her right. Carefully, Ivy did the same. Dorothy couldn't think of what to say, and she scanned the room for ideas. "I have a book over there you might find interesting. It's a first edition of *The Wizard of Oz*. On that round table. Why not bring it here. No, not that one, the other, with the red leather binding."

One of the girl's socks was completely muddy, as though she had stepped in a deep hole. Ivy brought the book back and began looking through it. She handled the book carefully, Dorothy was pleased to note, turning the pages with gentle respect. "The illustrations are by W.W. Denslow. Look closely and you will see he signed his name with a seahorse for the 'S'. Isn't that clever?"

"Shouldn't this be in a museum?"

"Well, it would mean a lot to a collector, I'm sure. And it's worth a significant amount of money, I suppose. But I don't really need the money and I like beautiful things. Don't you think it's beautiful?"

"It's fantastic," the child's face lit up in a most pleasing way. It almost removed the puffy evidence of her earlier tears.

They finished their tea and Dorothy showed her how to polish silver. She was an attentive student and worked hard. Half an hour later the tea set sparkled. They stood back, admiring their work.

"Do you think we should call your mother and let her know you're here?"

"My mother works at Wilton's until six." It was four-ten.

"Well, your father then. Tom's finished work early afternoon, isn't he?"

"Can't I just stay here for a little while? Then I'll go home."

"I'm sure those girls have long since lost interest or have found a small animal to torture."

Ivy's eyes went wide.

"I'm joking, dear. I'm sure they wouldn't really hurt an animal."

"Oh," said Ivy, who did not look quite so sure.

"Do you want to tell me what happened?" Oh why, thought Dorothy, have I asked that? "Of course, you don't have to tell me if you don't want to."

Ivy said nothing for a moment, folding the polishing cloth carefully, unfolding it and then folding it again. "I don't know what to do," she said.

"Perhaps you'd better tell me. Sit down."

"It was stupid. I knew I shouldn't have gone. But Cathy can be so nice sometimes."

Cathy Watson, it seemed, had persuaded Ivy to walk home from school with her and Gelsey through the woods that ran in a wide swath between Elm and Woodbridge. Many of the children who lived on the far side of the forest chose to take the short cut rather than to walk the long way round. A rutted path ran to the Stony Creek, leading to a bridge of large rocks on which they could cross.

"The water's high this time of year. It was really slippery," said Ivy. "We had to be careful and go from stone to stone. Cathy went first and she never slipped. She told me to be careful." Ivy frowned and picked at the knee of her jeans. "Gelsey laughed. I didn't know what was funny. And then Cathy looked at me and her face was all weird, like."

"Like what, dear? I don't know what 'weird' means in this context. Be specific."

Ivy looked at Dorothy and it was clear she was trying to find the right words. Dorothy felt a flicker of respect. She liked young people you could treat as adults.

"Well," said Ivy after a minute, "Cathy's smile was there one minute, the pretty one, but then it was gone. She looked mean. She looked . . . sneaky. I hate that look."

"You've seen it before then."

Ivy nodded. "We were a long way in the woods. Cathy stopped. She was on this big rock in the centre of a swampy part. 'Well,' she said. 'Well, well.'" Ivy's voice was sing-song, taunting, imitating the other girl. "'Look at this. You can't pass, can you?' I looked behind me, to go back, you know, but Gelsey was there. 'Come on, Cathy. Move,' I said. She just danced around on the rock and laughed at me. She said, I wasn't her friend, not really. I said I was and she said I had to prove it. She said I had to cover my shoes in mud. And I said I didn't want to, but Gelsey said I had to. 'Of course you don't *want* to,' Cathy said. 'If it was something you *wanted* to do, it wouldn't prove anything, would it?' I said why did I have to prove anything and Cathy said, 'Because if you don't, something bad might happen.'" Ivy hung her head. "It scared me. The look in Cathy's eyes like that. Snakey-like."

"Reptilian," said Dorothy.

"Reptilian," repeated Ivy, nodding. She paused for a moment, as if to hold on to the word. "Then she said, 'If you want to be my friend you will do this.'" Ivy hesitated. "Cathy has a lot of friends. She kept saying do it, do it, do it."

"And so you did it," said Dorothy, gently.

"I used a stick. I smeared it with mud and put some on the side of my shoes, but that wasn't enough. And then she picked up a stick of her own, a big one, and so did Gelsey and she said I better do it." Ivy's eyes flashed with tears. "I didn't want to do it."

"And then what happened?" Dorothy handed Ivy a tissue.

"She pushed me with the stick. Hard. I almost fell back, but I didn't. I had to step down though, one foot into the mud. It came up over my left foot right to the ankle. Then Gelsey jumped onto her rock and pushed me the rest of the way so I had to either fall down or put the other foot down. I was way deep in the mud. I tried to pull my foot out, but my shoe came off and then I had to pull *that* out. They laughed at me and said, 'come on, come on,' like I was going to fight them or something." She was crying hard again. "So I came back to town and was going to go around the long way, but then they followed me back here and I didn't know what they were going to do. . ." her voice trailed off, hiccupping.

"Don't cry, dear. It doesn't help, you know." Dorothy handed her another tissue. "I'll have a talk with your mother."

"No! Please. She'll get mad and she'll yell at them or their moms and then they'll get even madder and—"

"All right, Ivy. Really. You mustn't get hysterical."

Ivy looked at her, and blinked. "I'm not hysterical, Mrs. Carlisle. I would *never* get hysterical."

"I'm glad to hear it." Dorothy made a show of blowing her nose in order to hide her amusement. Oh, she had insulted the little girl. And Dorothy, seeing the frown, the pursed lips and the flush of indignation, liked her better for it. Pride in excess was a bad thing, but a little, judiciously applied, could steel up a backbone quite nicely.

"It's just I'm, I don't know, mad, I guess," said Ivy.

"Well, with some good reason."

"What time is it, please?"

"Just after four-thirty."

"I better go. Thanks for letting me stay here, and for the tea and all."

"Thank you for polishing the silver. It was most helpful."

Ivy gathered up her schoolbooks and her coat. As she was opening the door she turned back. "Do you think, sometime, I don't know . . ."

"What is it, Ivy? Speak up."

"Could I come back, and maybe help you again?"

"I don't need much help, dear, but thank you."

The girl blushed deeply and she dropped her eyes.

"Well, sometimes, I could use a hand dusting, I suppose. Once in a while. Occasionally."

"I can do that. I'm an excellent duster."

And with that the girl was gone, looking quickly up and down the street and then dashing off, leaving Dorothy to scowl at the door and wonder what on earth she was letting herself in for.

CHAPTER SIX

"Goodnight, sweetpea," Tom said, and kissed Ivy goodnight. She pattered out of the room. Tom looked at his watch. 8:20, and although he didn't usually go to bed for another hour, already he was falling asleep in his chair. He glanced at Patty, who sat at the far end of the couch with a glass of wine in her hand, staring at the television set. What was on? Something about a crime scene in some big city, bits of flesh and bone and close-up shots of half-digested stomach contents. Why did she find it so fascinating? Or did she? She sat there, her legs tucked up, her turtleneck pulled over her chin, folded in on herself. How long had it been since they'd necked on the couch after the kids had gone to bed? Fallen asleep in each other's arms? They had time for themselves right this instant, Bobby was out with friends and Ivy upstairs now. Why was it so difficult to simply cross the room and kiss her?

As though she sensed his eyes on her, she drank from her glass and glanced at him from the corner of her eye. She said nothing, merely locked her gaze on the set again. A shadow caught Tom's attention and it was then he realized he hadn't actually heard Ivy's feet going up the stairs. He cocked his head, listened, but there was only the sound of the television and the silence of the house.

"I'll be right back," he said.

He poked his head around the doorway. Ivy stood at the bottom of the stairs near the kitchen. She looked at her feet. Her hands were clenched. She glanced up at the top of the stairs and then down at her feet again.

"What'cha doin'?"

Ivy's head snapped around and her mouth opened, but no sound came out.

Tom went to her. "What's the problem?"

"Nothing," she said, blushing furiously.

He knelt down and put his hands on her arms. "Something got you spooked?"

43

She shook her head.

"You can tell me, you know that, right? I am extremely good at dealing with spooky things." He smiled and waited. From the living room came the bass-heavy theme song for the crime show.

Ivy looked to the top of the stairs again. "I don't know. There's something. . . up there."

"What kind of something?"

She squirmed. "Bad. You know."

Tom looked up the staircase, at the twist in the stairs, and saw how the darkness of the upstairs hall seemed to spill towards them. He saw how it must look to a little girl whose parents had not taken her up to bed in a very long time.

"Light switch for the hall's a long way away, huh?" he said.

"Yeah, but if I get to the switch quick enough . . ." She shrugged.

"I see. Well, how about I go up with you tonight?"

"Okay."

They started up the steps, her hand hidden in his. When they got to the landing she reached up and turned on the light, keeping her eyes turned from the hall.

"Better?" Tom said.

"Yes." She sounded unconvinced.

"I think we better fix some new lights up here, don't you?"

"Maybe."

"Tell you what, I'll hang around for a few minutes and tuck you in, how's that?"

He was rewarded with her smile. She scampered quickly down the hall to the bathroom and when she came out again a few minutes later he walked her to her bedroom and sat on the small bed while she changed into her pajamas, the ones with pink rabbits all over them. Tom pulled back the blankets and she hopped in.

"Better?"

"Thanks, Daddy. I get scared, just sometimes. It's better now." She took his hand and stroked the back of it, so the hairs lay flat and smooth. "The worst, though, you know, really the worst?"

"What's the worst?"

"It's when I come out of the bathroom, because I have to switch the light out there, you know, at that end of the hall and run down here." She

44

stopped patting his hand and instead picked and smoothed and worried the sheet without looking at him.

"Sweetie, why didn't you tell us?"

She shrugged. "I don't know."

"You know there isn't really anything up here, don't you?"

"I know. I'm not a little kid, Dad."

"But still, right?"

"But still."

"Okay. Here's what we're going to do. Tomorrow, I'm going to fix up another light switch, right outside your room, so you don't have to go down the hall in the dark. And I can put a night-light in here if you want one."

"No. That's just for babies."

"Not at all. Lots of people prefer to sleep with a little light."

She looked skeptical and toyed with the ends of her hair. "I saw on a TV show once, about this man who gets left behind in a cave, because his leg's broken. But there are saber-toothed tigers in the cave, left over from prehistoric times, right? And the others say they'll come back for him the next day, after they get help, and when they come back he's crazy from being afraid and his hair is all white, completely all white. Which is what happens from being that scared, right?"

"Well, I suppose that could happen, but you'd have to be really, really, afraid, Ivy. Are you that afraid?"

"I only checked my hair once."

He hesitated asking the question that must be asked. "Why don't you call Mom?"

Ivy kept playing with the ends of her hair.

"Hang on a minute. I'll be right back."

He had something hidden in his hand when he returned. "I'm going to check on you every night before I go to work, okay? And Mom'll check too, and if you ever feel in any way even a little frightened, you blow on this, okay?" He took her hand and dropped a long silver whistle on a braided cord in her palm. "That used to be your grandfather's whistle, from when he was a Scout leader. It blows louder than anything. You give a blast on that and one or the other of us will come running. Okay?"

"Okay."

"Think you can sleep?"

45

"Uh-huh."

"I'll leave the hall light on, okay?" He kissed her on the top of her head, which smelled of her special coconut shampoo. Ivy's hair tangled so.

"I love you, Daddy."

"I love you, Ivy."

He went back downstairs to the living room.

"Why didn't you tell me Ivy's so scared of the dark?" he said.

"She is? I didn't know that." Patty frowned and raised an eyebrow. "This must be something new. She tell you that?"

"I don't think it's new."

"It must be. I would have noticed."

"Well, she's sure as hell scared now. Checking her hair to see if it's turned white, for God's sake."

"No! Really? I used to be like that when I was a kid. Scared of everything."

"You're going to have to keep an eye on her when I'm not here. Check on her a couple of times a night. I promised her you would. And I said I'd fix up a new light switch, so she doesn't have to go down the hall in the dark."

"Don't fuss over her too much, Tom. She's got to grow out of it."

"I won't have her being afraid. I gave her Dad's old Scout whistle to blow in case she gets scared. Just so you know. I don't think she'll use it. More like a talisman to keep the bogeymen away."

"What did you do that for? She blows on that thing and I'll have a heart attack." She turned back to the ghostly morgue on the television screen.

He checked on Ivy before he left for work. She slept with the whistle in her hand and the cord around her neck. He told himself it was all right, that she wouldn't strangle as she slept. *But she might. I should take it off. But what if she loses it in the bed and wakes up frightened? I said it would be there. Better to leave it.* He made a move toward the bed, and then stopped, started again. He shook his head to clear away the cobwebbed indecision. *Christ, get a grip.* Tomorrow he'd get her a nightlight, fix the switches. He'd build a moat around her bed if necessary.

Two days later, Tom was getting gas at Ed's Garage, talking with Ed about the possibility of a poker game one of these nights. Both men leaned with their backs against the truck as the pump clicked away. Ed was a wiry little guy with abnormally hairy ears. Ivy called him an elf and had been afraid of him until recently.

"You wanna get out of the house more often," said Ed. "Guys are starting to think you're whipped."

"It's not Patty. It's just the hours. I'm dead by nine o'clock. I'd fall asleep in my beer."

"Maybe you'd finally lose once in a while then."

Another car pulled up and Ed called for Bill Bodine. "Where is that asshole? Supposed to be changing oil for Pataki, but do you see him anywhere? Probably in the can with a joint again. I'd fire his ass if he wasn't such a good mechanic. Don't go. I want to pin down a date." And he stepped away to serve his customer.

Tom turned and unhitched the nozzle from the gas tank when the pump hit twenty-five dollars.

"Hey, Tom, long time no see," a woman's voice said. He looked up to see Rita Kruppman—correction—Rita *Cronin* standing in front of him, tossing her car keys from one hand to the other. Rita was tall and lean, with dark honey-blond hair pulled back into a simple ponytail. Her face was make–up free, covered with more freckles than ever and her eyes clear and blue.

"Hi, Rita," he gave her a peck on the cheek, "how are you?"

"Well. Fair I guess. Holding up."

"Oh? Kids okay?" Tom looked past her into the blue SUV she was driving these days. Rita's freckled twins, Gabrielle and James, sat in the back, both with little headphones in their ears. They stared at him with bored expressions.

"They're thirteen."

"Right."

Tom noticed Ed looking at him. Ed grinned and winked.

"You all right?" She looked in rude good health. "Not sick or anything?"

"You must be the only person in town who doesn't get the gossip."

"Meaning?"

"Tom, Harry and I are divorcing." She dropped her eyes and went pink between the freckles.

"Oh, man. Rita. I'm really sorry. I thought you guys were doing great."

47

"Yes, well, so did I. He said he felt stifled, that he needed to toss, and I'm quoting here, 'a grenade into the trench of our marriage'. Sadly, he forgot the children and I were still living in that trench."

"Ouch."

"No other woman, or so he says. He's moving to Utah. Maybe he saw Brokeback Mountain and got ideas."

"Meaning?"

Rita shrugged, looked at Tom pointedly.

"No way. Harry's gay? Come on, Harry's not gay." Tom had played football with Harry. It wasn't possible; the guy was a linebacker in high school.

"Well, if he is, he couldn't very well live in this town, now could he?" Rita shook her head. "I don't know. I really don't. Let's just say the twins were a miracle."

Tom was speechless. He jingled the coins in his pockets.

"Oh, shit. Too much information. Sorry."

"It's all right. I'm just kind of shocked."

"You and me both. Don't say anything about that last bit, will you? I don't even know why I told you."

"No, course not."

"The good news is he left us set for cash."

"That's good. You still teaching?"

"Which really, is what I wanted to talk to you about."

"School?"

"Well, Ivy, actually."

"What about her? I didn't think you were teaching her this year."

"I'm not, but, Tom, well, I've seen some things around the school and I wasn't going to mention anything. I mean, it's not anything serious. It's just that Ivy's such a sweet kid, and so smart."

"Thanks."

"But has she talked to you about getting picked on?"

"No." Tom's stomach suddenly felt sour. He looked around and realized Ed had disappeared into the office. Why? Discretion? About what? Ivy or Rita? "What do you mean, picked on? Bullying?"

"No, no, nothing that serious. Just some girls who think they're special looking for someone to, I don't know, set apart. You remember how it was at school, one week it would be the kid who'd let loose a loud fart and everybody teased him, the next somebody had a huge pimple—you know what kids can be like and, I'm sad to say, especially girls."

"What are they picking on Ivy for? And why isn't the school doing anything about it? Nobody's called us. Nobody's told us a damn thing."

"Hey, don't shoot the messenger, Tom. If we thought it was really serious, of course the school would be in touch. It's not like that. I just thought you should know. It'll all blow over, of course, and next week I'm sure they'll be on to somebody else. You know. . . She's so sweet. . ."
Rita reached out and put her hand on his arm and then took it away again. Gabriella rolled down the window and yelled, "Mom, I'm going to be late!"

"Hang on a minute! Look Tom, it's all schoolyard nonsense. No one holds any store by it. It's all for effect."

"I'll talk to her."

"I know you will. You're a fantastic father."

Gabrielle hollered again. "I have to go."

"Rita, listen, I'm really sorry about Harry."

She looked at him, her expression sad and weary. "Life just doesn't turn out like we planned, does it, Tom? See you around."

Tom paid Ed, not really listening to what he was saying about poker or how good Rita looked these days, now that she was single again. All Tom could think was Ivy, getting teased like that and not saying anything. He didn't have the faintest idea how to deal with it. Driving along Franklin, he scowled at every face he saw. The world was full of shadows, places where things were happening that he couldn't see. So much could happen when you weren't looking, when you weren't paying attention. Look what happened to Rita and Harry. Look how that ended up. A horn sounded and Tom slammed on the brake just as he was about to run a red light. The driver in a landscaping truck swore as he passed. Tom shook his head, realized he was trembling. See? Just like that, you weren't looking and then everything changed.

CHAPTER SEVEN

*Proverbs 11:19. **As righteousness leads to life, so he that pursues evil pursues it to his own death.** When a good man dies he not only goes to heaven, drawn thither by the natural forces of spiritual gravity, by the approval of God and angels, but when a good man dies he goes to heaven by the common consent of every intelligent creature in the world. When a bad man dies he not only goes to hell, drawn thither by the natural forces of spiritual gravity, not only by the approval of God and His angels, but when a bad man dies he goes to hell by the common consent of every man in the world."* — **Reverend Sam P. Jones – 1885, visiting preacher, Church of Christ Returning**

Albert stepped into Mavericks first, with Bobby on his heels. Since that day by the bridge, Albert managed to run into Bobby six or seven times as the kid walked home from school. He was always alone, except for one instance, when Bobby had been with a group of jocks who clearly only tolerated the skinny, sunken-chest boy. On that occasion Albert passed on by with only a toot of the truck horn. The other times they'd gone for a drive, talking about Bobby's family, mostly. He said his little sister was a prissy pain in the ass. According to Bobby, neither of his parents gave a shit what he did as long as he didn't get into trouble. There was trouble in the Evans' marriage, apparently, but Bobby wouldn't elaborate. Albert didn't push. There was no rush. And today was a big day. Today he'd get the kid his first beer in a real bar.

Maverick's was a long room—the ancient, battered wooden bar on one side, with a mirror behind it, and a few tables on the other. In the murky light beyond that lurked a row of booths, tall backed, favored spot of those wanting to do a little quiet business in private. A cigarette-burned pool table and a few stools were tucked into an alcove off the bar. Stevie Ray Vaughn's guitar moaned from the speakers mounted on the walls. A small television sat on a shelf behind the bar, turned to a boxing match. The floor was blotchy with various stains, some darker than others and if you looked in the corners you would find piles of dust, ash, hair and mouse turds dating back to the late eighteen hundreds when the place first opened. A window stood on either side of the padded vinyl door, and the bent venetian blinds permitted only slats of mote-strewn light. The room was empty at four o'clock in the afternoon, before the shift workers from the paint factory and the county crews came in for their wind-down Rolling Rock just after five. Finn the bartender was the only guy in the place, filling plastic bowls with peanuts and pretzels. The air reeked of old beer and last night's cigarettes. Finn was a man with a permanent frown and deep pouches under his pale eyes, characteristics gained from too many late nights and too many disappointments concerning the nature of man. When he saw Albert come through the door he nodded, as though expecting him, and then he saw Bobby.

"He can't come in here, Erskine," he said.

"You want what you want, or not?" Albert slid a paper bag across the bar, which Finn quickly grabbed and tucked into some crevice below the bar. Albert took the bills Finn handed him, counting them before he put them in the pocket of his decrepit leather jacket. "Where are your manners, Finn? Don't you even say thank you?"

"I'm eternally grateful, but like I said," the bartender pointed at Bobby, who still stood by the door, "He can't come in here."

"Don't be like that, now, Finn. He's eighteen," said Albert, while Bobby rocked back and forth on his heels, his hands deep in the pockets of his army surplus jacket.

Finn snorted. "Even if that were true, it doesn't mean shit, now does it, since the legal age is twenty-one?"

"Kid can have a fucking soda, can't he?" said Albert.

"Sure he can. Take him over to Gus's Corner," Finn said, naming the diner a few doors down the street.

"I can't get a beer in Gus's. Come on, man, don't be a hard ass. It's not like he's the first underage guy ever been in here, now is it?"

"This isn't the fucking Olive Garden. Who is he? He's not one of your cousins." Finn looked Bobby over. "Aren't you—"

"You're worried about too many Erskines in one place? Is that it?"

"I don't care, man, let's go," said Bobby.

51

"Don't make a fucking federal case, Erskine."

"Me? That's rich. I just come in with the kid to get a fucking beer."

"Sit at the back. You see a uniform walk through that door you get the fuck out like your ass was on fire. Clear?"

Albert clapped Bobby on the back. "You're a real prince, Finn, a real prince. Bring us a Bud and a Coke. And bring some peanuts and a pack of chips."

Albert and Bobby sat in a split-leather booth at the back, near the bathroom fumes of piss, the under-note of vomit and whiff of rotting garbage from the alley. Bobby faced Albert, where he couldn't be seen from the door. Finn put the beer bottle, with a glass upturned on top of it, and another glass of Coke on the bar, next to a bowl of nuts and a plastic package of chips.

"Come and get it," he said, and turned back to the two men knocking the crap out of each other on the television.

Albert stared at his back for a minute, willing him to turn around. "Fucktard," he said under his breath, and then fished in his pocket for a couple of bills. "Go get it, Bobby."

When he'd fetched their food and drink, Albert pushed aside the Coke and poured half his beer into the glass. "Here," he said.

"You sure it's okay?" said Bobby, looking around the corner of the booth in Finn's direction.

"Drink the goddam beer," said Albert.

"Why are you pissed off at me?"

"I'm not pissed off at you. Fucking Finn. He expects me to show up here every week with his weed, special delivery, like I'm a fucking UPS guy, and I do, man, I do. I am reliable, a dependable businessman. And then I get attitude. What the fuck's that about?"

"Maybe he's just having a day."

"Maybe we're all just having a day." Albert scowled into his beer.

The fact was, it was bad at the compound. The Others, what with their new enterprise, were getting more customers than the bootleg used to bring in. What did they do, have a newsletter or something? How did people know? All these wild-eyed, scraggle-toothed, skin-rotting tweakers willing to do pretty much anything for a fix. The Uncles were picking out some of the prettier girls, getting them to trade sex for meth. One of the side effects of meth was an increased sex drive, along with the paranoia and compulsive behavior—the hour after hour of going through the complicated rituals of cooking the drug, driving across the state looking for pharmacies where they could get cold medicine without being noticed. Yeah, they were all having a day.

"So, you like, sell dope?" Bobby kept his voice very low, leaning forward.

Albert leaned back and crossed his arms over his chest, staring at Bobby until Bobby dropped his eyes and sat back as well.

"Maybe," said Albert.

"Maybe I want to buy some," Bobby said.

Albert laughed so loud Finn turned and looked at him. "Jesus, kid, you are something else, you know that? What do you want to buy? Crank? Hillbilly heroin? Tootsies? Casper? How much? You got the cash, little brother?"

"I don't know. A couple of joints maybe."

"Hell, I'll give you a couple of joints. Between friends, right?"

"Yeah?"

Albert leaned forward and grabbed Bobby's upper arm.

"Hey," Bobby said, trying to pull away.

"Listen, I ever catch you doing crank or oxy or any of that other shit, I'll break you in half, you got that?" Albert's face was close to Bobby's and he could smell the cigarettes on the teenager's breath. "I sell a little grass, homegrown, and that's all I sell. Fucking slammers and bulb babies are a blight. Zombies, man, that's all they are."

"I don't do that stuff."

The boy's eyes darted sideways and downwards, and Albert could see the confusion. There was a little bead of sweat on his upper lip, on that soft little fuzz the kid probably shaved hoping it would grow in thicker. He likely didn't even have pubic hair yet.

"Come on, man. Honest," Bobby said. "Let go of my fucking arm."

Albert smiled and patted the side of the boy's soft face. "You're a good kid, I know that. It's just that I care about you, okay? I don't want to see you fucking up your life. There's things a man can do, and things a man can't. It's like a code, right?"

Bobby rubbed his arm. "A code?"

"Yeah, a code," said Albert, warming to the subject. He liked giving Bobby Evans little lectures, liked the way the boy listened, soaking it all in and not interrupting like the kids up at the compound did. They had no respect. Then again, who could blame them? That was the mountain. This was here and the two were not the same in any way. He shook a cigarette out of his pack, lit it and inhaled the smoke deep, enjoyed the slight lightheadedness from that first hit. "You know what a code is, right? Okay, so it's like every man has to develop his own personal code of conduct. He has to decide how he's going to be, what he's willing to do and what he's not, and he can't break that code, can't let anybody make him break that code, or he's not a man. You get that?"

"Yeah, I guess." Bobby chewed at his thumbnail.

"Don't fucking do that. You look like a fucktard."

"Sorry."

"So, what's your code going to be, young Bobby?"

"I don't know, what's yours?"

"Well, I could tell you, but you have to come up with your own. You can't adopt another man's code." How could he possibly explain his code? How he'd built it slap by slap, bruise by bruise? You don't let yourself sleep in your own fucking vomit. You don't shack up with a woman who tosses her used sanitary napkins in the stove. You keep your secrets to yourself and you keep your weaknesses a secret and your hurts a secret and your dreams you bury double deep. He'd had that list by the time he was ten. "You think about it," Albert said, and he wanted another drink more than anything all of a sudden.

The door opened and four men came in, wearing the city-issue overalls of road crew workers. They were laughing. Finn greeted them warmly, shook hands with each.

"Drink up. I'm getting another beer," said Albert. "And then I'll tell you how to grow some killer weed, if you're interested, that is. You interested?"

"Yeah," said Bobby, and he smiled that goofy smile and picked at a pimple on his chin. The kid was full of bad habits.

When he came back, Albert launched into a long sermon on the way to increase the THC content of marijuana plants using a growth changer called colchicine. "You soak the seeds in this solution, right? Maybe some of the seeds die, maybe most of them, but the ones who survive will be fucking superweed. It's all about the number of females," he said, "But then ain't it always?" And he chuckled, and the kid chuckled with him, as though he knew exactly what Albert meant.

It was long gone dark when Albert drove back into the compound and he passed a car as he did. A car he recognized. The good Dr. Hawthorne.

"Fuck," said Albert to no one in particular.

When he got to the cabin Toots and Joe were squatting in the shadows by the forsythia bush.

"What's going on?" he said.

"Jill," said Toots.

"What about her?"

"She got knocked up again."

"That why Hawthorne was here?"

"Yeah. She's bleeding some, though," said Joe. "I saw it."

"Where is she?"

"At her place. Jack's with her."

"She have to go to the hospital?"

Toots shrugged. "I don't think so. But she sure is crying."

Albert unlocked the cabin door and got a bottle of whiskey from his trunk. "Take this over to her, Toots, but don't let the rest of 'em see you, yeah?"

"Okay," the little girl reached out for it and Albert noticed there was a burn on her arm.

"Where'd you get that?"

She pulled her sleeve down and shrugged, saying nothing.

"Yeah, all right. Just make sure Hawthorne didn't give her any pain killers before she drinks that, all right?" He took her upper arm firmly. "Make sure, Toots."

"Hawthorne didn't give her no pain killers," she said. "He never does."

CHAPTER EIGHT

It was one of those brilliant first days of true spring when the world heaved itself out of the long silver somnolence of winter. The temperature soared, and the air carried the fragrance of honeysuckle, crab apple and cherry blossoms. The clouds in the blue sky fairly sparkled and the promise of green was a joyful aura around the trees. Dorothy had closed up the shop for an hour at lunch, and gone for a long walk by the river. Everyone, it seemed, had the same idea and what she had anticipated would be a solitary meander turned out to be a stop-and-chat with half the town. Her mood was so buoyant, nearly giddy, in fact, that she didn't even feel this as an imposition. *Hello. How are you? Isn't it splendid? Oh, yes, a wonderful day. No, there won't be many more like this. Take advantage of it.*

She wore a black sweater-jacket over her blouse. The warmth on the back of her neck, below the line of her short-cut gray hair, was delicious. She slowly rolled her head from side to side. Because she'd guessed it would be muddy, she had on her old green Wellington boots, the perfect thing for puddles and muck and tromping about the moors, and between greetings she imagined that was exactly where she was—out on the moors of Yorkshire or Wales, perhaps, somewhere Dylan Thomas-y, full of windy boys and a bit. . .

By the time she turned back up River Road her cheeks were rosy and her eyes bright. She felt all was well with the world. There was no particular reason to dash back to the store. Why not take one last zip around the block? She set off up Main Street, and along Spring Street to Spruce, Spruce to Moore, past Jefferson High School, where some of the windows were open. The teacher's voice carried and she could just make out the word 'algebra,' and smiled, pitying children struggling to pay attention to that sort of thing on a day like this.

She thought about Ivy, who would be in her classes at the middle school around the corner. Ivy had taken to dropping in to the store three, sometimes four, afternoons a week. She would look in the window and then tap on the glass door, always waiting for an invitation to come in, as though the store were not a public place. She never stayed too long—no more than an hour—and always helped. Although it surprised Dorothy to admit it, she had begun to look forward to these brief visits. The girl was bright, and helpful, and clearly at odds with something. There seemed to be trouble between her parents, a topic Dorothy did not particularly want to discuss. It smacked of gossip and seemed prurient. But clearly the girl wasn't getting much attention at home. Dorothy was sure the visits wouldn't last—Ivy would become bored spending time with an old lady eventually—but it was oddly pleasant for the moment.

She turned down Spruce, and was passing the Italian Garden Pizzeria when she became aware of something on the edge of her senses. Laughter. Yes, it was familiar laughter that drew her attention, coming from the passageway between the Pizzeria and Pretty-as-a-Picture Dresses. A voice. Two voices. One raised in inquiry. That laugh again.

Dorothy stopped and turned toward the sound. The alley was darker, shielded as it was by buildings on either side—a pocket of shadow, smelling of pizza ovens and refuse. A figure at the end—no two—hunkered down by a dumpster, one smaller than the other. The glint of something, a flame . . .

"Who is that?" the sound of her voice surprised her. How authoritative she sounded. "Who's there?"

The smaller figure skittered. Startled and no doubt guilty. Stood. Dorothy, sun-blind, could make out no features. "I said, who is that? What are you doing?"

"Nothing." The larger figure still crouched, bestial, in the corner. The acrid scent of burning wafted. The figure, clearly a man, raised something to his lips. A bottle.

"Do you want me to call the police? Come out here this instant." She should go into the dress shop. Have Doris Heaney call Carl. But on what complaint?

"We're not bothering you." She must be only a silhouette to them, with the sun behind her, but perhaps not.

"Albert . . ." The other one spoke at last. "Maybe we should go."

"Albert who? You are very rude, whoever you are. Is that Albert Erskine? Albert?"

"Shit." It was said quietly, almost as though he didn't want her to

57

hear. The figure stood and he was tall, much taller than the other. He drank from the bottle again and wiped his mouth on his sleeve.

"Albert Erskine, do not be absurd. Come out here."

"Mrs. Carlisle?"

"Yes, it's Dorothy Carlisle, and who is that with you?"

Her eyes adjusted to the shadows. Someone smaller, frailer. Whereas Albert was a collection of muscled slabs, thick and layered, the other was all knots of bone and angles. The small one, no more than a boy, put his head toward Albert and said something. Albert shrugged and the boy walked toward Dorothy. His gait was jerky and uneven. She fought the impulse to back away. As he neared, she saw it was Bobby Evans, Ivy's brother, his eyes downcast on his big sneakered feet, his shoulders held up tight, hands in pockets.

"Hi, Mrs. Carlisle," he said. Another laugh from Albert. And that smell. It might be marijuana. Something else though, in that smoke.

"Are you lighting fires? You should be in school, young man," Dorothy said to Bobby. "I've a mind to tell your father." What on earth was going on in that family? Wasn't anyone paying attention to the children at all? She would have to have a little chat with Tom Evans when she next saw him.

Albert walked toward her slowly and as he did, he slipped the bottle inside his battered leather jacket. He stopped directly in front of her, forcing her to look up at him. He had grown a goatee since last she'd seen him. It accentuated the hollow cheeks, the sharp bones. His hair fell over his brows and curled around his ears. Sunlight glittered off the lenses of his silver metal-rimmed sunglasses. He now used his middle finger (she noticed a black line of grime under the nail) to push them up the bridge of his nose.

"Oh, Albert, what are you doing back there?"

"Burning trash. Nothing. Didn't know it was you." His breath stank of alcohol.

"Albert, listen to me. There has been a break-in at Wilton's. If you don't want people thinking you had something to do with that, it would be prudent not to hang around back alleys, don't you think?"

"I didn't rob Wilton's." He lowered his chin so she could see his eyes more clearly, his thin eyebrows frowning. "You saying I robbed Wilton's?"

"No. I am not saying that. What I'm saying is if people see you

58

loitering in alleys they will call Carl. I'm sure you don't want to spend a beautiful day like this answering questions at the police station."

Albert ran his tongue over his lips and smiled in a rather sheepish manner. Dorothy thought, not for the first time, how much she'd like to get him to a dentist. "Naw, you're right," he said. "You worried about me, Mrs. Carlisle? That it?"

"It's obvious you've been drinking and you are not yourself. I'd hate to think you were giving alcohol, or anything else you shouldn't, to a minor. You and I both know how smart you are. Don't waste it, Albert. How many times have I said that to you?"

"Too many times, maybe," he mumbled, not meeting her gaze now.

"I should probably say it more. You ought to attend those night classes at the high school. Get your GED. You should never have dropped out of school. It's a waste of a good mind."

"Give me a break."

"You're not like . . . well, you have a chance, Albert. I believe that."

"Not like the rest of the Erskines, huh?" His eyes snapped.

They were so touchy, all the Erskines. Hair-trigger the bunch of them. And maybe Dorothy didn't blame them. "Do you want to tell me what you're doing just now?"

"Nope," he laughed. "Go see for yourself if you want, but you know what they say about curiosity. Have a nice day, Mrs. Carlisle." With that he ambled down the street, as though he hadn't a care in the world. Bobby Evans followed him.

Dorothy watched them for a moment and then looked back into the alley. She should just go and call Carl. Let him handle it. That was undoubtedly the sensible thing to do. But she hated to call the police on Albert Erskine, and wasn't completely sure Carl Whitford would care very much. Boys in an alley, one of them truant from school on a beautiful spring day. She knew it was probably misguided, but she had a soft spot for Albert. So much worked against him in this town. She had watched him grow up from a skinny young boy with all those bruises. She'd even called Children's Services once, when his little face had worn the reddened, puffy evidence of a beating, but nothing had come of it. It was the mountain, everyone said. What do you expect? She didn't want to be another one of the people against him. She wanted him to be better; she wanted him to rise up against the odds and break free of his past. If you expected the best of people, wouldn't they struggle to meet those expectations? And if public opinion expected the worst, well, she chose not to be among them.

The smoke in the back of the alley had disappeared now, although the smell lingered. Either she had stopped them from truly setting a fire, or the fire had gone out. It would only take a moment to check and they were, after all, gone. There was no danger now, surely, and probably there never had been any. It was only Albert Erskine and Bobby Evans, for heaven's sake.

It was chilly in the alley, out of the sun. Boxes lay scattered on the ground against the wall of the pizzeria in front of the dumpster. Whatever the boys had burned lay behind the dumpster, past the back entrance of the restaurant. A pile of newspaper, charred around the edges. The fire hadn't caught, then. Just some old papers and cardboard boxes, foolish mischief for which twenty-two year old Albert was far too old. But something else, in the pile. Dorothy caught her breath and she dropped her plastic bag of berries and cake. Fur there. Tortoiseshell fur. A cat? It couldn't be they had killed a cat. Oh, Lord. *Curiosity killed the cat.* She couldn't help herself, she bent forward to look more closely and when she did her stomach turned and she jumped back. Maggots in the sunken eyes, the body shrunken, withered. Long dead.

Dorothy turned back to the warm brightness of the sidewalk, abandoning her shopping. There was no sign of Albert. All she wanted to do was go back to her own little shop. Her mind snapped and cracked with questions as she hurried along. They hadn't killed the cat, then. But why try and burn it? It was disgusting. Had they found the carcass there? But then what had they been doing in the alley to begin with? Albert and the Evans boy. It didn't ring true. Albert was at least six years older than Bobby Evans. What would he want with a boy that age?

Dorothy did not believe half the stories she heard about the Erskine clan. The Erskine women, whenever she did see them in town, always looked so haggard and worn, frightened and ashamed of their meagre purchases. For the past twenty years, every few months or so, Dorothy (and William when he was alive) had driven up to North Mountain and the Erskine's compound in the wee hours of the night, waiting until they were sure everyone would be asleep. She left a box of used clothes, powdered milk, children's toys, canned goods, peanut butter, bars of soap and toothpaste, thick socks and mittens and scarves and oatmeal and anything else she thought they might be able to use. Years back, when she overheard one of the teachers mentioning how smart Albert was, and what a shame it was to waste brains on someone like that, she began including books—*Robinson Crusoe, Treasure Island, Tom Sawyer, Catcher in the Rye.* Dorothy had hoped she was helping, in some way. Not enough. Never enough.

When she arrived at the shop she looked around at the Queen Anne and Windsor chairs, the elegant little Federal and Empire tables, the silver tea-sets and cobalt salt holders and sets of spoons—all the lovely items of beauty and comfort.

First Ivy and now Bobby. Oh, how she wanted to lay in a bath full of lavender bubbles. She wrote a note in case Ivy came by, saying she had closed up early for a doctor's appointment, and taped it to the door. Then she switched off the lights, locked the door and went home.

As far as she was concerned, this day was over.

CHAPTER NINE

Tom had the truck loaded by four a.m. and headed out for his first delivery over in Argyle, at the Mr. Greenjeans Grocery chain. It was half an hour's drive along the highway in the dark before dawn. He had to be careful of three things: drunks, dozers, and deer. Because the traffic was sparse, he could usually spot a drunk weaving from a long way off. Dozers were more problematic. A guy could be driving along with the window open to keep himself awake one minute and be dead asleep the next, swerving into Tom's lane for a head-on with no reaction time. Deer made him drive slower than his boss would like. Tom had hit a deer once. A doe. It had taken her forty-seven minutes to die and Tom had sat with her the whole time, listening to the hollow bone-whistle of her bleat, nasal and low. He'd never forgotten the sound and didn't want to hear it again. Bucks were a different story. If you hit a hulker you were just as likely to be the one dead. Antlers through the windshield and you're slashed to pieces. Impaled if you were unlucky. Even with a doe, in a smaller car, the hooves could be deadly. They tended to come right in through the windshield at face level. Sure, in the delivery truck he had the advantages of weight and height, but still. People asked him if he had a problem staying awake. "Ah, no. Not really," he said.

Patty's face appeared in his mind's eye and he wanted to be home, to be snuggled up against his wife's delicate spine, his arm around her, cradling a soft breast, adjusting his breathing to hers.

He remembered that night he found her singing in a bar in New York. He'd come to the city planning to ship out on a merchant ship or maybe even join the Navy. He'd worked at the cement factory before it closed, and then at the paint factory after that and in both places for a hell of a lot longer than he'd intended. After his father succumbed to the ragged agony of his sinus cancer—his eyes pushed out of his head by the tumors, blind and moaning, high as a kite on morphine—Tom couldn't leave his mother alone. Maureen Evans was so lost, so overwhelmed by every form to be filled out, every bill to be paid, and frightened by every scratchy tree branch on the side of the house. One day had rolled into the next and Tom found himself on the far side of thirty. Then one day his mother didn't come down for breakfast and when he went up to check on her she was in bed, the pink and yellow chenille comforter tidy, lying on her side with her hands tucked under her cheek like a little girl who'd fallen asleep during her bedtime prayers. The room smelled of feces. She wore a flannel nightdress with roses on it, and she was stone cold. He knelt beside the bed and tried to pray and found he couldn't. He took her hand and cried a little, kissed her cheek and went to phone Carl at the sheriff's office. And that was that.

He buried her and everyone agreed the service was nice and the minister said kind things and people brought casseroles around for a while. He dusted the house and gave away her clothes to the church rummage and every evening he sat in the same chair his father had sat in.

Although he'd fooled around with a couple of local girls, dating Rita Kruppman for nearly five years, he'd never felt the pull to the altar. Rita was a fun girl, a tall raw-boned tomboy with a spatter of freckles across her broad shoulders and a sort of cute twisted nose she earned when she got walloped by her older brother Melvin's elbow during a family game of touch football one Thanksgiving years ago. They had that in common, broken noses, although he'd broken his falling from his bike onto a curb when he was seven. He liked Rita well enough, and she wanted all the things a girl is supposed to want, in terms of family and such, but he kept putting her off.

After his mother died and there was no longer any good reason to delay, Rita told him it was a wedding or nothing. He couldn't argue with her; he had no right to lead her on. She didn't take it nearly as hard as he thought she might, which made him laugh, after all, who did he think he was? When she married Harry Cronin he shook Harry's hand and kissed Rita's cheek and danced with her at the reception and gave them a place setting from a china pattern she'd picked out at Field Hardware and Homegoods. And that was that, too; which was when he decided to go off to New York City and see what all the fuss was about out in the wide, wide world.

On his second day in The Big Apple, just as evening approached, he meandered along 4th Street and found himself in Greenwich Village, a neighborhood of townhouses with tiny gardens, fancy clothing stores and trendy-looking eateries. He caught glimpses of leafy courtyards. An AIDs information clinic. Art galleries exhibiting bizarrely abstract works at which he tried not to gawk. Shops selling jewelry from around the world, and vintage (not used) clothing shops. The bookstores were bustling, the markets looked inviting. He walked along Bleeker Street to Christopher and down to Hudson, ambling, taking it all in. The streets were just coming alive and music drifted from the bars. The women wore tight black pants or blue jeans and their hair styles were either cut choppily close to their heads, or hanging straight and long and silky. Expensive, salon-streaked blondes and some with hair the color of ebony, Black girls with fantastical, architectural hairdos, cornstarch-skinned girls with hair of pink, or blue. Their eyes were ringed with black. Their ears were pierced and so were their eyebrows and their lips. The men looked pretty much the same. To Tom, who did not smoke, it seemed as though everyone else did.

He stepped unthinkingly into the street to take a better look at an interesting marble façade. A car horn jolted him from his reveries with a harsh, heart-thumping jolt and a bearded man in a black BMW swore at him—*fucking asshole!* He jumped back onto the sidewalk. So many cars, so many people. It might have been hunger, or a more general alienation, but he felt dizzy. He bent over, trying to get some blood back into his head. He took deep breaths and stood up slowly, blinking. Then he heard someone singing.

He knew the song, an old Irish ballad his mother used to hum. The voice was a hook; it pulled him by the ear and it drew him down the street to the open door of a smoky bar with the head of a white horse painted on its windows. Only later would he think how he had fallen under Patty's spell before he even saw her.

The inside was dark and oak panelled. A postage-stamp stage was crowded with musical equipment—a drum kit and microphones and amps—and in front of this stood a tiny girl, with a mass of blond curls flying around her head. She wore a long skirt, made of some gauzy Indian fabric, dark green with silver thread running through it, a white blouse with a drawstring neckline and long loose sleeves. It was an odd outfit, in this crowd of tattoos and black-on-black. The outline of her legs as the lights from behind her shone through the skirt's thin material mesmerized him. He wanted to run his hands under the material, feel the bones of her knees. A tidal bore of desire overcame him, the intensity of which was completely unknown, a voluptuous sensation not unlike drowning.

"Sit down, man, you're blocking the view," someone said, and so he took a seat at a table near the stage.

Her voice was bird song. Her voice was a mermaid singing. Her voice was perfume and wine and a soft feather against his cheek.

He ordered a beer. People chatted around him, half listening. They clinked glasses and coffee cups and ashtrays and he wanted them to stop, to pay attention to her, to respect her. A jewelry box lay on a stool beside her, the kind with a little plastic ballerina that popped up when, as now, the lid was open. Something about that box, the innocence of it, pierced him. A guy with thin legs and huge, military-style ox-blood boots flipped a quarter into it on the way to the bathroom. She smiled at the guy. Tom put a dollar in the box and her smile flowed over him like honey. He listened to her sing five or six more songs. He emptied his pockets of change.

"C'mon, Patty," someone said. "Time for the next set."

She closed her little jewelry box, looked Tom straight in the eye and said, "I'm hungry."

He bought her dinner, and she ate with clear purpose, hunched over her food, making tiny smacking noises with her glistening lips. She put large pieces on her fork and thick slabs of butter on her bread. She ate a 16oz. rib-eye cooked medium rare with the red juices pooling at the edge of the heavy white plate and lots of pepper. She ate two baked potatoes smothered in sour cream and salad and pecan pie with vanilla ice cream. When she was done she'd licked her fingers one by one, sucking for a moment on her thumb. He watched her over a beer. She ate his French fries. He couldn't eat—all his senses were full of her. He asked her to come with him, back to his room. She shrugged her shoulders and said, "Why not?"

In his room overlooking the street, she stood with one hand pressed up against the window glass, her back to him. She told him her story. She was barely twenty and living in a haphazard relationship with a few people. They were 'authentic,' she said. Poets and musicians. They were starting a newspaper. She sang for her supper. They lived in a cold-water flat in Alphabet City, but would probably be evicted soon. She told him there had been a couple of men in her life, in her bed. He thought there might be more. He didn't care.

He felt enormous next to her, all hands and feet and bony shoulders. When he held her in his arms he felt he held blown glass covered in velvet. He touched his tongue to a tiny mole on the inside of her elbow and tasted vanilla. He circled her upper arm with his thumb and middle finger, marvelling at her delicacy, at the precision of her structure.

Now, driving on this deserted road in the middle of the night, he shifted uncomfortably, trying to rearrange his sudden erection. "Miles, to go, pal. Miles to go," he said.

That afternoon, as Tom pulled into the driveway, he was surprised to see Patty's dented Pinto already there. He had stopped into Ed's Garage to get the spark plugs on the truck changed, then grabbed a quick burger down at Gus's Corner. It was three o'clock in the afternoon. Patty should be at work by now. Was she sick, he wondered? Something wrong with one of the kids? Ivy? The teasing? He'd tried to talk to Ivy about it, but she'd just laughed him off, said nobody was teasing her, what would they tease her about? He had to get a cell phone.

Rascal barked even before he closed the truck door. His bark sounded normal, just his usual dopey glee, nothing alarming. Still, Tom jogged up the steps. As he opened the door Rascal jumped up to greet him. Patty's singing came from the kitchen. Nothing amiss then. When had he become such a Cassandra, expecting the worst?

"But the sea is wide . . . and I can't cross over. . ." It was a sad song, but Patty's voice rang out as pure as clear water.

He went into the kitchen and found her fussing with pots and pans. When she heard him she turned, and gave him a big grin.

"I quit my job! Just like that. It came to me during my coffee break. I don't have to do this. I'm not a prisoner. I just washed my mug out in the sink and I walked back into Mr. Wilton's office, turned in my smock and said I wasn't coming back."

Patty twirled around the kitchen holding a wooden spoon in one hand and pot lid in the other. She wore a white, ankle-length dress he hadn't seen in a long time. Her feet were bare.

"Free! I'm free! Free at last! Thank God almighty I'm free at last!" She spun over to him, smiling. Glowing. Then stopped. "Why are you

66

looking at me that way? It was your idea. You said I could quit if I wanted to." The wooden spoon and lid dangled from the ends of her arms.

"Sure. It's great," He tried to mean it, tried not to think about bills and clothes for the kids who grew out of them almost as soon as their arms were through the sleeves. "I just thought maybe it was something you'd do next year, or sometime . . ."

"You said I could."

It was as though a screen door slammed. He saw her face there, behind a defensive metallic haze, her features fuzzy and guarded. He wanted more than anything for her not to hide herself. "And I meant it." He reached out to brush a curl out of her eyes, but she pulled back. "I meant it, Patty. We'll be fine. The most important thing is that you're happy. We'll manage."

She regarded him sternly, the way she looked at Bobby to see if he were fibbing. Then she smiled. "It's going to be better around here. You'll see, Tom. The house will be clean and I'll plant a garden next month and grow our own vegetables. I'll bake bread. Won't that be great?"

She threw her arms around his neck, stood on tiptoe and kissed him in the soft hollow where his throat met his shoulder. He shivered and his arms went around her. She squirmed away and was back at the sink, gone so quickly he wondered if he'd only imagined the sensation of her lips on his skin, the smell of patchouli in her hair.

She made a celebration dinner. Chicken with lemons, green beans with almonds, rice and cheesecake, a bottle of cheap red wine which only she drank. It was disorienting to have such a strangely formal dinner in this old house. Ivy made them light candles and wanted Patty to blow them out and make a wish.

"It's not a birthday," said Patty, laughing.

"Then it's an un-birthday," said Ivy.

"Both your Dad and I will be home now, when you get back from school," Patty said.

"I want my own car next year," said Bobby.

"We'll talk about that when you get your license," said Tom.

"And then you can work for it," said Patty.

"You don't need your car now," said Bobby. "Since you're not working anymore."

It changed in an instant. A sudden drop in temperature. A crackle of electricity. A draft. Ivy laid her fork on the table and clasped her hands in her lap. Patty's mouth pulled down, the lines running from her nose deepened. "Listen, you—"

"Come on, now," said Tom. "Not tonight. Celebration, right? No point in talking about cars just yet, anyhow. You don't even start driver's ed until next fall."

Bobby mashed his beans into green mush. "I'm just saying."

"It's all right, son. Every boy needs a car. I get it. When the time comes." He patted his wife's arm. "Great dinner, baby. Really first rate."

Tom looked at the festive dinner and tried to get in the spirit of the thing. The candles in Chianti bottles. The kitchen transformed through the miracle of soft lighting to a place where even Bobby sat up a bit straighter and was willing to let an argument go.

"What is this?" Ivy said, holding up her fork with a beige sliver on it.

"It's an almond, silly. You like almonds," said Patty.

"No, I don't think I do," she said and put her fork down, scraping the almond slice onto the rim of her plate.

"I like them," said Bobby. "I'll eat hers."

Tom tried not to think about money. No treats, no dinners out, and certainly no college for the kids. Bobby hardly seemed interested in college, but maybe. No chance now, though, even if his grades improved. Not on Tom's salary. Unless he doubled up with a second job. Part-time maybe. At least in the warm months. Landscaping. He could handle that. Put something away. He chewed a mouthful of sticky, sweet-sour chicken and smiled at his wife.

Ivy became very quiet, even for Ivy, and in a way that was different from Bobby's sulking silence. Ivy guarded herself, held herself close. She watched her mother as though at any moment Patty might do something else unexpected. The girl pushed beans around on her plate, built a nest for them in a pile of rice, and smiled whenever Patty looked in her direction.

All through dinner Patty chattered away about what she'd do with all her time now. Read Chekhov and Shakespeare. Grow tomatoes and sweet peas and maybe even potatoes. Take up quilting, or no, maybe she'd become a weaver. "I'll bet you could make me a loom," she said.

"I don't know anything about looms," Tom said.

"You can learn. We can all learn new things. Maybe I'll move this stuff out of the dining room. We could put it in the shed. Then I could make it a studio or something."

"That dining room suite's from my parents, Patty. It's good walnut. I don't want it out in the shed."

She folded her arms across her chest. "Well, somewhere else then. You could turn the shed into a workshop for me. You could, couldn't you?"

After the cheesecake was finished, Bobby stood up, and said he was going out. Tom said he was not. Bobby said he was meeting his friends. Tom said he was doing his homework. Bobby said he didn't have any. Tom said he doubted that.

"You want me to call up your teachers tomorrow and ask?"

Bobby held his ground, glared at Tom. His expression matched that of the blond rapper stenciled to the front of his tee shirt, some absurdly rich kid named after a candy, from what Tom remembered.

"Up to you," said Tom.

"This family's whacked," said Bobby and he stomped up to his room and slammed the door.

"I've done my homework," said Ivy.

"Never doubted it for a moment, sweetpea."

"Are you going to help me with these dishes?" said Patty.

And so he and Ivy did the dishes while Patty watched television. Ivy stood on a little stool and carefully dried each plate, each piece of cutlery, each glass, polishing each one and holding the glasses up to the light to make sure there were no spots. When they finished, they joined Patty in the living room and watched a program in which two sets of neighbors redecorated each other's houses. Tom picked at the duct tape covering the tear in the arm of his lounge chair. Ivy laid on the floor, hugging a pillow, her expression intent, as though she really cared about valences and ottomans and shades of blue paint. Patty sat cross-legged on the plaid couch, sipping wine. At last it was time for Ivy to go to bed. She kissed them both and said goodnight.

After a few minutes, Tom went up stairs to check on her. As he passed Bobby's door he heard his son singing a horribly off-key version of something he supposed the boy must be listening to through headphones. He caught a whiff of incense with a possible under-note of cigarette, wondered if he should look in, but then decided against it. Let the kid think he was getting away with something small.

Ivy was already in bed, reading a book called *A Wrinkle in Time*.

"You all right, sweetie?"

"Sure. The new light helps a lot. You don't have to check on me all the time, you know."

"I like to check on you. Good book?"

"Very," she said.

"Don't read too late, okay?" he said, kissing her head.

He went back downstairs to the living room.

"She still scared of the dark?" said Patty. "She's an awfully timid kid, isn't she? You'd think she'd be over it at her age."

"She's fine."

He considered sitting next to her on the couch. She was a little bundle of knees and elbows and he didn't know how he'd get purchase on her if he did. "Patty," he said as he perched on the edge of his lounger. "Are you happy?"

"What kind of question is that?"

"I want you to be happy. Is quitting this job going to make you happy? Happier?"

Patty got up, walked over to him and plopped herself down on his lap. "You're the sweetest old thing, you know that?"

"Patty," he faltered and started again. "I feel like we're drifting."

She took another sip from her glass and played with the button on his shirt. "The thing is, I'm just stuck, you know? It was like the whole world was going by my cash register, doing things, on their way somewhere and there I was, punching cash register buttons. Wasting time."

"I don't think having a family is wasting time."

She put her glass on the table, put her hands up on either side of his face and kissed him on the forehead. "You never feel cooped up, do you?"

"You feel cooped up?"

"Well, no, not really, not like that. But you know . . . we could go somewhere."

"Sure, we'll take a vacation in the summer. Maybe go camping. The kids might like that."

She stood up, walked away from him and stood at the window looking out at her reflection looking back at her. "That's not what I meant."

"What did you mean?"

"I don't know," she said.

And try as he might, for the couple of hours before he had to sleep, he couldn't think of anything else to say. He tried to concentrate on the kinetic television dialogue of people who were supposed to be running the White House but who never seemed to stop walking around long enough to actually get anything done, but he could hardly hear the actors' voices, so loud were his thoughts as they flung themselves against the bones of his skull.

CHAPTER TEN

Do not be blind to what is among you. Those who flaunt their wickedness, their sloth, their drunkenness. They say they are as good as Christians, but it is nearer the truth to say that they are almost as bad as devils! Their common purpose to war against God compels them to act in concert. Did not the devils go in concert into the man possessed with a legion of devils as we learn in the gospel history? While they withstand God, they are only like devils in hell. Carry this message, I charge you, to the impenitent – tell them you know their evil and will not be fooled by the voice of Satan. Tell them they are cast away from you as our Savior cast aside the legion of devils – swine unto swine. We know them for what they are. Blasphemers. Evil men. — **Reverend Joshua Cotton, Church of Christ Returning, 1906**

On Thursday evening just after seven o'clock, Albert, with Bobby in the passenger seat, eased his truck into Stan Mertus's driveway. Stan had left word at the Maverick he wanted to see Albert, which Albert understood to mean Stan wanted a delivery. The backpack on Bobby's lap contained two ounces of prime weed.

Stan and his brother Petey lived in a somewhat dilapidated stucco bungalow. Their father had bought the house cheap back in the sixties after the old war veteran who'd built it hanged himself from the bathroom door and nobody else wanted to buy it. Mrs. Mertus had died shortly after that and Mr. Mertus, a drunk and a bully, had disappeared a few years ago, gone to Nobody-Knew-Where-And-Even-Fewer-Cared. The bungalow's front yard was a scrap heap of tires, rusty tools, an old Chevy up on blocks, a couple of bikes under tarps, a can of motor oil, an old metal garden chair draped with chains, an over-turned garbage can, and, incongruously, a life-sized plastic deer. Painted pink. Both ears missing.

"You coming?" Albert said to Bobby.

"Sure. Yeah."

"Take the backpack."

Stan's wide face appeared in the window, which sported a bed sheet curtain. Given his own living situation, Albert was immune to deficiencies of architecture and aesthetics, and he strode across the uneven, debris-clogged walkway on legs well accustomed to navigating treacherous surfaces. Bobby tiptoed around an abandoned carburetor, several beer bottles, a crankshaft and a leaking can of motor oil.

Stan opened the door and absentmindedly clawed through his shaggy black beard. "Hey," he said.

"Jesus, man, you're fatter every time I see you," said Albert.

Stan grabbed his belly with both hands. "Good living," he said. "Come on in. What's that with you?"

"That is Bobby Evans. Say hello, Bobby."

"Hey," said Bobby.

"Uh-huh," said Stan.

Stan went into the house; Albert and Bobby followed. Stan Mertus liked to call himself a biker. He often, as now, wore a bandana around his head, thick-soled motorcycle boots and, regardless of the weather, a leather jacket acquired from a pawn shop in New York City, which he thought gave him allure. Stan tinkered with motorcycles, occasionally for pay. He wasn't a half-bad mechanic, truth be told, and he had a fine reputation for bikes. The problem was that Stan Mertus was wet-sack-of-cement lazy, and was far happier stoned out of his gourd, figuring out the subliminal messages in television commercials than he was in honest enterprise. But then, thought Albert, who wasn't, if they could get away with it? Selling a little dope was a hell of a lot easier, and more profitable, than digging a grave or repairing potholes out on the highway.

In the living room, Keith Keyes, a friend of Stan's who Albert had heard was sleeping on the couch these days, sat in a vinyl-covered rocker with metal runners. The fungal-green linoleum beneath the chair was gouged and scarred. Keith had the long brown curls, soft lips and smooth skin teenage girls went crazy for. He watched a NASCAR race on a television set on a two-tiered table on which were also displayed three framed photographs: one of a baby in a white baptismal dress, one of a young couple dressed in the style of the 1980s—he with teased up hair and skin-tight leopard print pants, she with enormous shoulder pads and the same hair—and one of two small boys wearing matching overalls. The only adornment on the walls was a large photo of a Kenworth truck superimposed on a mirror. Through an archway, Stan's little brother, Petey, stood in front of the open refrigerator with a disappointed look on his face.

"Hey," said Keith, "grab a seat."

Albert sat on an old plaid couch pushed against the wall and Bobby sat next to him while Stan disappeared into the bedroom, saying, "I'll get my cash."

Albert didn't much like the way he said it, as though the business they had should be conducted quickly and Albert should, by this reasoning, be gone quickly. He put his feet up on the water-ring-stained coffee table. Electrical tape held one of the legs together.

"How you doing?" he said to Keith. "What you up to these days?"

"Nothing much."

"Keith got his heart broken," said Petey, chewing on a piece of white bread smeared with bright yellow mustard. He was a miniature version of Stan, one hundred pounds lighter and minus the facial hair.

"Fuck you," said Keith.

"Hey, no shame in it," said Stan, who had come back into the room with his wallet. "Happens to all of us sometime."

"Never happened to you." Keith peeled the label off a bottle of beer.

"I am incapable of love," said Stan. He pulled at his beard in an attempt, Albert thought, to keep the smile from his lips.

Keith snorted. "You're lucky."

Albert considered Keith Keyes a wuss. All broken up over a bitch. Guy should be embarrassed. He remembered a time he'd seen Keith and Stan Mertus down at the Italian Garden Pizzeria. Keith had obviously had a cold—nose red and dripping, sneezing. He coughed, little prissy *uh-huh, uh-huh, uh-huhs*, holding his hand up to his chest. "I think I might need antibodies," he said and Stan, his hands black with grease and motor oil, his overalls strained and straining across his beer belly, looked disgusted. "Antibiotics. And for Chrissake, man, buck up. You haven't got fucking *pneumonia*," he said. Keith had looked so hurt, and so pathetic, and so full of self-pity.

"Yeah, I heard you and Jayne—it was Jayne right?—I heard you broke up," Albert said. "That's a tough one. Hey, you got another beer?"

"You want a beer?" said Petey.

"Yeah. I would like a beer. How about you, Bobby, you want a beer?"

"Okay," said Bobby.

"You got my message?" said Stan. He dragged a metal-legged chair from the kitchen and sat, heavily, straddling it.

"That's why I'm here. What did you think? I dropped in because I heard Stan Mertus was receiving this afternoon?"

Bobby giggled behind his hand.

"What? What's that mean?" Stan glared at Bobby. "What are you fucking laughing at?"

"Nothing."

"I'll get you guys a beer," said Petey.

"Thanks," he said. "Mighty white of you."

"You got the dope, or what?" said Stan.

"What's the hurry? Why don't we have a taste first, see if the quality's up to your standards?"

"All right," said Keith, rubbing his hands in anticipation.

Petey returned with the beers and Albert rolled a joint. They passed it around and all conversation quieted while they inhaled, held their breath, exhaled. Albert watched Stan's shoulders relax.

"So, what happened, anyway?" Albert said to Keith.

"About?"

"Your old lady."

"Don't get him started," said Stan.

"I'm interested. Might be good to talk about it."

"All he fucking does is talk about it." Stan took a mighty hit into his lungs and stifled a cough. "Good shit," he said, with the croak of contained air.

"C'mon, Stan," said Petey.

"Yeah, c'mon, Stan." Albert leaned back on the couch and dared, with his slitted eyes, for Stan to piss him off. It was amazing what you could do to people when they needed you. Amazing what sort of disrespect they'd tolerate when you had the best grass in town. Stan took another hit before passing the joint along, but said nothing. "So tell me, Keith, this Jayne, she a bitch, or what?"

Keith drooped like a basset hound. "I was good to her, man. I was really good to her. You know, we were together for five years and I never once screwed around on her. Never once."

"What about Wendy Boyer?" said Stan.

"That wasn't nothing. Just a blow job at a party. Nothing." Keith rolled up the beer label he'd peeled off the bottle into little pellets and flicked them across the room with his thumb and forefinger.

Albert watched Keith settle in to a puddle of self-pity. He began to mumble about how Jayne would come back one day, when she saw what she'd passed up. Albert stopped listening. Stan grabbed the remote and raised the volume on the television just as Keith was saying he'd never hit Jayne, nothing like that. Although he no longer paid attention to the words, Albert watched Keith's face. Shit, he thought, the pussy might actually cry. What kind of girl could do that to a guy? She had to be one hell of a fuck. Little bird-like Jayne Miller. He knew her from around town. She was a waitress at Gus's Corner. Little sparrow of a thing. He remembered she'd poured him an extra cup of coffee one cold morning. Smiled at him, as if he was just a regular townie, and not a fucking Erskine. She was all right, he thought. Better off without this fucktard.

The weed slipped around in his own head now, and he'd barely inhaled, just enough to be sociable. Never get foggy where business was concerned, that was his rule. He figured the others must be pretty gone. Bobby had a half-mast stupid-ass grin on his face.

The door opened and all heads turned. Stan turned the set off. "Fuck," Albert said, and slipped the baggie of grass between the couch cushions. They hadn't heard anyone pull up over the drone of race cars on the screen. Stupid. His own fucking fault, not paying attention. Daydreaming about some waitress for Christ sake.

The figure at the door was tall and well built. His head was bald as a bullet and a knife-shaped tattoo adorned his neck. Albert recognized Bill Corkum.

"Yeah, it's all right," said Stan. "It's just Bill."

It wasn't all right for Albert. The Corkums lived in the no-man's land between town and mountain, considered mountain people by the townies, but not by the Erskines. The Corkums had aspirations. Bill Corkum worked at Kroeler's Paint as a mixer or something.

"Hey." Bill did not smile, did not come any further in the room. "This a bad time?" His eyes took in the room. He nodded at Albert. When he noticed Keith his eyes flickered with something Albert couldn't quite gauge. "Keith," he said. "How you doing?"

Keith did not reply, wouldn't even look at the guy.

Stan rose from his chair, "Bill? What do you want? You ain't got a fucking phone? You can't call first?"

"Hey, I'm trying to give you some business. You want it or not? I got a carburetor problem. I can take it up to Ed's though, you prefer. No skin off my ass." His voice was calm, smooth.

"I'm kinda busy right now, Bill."

"1988 Harley FXR. Edlebrock heads, end dual carb, Andrews cam, Crane ignition. Might need a new carb. Only runs with the enrichening lever pulled out. Maybe just needs the jets unplugged."

Stan's eyes lit up. "You got a 1988 Harley? How much you pay? Where you buy it from? You better pray it wasn't Darryl up in Cranshaw. He'd rip off his mother."

"Wasn't Darryl, and I'm not telling you what I paid. You'll tell me it was too much no matter what it was, you jealous bastard."

"Probably was. Let me take a look. Might be a problem in the float."

"Stan," said Albert, standing. "We should finish our business before you move on to other things."

"What? Yeah, all right." Stan pulled out his wallet again and rifled through the bills, counting and recounting before handing some to Albert.

Albert put the money in his pocket without counting and handed Stan the baggie. "I trust you," he said.

"You selling meth, too?" Bill folded his arms across his chest, putting his fists under his biceps to make them look bigger. "Family affair?"

"You hitting?" said Albert. Bill didn't have the telltale twitch-and-fidget of a tweaker, but you never knew. "I always knew you Corkums were dumb."

"Is that so? Hey, no lab on our slab, if you know what I mean."

"Shit," said Keith, although he didn't sound completely displeased by the sudden tension in the room.

Bobby stood up, pale, but game, like a little terrier. Would have been laughable in other circumstances.

"Sit," said Albert. "Now." He pointed at the couch. The boy did as he was told. Stan, Keith and Petey went quiet, like they were watching two pit bulls square off. No matter how good it would feel to lay Bill Corkum out, to finish the job someone else had started on that incisor,

Albert would not entertain these assholes. He inhaled deeply and let it out. "Don't know where you get your information from, Bill," he said. "And I don't give a shit. But let's be clear. I am strictly a weed man. Now, if you're interested in that, well, maybe we can do business."

Bill moved his mouth like he was chewing on something. Without turning his head, Albert glanced to his right, at Stan and Petey, and to his left, at Bobby and Keith. Then he locked on to Bill's eyes and held them, his eyebrow cocked. *Not in front of the townies, Bill.*

Bill opened his mouth as though to say something, but apparently thought better of it. He laughed. "Listen, I'm too goddamn lazy to work on that patch the way you do. You always have some excellent shit, am I right, boys?" He spread his arms wide to include the whole room.

"Sure," said Petey. "Great stuff."

"I get all the speed I need on that bike out there." He looked at Albert. "I'll be happy to take some weed off your hands, though."

"I don't have any more shit here," said Albert. "You want some, we can make an arrangement. Meet later. You get in touch."

"Give me your cell," said Bill.

"Don't use a cell," said Albert. "You leave a message at Mavericks like everybody else."

"You don't have a cell? Who doesn't have a fucking cell?" said Bill, and his voice was less friendly now, more annoyed. "You putting me off?"

Bill was about as sharp as a log. None of the Erskines had credit and weren't likely to get any and had no bank accounts. Just one more way for people to find out things about you. It was a strictly cash lifestyle. He might have used a prepaid, but constantly replacing them was a pain, and there was no reception on the mountain. Besides, Albert didn't want people being able to call him whenever they felt like it. "That's the way it is. I do business the way I do business and if you don't like it, I don't give a flying rat shit."

Bobby stood up again. "That's right," he said.

Albert whipped around and, with one hand in the center of the boy's chest, pushed him back onto the couch. "I didn't tell you to get the fuck up."

"Come on, now. I haven't got all goddamn day," said Stan. "You want me to look at this bike or not? Don't matter to me."

"Yeah, look at it," said Bill, his eyes still on Albert.

Stan grabbed his arm. "Well, then, let's go."

Bill shook him off.

"Albert, thanks," said Stan. "Bill. Now or never."

Bill chewed on the inside of his mouth again, and then smiled. "You're right. Better outside. Air's fresher. And hey, I got me a pretty new bike out there. Aren't I lucky? The things some men get. See ya'll." He raised his hand to his forehead and gave Keith a quick salute. "See you around, Keith." And he turned and followed Stan into the yard.

You just can't educate some people. "Come on, Bobby, we're done here," Albert said.

The two passed Bill and Stan standing on the bed of a truck looking over a red and chrome bike. Neither party said a word. Once inside his own truck cab Albert gunned the engine and then slid off down the road. He watched the motorcycle and the two men in his rear view mirror until the road turned.

"How come you don't like that guy?" Bobby said.

"It's complicated."

"You were great. I thought you were going to pop that guy. Why didn't you just do it?" He smacked a fist into a palm, his cheeks flushed.

"Why would I pop that guy, Bobby, you tell me that? You want to see that, huh? What do you think this is, the fucking Gladiators or something? I'm beginning to think you aren't old enough to run with the big dogs after all. I'm beginning to think you're just pussy wet. Or maybe you can't hold your drugs, is that it?" His voice rose and he was yelling now. "I got business in there, you got that? *Serious business.* And nobody messes with my business, not even you. Standing up like that. What the fuck did you think you were going to do, all hundred and twenty pounds of you?"

"I was just trying to have your back, Albert."

"Yeah, well, don't try and help me, all right? I have a reputation that I am not going to get fucked because of some kid who wants to get his ass kicked."

Bobby sulked, hunched up in the corner of the seat, all the fight gone out of him.

"Do you fucking hear me?"

"I hear you."

"And?"

79

"Sorry."

"I'll say you're fucking sorry. One sorry little shit. Don't talk to me, all right? Just keep your mouth shut."

They drove some way in silence, Bobby twisting the corner of his jacket between his fingers. Albert's mind raced. It could have gone wrong back there. Stan was a steady customer, one he didn't want to lose and, frankly, he didn't want to start shit with the Corkums. There was a loose sort of alliance between mountain people. Each one knew the other looked down on them, felt superior, but they kept things civil since all held such a dubious position in town. They were like packs of half-wild dogs, gnawing away at the edges of things, finding it easier to hunt together than to tear each other apart over a kill. But what would young Bobby, middle class townie that he was, know about such treaties?

It took a couple of miles for Albert to calm down and realize Bobby was snuffling and sniffing. "Are you *crying?*"

The boy put his knuckles to his face and dug at his eyes, grinding the tears in more than wiping them away. "No," he said.

"Yes, you are. Jesus Christ." Albert pinched the bridge of his nose and concentrated on the road, a long thin line of country road going nowhere in particular. Albert pulled over to the shoulder, nothing but stubble-rough fields on either side. The sky looked like bluish milk—thick and close.

"You want me to get out?" snuffled Bobby, not looking at him.

"No, I don't want you to get out."

Bobby wiped at his nose with his sleeve and looked out the window. "Can I have a smoke?" he said.

Albert gave him one, lit one himself. "Man, if you get this bent out of shape by a little disagreement between friends, well, I don't know." He blew a smoke ring toward the rear view mirror. Having a friend was complicated. How did people manage it?

"It's not that. It's my parents," Bobby said at last. He looked over at Albert as though waiting for him to make a joke. Albert merely raised an eyebrow and rolled down the window for the smoke to escape.

"You can tell me, Bobby. It's all right."

"They're all fucked up. Fighting all the time. I don't know. Something's up with my mother. The guys at school. They're saying shit about her."

"What kind of shit?"

"Like my old man's blind. That she's cheating on him. I hate it there. I wish I didn't live there."

Now, this was something Albert knew a thing or two about. "Bobby, young Bobby," he said, with a wide grin, "welcome to the real world, my man. Step right up. Learn to take it, young Bobby, because the shit keeps coming and if you don't learn to swim in it you'll drown with a mouth full of crap. I appreciate you telling me your secrets, I do. And maybe it's time I told you a few of my own. Why do you think I don't take you up to my place? I got some stories to tell you, young Bobby, stories that will make you glad you got the family you got. But more important than that, I'm going teach you how to live beyond them all. That's right. You are going to learn to live in spite of them, not just to spite them, if you know what I mean." He leaned over and put his arm around the boy's shaking shoulders, felt how he was all bone and nerves. "It'll be all right, Bobby-boy, it'll be all right. You got an older brother, now. You understand? An older brother."

CHAPTER ELEVEN

The morning's rain had stopped, but the sky was still heavy. Ivy walked along Bank to Elm Street and turned left. She didn't go through the forest short-cut anymore. She carried her science project, a box of twenty-nine properly labeled rocks, as well as the ten-page report she had written with no help from anyone. She had not only labeled everything, but classified each rock: igneous, sedimentary, metamorphic, and minerals.

"Gelsey, do you think Ivy's ignoring us?"

Cathy and Gelsey had been behind her since she left school.

"She must be, or else she's just retarded."

Ivy would not turn around. She would ignore them. She concentrated on the warm glow of Mrs. Sergeant's praise. When the teacher had said how good her project was she hadn't been able to keep the smile off her face no matter how she tried.

Something struck her between the shoulder blades. Something small, a pebble, probably, and it didn't really hurt, not through her raincoat, but she flinched.

"Hey, turn around," Cathy called. "Are you a retard?"

Another pebble. She kept her pace steady, shifting the heavy box from one hip to another. She thought of the rocks' physical properties: *color*, which was self-explanatory; *luster* (the way a mineral reflected light), *hardness* (measured using Mohs Scale of Hardness with diamond being the hardest at 10, and talc being the softest at 1); *cleavage*, a word which resulted in much giggling, something Ivy found very immature; and *streak*, the color a mineral rubs onto a white porcelain plate after the mineral's been ground to a powder. There were so many words here to love: the regal sounding *galena*, the religious sounding *hematite*, magical *metamorphic*, warrior-like *anthracite*, scholarly *bituminous*, and quiet little *shale*. She made an incantation of them, and they transported her to deserts and caves, deep hollow-hearted canyons and twinkling stream beds.

Something else hit her back. Softer. The smell. The laughter. Dog poop.

"Oh, my, what a smelly retard." Giggling.

A car horn blared, and Ivy nearly dropped her box. A truck rolled to a stop next to her. Someone got out. She recognized him. It was Albert Erskine, scary Albert Erskine. He wore a leather jacket, like some old-time biker, and carried a baseball bat. He stalked toward Gelsey and Cathy, who were frozen on the sidewalk, mouths open. Gelsey held a plastic bag from which another piece of dog shit fell.

"You little brats," snarled Albert. "Don't you run. Don't make me chase you. What the fuck are you doing?"

"Nothing," mumbled Cathy.

"Hey, Ivy. This should be good." Bobby's face grinned from the truck's open passenger window, his arms dangling, drumming lightly on the door panel. The green of Bobby's camouflage jacket was nearly the same sludgy color of the truck.

"What's he doing?" said Ivy. "What are you doing with him?"

Bobby rested his forearms on the lowered windowsill and lay his chin on his arms. He had a loopy grin on his face. "Hanging. Hanging loose," he laughed.

Albert was within grabbing distance of the two girls now. He loomed over them. Ivy, her stomach flipping, looked around to see if anyone would come, if anyone would stop Albert Erskine from killing Cathy and Gelsey. There was nobody.

"Make him stop," she said.

Albert bent down so his face was close to the girls'. They stepped back and he made an *eh-eh* noise, like they were misbehaving dogs. "If I ever see you near Ivy Evans again, I will be forced to come to your house some really dark night and I won't bring a bat, I'll bring an axe. And what do you think I'll do with that axe?"

Cathy's face went white. "I'm going to tell my father."

"I hope you do. And when you do, and he comes looking for me, I'll tell him what a little cunt his shit-throwing daughter is, and then I'll scoop out his eyes with a rusty spoon." Gelsey started to cry. "I know where you live you little bitches. Now, say you're sorry."

"We're sorry."

"Not to me, you idiot. Say you're sorry to Ivy."

"We're sorry."

"And you're never going to bother her again, are you?"

"No."

"That's what I thought. Now. Take that shit you've dropped and wipe it on your hands. Yeah, that's right. Do it. Right now. Very good. And just be glad I don't make you eat it. This time. If there's a next time, remember, it's going to be different. Now get the fuck out of here."

Cathy and Gelsey ran down the street as though chased by a rabid pit bull. Albert turned and smiled at Ivy. "I don't think they'll do that again, but if they do, you tell 'em Albert's watching."

"Say thank you, Ivy," said Bobby. He raised a cigarette to his lips, smoked almost down to the filter, and inhaled deeply.

Everything looked like it was far away, like in a movie. Nothing made any sense. Not Bobby in a truck with Albert Erskine, not seeing Cathy meekly rub dog poop between her palms, certainly not being defended by an Erskine. She had no idea what this meant for tomorrow. What was she supposed to do now? "You smoke?" she said, "Dad's gonna kill you!"

"And who's going to tell him?" said Bobby as he flicked the butt into the street. "Say thank you."

"Thank you."

"Hop in," said Albert.

"No, thanks. I'll walk."

"Get in, Ivy." Bobby opened the door and stepped out, then reached back into the truck and pulled out a handful of "McDonald's" napkins. He cleaned off the back of her coat, and ushered her into the middle seat. "Ivy, this is Albert."

"Hello," said Ivy, not looking at him.

"Hey, honey," said Albert, getting back into the truck. "I'm not going to bite. Get in."

It seemed rude not to, especially since he had rescued her. She sat in the middle, her feet dangling near the gearbox with the rock collection on her lap. Albert was smoking and she coughed. The polite thing to do would be to throw the cigarette out, but there you were. She was a bit dizzy from the smoke, and from what had happened. Thick gray electrical tape bound a split in the seat underneath her and it had rolled up at the corners. It was uncomfortable and she shifted around. The underside of the tape stuck to her tights. The cab was strewn with junk: empty plastic cassette cases, empty pop cans and cigarette packs, as well as a few squashed butts, fast food wrappers and a couple of tattered paperbacks.

She could only read the title of one. *The Grapes of Wrath*. Music played on the radio, something sharp with electric guitars and a screaming singer. Bobby drummed his thumbs on his knees. Albert caught her looking at him and grinned, that same mongrel grin all the Erskines had. Not that they all looked the same, some didn't look like they were related at all, but some others looked so much alike you thought they might be older or younger versions of themselves. Most of them had that smile, though. It made her feel wriggly inside. Was she supposed to think of him as her hero? She glanced at Bobby, smirking behind his hand. The heat from Albert's leg oozed onto hers, even through his pants. He emanated a strange warmth that was at once both disturbing and intriguing.

She focused on the word *emanated*. She had recently learned it and loved the way the sound rolled over her lips to the back of her throat, the roof of her mouth, and then tucked between her teeth. She practiced now, silently, moving her lips and tongue through the word's dance.

"What you thinking, there, little sister?" said Albert.

"Nothing."

"Your lips were moving," he said.

"Shouldn't you be watching the road?" she said.

He laughed and looked at her long enough so that flame crawled up her cheek. "I'm a talented guy. I can do more than one thing at a time."

Bobby played around with the radio and then switched it off. After a few minutes the silence in the truck felt like not silence at all, but like they—or not *they* but Albert—was listening to her, even though she wasn't speaking. She tried to nudge Bobby with her elbow to make him say something, but he was too involved with whatever was going on inside his head.

Obsidian, she thought. Scoria. Igneous. Apache tears. Cinnabar. Coquina. Scoria—a much better word than slag.

"So," said Albert. "Where do you want to go?"

Ivy's eyes flew wide. "Aren't you taking me home?"

"Of course we're taking you home, pipsqueak. You think we want to hang out with a little kid?" said Bobby.

"I don't know," said Albert, his eyes on the road, not looking at her at all, which seemed strange now, as though he were not looking at her on purpose. "Maybe Ivy would like to go for a drive before we take her home. Make sure her little friends got the message."

"Are you kidding?" said Bobby. He laughed, like it was a joke because, Ivy thought, it had to be a joke, didn't it?

"Yeah, of course I'm kidding. We're taking you home, little sister. No worries. I'm not the big bad wolf, you know."

"I know that," said Ivy.

"Oh, you do, huh?" And still Albert looked straight ahead. "Well, let's not tell your pals, okay?"

"We could go shoot some pool," said Bobby. He sounded a little put out, a little whiney, which made Ivy feel slightly proud for some reason, as if she had something Bobby wanted, but it wasn't a nice proud feeling, like when she looked at her rock collection and was proud of how perfect they all were, but a slithery sort of proud, that didn't feel good at all.

"I guess. Not for long. I got things to do," said Albert.

"Yeah?" said Bobby.

"Yeah, fuck," said Albert and Ivy jumped at the bad word.

Biotite. Basalt. Graphite. Gypsum.

"I got things to do. Money to make, people to see."

Bobby stopped drumming his fingers and sunk lower in the seat. "I could help, maybe."

"Help?" Albert took his eyes off the road and looked at Bobby over Ivy's head. "Help, huh? Maybe. Not today."

"Okay. Okay," said Bobby, his chin tucked into his jacket.

Albert's eyes went back to the road. "We'll go for a while," he said.

They were driving down Elm now, passing Farmhouse Antiques. Seeing the store sent a rush of longing careening from the center of Ivy's chest along her arms and into her fingertips like electricity. "Stop! I forgot. I have to go see Mrs. Carlisle. You have to let me out."

"What are you going to see her for?" said Bobby.

Albert turned on to Quaker. Ivy sat forward and banged on the dashboard. "Stop, Albert. I have to get out. Stop."

"Hey, hey, all right, simmer down," said Albert. He slowed the truck, and pulled over. The driver of a car behind them beeped his horn and Albert stuck his finger out the window and flipped the other driver the bird. He looked at Ivy and his face wore an annoyed expression, the pressed together lips turned up at the corners. "You want out, huh?"

"I promised I'd help her," said Ivy.

"With what?" asked Bobby.

With both Bobby and Albert's attention centered on her she fidgeted and worried she was about to cry. It felt hot inside the cab suddenly and the cigarette smoke made her queasy. Her skin was clammy. Albert's leg was too close to hers. She didn't want him touching her. She pushed at Bobby. "In the store, dusting and stuff, let me out, Bobby. Let me out."

"Let her out," said Albert.

"Geez, all right. Don't freak out. What's wrong with you?" Bobby opened the door and she scooted over. As she did she glanced back at Albert. He wasn't looking at her at all, just staring out the windshield. She scrambled down, careful not to drop her rock collection. The solid ground felt like a welcome mat under her feet.

Bobby held the door. "Mom and Dad know where you are?"

"Do they know where *you* are?" she said, bold again, now that she was out of the truck.

"Like they give a shit," said Bobby. "But you keep your mouth shut, Ivy, and so will I."

"They're not going to mind me visiting Mrs. Carlisle."

"You think your parents would mind your brother hanging out with me?" said Albert from behind her.

She shuffled her feet and didn't look at him. "I don't know."

"You mind your own business, Ivy," said Bobby, glaring at her. "I don't know why we even helped you. Trying to do something nice for anybody in this family is a waste of time."

And she felt sorry then, for she saw that he had been trying to show off his new friend. His new friend who protected her. Maybe she had been rude for no reason. "I won't tell," she said.

"Yeah, well. When you going home?" He climbed back into the truck cab.

"Soon. About an hour, I guess."

"Tell Mom I might not be back before dinner," said Bobby.

"What if she asks where you are?"

"Like *that's* going to happen. Better you should ask her where she's been."

"What does that mean?" she said.

"Nothing, just tell her I'm at a friend's house."

"All right," said Ivy and stepped on to the sidewalk. But then, now that there was distance between them, she remembered her manners. "Oh, and thank you, Albert. Thank you for what you did."

Albert Erskine stopped grinning then and leaned forward in front of Bobby. "You're welcome, little sister," he said. "Anytime. But I don't think they'll be bothering you anymore." His voice, like his expression, was solemn. For a moment, their eyes held, and what she saw in Albert's eyes jolted Ivy, for it wasn't at all what she expected. It wasn't scary at all. It was far away, and kind of locked down, and unutterably sad.

Then he turned away and the truck jumped forward and Ivy was left on the sidewalk, wondering how it was possible to be so uncomfortable around a person one moment, and want to give them a hug the next.

She put her hand inside her collar and pulled up the string with the Boy Scout whistle her father had given her. She felt the metal, smooth and warm from being next to her skin. It felt alive and she was sure it had power to keep her safe.

Dorothy was rearranging some of the plates in a corner cabinet enjoying the reassuring coziness of her shop, the dust motes floating through the beeswax-scented air. Ivy came through the door carrying a flat box and with a most peculiar expression on her face.

"Hello, dear." Dorothy was no longer surprised to see the girl at her door. Poor little mouse. Her face was quite pained. From what she'd told Dorothy, meted out in scrips and scraps, she was this year's goat. There was one every year, chosen, if she remembered correctly, for any number of arbitrary reasons. Although she had yet to hear from Ivy herself what the reason was in her case, Dorothy couldn't help but wonder if her slightly eccentric mother didn't have something to do with it, although she didn't wish to look too closely at this scenario. There were rumors and if Dorothy, an adult who did her best to avoid hearing things, had heard them, it was more than probable they had filtered down to the schoolyard. Well, she wouldn't push the girl.

"Hi," said Ivy. "Are you busy?"

"Not too busy for you, dear." How were some children able to wheedle into your heart against your will? And what was the expression on the girl's face? Something to do with that box? "Take your coat off. What are you carrying there?"

"It's my rock collection. I did it for science class."

"Do you care to show me?"

A flush of pink pride radiated from Ivy. "Okay."

"Well then, tea I think," said Dorothy.

Over tea and homemade oatmeal cookies, Dorothy got a short lecture on the kinds of rocks there were and how one told them apart and what their properties were. She was amused and charmed by the delight Ivy took in her recitation and in the sound of words. In the coquina sample, Ivy pointed out the visible fossil shells. "It's composed mainly of marine or freshwater mollusk shells and shell fragments cemented together with calcium carbonate," she said seriously.

"Wherever did you find so many interesting specimens?"

"Oh, I didn't find them," she said, sounding very disappointed indeed. "I'm not old enough to go by myself and nobody else is really interested. It's kind of a geek thing, I guess. But I got an A+ for my project."

"You are to be congratulated, then. There is nothing remotely geeky about an A+."

"I guess." She shrugged, but looked pleased.

"So, if you don't hunt for the specimens yourself, how do you come by them?"

"There are rock stores, but not around here. So I buy them off the internet. It's expensive, though, for the best ones. There's this one called plumbogummite from China that sells for hundreds and hundreds of dollars. But most aren't that much. There's this stone called selenite from Algeria that looks like a rose. It costs $15.00 and I'm saving up. I want to go to the old quarry. You can find all sorts of things there, even stuff like azurite and datolite. Aurite is blue, of course, sometimes there's yellow in it, too, and that's because it's mixed with malachite."

"Ivy, I have to say, I couldn't help but notice that you were upset when you came in. Was Cathy teasing you about your collection?" Watching Ivy's face fall, Dorothy could have kicked herself.

"No, not like that, but it's kind of about her."

"Do you want to tell me?"

"I don't know. My brother was with someone. I didn't like him. Or I don't think I did. But he kind of helped me. I don't know. He's weird."

"Who, your brother?"

"Yeah," Ivy rolled her eyes and grinned, "I'll say. But I meant the other guy."

"Who is that?"

"I promised I wouldn't tell." She bit her lip. "Bobby was in the guy's truck. An older guy." She told an edited version of what had happened. Bobby's friend had chased the girls away, and gave her a lift.

Dorothy considered. Someone Ivy wasn't supposed to say was with her brother. Someone with a truck. It didn't take much for Dorothy to figure out whose truck they were discussing. Seeing Albert Erskine with Bobby Evans was one thing, thinking about Ivy in a truck with him was something else. But he had helped her.

"It was nice of him, wasn't it, to defend you?"

"Sure."

"Still, Ivy, if ever you are uncomfortable with someone, you mustn't go with them. Surely your parents have told you this." Dorothy was out of her depth here. This was a parent's job. Someone would have to be told, or perhaps they knew? What then? There was no comprehending what went on in other people's houses.

"Sure. But Bobby's friends with this guy. So it's all right, isn't it?"

"I think you have to talk to your parents about this, dear."

"But I can't tell them. I promised." She broke a cookie up into small pieces, but didn't eat it. "I promised."

"There are some promises which are perfectly all right to break, I think, particularly if you believe something dangerous is going on."

"Like what?"

Yes, like what, exactly? What was she suggesting? What gossip was she spreading here, and to a child? It wouldn't do. "Oh, I don't know, Ivy. I just think you shouldn't go in cars with older boys, even if they are with your brother, and especially if they make you uncomfortable."

"I just didn't want to go for a drive, is all." Her voice sounded defensive now. She put the lid back on her rock collection.

"Ivy, how would you like to earn some money for your rock collection?" It seemed there was no end to the surprising things Dorothy might find herself saying.

"Sure, how?" Ivy popped a piece of cookie into her mouth.

"Well, since you're here so often, which I find very generous, and since you help so much, I'm simply going to have to start paying you."

"Paying me? To come here?"

"Absolutely. You'll have to work for it, of course. But it's only what you've been doing. Polishing silver and dusting and so forth. Yes. I think that's a good idea. What do you say?"

"Sure!"

"You could come here whenever you wanted, and I would pay you . . . what do you think is fair?"

"A dollar an hour?" Her eyes were wide, and her mouth slightly open.

"Oh, perhaps a bit more than that." Dorothy considered, tilted her head, and said, "Let's see. School ends at 3:30 and if you're here by 3:45 and then we have tea and you work for an hour or so, I think that's worth three dollars, don't you?"

"If I came every day I could get the selenite in a week!"

"That seems right. But I do think we need to arrange this with your parents. They need to say it's all right and we have to think about how you'll get home. I don't think it's a good idea for you to walk home alone, do you?"

"I do it every day."

"Still, I think, if it's all right with you, I'll just give your parents a call. What do you think?"

"I guess," she said, but she looked worried.

Dorothy patted Ivy's arm as she rose to use the phone. "I might just as well call them right now, don't you agree?"

CHAPTER TWELVE

Before he went home, Tom stopped off at Wilton's to get some things Patty had asked for. He was in the produce department under the fluorescent lights, his hands damp and slightly chilly from the sprinkler intermittently freshening the greens. He picked flat-leaf parsley and put it in a plastic bag. He had turned to the tomatoes and was picking through, feeling for invisible soft spots, enjoying the heft and weight of them warming in his palm, when Dorothy Carlisle tapped him on the shoulder. She wore a grayish blue, soft-looking turtleneck that made her eyes, which were focused on Tom with their usual acuity, appear steely. She was a woman whose face was transformed by a smile—she became impish, girlish, even with that short gray hair. Now, however, she was not smiling and the lines around her mouth set hard, making her look as severe as any British schoolmistress. She carried a basket containing asparagus, eggs and a bunch of fresh basil that perfumed the air between them. Dorothy Carlisle had been much on Tom's mind since her phone call a few days ago.

"Hi, Mrs. Carlisle, how are you? I've been meaning to pop into the shop and thank you for spending time with Ivy. It means a lot to me. Ivy never knew my mother, never had a grandmother and I think she feels a bit like that around you—not that you're old or anything, but, well, that wasn't the wrong thing to say was it?"

Her face did then break into that transforming smile. "I am so an old lady, Tom. But one thing I am not is vain about my age. And I'm delighted you don't mind Ivy helping me. I've been worried I overstepped my boundaries. Patty didn't sound, well, she didn't sound. . ." She waved her hands in the air as though trying to gather words.

"That's just Patty, Mrs. Carlisle. She's maybe a little touchy about people thinking she's not a good mother or something."

"I never meant to imply that."

"No, no. But not knowing Ivy was coming round to you, and this teasing business. Rita Cronin mentioned it to me before you did, and I spoke to Ivy about it, but, I should have taken it more seriously. It's such a small town, you don't think of bullying as going on here. More a big city thing, you know? Anyway, I called the school. Mrs. Sergeant said she'd keep an eye out. She thinks it's died down, just a passing thing between kids. Cathy Watson, she's quite a piece of work, I guess."

"It does seem that way. But I hope Patty doesn't think I was judging her in any way. Perhaps I should call her again?"

"No. No. You don't need to do that." He hesitated, remembering what Patty had said when he got off the phone, *interfering old witch! Who does she think she is, taking my kid in like she's some kind of trailer park stray?* It had taken him some time to persuade her it was nice for Ivy to have a grandmotherly figure. When Mrs. Carlisle had dropped her off, watching from the driver's seat of her boxy brown Volvo station wagon to make sure Ivy got inside the house safely, Tom had been the one to thank her. Patty said only that if Ivy preferred being with somebody else there wasn't much she could do about it. Tom put Ivy to bed that night and told his daughter her mom didn't mean it when she said such things, she was just afraid Ivy didn't love her. And Ivy said she knew. "Mom's always afraid people don't love her enough," she'd said, and those words had kept him up all night, watching Patty sleep with her fist curled in front of her mouth and her legs restless under the sheets. And now, he said to Dorothy, "You can imagine how it is for her, this not being her town, not really."

"Yes, I can. We are not a welcoming people. And it is hard to keep track of children nowadays I imagine." Dorothy rearranged the eggs and herbs in her basket. "How is Bobby? I see him around town sometimes."

Tom shrugged. "He's a teenager. Doesn't want to talk to his old man any more, that's for sure. But then, I don't suppose I had much to say to my Dad when I was his age. He'll be all right. He's taken up basketball after school. Plays nearly every day and we hardly see him. Never thought he was one for sports but I'm glad. Maybe it'll put some meat on him."

"Ah," said Dorothy. "Well, that's good then."

"Listen, Mrs. Carlisle, I wonder if maybe . . ."

"What is it, Tom?"

"I shouldn't ask. But . . ."

"Oh my, just out with it, dear."

"Would you consider babysitting for us some night?" He threw his

93

hand up as soon as the words were out of his mouth. "Naw, forget I asked. I..."

"I think that might be arranged."

"Really? Because it's our anniversary coming up and we haven't had much time alone lately and I don't know who I could trust with Ivy. Bobby's old enough to be left alone for a while, but I don't like to leave Ivy, even if Bobby is home, and, look . . . I'd really appreciate it." He knew how desperate he must sound.

"Oh, wedding anniversary is it? Well, I understand. William always made quite a production out of such things. I sometimes wonder if men aren't more romantic than women. When is it, exactly?"

"To be honest, I haven't planned anything. I wasn't sure I could make it happen. Couple of Saturdays from now. I need to make a reservation somewhere."

"Yes. Good idea." She paused and considered the contents of her basket for a moment. "Here's what I'm thinking, Tom. Perhaps Ivy should stay the night. Better than keeping her up late or having you hurry back from your dinner."

Half an hour later, with a bag of groceries under each arm, Tom used his leg to fend off the dog's exuberance as he stepped in the door and called for Patty.

"Get down, Rascal. Okay. Good boy. Yes, I love you, too. Now get down!" No answer from Patty. What was that sound? He called again and realized it was the upstairs shower. God, she was only getting around to taking a shower now? He stepped around Rascal, sidestepping to avoid tripping on his wriggling frame, and put the bags of groceries on the kitchen table. Cereal, peanut butter, yogurt, pop, bread, hamburger, chicken legs, carrots, tomatoes, parsley, cucumber, cheese, milk, fish fingers, spaghetti sauce, rice, ice cream. There wasn't much already in the fridge, which smelled of something gone off, milk maybe. He pinched open the cardboard carton and put it to his nose, jerking his head away quickly and pouring the lumpy milk into the sink, one side of which was filled with dirty breakfast dishes. He tossed out old mushy lettuce, a mouldy piece of cheese and something fuzzy and unidentifiable in a plastic container. He couldn't figure out what Patty did all day long. The

94

counter was sticky and crumbs crunched underfoot. Rascal sat next to his plastic dish. Hardened food caked the sides and the water bowl was empty. Tom opened a cupboard and pulled out a can of dog food. Rascal cocked his head and barked in an accusatory way.

"Nobody fed you, again, huh? Sorry, pal."

Tom cleaned out the dish, scraping at the dry hard bits with his thumbnail, and spooned in fresh food. He rinsed the water bowl and filled that too. Rascal danced with joy, toenails ticking on the crumb-scattered linoleum. Dogs, thought Tom, were so forgiving.

He left Rascal to his dinner and climbed the stairs.

"Patty," he called, not wanting to frighten her, "It's me."

The water turned off as he stepped onto the landing. "Patty, you hear me?"

"I hear you," she called back. "You do the groceries?"

"Yup.."

"You put them away?"

"Yes, I put them away. Listen, I have to talk to you about something."

He stepped into the steamy bathroom. Patty stood before him wrapped in a towel, her wet, darkened hair streaming around her shoulders. He reached for her, put his arms around her and gathered her close. She smelled of lemon shampoo and soap. Her skin was like that of a porpoise—gleaming and smooth.

"You'll get all wet. What's the matter with you?" She pushed him back.

He sighed and sat on the toilet seat. Rascal came in, having gulped down his food in the way of all dogs and sat between Tom's legs, pushing at his knee with his knobbly head, wanting his ears scratched. Tom obliged. The dog burped extravagantly, casting a meaty smell into the air. Tom waved it away. "You know we got an anniversary coming up. What would you say to a fancy dinner out on the town?"

Patty rubbed a spot clear of fog and regarded herself in the mirror, pushing up the skin at the corner of her eyes. He knew she worried about getting older, but he couldn't see it. She was Patty, always beautiful, always young.

"You hate going out for dinner."

She bent over and twisted a green towel around her hair, flipping it back up and tucking the ends in to form a turban. The towel made her eyes look even greener than usual. She pulled a pair of tweezers from the vanity drawer and plucked at her brows.

"What would you say to someplace fancy?" Ed Carlaw had told him about the Blue Moon. He took his own wife there from time to time. Nice, Ed had said, with tablecloths and daisies in little vases next to a candle on every table.

"Oh, I don't know." Patty walked out of the bathroom and Tom followed.

"What do you mean, you don't know?" Rascal's ears flicked forward, and then he disappeared downstairs.

"The four of us at the Olive Garden isn't exactly my idea of romance." In the bedroom now, Patty opened a top drawer on the white painted pine bureau and pulled out clean underwear. She dropped her towel on the floor and lifted first one leg and then the other to step into her panties. She pointed her toes. There were goose bumps on the skin of her arms and legs, on her ribs and stomach. Tom wanted to pick her up and carry her to the bed and lay her down and put his body over hers until she was warm again. He wanted to run his tongue over the dark line that went from her belly button into her pubic hair. But there he was, standing in the doorway like an intruder and she was already unravelling the turban, pulling a sweatshirt over her head, covering those breasts, which were softer and riper than when he'd first met her, covering those rosy nipples that tasted like vanilla, pulling jeans over the curve of her hips, and if she noticed him looking at her, noticed the hunger in his eyes, she gave no sign.

He walked over and wrapped his arms around her from behind. "No kids. The Blue Moon Restaurant. Just you and me out as late as we like," he whispered in her ear.

"Bobby won't want to watch Ivy. He's always out these days." She stood passively.

"That's part of the surprise. Dorothy Carlisle's offered to take Ivy for the night. Sleep over. Bobby's old enough to be by himself for a while."

Patty turned in his arms and looked up at him. "I don't know about that woman."

"I've known her all my life. She's fine."

Patty grinned. "Might be just what we need."

"I agree," Tom said, and kissed her.

Two weeks later, Patty stood in front of the bathroom mirror and, having just applied lipstick in a shade indicated in a little gold sticker on the end of the black cylinder as *'Seduction.'* She stuck her index finger in her mouth up to the knuckle and then pulled it out again.

"Why do you do that?" Ivy sat on the side of the tub watching her mother's preparations.

"A good trick for you to remember, kidlet." Patty held her finger up to show Ivy the circle of red. "You'll never get lipstick on your teeth, see?"

"I don't think I'll ever wear lipstick."

"No? Why not?"

"It's kind of gummy. But," she added quickly, "it looks pretty on you."

Patty wore a green halter-top, the color of a new leaf, and a black skirt with a fluted hem that fell just above the knee. She ran her thumb inside the waistband. "This skirt is so old. I've gained weight. I look like a sausage."

"No, you don't. You look beautiful." Tom stood in the doorway, leaning against the doorframe with a big grin on his face. He, too, was dressed up in flannel pants that were only slightly too short, a white shirt and blue tie under a blazer.

She cast him a skeptical look. "You'd say that no matter what."

"Yes, I would, and it would be true."

Patty snorted, but she looked pleased. Ivy giggled.

Tom crossed the bathroom in two steps and picked Ivy up with one arm. The other he put around Patty. "My two beautiful girls," he said, and kissed them.

"Get off!" said Patty, though she sounded happy, "You're wrecking my makeup! Tom! Stop it!"

Tom put Ivy down. "Ready, then?" he said. "Mrs. Carlisle's expecting you at six."

They passed Bobby's closed door. Tom knocked but received no reply so he opened the door.

"Bobby, we're going."

Bobby's back was to the door, as he hunched close to the computer monitor. Tom couldn't see what was on the screen, only the chill, eerie light around the boy's head. Bobby's hand on the mouse jiggled and jolted in tiny, furious movements.

"Hey," Tom said. "Hey, hello!"

Bobby started and then let go of the mouse. "Shit," he said, and pressed a button. He pushed his chair back and turned to face his father. The screen flickered and the image of a swimming shark appeared. "What?"

"We're going."

"Fine."

"You sure you're going to be all right here alone?"

"Dad, I'm not a little kid. Besides, I might go out myself."

"I don't think so. I want you home, pal."

Bobby shrugged. "Fine."

Patty called from downstairs that they were going to be late for their reservations.

"Don't spend all your time playing games, okay? And no friends over."

Bobby turned back to the computer. "Got it. Have a nice time."

Fifteen minutes later they arrived at Dorothy Carlisle's and Tom walked Ivy up to the door. Ivy carried a little round overnight case that had been Patty's. It was pink and had an oval strap. Ivy insisted on carrying it herself, proud and straight-backed on this, her first night away from home. Dorothy waited for them in the open doorway.

"Well, good evening, Ivy, Tom. This is going to be lovely."

"Nice of you to take her, Mrs. C."

"Nonsense. I'm happy for the company. We shall have great fun. Rice crispy squares are in the offing and then Ivy is going to beat the pants off me at Crazy Eights."

"No, I won't," laughed Ivy. "I'll let you win."

"Oh, you mustn't do that, young lady. And I shall be watching you closely. Besides, once you trounce me, I will have the opportunity to return the flogging at a game of scrabble."

"Sounds like you've got it all planned," said Tom.

"What is that around your neck, dear?" Dorothy asked Ivy.

"That's my whistle. From Dad." Her skin turned faintly pink. "It's a kind of protection."

"A Boy Scout whistle, isn't it? Oh, very sensible. My husband was a Boy Scout Leader, you know, and he had one of those. Loud enough to call up the cavalry if I recall and excellent if one is lost in the woods." She turned to Tom. "Now, you and Patty have a wonderful evening." Dorothy ushered Ivy inside. "And don't worry about us at all. I'll drop Ivy by in the morning after breakfast. Waffles, I think, don't you?" she said, addressing this last bit to Ivy.

"They're like pancakes, aren't they?" said Ivy.

"Far superior, to my mind, if made correctly. Now, off you go, Tom, off you go. Your wife is waiting for you."

"Thanks, Mrs. C. Really. Thanks a lot."

She shooed him and closed the door.

As Tom got back into the car he saw Dorothy and Ivy at the window, waving. He waved back as he started the car up again. "You could at least wave," he said as he backed out of the drive.

"I waved. I waved. She's got a nice house," said Patty, with a trace of wistfulness as she gazed at the small white front-gabled gothic revival with dark green scalloped gable trim and finial and a graceful porch with flattened arches. A neatly trimmed boxwood hedge ran along the sidewalk and a climbing rose grew up along the porch columns. A brass wind chime tinkled prettily in the evening air.

"Maybe we should plant a climbing rose." Tom set the car towards the Delaware River.

Although Tom had not corrected Dorothy when she said 'wedding anniversary' it was not, in fact, the anniversary of their wedding, since Patty had resolutely refused to marry him. Rather, it was the sixteenth anniversary of the night she'd agreed to come back to Gideon with him. Every year since then Tom had marked the day in some way. A rose on her pillow, a bottle of perfume, an impromptu bottle of wine and a waltz in the kitchen, a picnic if the weather permitted, and occasionally, a dinner out, like tonight. But tonight, Tom was hoping, would be even more special. Until he'd talked to Mrs. Carlisle he hadn't known exactly how it would happen, only that he'd saved for months for this dinner. Doing without lunches and without a couple of beers after work with the boys. He'd done without new underwear and without new work gloves. They would have wine with dinner and dessert and anything else she wanted.

During the forty-five minute drive he tried to keep the conversation going. He talked about the kids: Ivy and her interest in rock collecting, what a strange hobby that was for a girl; about Bobby's sudden interest in basketball and some new group of friends he seemed to be with all the time; how he'd like to know a bit more about them. Maybe they could watch him play some time? Sure, she said, sometime. Well, Tom said he was pleased Bobby had new friends. And then he tried to find something else to say, but couldn't and so the last minutes of the drive were spent in silence, watching out for deer.

When they'd arrived at the Blue Moon and parked the car, Tom made Patty wait until he went around and opened the door and made her take his arm so her heels wouldn't slip in the gravel pathway. He held the restaurant door open and bowed slightly, clicking his heels. He was rewarded when she laughed and told him not to be an ass, and he felt the evening might be fine, after all.

They were seated at a good table halfway down the room, not too close to the swinging doors of the kitchen, or to the hall leading to the bathroom in the back. Tom held Patty's chair. The room was filled—lots of couples and a few families, who were set up near the back where the noise of children wouldn't bother anyone, and a couple of tables of friends. The lighting was low and jazz piano drifted from speakers suspended in the corners of the room. The tablecloths were white and the water glasses were cobalt blue with gold moons on them. Small white candles in gold holders sent light glinting off the moons and the water and Patty's green eyes. The waiter asked if they wanted a drink before dinner and Patty said yes please, she'd have a Manhattan, and Tom had a scotch and soda. They looked over the menu.

"How about oysters to start?" he said.

"Oysters?" She made the suggestion sound sexual. "Oh, you want me to have oysters, do you?"

He couldn't tell if her teasing was in fun, or if she was irritated. "Might be interesting," he said.

"Can I have the lamb?" she asked and read from the menu, "Roast baby rack of New Zealand lamb with mustard and basil crust. Piquillo pepper and hummus tortilla, roast garlic and green peppercorn au jus."

"Sounds good, maybe I'll have that myself, although I don't know what the hell piquillo pepper is, do you?"

"No idea."

"No oysters?"

"I'll have a salad. I need to lose weight."

Tom reached across and took her hand. "You're the size of nothing. You don't need to lose weight." He brought her hand up to his mouth and kissed her palm. It smelled of roses. "Change nothing. You're perfect."

"Why do you love me so much?"

"How could I not?"

The waiter arrived and brought their drinks. He said he'd be back to take their orders and Tom said they were in no hurry whatsoever. Patty sipped her drink and said it was good, so good she might have two. Tom proposed a toast. "To us," he said, raising his glass. "To you. To another fifty years together."

The light from the candle flashed in her hair, in her eyes and on the drop of liquid on her bottom lip. "To us," she said.

They ordered wine to go with the meal. Red wine. A Shiraz the waiter recommended. The food, when it came, was served on white and gold plates and was fragrant with basil and pepper and the jus from the lamb pooled against the hummus. They talked about how good the food was and drank their wine. Knowing he was driving, Tom only had one glass and Patty drank the rest. Maybe that was what made her mood change. One minute they were talking about putting in a vegetable garden in the back of the house and the next Patty said, what was the point?

"I mean, why bother with any of this?"

"Bother with what? Gardening?"

"Sure, that's it." She snorted. "Gardening."

"I thought you liked that climbing rose at Mrs. Carlisle's. It did make the house look nice. I've kind of let our yard go of late. Used to be real pretty when my mother took care of it."

"Of course, I'll never be as good as your sainted mother," said Patty, pouring herself more wine.

"That's not what I meant."

"Have you ever thought what it's like for me, living in a dead woman's house? Sleeping in a dead woman's bedroom?"

"I thought that's why we got all new furniture and painted—"

"We got *some* new furniture. Some. And that was sixteen years ago. It's hardly new now." She put her fork down. "Why can't we have anything new? You sit in that chair of your father's every night. It's actually disgusting, now I think about it. It's like all the molecules and cells of these dead people are still around, and you're morphing into them. I'm morphing into them."

"You want me to get rid of the chair?" It was like having a handful of water, watching it slither through his fingers with no idea how to stop it.

"Oh, God, Tom. It's not the fucking chair."

A woman at the next table glanced over at them. Tom's eyes met hers for a second and he could have sworn he saw pity in her expression. "Then what is it?" he said quietly.

"Forget it."

"No, I want to know."

"Well, maybe I don't feel like talking about it. Maybe I don't feel like talking much at all. Maybe I'm all talked out, Tom. Jesus. Everything is such a battle with you. We just don't see things the same way, do we? Maybe that was what I liked about you. We're so goddamn different. You remember that night we first met?"

Liked? *Past tense*? "Every minute of it."

"You looked like such a hick. A big corn fed hick right off the plow." She chuckled. "Everybody looked at you when you walked into the Horse, wondering what tour bus you'd fallen off."

"I never claimed to be anything but what I am."

"I know. I couldn't believe it when you sat front and center and wouldn't be budged. You made me feel self-conscious, did you know that? You made me feel like you were hunting me or something. But then, I figured I'd keep singing as long as you were handing out the cash." She looked at him as though she didn't see him every single day, like she didn't sleep next to him. "I never figured I'd end up here."

He knew then the question he had hoped to ask again, and hoped maybe, just maybe she'd answer differently than the other times he'd asked it, would go unspoken. He felt it drift down like a body sinking in water, down to settle at the silty bottom.

They were supposed to be talking about what was right. How right they were together and how much they meant to each other. He could see now how foolish he had been to think of asking her, again, to marry him. It had been years since he'd brought it up, so long perhaps even he'd thought it no longer mattered—so many people never bothered these days, as Patty assured him. But to him it did matter. And he was slightly ashamed of that knowledge, for what did a paper mean? Was it ownership he was seeking? Some sort of legal right? Something he could brandish if need be? She would throw her food in his face if she knew what he was thinking. But he wasn't the only one, surely, who cared about such things? Married mattered in this town. Not married was merely shacked up. And then there were the kids. Nobody had ever said anything to him, but that didn't mean they hadn't said anything. Neither Ivy nor Bobby had ever asked to see wedding pictures, but they would one day. It was a wonder they hadn't already.

So, no question tonight, or at least not *the* question. But certainly others must be asked. "If not here, then where did you figure you'd end up, Patty?" Every word out of his mouth felt like something sticky pulled from between his teeth.

"Honestly? I don't know, Tom."

His throat closed over. He hadn't expected it, this strangling emotion. He removed his hand from the stem of his wine glass, afraid it might snap. "Excuse me," he said, in a choked voice, and stood.

"Tom?"

"I'll be right back."

In the men's room, he sat on a toilet while tears burned and finally fell down his cheeks. He pressed the palms of his hands into his eyes until geometric patterns collided behind his lids. His chest was on fire and he briefly wondered if he was having a heart attack and then wondered if he cared. They would end up like all the other couples, sitting across from each other at brightly lit tables in the food court at the shopping mall, staring at their food, not talking, not touching. It was enough to make you want to stick a fork in your eye. In fact, he could picture just that. One moment you're sitting there at your weekly outing to the mall, poking at the lunch special of chicken-noodle soup and salad, having just picked up those boxes of cereal on special at the Piggly-Wiggly, wearing your orthopedic sneakers and Depends, and one of you just snaps under the weight of all the unrealized dreams. One of you picks up the fork, wipes it on a napkin, and ends it all. Death by heavy sag of the dream deferred. Nod to Langston Hughes. You had to laugh, didn't you?

He couldn't sit in the john all night. He wiped his eyes with toilet tissue and stepped out of the stall, thankful no one else was in the bathroom. He ran cold water over his eyes and, looking in the mirror, he thought he would do. It wasn't such a bad face, was it? Not an altogether unattractive face, surely. He turned sideways to the mirror. No gut. Shoulders still broad. Arms still muscular. He splayed his fingers and regarded his hands. Meat packers, his father used to call them. "Shame you don't like football, boy," his father had said. "You'd make a hell of

103

a wide receiver with hands like that." But he hadn't liked football, had he? Hadn't liked the bone crushing violence he could very possibly do to another boy. You had to be careful with strength. You had to know when to use it, and when to keep it tucked up under your arm.

As he stepped out of the men's room, he saw Patty had turned in her chair, as though about to get up. He saw the worry in her face. Such beautiful worry. The fire in his chest died down to embers. She worried about him, and that was something.

She stood up, the way a man would when a woman approaches the table. As he came near her he saw there were tears in her eyes as well, her cheeks bright with wine flush. She put her arms up like a child, up around his neck and she nuzzled there. "I'm sorry, baby. Don't pay any attention to me. I'm a bitch, ruining this wonderful night. It's the wine. Forgive me?"

And he very nearly said, marry me. Instead, he said, "Come on, no harm done. Let's finish dinner. What do you want for dessert? We have to have dessert."

They took their seats on opposite sides of the table and avoided each other's eyes while the waiter refilled their water glasses and then poured the remainder of the wine equally between them.

On the drive home, she refused to wear her seatbelt, snuggled next to him, and said she didn't care if they did hit a deer and she died now, because there really was nowhere else she'd rather be and no one she'd rather be with. He let her snuggle there on his shoulder and let her hand draw patterns on his thigh.

When they got home she stepped inside the door and let her coat crumple to the floor, then untied the halter top from around her neck and let it slither to her waist, revealing the lacy strapless bra she wore underneath. "Make love to me, Tom," she said.

"Patty! Bobby's upstairs."

"He's either in front of the computer or he's asleep. You know Bobby."

He didn't bother to take off his coat. He picked her up and carried her up the stairs. They passed Bobby's door. Dark. A light snore. He kept going. He lay her down on the bed and stripped off his clothes, scattering them around him on the floor like so many skins, his erection nearly painful, too urgent to be contained. She made a motion to take off her skirt, but he shook his head and she lay back. He took off one of her shoes and then the other and rolled her pantyhose down her legs and lifted her foot and ran his tongue along her instep. She rose up on her elbows and watched him. He rolled her over and placed his hand on the middle of her back, pinning her gently there, the span of his fingers nearly covering the expanse of her skin. He undid the zipper on her skirt, the buttons on the base of the halter-top and then rolled her back and lifted her, so he could slip the skirt from her hips. She felt as light as balsa wood and the scent of roses and amber came from her. He began again at her foot and worked his mouth slowly up her calf to the inside of her knee. She moaned then, and covered her eyes with her arm. Tom took her arm away. "Look at me," he said, and she did, her expression a little frightened, vulnerable and slightly lost. Her lower lip, he thought, trembled ever so slightly. It occurred to him that he wouldn't mind making her cry. He lowered his mouth to hers and she flicked her hot, pointed tongue against his lip. The lace of her panties was damp under his fingers and he moved it aside, anxious to feel the softness, the heat of her. She arched her back.

After that, it was all sensation and texture and smell and the sound of sighing and sharp cries. He moved into her as into a lake of warm honey and drowned there, his mouth filled with her taste and his ears filled with her moans and his skin flame and electricity wherever they met and his nostrils full of the scent of crushed roses.

CHAPTER THIRTEEN

In the morning, he woke late and found her already up. The smell of coffee and the radio news ascended from the kitchen. He pulled on sweatpants and went to the bathroom. His penis was sore and the sensation made him smile. Such a good sore. He hoped she was limping. He wanted a mark on her and was not, for once, ashamed of this desire. He felt, albeit with a semi-sheepish self-awareness, as though he wanted to strut, wanted to throw out his chest and tuck his thumbs in his pants. He flushed the toilet, brushed his teeth and washed his face, rubbing his hand over stubble, which he decided he wouldn't bother to shave. Not today.

When he came into the kitchen he was surprised to find Patty sitting at the table, a coffee cup between her hands, a bare foot tucked up underneath her, staring intently into the black liquid. He had, he realized, expected to find her humming, dancing, ready to spring into his arms.

"Hey, beautiful," he said.

She smiled. Warm, but not the smile for which he had hoped. "Hey. You want coffee?"

"Sure. We alone?"

"You just missed Bobby. Cranky this morning. I think he heard us last night."

"It's good for him to know his parents are in love." Tom came around beside her, squatted, and put his arms around her, nuzzling her neck. She put her arms around him and held on. "I love you," he said.

"I love you, too," she said, in the sort of voice she hadn't used last night, the sort of voice one might use for a child, or a favored pet.

"Want to go back upstairs? Ivy won't be back for a while yet." He waggled his eyebrows.

"What am I going to do with you?" She took his face between her hands and kissed him.

"I can think of a thing or two."

She squirmed out of his arms and stood up, the belt of her housecoat

106

dragging across the floor, picking up crumbs. "What do you want for breakfast? I can scramble up some eggs."

Tom stayed where he was for a moment, one arm on the back of the empty chair and one arm on the table. He hung his head. There was a split in the seat of the chair and some of the grayish-yellow stuffing spilled out like fat from a deep wound.

"You want to go to a movie or something today?" he said.

"No, I don't think so. I've got to get new heels on my shoes and pick up some new socks and underwear for the kids. And we need a few things from Wilton's."

She opened the fridge door, and a chill draft encircled his bare ankles. Eggs and butter, milk and some pre-grated cheddar. Pan and plates, another mug for his coffee. She was all efficiency and resolution there in the chill florescent light of the kitchen. Her bathrobe might just as well been made out of razor-wire.

"What's wrong?"

"Nothing's wrong. Why are you starting up? We had such a nice time last night, Tom. Don't spoil it." She kept her back to him, her eyes on the frying pan.

"I don't get you."

He waited for an answer. But there wasn't any answer. Just the splatter of grease in the pan. Tom sat in the chair she'd vacated; it was still warm from her backside. He considered throwing the cup she'd left against the wall, but he didn't have the energy for that, or all that would come after. He didn't know what the hell had happened between last night and this morning. Didn't know if he had the ambition to try and find out, to shred his skin trying to breech her defenses yet again. He only knew he wasn't at all hungry. The smell of the food made him faintly queasy.

Still, when the eggs were in front of him there seemed nothing else to do; he put the fork to his mouth. They were rubbery and too salty. When he asked her where hers were, Patty said she'd already eaten.

"I'm going to get dressed," she said and left the kitchen without looking at him.

He chewed the eggs, tasting the alien metallic chemicals of the cheese that wasn't cheese at all, just a cheap imitation of cheese. When he'd eaten not quite half what was on his plate he realized if he ate one more bite he would vomit. He threw the rest in the garbage and returned to his chair, and to his bitter cup of coffee. He listened to his wife moving around above him, and then her steps on the stairs and the rattle of her keys.

"Okay, Tom. I'm off. You need anything at the store?"

"Not a thing," he said. She closed the door and he wondered if she'd even heard him. The car started up and pulled out of the drive and then the silence of the house descended. The husky hum of the refrigerator sounded like whispers, as though ghosts haunted the house, speaking through the white noise of appliances. He sat a little while longer and saw that sitting would change nothing. He went upstairs to shave. Ivy would be home soon. It occurred to him he had no idea where Bobby was.

An hour later, Dorothy dropped Ivy off at the house. Again, she didn't come up to the door, just beeped and waved from the car. Ivy trotted up the steps and threw her arms around him. Her eyes were bright pieces of dark amber, and she chattered away about the pretty crystal glass Mrs. Carlisle had let her use for milk, fragile as the wing of a moth, and the paintings in the house, some of Mrs. Carlisle's own ancestors, and about the minerals she'd be able to buy with the money Mrs. Carlisle paid her and about when would he take her out rockhounding, as she called it, and he half listened and tried to say the right things and probably didn't. She went up to her room to put her things away and Tom sat in the kitchen for a while and then went out to the garage, with Rascal on his heels. He couldn't think of anything else to do, so he began cleaning up his work shelves, banging things about with perhaps more vigor than was strictly required.

At dinner that night, it was just the three of them. They set a place for Bobby but he didn't appear. Dinner was hamburger fried in a pan with a topping of processed cheese, which sat greasy and wet on the plates, and some raw carrots and nobody enjoyed it.

When Bobby hadn't come home by seven Tom cleared the dishes, put his son's dinner in a plastic leftover container in the refrigerator, and began washing the dishes. Patty went to her station on the couch in front of the television and Ivy went to her room to do her homework, and when Tom had left the dishes to drain on the rack, he sat in the kitchen, nursing a beer and waiting for his son to come home.

Patty went up to bed at ten without kissing him, without touching him at all and without even looking at him sitting there at the kitchen table, and he didn't know what he'd done that was so wrong. He should be in bed himself, but knew he wouldn't be able to sleep. He got up and turned off the overhead light, leaving only the bulb from the stove hood to cast an oily glow. He felt better in the half-light—less exposed.

Soon it was nearly eleven. Rascal pricked up his ears and barked and headlights flashed along the wall. Tom rose and went to the window, tried to see who was in the truck as it drove away, but couldn't, only saw Bobby slouching up towards the house, his hand over his mouth as though checking his breath.

The front door opened, admitting a gust of night wind that smelled of pinesap with an under-note of truck exhaust. Tom stood directly inside the vestibule and was gratified to see this startled his son.

"Where have you been?" said Tom.

"Nowhere."

"Close the door. That is not an answer. Try another."

Bobby stood with his back against the door, his eyes flickering, jittery in their sockets. His eyes were red. Now that the smell of night had dissipated in the interior funk of cooking smells, another odor was evident: cigarettes and that of smoke from neither tobacco nor campfire.

"I've just been with friends." Bobby's breath carried the yeasty musk of beer.

"What friends?"

"Friends from school."

"I want their names."

"What the hell is this? An interrogation?" Bobby's voice rang shrill and his skin mottled. "Why should I have to tell you anything?"

"Because you are fifteen and I am your father."

Bobby ran his tongue over his teeth. "Just some guys from school."

"You're drinking and smoking grass."

A stupid grin. "No, I'm not."

"Don't lie to me. You reek of it."

Bobby just stood there, a grin coming and going on his face like a crawling worm. He wiped at his mouth, struggling not to laugh. It was very hard not to slap him.

How did the father look to the son? Tom tried to be intimidating, to loom, to assert, and yet, stoned as Bobby undoubtedly was, how did he look? A big clown, lumpish, slow and dim, laughable in his gravity.

Encysted deep in every father is the son he once was, who compares everything he does to what his own father did—the old king is dead, long live the king. The distant image of himself as a boy, not much older than Bobby, swaying and unsteady from a night of drinking out in the woods with the football team (that night Rita Kruppman had taken her blouse off on a dare from Ed Carlaw and she'd blazed in the mystical white gleam of her bra in the moonlight). His own father had stood almost exactly where Tom stood now, wearing his raggedy brown bathrobe, his head a glinting orb under the hall light, demanding to know who Tom thought he was, a big man, a real man, just because he could down a few beers and make a puking fool of himself? The implication, not lost on young Tom, was that perhaps he would never be a real man at all, no matter how much he drank, or didn't. It had infuriated Tom then, and he swore in his inebriated swagger he'd never let the old man know anything about him, even as the shame, the truth of his own ridiculous adolescence became apparent. And so Tom had vowed to be a different kind of father, and yet here he was, in the same hall, pressing down on his son with that same age-old superior masculinity. An urge to pick his son up and hold him to his chest swept over him; to hold him until the need for all this fell away, dissolved in the sound of synchronized heartbeats.

And then Bobby said, in a voice that seemed exploratory rather than purely defiant, "Fuck you."

"What did you say?" said Tom, whose hands had formed fists the size of axe heads.

Bobby did not answer. The words hung sharp and rusty in the air between them.

"Say it again," said Tom. "You go on and say that to me again."

Bobby, thin as a feral cat, diminished in the hulking possibility of being struck down, struck dumb, struck dead by his father's shock and fury, stood silent, but stood his ground. He looked like a cornered stray. He looked like his mother.

"Jesus Christ," said Tom. "What's happening to us?"

CHAPTER FOURTEEN

I am against sin, brothers and sisters and I know you are, too. I know you are on the train to heaven and not on the hell-bound train. You know that poem?

Tom Gray lay down on the bar room floor
He drank so much he could drink no more
So he fell to sleep with a troubled brain
And dreamed that he rode on a Hell-Bound Train
The engine with blood was red and damp
For fuel an imp was shoveling bones
While from the fiery furnace rang a million groans.
The boiler was filled with lager beer
And the Devil himself was the engineer.

He said, You have laid up gold which canker and rusts
And given free vent to your fleshy lust
You have drank, and rioted, and murdered, and lied
And mocked at God in your Hell-Bound pride
You have paid full fare so I'll carry you through
It is only just you should get your due
Why, every laborer expects his hire
So I'll land you safe in the lake of fire.

That's right, brothers! That's right, sisters! That's where they're going, those who truck with Satan, who turn God's green mountain into a cesspit of moonshine and unnatural, ungodly practices. Paint your doorway with the blood of the Lamb, my neighbors, and let evil just pass on by.
— **Reverend. Clarence Goodall, Church of Christ Returning, 1925**

On Saturday afternoon, Gus's Corner Restaurant was crowded with high school students lingering over fries and a pop. When Albert Erskine walked in with Bobby Evans in tow, the students stopped talking, nudged one another, gestured with their chins, and whispered behind their hands. Bobby walked with a little bounce, a little strut in his step. Albert chuckled; Bobby gained street cred being seen with him. They walked through the tables to a booth, Bobby nodding at this kid or that. One of the two waitresses, Carol Everett, a twenty-nine year old blonde whose pudginess began under her eye sockets and continued to the ends of her fleshy fingertips, stood behind the counter near the cash register, fussing with the pyramids of ice cream dishes, glasses, cups and saucers on the shelves, surreptitiously glancing at herself in the mirror that ran the length of the counter. Albert caught her eye and winked. Her mouth hung open. Albert and Bobby slid into a back booth, Albert with his back to the wall, on which someone had scratched, *"To some it's a six pack—to me it's a support group."*

The other waitress, Jayne Miller, popped up from behind the counter and came over. "Hey, how are you two?"

"Can't complain now I'm looking at you," said Albert.

She smiled and Albert tried to think of something even wittier to say. Jayne had chin-length, gently curling dark hair that he imagined she shook effortlessly into place in the morning, forming a flattering halo of soft curls around her elfish face. It was the kind of hair he thought of as belonging to French girls, girls from Paris. Girls who knew how to tease a guy. Her gray eyes, pale enough to note, gave her an air of wisdom Albert was not completely convinced she merited, but they were absorbing.

"Sweet," she said. "What can I get you?"

"Burger, fries, and a coffee," said Albert. "He'll have the same."

"I want a Coke."

"He'll have a Coke."

"Coming right up."

Albert watched her walk away. She was slender in her A-line white uniform and her legs and arms were very thin, like a dancer, or a gymnast, but she was not without some intriguing curves. It was because of Jayne that Albert had agreed to Bobby's suggestion they come to Gus's. Normally, he preferred the dim, licensed interior of Maverick's, but Jayne Miller had been on his mind ever since that afternoon at Stan Mertus's,

112

when her ex-boyfriend Keith had been so broken-hearted. There was something about a girl who could reduce a guy to that sniveling mess. Something challenging. Something that indicated she had taste and spine. Albert had walked past Gus's a few times in the past week. Just checking her out. He'd had a few daydreams. Dreams about a clean little apartment somewhere with African violets on the windowsill and a big bed with this girl's tousled head peeking from the covers. The sound of kids voices in the other room. Toots and Kenny and Ruby, playing and laughing; Griff and Frankie, unafraid of what would happen that day. He'd thought about dropping in and sitting at the counter and maybe asking her out sometime, maybe go for a drink at Maverick's. And he'd started to, once or twice, and then hadn't. She made him shy. There, he admitted it. He wasn't used to feeling this way, didn't get it, but it was the truth. Him, Albert Erskine, shy around a fucking girl. There had been more than one night since then when he'd fallen asleep with his hand around his dick and the image of this girl in his head. And then Bobby had suggested coming here and here they were.

She returned with their order a few minutes later, and Albert was sure she would have stayed and talked, but Pataki, the owner, yelled for her from the pass-through. She rolled her eyes and smiled at Albert again. He'd never liked Pataki.

"I don't know what the fuck's wrong with my Dad," said Bobby. "He's like, gone all weird."

"Why, because he busted you for smoking dope?" Bobby had told him what happened. He'd thought he was going to get grounded for sure, but then apparently Tom Evans had kind of deflated and backed down. Told Bobby nothing more than to pull himself together before it was too late.

"No, and I'd like to see him try anyway." Bobby scowled but only succeeded in looking like a spoiled kid. He swirled a soggy French fry in a puddle of ketchup.

Albert bit into his burger and watched Jayne bend over to pick up a fork someone had dropped, noted the rounded swell of her ass under the uniform, and the lack of panty line. She must be wearing a thong, he thought, and his dick twitched in his jeans.

"Anyway, my mother smokes dope," Bobby was saying. "I know she does, I saw the roach, and it sure as hell wasn't Ivy's. They're such fucking hypocrites."

"Your old lady smokes weed? Where does she get it from?"

Bobby sucked on his straw and pulled it out of the soda, his finger against the end so the liquid stayed in the straw, then he let it drain out. "I don't know. But I've seen her come out of the bathroom after she's been in there for a damn hour, saying she's reading. She's stoned. I can't believe he doesn't know."

"Maybe he does know. Maybe he smokes with her."

Bobby laughed. "My old man? Are you kidding? I'm surprised he even knows what grass is." He shook his head, grinning. "My father, Chinese-eyed. That'd be something to see."

The door opened and Bill Corkum stepped in. As he ran his hand over his shaved head, he looked around, his eyes pausing on Albert for only a nano-second before coming to rest on Jayne, who stood behind the counter. He smiled, walked to the end and took a seat where Albert imagined he could keep an eye on him and Bobby. Albert finished the last of his burger and pushed the plate away. So, that's why Bill had looked at Keith so funny that afternoon. He was trying to stick it to his old lady, huh? Well, Jayne wouldn't go for that shit. Not Bill Corkum. Bobby hadn't noticed Bill; he was folding creases into his placemat and mumbling about his mother.

"You not working?" said Jayne to Bill.

"Mixer broke down again. Told us to take lunch."

"Must be hard working at Kroeler's," said Jayne.

"Naw, it ain't hard."

"You like it?"

Bill laughed. "No, girl, I don't *like* it, I *do* it. So, you coming to Aunt Gerry's tonight?" he said, popping a toothpick in between his teeth.

"I have no idea what you're talking about."

"Eating. Food. At the house."

"No," Jayne laughed. "How could I do that?"

And Albert thought, *smart girl.*

"Which means what, exactly?" said Bill.

And Albert thought, it means she's not going to fuck you, pal.

The bell rang in the kitchen. "Table six up. Table nine up," Pataki yelled.

"Excuse me," said Albert. "Can I get some more coffee, please? If you're not too busy."

Blushing furiously Jayne said, "I gotta go. I'll be right with you, Albert."

Bill did not look at Albert. Jayne picked up two meatball sandwiches and one grilled cheese and bacon and delivered them to the waiting customers. As she circled round, she stopped to grab the coffee pot and came to Albert and Bobby's table. Albert leaned over the table, drumming his fingers on the surface.

"Can I get you anything else?" said Jayne, pouring the coffee.

"Whatcha got?" said Albert, smiling at her with that smile he knew was his best feature.

"Well," Jayne said, smiling back, "we've got pies—apple, blueberry, cherry."

"I think I'll have a cherry," said Albert. "Bobby, you want anything else?"

"Naw," said Bobby. He dangled his dripping straw over a pile of salt in the middle of his ketchup-stained plate.

"So have another Coke, and stop playing with the fucking straw," said Albert.

"Coming right up," said Jayne.

Carol stood by the register, facing the mirror, pressing lightly at a pimple on her chin. Jayne whispered something to her as she walked past and Carol gave her a dirty look, one hand caressing the small gold cross around her neck. Jayne cut the cherry pie, licking her thumb afterwards, pulled a fresh Coke from the soda gun and brought the order to Albert and Bobby. Before Albert could say more than thank you, she ducked back around the counter in front of Bill. "Okay Bill, what can I get you?"

"How come you won't come to supper? Not town enough for you?" He grinned at her, his tone teasing.

"Are you the cook?"

"*Hell*, no."

"Well, I can't just go to supper at someone's house when they don't even know I'm coming. A person just can't barge in like that." She stood with pencil poised. "What can I get you?"

A gaggle of boys at the register pushed and shoved as each one tried to pawn the check off on someone else. They waved their goodbye's to Jayne and she waved back. The restaurant was quieter now, only a few girls left, and they looked about to follow the boys, disappointed they hadn't been asked.

"Give me some fries and coffee, lots of cream," Bill said.

She fetched the coffee pot and a heavy mug and as she put the cup down Bill took her hand. A flush of proprietary jealousy sat in the pit of Albert's stomach like a frozen rock.

"Listen," Bill was saying, "you don't get it. My Auntie Gerry don't care. One more ain't going to make a bit of difference."

Jayne took her hand back, but not, Albert noticed, without a friendly little squeeze. "She run a restaurant, or what?"

"Feels that way, but it's all family."

Bobby, who was also listening now, muttered "I'll bet," and Albert glared at him so that he shut up. The kid didn't get it. You kept your mouth shut—that was the way you learned. You let people tell you things they didn't know they were telling you. It was an art he'd learned, growing up in a place where your life depended on recognizing the slightest change in vocal inflection, the smallest shift in conversational subject. An unintended glance could tell you where someone stashed a bottle, or some extra cash, or a hoard of bread and baloney. And if you talked too much and missed the clues, the bruises and blood were your own fault.

"She's a pretty great lady. Come on, meet her."

"I don't think so." Jayne blushed prettily.

Albert was happy to see her looking uncomfortable. He thought he'd let her squirm for a few more minutes and then step in.

"Too mountain for you?" said Bill.

The bell in the kitchen rang. "Table fifteen up."

"You flatter yourself, Bill Corkum," she said, walking away.

"You're killing me!" he called after her. "I heard you were a heartbreaker!"

"Guess that's one name for it," said a familiar voice.

Albert watched as Keith Keyes walked through the door and Jayne stopped in her tracks.

"Hi, Jayne," Keith took a table in the window. He ordered fries, grilled cheese and a Coke.

"This should be interesting," said Albert.

Bill stayed in his seat, but all the jokiness of a moment before disappeared. He sat straight, his forearms placed before him on the counter. His left leg was flat on the floor, but his right one was cocked, in a stance Albert recognized as one designed for the fastest upward movement, if required.

"Keith," said Jayne, in a flat voice.

116

She picked up Albert's order from the window, and Pataki stuck his head out. A goatish little man, he sported a tidy moustache that was better suited to a tango dancer. One of Gideon's few 'foreigners', Gus Pataki never seemed to leave his restaurant. He spoke with the myth-laden accent of his Greek homeland and had married Alice Sully, a local girl. They lived in one of the town's finer houses, on Washington Street, facing the Trout River, and it was widely agreed he couldn't possibly have made his money solely from Gus's, which was, after all, little more than a diner.

"We slowing?" Pataki asked, and Carol said they were.

Jayne busied herself putting on a new pot of coffee and didn't see Mr. Pataki come out of the kitchen. He took her by the elbow and gestured with his chin in Keith's direction. Albert strained to hear and even Bobby had stopped playing with his drink and turned around to watch.

"You see who's here?" said Pataki.

"I saw."

"You two getting back together? Going to kiss and make up?"

She looked at his hand on her elbow. She tried to move away but he gripped her tighter. Albert watched to see if Bill would rescue her, but Bill, although his shoulders bunched, stayed where he was. It was not what he, Albert, would have done. Albert considered going over and tearing Pataki's hands off Jayne. The idea made him snort.

"What?" said Bobby.

"Nothing."

The urge to intervene, like his early twinge of jealousy, took him off guard. Perhaps it was because Jayne reminded him a little of his ten-year-old cousin, Toots. Something about Jayne's independence, maybe, or her skinny legs. But then, Jayne's weren't blotchy with bruises, were they? An acid wave of guilt washed over him.

"No, we are not getting back together," Jayne said, in a voice loud enough to carry across the restaurant. "Can I have my arm back?"

"You want me to toss him out?" said Pataki. "I can do it, you know. Wouldn't bother me, if you wanted me to do you a favor like that."

What was it about this little chick that got all the roosters so riled up? Albert mused.

She pulled away, fast and neat, leaving Pataki holding air. The motion looked as if she was drawing back to slap him, and Albert was surprised when Pataki flinched ever so slightly. Albert's admiration for Jayne grew, and again, she reminded him of Toots.

"Thanks, but there's no need," she said.

Pataki scowled and hefted up his pants. "I don't want no trouble here, Jayne. Troublemakers got no place working here."

"Hey, hey," said Bobby.

"Mind your business," said Albert.

"Oh, like you're minding yours?"

"This might be my business," said Albert.

Pataki caught her arm and leaned in close to her ear. He wasn't much taller than she was. He whispered something and Jayne looked dangerously close to tears.

Pataki let her go and brushed off his sleeves. "Now you apologize and get back to work."

"Sorry," she said.

Pataki disappeared into the kitchen, and must have slammed a pot against something metal, for a loud bang made them all jump. Keith remained with his gaze fixed out the window, concentrating on the street as if there was a parade going by. Carol put a grilled cheese, fries and cola down in front of him, but he ignored her.

It was all working out pretty well. If Albert played his cards right, if he asked her out now, pissed as she was, he'd bet money she'd say yes.

Jayne looked blankly around her as though wondering how to get out of the place. Albert tried to catch her eye, and she looked at him, but he wasn't altogether sure she saw him. He winked at her, subtly, a thing just between the two of them. Letting her know he was here for her. After all, didn't he understand better than most what it was to have people look down on you? Make comments about you? He could be good for this girl.

Jayne blinked twice and walked over to Bill. She put her hand on his shoulder and a surge of electricity ran down Albert's arms, so strong his hands jerked from where they rested on his thighs.

"I can't make it for dinner tonight," she said in a steady voice. "Would another night be possible?" She said it loud enough to be heard throughout the room.

The air around Albert got colder. This happened sometimes, when he got angry. It was as if his body temperature spiked so fast that in comparison the air felt cold, as if he ran a fever of anger. He couldn't figure out just who he was angriest at: himself, for missing his opportunity, or Bill, for taking his. Or maybe it was Jayne—all those points she'd racked up for dignity and pride, she was willing to throw away on Bill Corkum. Stupid little slut. And he'd fantasized she'd be the one to . . . to what? Fuck that. Fuck her. And maybe he would one day. A mercy fuck.

"What about Friday?" said Bill, also loudly, and grinning.

Albert knew if Bill so much as glanced in his direction he was going to jump up out of this booth and slam his rival's bony chin into the counter. He hoped Bill would look at him, hoped he would hold his winner's smirk long enough to let Albert smear it off in blood and bits of tooth and bone.

"Lovely. What time?" said Jayne.

"I'll swing by and pick you up after I finish up work, okay?" he said.

"Hey! You! I want my check," Albert called.

Startled, Jayne turned to him. "But you haven't touched your pie."

"It's fucking crap. Give me my bill or I'm leaving anyway."

"Fine, take it." She pulled the little yellow pad from her pocket, ripped off the bill, came to him and slapped it down on the table. It was for eight-fifty. He threw down eight dollars.

"Pay at the register," she said, and he ignored her.

He stood and strode to the door without even glancing at Bill. Bobby said something he didn't catch and then laughed, following him.

"You're short!" called Jayne.

"So fucking sue me," he called back.

"What's your problem? Albert? *Albert!*"

Outside he walked down the street without stopping to see if Bobby followed. The air carried a trace of the fried meat and oil from Gus's kitchen, and under it the tang of springtime dog shit and wet newspapers. The sound of reggae music wafted from Danny's Records and he glanced in. A pretty girl stood flipping through the bins of CD's and collector vinyl. He hated her on sight, with her perfect cheerleader's nose and pert ass. And then there Bobby was, trotting beside him.

"Wow, what are you so pissed at?"

"I fucking hate that place. No class. I don't know why you wanted to go there. I'm never fucking going there again. All that bullshit. Who needs it?" A pain shot up from his instep and he'd taken another step, endured another flash of pain, before he realized he had a stone in his boot. He sat down on the curb, next to the clogged up leaves in the drain, the cigarette butts and the dust, and pulled his boot off while Bobby watched him, his hands shoved deep in his pockets. Albert held the boot upside down and a small, sharp stone fell into his palm. "How does that fucking happen?" he yelled. "I mean, how does it get the fuck in there?" He threw it at a passing car and was only minimally satisfied with the *ting* it made when it hit the side. It would have pleased him more if the driver had stopped. A stone in his shoe was just like goddamn life, he thought. You didn't put it there and you didn't want it and you couldn't see it, and then *wham!* it cut into your instep and made you bleed.

"You okay?" said Bobby.

"I'm a fucking carnival," said Albert, and in that moment all he was left with was a huge gaping pit of loneliness, just a black bottomless space on the ground around him in every direction. He would never admit it to anyone, and maybe he didn't want to admit it even to himself, but for a while now, and certainly for a few minutes there Albert had wondered about the future in a way he hadn't before. Permitted himself to think in terms of possibilities. He hadn't seen it coming, because he'd never really had a crush on anyone before, not in all the years of his being alive. He'd banged a good number of girls. He'd even seen a few for a couple of months at a time, mountain slags, mostly, and one or two too stupid to figure out they were nothing more than booty calls, but for some reason that skinny little bitch of a waitress had been different. Why? Because she'd given him a couple of free coffees? Because she didn't look at him the same way other people did? Because she'd had the good sense to drop that loser, Keith Keyes? Well, who was the loser now, huh? Who was the fucking loser now? He was a carnival all right, a fucking freak show.

Albert pulled his boot back on and stood on the sidewalk, tired down to his bones. He wanted to go back to the cabin and get good and drunk and sleep for about a hundred years. But he knew as soon as he got back there he'd feel like a trapped wolf. He was wiped out and restless all at once. He needed something to do, to plan, a project to get his mind off this self-indulgent shit. He started walking, kicking at stray stones on the sidewalk, crushing a can under his heel with one satisfying crunch. Then he stopped, the tips of his fingers tingling for something to do, for something to take the edge off.

"You know what, son?" he said to Bobby. "I think you might be ready. I think you might finally be ready to step into the game." And, his decision being made, he felt better.

CHAPTER FIFTEEN

A wide, slow moving line of thunderstorms battered Gideon all morning and afternoon. Driving home took Tom longer than usual since two of the roads were blocked with downed trees. At the outskirts of town a power line danced across the street, spitting sparks like a furious cobra and the traffic lights were out. The temperature dropped and for May it was chilly, with a pewter sky and still-roiling clouds. Tom pulled into the driveway. A stray burst of sunlight flashed from between the dark clouds, briefly blinding him. Everything smelled of electricity. Although the rain had stopped, the wind was still high and the trees whipped and creaked. The sickly maple had succumbed at last. It lay on its side across the lawn, but it looked as though two branches had broken off first. One had hit the fence on the side of the house and broken through the top rail. Another lay near the garage. It was a big limb, a good six feet or more, far enough from the mother tree to make Tom wonder how the hell it had got there. Patty's car was visible through the windows in the garage and he thanked god she'd had the foresight not to take it out on one of her rambles today. A gust came up out of nowhere and a metal watering can bounced and rattled across the walk. He looked up. The sky had that ominous tinge of green you never wanted to see. The weather report on the radio had said the worst of it was over, but Tom wasn't so sure. Rascal barked from inside the house. The door opened and Ivy stepped out.

"Hey, Munchkin. What are you doing home?"

She wore a blue jumper and a white turtleneck. She was barefoot and, although her feet were clean, her shins showed spatters of dark muck. Her hair was pulled back into a messy braid she must have done herself.

"Get back inside. Go on," he said, his voice tight with worry he hoped didn't sound like irritation. She was all skinny arms and legs, fragile elbows and knees. He gently pushed her inside and closed the door against the suck of wind. "So, what are you doing home? Are you sick, sweetpea? The school close because of the storm?" He couldn't believe the school would send the kids home in this weather.

The expression on Ivy's face puzzled him. She looked very serious, almost angry, and he wondered for a moment if she and Patty had had an argument. But there was something else. There was worry in the way her forehead puckered and in the narrowing of her dark eyes. Tom felt a jolt, as though some great hand shook him. "You okay, sweetie? Everything all right?"

"Daddy . . ." she said in a whisper, as though she were afraid to make any sound at all, afraid of what the merest ripple in the air would do. "Mommy . . ."

"What about Mommy? Is she okay? Ivy, tell me!"

"She's not here."

"Not here? Where is she?"

"Her things aren't here either."

An avalanche of understanding rolled over him, a frigid tumbling of his senses, so that for several seconds he didn't know whether he was standing or had fallen, didn't know where up was, or down. Without thinking, he scooped Ivy up in his arms and she put her hands over her head as he narrowly missed whacking her skull on the doorjamb. "Patty! Patty!" He raced, holding her in his arms as though each room was on fire, from one room to the other, and was aware of very little other than the emptiness of each space. The dog slinked behind the couch. In the kitchen, he stopped. Bobby sat at the kitchen table, a half eaten grilled cheese sandwich on a plate in front of him. His son stared at the plate, at the greasy, congealing sandwich, not looking at Tom. And then Tom moved on, bellowing now, calling for her, room by room . . .

Everywhere he looked were discarded things—shoes and rubber boots and backpacks, magazines, a Barbie doll, a toy truck, a glass with half an inch of crystallizing red wine staining the sides. Everything looked left behind, forgotten, cast away.

"Daddy, you're hurting me," said Ivy, softly, so softly it was the only thing that got through to him.

"I'm sorry, baby, I'm sorry." He kissed her head and put her down and then he ran upstairs and roared into the bedroom he had shared with his wife, into the room where on the anniversary of their beginning he had made her writhe and moan on the bed, calling out his name. He tore open the closet door. His clothes were pushed to one side. And on her side: empty hangers, skeletons where the flesh of cloth had been. Scraps left behind. A blue lace scarf he'd given her as a birthday present ten years ago. A yellow sandal. A T-shirt. He quickly scanned the room. Drawers half closed. A pair of corduroy pants abandoned. Detritus. Flotsam. He fell to his knees and reached to the back of the closet, groping blindly past his own clumsy enormous shoes and her empty shoeboxes, a plastic package of sanitary napkins, a pile of tattered, swollen paperbacks Patty read in the bath, two ties, fallen and forgotten. Then his fingers found the jewelry box with the little dancer inside, the very one she'd put on the stool in front of her the day he'd first seen her, there to collect coins in return for her song. The one they used as a sort of sentimental savings account. Ten dollars here, thirty there. It grew over the years. They'd been saving for something special, or so he thought. He had used the talisman of the box, place of his first offering to her, as their promise to the future.

He held the box in his hands and dared not open it. Knew by the weight what was not there. By the feather-light, bird-has-flown weight of it, he knew what he would find. Not find. He was tempted, sorely tempted, to crush the box. He could do it, too. Mash the thing with his bare hands to a crumple of cardboard and metal winding gears. He lifted the lid and was startled, and felt a fool, when the little dancer began to twirl to the tinkle-y strains of Chopin. Nothing. A bobby-pin. A lone cuff-link, brass with an enamel thistle. Furry bits of ancient dust. Less than nothing. He closed the lid, gently, and put the box back into the shadowed recesses of the closet.

He sat on the unmade bed, in the imprint her body had made. He would go downstairs. He would find out what Bobby knew. And then he started, for it came to him that he had noticed something, registered it down in the little lizard part of his brain. Patty's car in the garage. That tree limb. Pushed up against the garage. Knowledge of what that meant stood briefly outlined in his mind and then panicked, tried to slip back into the shadows of his frantic thoughts. But he'd seen it now. Could not ignore it. He knew Patty had not walked away alone, knew that as surely as if he'd been there to see her leave himself. Someone had come with a car of their own. A tree limb blocked their path. Someone had moved that tree limb from where it had most likely fallen across the road. Moved it out of the way, against the side of the garage, so the car could be driven away. It was too big for her to lift herself. Someone had helped her. He imagined a Paul Bunyan who could toss aside a tree limb as if flicking away a used match. No obstacle too large to stand in his way. Someone who hadn't even come up to the house, probably, but had the power to draw her to him. Might it have been a woman, a friend who had taken one end while she took the other, both of them struggling with the weight and bulk? He considered. It was no woman.

Tom tried to think back over the past few days, the past few weeks; he re-ran every argument, every harsh word that had flown through the house like glass shards in a windstorm. Found no clue to give him purchase. Found every clue to confirm she was leaving him, but nothing told him with whom. Faces flashed in his mind's eye. Men he knew well, men he knew hardly at all, friends and acquaintances, men at the garage, at the market, in the stores. The world seemed filled with men capable of any sort of deceit. He recalled the way conversations cut off when he entered certain places: the loading docks of certain stores, his own company's lunch room. The room spun. He sat on the edge of the bed, his head between his knees, afraid he was about to pass out.

"Daddy?" Ivy and Bobby stood in the doorway. Tom was ashamed then, for he had forgotten he had children. Bobby kept his eyes on the floor, as though he was guilty of something. Was he? Did he know something? Ivy held her brother's hand and it was evidence of Bobby's anxiety that he let her.

Tom opened his arms wide. "Come here," he said. Ivy hesitated, and then ran for him, throwing herself into his arms. Sobbing. He held her on his knee and patted her, feeling her skull, so easily cupped in his hand. Instinct made him want to hold her tightly, but he was afraid of crushing her. Bobby hung in the doorway, his hands in his pockets now.

"Son . . ." The boy looked at a spot somewhere near Tom's face. ". . . come here."

Bobby slouched over to the bed and sat at the end, one leg hooked up under his skinny behind.

After a while Ivy's crying turned to hiccups. She held onto the Boy Scout whistle she wore around her neck. A lot of good that had done, thought Tom. He produced a tissue from his pocket and she wiped her eyes and blew her nose.

"What happened?" Tom said. "Bobby, was Mom gone when you got up this morning?"

Bobby shook his head.

"She was here, then?"

Ivy nodded. That was good. He'd had visions of them waking up to an empty house. "Okay. Okay. Did anything happen this morning? I mean anything at all?" He would have given anything to have someone else to ask.

"There was a storm." Ivy twisted the tissue in her hand.

"I know. It's all right, baby. Everything's fine. Did Mommy say anything to you? Did she leave a note? Did she say where she was going? To the store, maybe? Or when she'd be back?"

Ivy shook her head. Tom willed himself to breathe in to the count of five, breathe out to the count of five. "Tell me what happened."

"You and Mommy had a fight last night."

"You're always fighting," said Bobby.

"I know, but that happens sometimes, people fight. It doesn't mean anything. Tell me about this morning."

Ivy raised her eyes to her father's and screwed up on the side of her mouth, one eyebrow raised. It was a look Tom knew well, older than her years, disapproving. "She said sometimes she thought I was the mother around here, because I take such good care of you and Bobby."

"You're just a kid," said Bobby.

"All right," said Tom.

"I knew something was up," said Bobby.

"What do you mean?"

"She was funny. I don't know. Antsy." Bobby shrugged.

"What does that mean?" It was hard not to raise his voice, not to shake his son.

"Like she wanted us gone."

"Anyway," said Ivy, dragging the word like it was made up of three distinct syllables. "It was Bobby's idea."

"What was?"

"We left for school, but we didn't go to school."

"You didn't."

"I just figured, all right?" Bobby said.

"What? For God sake, Bobby, what did you figure?"

Bobby rose and faced his father. "I figured out what was going on, all right?"

Ivy pressed up against her father and his grip tightened around her.

125

"Tell me. Now."

"We waited around back of the house."

They stood out in the wind and the mud and the rain; Tom saw them as clearly as if he'd been there himself, stood out in the thunder and the flash in the strangely dark morning, the rain running into their hair, spattering mud against Ivy's white socks, Bobby's nose running; him wiping it off on his sleeve. Watching their mother. Knowing she was leaving. Leaning up against the weathered wood, trying to stay out of the wind. Had they done it before? "What were you waiting for?"

Ivy sighed heavily, her breath huffing out as though it was walking down a flight of stairs. "Until the car came and Mommy left."

"Who was in the car, Bobby?" And he wanted to ask, *Why didn't you stop her?*

Ivy squirmed off his knee. "Is she coming back?"

"Of course she is," said Tom, then he thought better of it. What good would it do, to lie to them now, to show them no one could be trusted, no one at all. "I hope so. Bobby, who was in the car?"

"I don't know." Bobby turned then, took a step toward the door.

Tom reached for his arm and was very careful not to hold him too tightly. He concentrated on this effort, for his fingers worked of their own free will and if they gained control he knew Bobby's arm could snap. "Look, I know somebody moved that broken branch. She couldn't have done it alone. It was somebody you knew, wasn't it? Was it a man?" He understood Bobby was frightened and defiant and nearly as full or fury as he was. Tom wanted to stop. "Bobby, this isn't a game. If you know who the man is, you have to tell me. Now. Listen to me. This is very important. I'm worried about your mother."

"Right." He nodded, but looked unconvinced.

"You have to tell me. You know that. Either you tell or Ivy will. You be the one. Don't make her do it. Who was in the car?" He released Bobby's arm.

"Some guy. I don't know." Bobby hugged himself as though cold.

The centre of Tom's chest constricted, tightened, easy enough to explain; and then a small pop, as though some muscle, some tendon, something necessary for holding his insides in their proper place, stretched beyond its limit. Whatever it was gave way softly, almost gently, and he felt like he was bleeding inside, his breath turning to blood in a broken vessel, leaking away down into his boots. It occurred to him he might very well die of love.

"Are you okay, Daddy?" Ivy's voice was far off somewhere.

"Yes, baby." What would they do, now? What would they do if she came back? What would happen to Ivy and Bobby in a town like this, with a mother who had run off with another man? But what would they do if she never came back? They would be the abandoned ones, the ones rejected, left behind, tainted forever. They would look at Ivy and Bobby for signs of badness, signs of cursed blood showing through. They would be tainted either way, with her return or her rejection. If he didn't love her so much, oh, how he could hate her.

"Are you mad at us? Don't be mad," said Ivy.

Her words brought him to the world and he saw Bobby had gone and his daughter was shaking. When he took her in his arms she almost vanished. He could put her in his pocket if he wanted. Keep her safe there. The problem was he couldn't feel her, couldn't get a sense of her in his arms. He'd gone numb, an icy radiating freeze from his heart to the end of his fingers. The rain had started again; it streamed against the windows with such force it was impossible to see past it.

CHAPTER SIXTEEN

Dorothy Carlisle was unable to concentrate on her reading. It was after four, nearly five, and she couldn't wait to close the shop, a feeling to which she was unaccustomed. But today nothing held her interest, not Rilke, not Homer, not Alice Munro, not Graham Greene. Ever since Tom Evans called to say his wife had, as they used to call it, "run off," Dorothy's mind was unable to settle on much of anything, not even those writers who had been her solace and refuge for decades.

Tom had called her several days after Patty disappeared, by which time it seemed clear even to him his wife would not be back any time soon. He was barely able to speak through his swallowed tears, his voice choked and halting. Practical matters precipitated the call, or so he told her, concerns about what to do with the kids when he had to return to work. Did he want Ivy to come and stay with her for a while, Dorothy had asked, and he went silent as though he had not considered that, and then said no, maybe it was selfish but he needed her with him. He had some time coming, some vacation. He would decide what to do and let her know. If he found a day job with regular hours, maybe she would look out for Ivy in the afternoon? She had said of course, of course. She said how sorry she was, and did he need anything, and surely Patty just wanted a little time alone and would be home soon, and all the other words one spoke in the hollow cave of loss. She had put the phone down softly, as though afraid a harsh gesture would transmit down the telephone line to Tom and crack open the thin, brittle shell of what remained of his reserve.

No one could ever accuse Dorothy Carlisle of being overly sentimental towards children, but there were some things Dorothy knew one simply did not do and deserting your children was very high up on that list. She imagined the Evans household, shut off in its shock and grief. Something like this was almost harder than a death. Death brought round the casseroles and condolences. She remembered when she was a child—a grandparent's death, her older brother lost in the Korean War—remembered the late night phone call, the telegram, the unexpected

128

knock on the door. The pots of coffee. The hushed voices. The sacred quiet of mourning. In contrast, she remembered, too, the sniggering whispers about a girl who lived down the road and had run off with a jazz clarinetist, only to return in disgrace less than a year later. There had been little kindness and certainly no sanctity over that pain. It was her own fault, people said. Her father should have locked her in her room, or beaten some sense into her. The family paid the steep price of shame and moved on within a few years, to no one knew where.

No one had much sympathy for the cuckold, which was, of course, what Tom was. *And not for the first time.* Dorothy clamped her hand over her mouth, as though afraid she might say the words out loud. Dorothy might be capable of keeping her thoughts to herself, but there were those in town for whom diplomacy was a foreign concept, and everyone knew what Gideonites thought of foreigners.

The next day, Ivy had come by after school, her eyes clouded with anxiety no child should ever have to experience, her shoulders set, and her posture at once defiant and vulnerable. She had come, she said, to tell Mrs. Carlisle she was needed at home, and that she was awfully sorry, but she would not be able to help in the store for a little while. Dorothy gathered the girl into her arms, and Ivy stiffened at first, and then collapsed into tears. She would not talk about it, though, and after a few minutes she pushed herself away from Dorothy, dried her eyes on her sleeve and said she had to get back, that her father needed her.

"I'll drive you," Dorothy had said.

"No, thank you," Ivy said with rigid formality. "I would really rather walk."

With that the little girl had gone and although Dorothy had called the house twice since, there was never any news. Tom answered the phone on the first half-ring, disappointment thick in his voice when he understood it was only Dorothy, and he told her they were coping, and that Ivy said hello, but no more. Dorothy thought she would give it another few days, and then she would go over there. It made her practically break out in hives just thinking about how intrusive this would be, and what an invasion of Tom Evan's privacy, but her worry outweighed her natural reticence to becoming involved in someone else's trouble. Far too late for remaining uninvolved. What she had begun that day, letting Ivy find refuge in her store from the bullying girls, she must see through. One does not, she told herself, see a job only half done.

Dorothy consulted the wall clock. Another half hour and she would leave. A grand total of six people, three sets of couples, had been in the shop that afternoon. It had been a virtual stampede by normal standards. Tourists who were, now the weather had finally turned warm again, beginning their annual spring migration through the small towns in the area. They swung through twice a year, once in the spring and once in the fall when they were referred to as "leaf peepers." Odious, most of them, sure they were being ripped off, trailing dripping ice cream cones and slurping coffee from plastic travel cups that appeared designed for enormous infants, only too happy to say in loud voices that they knew their antiques and would not be fooled by cheap imitation. It was enough to make one shut the doors until the season was over. Today, however, Dorothy hadn't minded the diversion and was happy enough to sell a lovely satinwood tea caddy for not much more than she'd paid for it, although she did refuse to sell the small bentwood chair, stamped Thonet of Vienna, because it was the chair she thought of as Ivy's.

Just as she gave up all notion of being drawn into Willa Cather's portrait of Nebraska pioneers, the door opened, and against all hope her heart leapt with the possibility it might be Ivy.

"You'll go blind reading in that light," said Mabel McQuaid.

"Hello, Mabel. I was just closing up, actually."

"That little Ivy Evans isn't here, is she? No? Good. I'm sure you've heard."

"I suppose I have." Dorothy closed *My Antonia* with a sharp *whack!*

"How's the little girl doing?" Mabel settled, without invitation, in an upholstered armchair with caryatid arm supports. With her crinkled décolletage plumping out from the neckline of her slightly too tight floral dress, and with that smear of pink lipstick on her teeth, Dorothy thought she looked like the Queen of Tarts.

"Mabel, I'm simply not going to gossip about this. Imagine what that family's going through and have a little pity."

"I admire the noble sentiment, Dot, really, but how on earth is Tom going to keep living here when his wife's run off? And you and I both know it's not the first time she's done this. I wouldn't be surprised if neither of those kids is his. What's wrong with that man? They need the church in their lives, they do."

Dorothy was, for once, utterly dumbfounded. Cramped between Mabel McQuaid's suggestion that Ivy and Bobby were not Tom's, and the information that, indeed, Patty Evans was with another man, Dorothy's verbal ability simply shut down. She didn't know which issue to address first and as her mind zigzagged between the possible options, Mabel McQuaid would not stop talking. She sat with her ankles crossed and her hands folded in her lap, and looked as though a crowbar wouldn't budge her.

"I mean, I actually wonder if Tom's not involved somehow. He can't possibly be that blind. Maybe they have some sort of arrangement, if you know what I mean. I wouldn't be surprised. It's the influence of Hollywood, for one thing. Everyone's been talking about it for months. It's one of the Corkums. The one that delivers oil. And other things, apparently." She snorted. "Oh, no, of course you haven't heard. Don't give me that look, you know what I mean. That's what happens when you make it so clear you don't want to hear any of the news around town. You're unprepared, aren't you, for when the inevitable happens? I dare say if you hadn't chased me out of here a while ago you might not be standing there like you are now with your mouth hanging open. She's been seen with him in practically every motel within fifty miles. You know, I always thought his people were all right, churchgoing, not the type for this sort of thing. He has a sister who's a geriatric aid and his mother was a terrific cleaning lady. She must be just mortified. Larry! That's it. His name's Larry. I used to let him cut my lawn in summer when he was a boy. Stocky, handsome in his own way. I'm almost sure it was him."

"You leave me speechless, Mabel." At some point Dorothy had risen and now stood with both hands pressed firmly on her desk, as though she was afraid if she didn't it might rise up of its own accord and hurl itself at the woman across from her. She looked down at her hands and saw her forearms were trembling.

Mabel leaned forward and said, in a slightly quieter voice, as though afraid of being overheard, "You don't suppose she's pregnant, do you?"

"Pregnant!"

"Well, you're the one who's made such a little pet out of the other one."

"The other *what*?"

"Don't get me wrong, I think you're a saint. I said as much to Reverend Hickland just the other day. You don't see the least bit of bad in anybody do you?"

"I wouldn't say that, Mabel. I wouldn't say that at all. You'd be amazed at what I see."

"You won't make me believe it. You are an angel to take an interest in that little girl. Look at the strikes she's got against her. A mother like that, a father—well, he calls himself that—who can't control his own wife. From the first day Patty Evans showed up you could see she'd break Tom's heart. He was such a good boy. Can you imagine what his mother would have thought of that Patty being in her house? It makes you wonder, of course, what will become of the little one. Or Bobby, for that matter. Timing's all wrong for him too, of course. Which makes Tom Evans either a saint, like you, or else he's the biggest fool in the world. I'm beginning to lean the other way, to be truthful. I mean, you fool me once, shame on you, but you fool me twice, shame on me, and now this. Oh, Dorothy, I'm sorry. You can't tell me you didn't consider it? Not even Bobby? But you must have noticed when she first arrived. You can count . . ."

"I never noticed anything like what you're implying, Mabel. It wasn't any of my business then and it isn't now. And it's not your business, either. Have some pity, for heaven's sake! Have some empathy!"

"Look at you. You look sick to your stomach. I shouldn't go on, I guess. I didn't mean any harm, honestly. I know you're close to the family these days."

"I am feeling sick." Dorothy moved out from behind the safety of the desk and flapped her hands at Mabel McQuaid, who stood, with a look on her face that indicated she was afraid Dorothy Carlisle might vomit on her. "Awfully, terribly sick. And I'm going home. Right now. Sorry, Mabel, but you'll have to leave."

In the Evans house that evening, Ivy stood on a stool at the sink and washed the dishes. Outside, the oak tree's long-fingered, wind-rattled shadows scrambled across the back yard and made her nervous. Her father was in the living room, sunk in his chair, smelling of beer, staring at but not watching the television. Ivy knew he wasn't watching because it was a television show on which people were forced to eat disgusting things like worms and cockroaches, and if he had been paying attention he would have changed the channel for sure.

Ivy was careful to rinse the dishes in hot water, getting all the soap off, before stacking them on the drain board. She changed the washing water often for she hated the feel of wet bits of food on her hands and as soon as something floated to the surface she emptied the water and began again. Something moved in the yard and she nearly dropped a glass. It took a moment for her to realize what she was looking at. It was only the fox, the beautiful red fox with the black legs. Ivy opened her mouth to call her dad, but then she thought better of it, knowing he wouldn't come. She watched the animal pad along the hedge-line, hunting for the baby rabbits who lived there, probably, or mice. She hated to think of her catching anything, for she loved the little wild rabbits, although she knew a fox had to eat, too, and may have babies of her own to feed.

Just a fox. Just the wind in the trees. Nothing to be afraid of.

But that, of course, wasn't true at all. Fear was a fact of life. It had been this way even before her mother left, although fear had been mostly relegated to night, then. That dark time when bad things came out. She had to observe certain rituals in order to control the bad things. Lights must be flicked on quickly; steps run up before shadows formed into things more solid than just a place where light wasn't. When her dad put in the new light switch, it had helped some. She hadn't checked her hair so often to see if it had turned white. But of course she hadn't told her father about the other things that scared her. Things about her parents' fights, the words that flew around the house like plates. She never told him about the bullying. No one followed her anymore, not since Albert Erskine threatened Gelsey and Cathy that day, but in school they whispered things as they passed her in the cafeteria, or in the hall, or from behind her in class. *Good never comes from bad, my mother says. Birds of a feather. Born in the blood. We don't want you here.* The broken-glass words were in her head all the time. *Your mother doesn't love you! You're so ugly she left you!*

A tumbler slipped from her fingers, splashed into the sink and hot water spattered her face and neck. She wiped it away and did not cry. It was important that she not cry in front of her father. When the fighting between her parents had been bad, she thought of the movie in which the little sorcerer's apprentice had let certain spells get out of control. Before he knew it a tide of water rose, threatening to drown them all. The normal things of the house—the brooms, the teapots, the pots and pans—became possessed by magic gone terribly wrong. You had to be so careful with spells. You had to know all the right words, and she'd never known them. So she had kept quiet. She didn't know how to name her fears, didn't know what the words might be for the vaporous wisps of worry that slid around the doorjambs and riffled the curtains. She wasn't even sure she wanted to know their names, for naming things gave them power.

She tried once, a few months back, to talk to Bobby. She wanted to know if he got scared, too. He laughed and told her she was crazy, then opened his mouth wide to show her the chewed up cookie he was eating. He was a teenager, and a boy, so of course he was oblivious to most things. He slept like a bear in hibernation; he never heard their mother when she wandered through the house as if she were a boat slipped from its mooring in the night.

Even now, when their mother floated out into far waters, mysterious and lost as a rudderless skiff, and left them all behind in the haunted house, Bobby seemed only to be more like himself, careless, loud, sullen and needy all at once. Although he added to this his anger. Anger at their dad, mostly, but at her, too. Like tonight. "I'm hungry," he whined, as though he was five and not fifteen.

"You want Spaghetti-O's and hot dogs?" she said.

"Are you kidding? What crap. I'm not eating kid's crap."

"Well, I'm hungry too, Bobby, why don't *you* make us something?"

"Fat chance, freak," he said, his face like a mask, "You want to take her place, play little mommy? Be my guest, but leave me out of it." And then he stomped out the door and slammed it behind him and still had not come home.

Maybe he was afraid after all.

Her father was certainly afraid. And that in itself was a new thing to be afraid of, for if he was afraid—her big, strong dad—then he couldn't reassure her any more, could he? How frightening it was, the way a person could be there one minute and gone the next. This is the way things are, though, she thought: uncertain, shifting, treacherous.

Ivy drained the water from the sink and shook powdered cleanser onto the enamel to clean it. She liked the feel of the scratchy powder, scouring away all traces of oily dirt, liked the sharp, medicinal smell of the bleach.

When she was done, she poked her head into the living room. Her father sat in his old lounger. Rascal lay sprawled on the carpet with his hind legs stretched out behind him and his muzzle resting on his crossed paws, but his eyes were fixed on Ivy's father, who in turn stared at the television. On the screen, a man wearing nothing but a bathing suit and a pair of goggles lay in something that looked like a coffin, while two

134

other men poured garbage cans full of rats over him and girls in bikinis squealed with disgust.

"Dad?"

"What is it, Ivy?"

"Do you want anything? A cup of tea?" She noticed the glass of whiskey in his hand then, and the bottle on the floor next to his chair.

"No. I don't want anything."

"I'm going to go up to my room, okay?"

"You do whatever you want."

Ivy did not want to do whatever she wanted. She wanted to be told what to do. She wanted to be told to do her homework, or come and sit on her father's knee, or get out the Parcheesi board, or something, anything that would make her believe she wasn't living in a house full of nothing but ghosts.

"Fine," she said, and turned away. Rascal roused and ran to the front door, toenails scratching on the linoleum. He wriggled and whined and Ivy let him out. The dog dove off the porch and raised a leg against the nearest shrub, releasing an apparently never-ending stream of urine. "Poor Rascal" she said. "Good boy." Her father, it seemed, was an invalid incapable of even letting the poor dog out. She waited and waited, such a long time even the dog looked embarrassed, but then, at last he was done and ran back into the house as if unwilling to leave the fragile, broken humans alone for longer than necessary. Not even the scent of fox in the night tempted him. "It's all right," said Ivy, closing the door and locking it, hoping Bobby had his keys, wherever he was. "It's all right."

She schlumped upstairs, Rascal trailing behind her. "Good boy," she said and took comfort in his warm fur under her fingers, the confident way he entered the dark hallway. Over the past weeks, the dog had become her shadow, following her around, sniffing in corners, looking for that absent-present person.

In her room, Ivy looked in the mirror above her dresser. She looked at her curling brown hair, looked at her skin, which wasn't like her mother's, not a freckle to be seen, and wasn't like her father's, nothing pinkly-burnt, not ever. And wasn't like her brother's, all milky pale, almost bluish sometimes. Even her mouth was different. Blubber mouth, they called her, fish lips, they called her. And her mother had said, "Pay no attention to them, they'll all be getting collagen injections to get what you've

135

got, all be getting tan out of a bottle to get what you got. Just like my grandmother, who was Spanish, you know, from Madrid." Maybe that was where her mother was. Dancing with the Spanish gypsies in Madrid.

Ivy took her rock collection from the shelf. She put the box on her bed and opened the lid. Each rock, so perfect, still, and serene, tucked up in its little compartment, nestled in a fluffy piece of cotton, snug as little bugs in little rugs. Each one knew its place and stayed there. Biotite next to calcite next to fluorite next to galena next to graphite next to gypsum next to hematite. She picked up the quartzite from its cubbyhole at the end of the third row, next to the slate. It was pinkish, like burnt skin or a piece of petrified meat. Tough but brittle, a hardness of 7 on the scale. Its parent rock was sandstone, but the grains would not rub off like sandstone. She held it, gripped it tight, tight, tight, wanted to feel it bite her. She had seen a man in a movie once who held a piece of glass in his hand, held it hard until the blood ran out from between his fingers. She wanted to feel that, wanted to feel hot blood in her hand instead of cold rock, rock whose parent was sandstone. Sandstone, a mineral held together by compaction, made up mostly of pieces of other rocks.

She opened her palm. The rock was still the rock, and her hand was still her hand, marked red, but not bleeding.

Stupid rock. Stupid hand.

Rascal sat and looked at her and cocked his head.

"What are you looking at? Stupid dog," she said. She thought she could throw the rock at Rascal and he'd still just sit there, waiting for something to happen, waiting for someone to feed him, to let him out, to play with him, to cut burrs from between the pads on his paws. He was like her father, day after day, waiting for the phone to ring, waiting to hear a key in a lock. Her father slept in the chair some nights. He had gone back to work, finally, but for days he'd called in sick, something he hadn't done ever before as far back as Ivy could remember. "She'll come home," he kept saying, "She'll be back. She loves us, loves you kids. She's just gone off for a wee break. She'll come home." That was the rosary he said, and for a day or two Ivy had tried to believe him, but she didn't, and after that she didn't think he believed it either, and then he pretty much stopped talking altogether. He went back to work, but when he came home he went straight for the chair, straight for the bottle. He ate if Ivy brought him food, changed his clothes once every couple of days, and then Ivy washed them. Just like she dusted and made beds and swept the floor, and picked up Bobby's towels from the bathroom floor and made her bed, but not Bobby's—let him take care of himself that much. And through it all her father sat with one eye on the television and the other on the car lights that went past the window, but never stopped.

Ivy wanted to shake him. Wanted him to be her father again.

Rascal cocked his head and whined. He opened his jaws, as though smiling at her, as though he was laughing. The one black patch over his eye looked like a target.

Ivy threw the rock, not at the dog, but at the mirror. It had not been her intention to throw the rock, and certainly not to throw it at the mirror. Still, she had thrown it, and time slowed oddly. She experienced a certain detached surprise as her arm made its arc, and as the stone sailed so unnaturally weightless through the air there was time to wonder whether this gesture would bring satisfaction, for she had seen on television, and read in books, that this is what people did when they were at the end of something, and could take no more of something, and so on. Then the miniscule meteor impacted against the mirror and, even though she had watched it happen, and so could not be taken unawares of its inevitability, the sharp and nearly shrieking sound, and the drama of the results—the shatter and scatter of it all—made her jump, and then she was instantly filled with regret as a spider-web of tinkling, distorted glass and silver-shiny backing, exploded into sparkling shards across the bureau, into the carpet, where surely tiny slivers would remain embedded for weeks, looking to punish her naked feet. The piece of quartzite bounced back and now lay, chipped, near her foot.

Rascal barked, and then whined.

She heard the ka-thump of her father's recliner snapping closed and his footfalls, somewhat unsteady on the stairs.

"Ivy! Ivy, are you all right? Ivy!"

She would not say anything. He would have to come all the way; he would have to make that effort. She wanted him to worry about her for a change.

And then he was in the door, one hand on either side of the jamb, his face red, his eyes wide. "Ivy? What happened?"

"Nothing," she said.

CHAPTER SEVENTEEN

I know times are tough, don't you think I don't know it. God knows it, too. He's standing there beside you when you're looking for honest work, trying to feed your babies, trying to pay your rent. He's got His hand on your back, propping you up in these hard times and you know it's true. We'll get through this, friends, like we got through the war and the influenza. We're not going to be like some around us, some I won't name—but surely God knows their names, knows the filthy cabins in which they sleep—stealing and cheating and fornicating and cursing the Lord's name. What does it say, friends, in The Book? It's says, **"Yea, the light of the wicked shall be put out, and the spark of his fire shall not shine."** *That's Job 18:15. He knew a thing or two, did old Job.* — **Reverend Clarence Goodall, Church of Christ Returning, 1936**

A chill wind blew from the northeast every day, the weirdest month of May Albert could remember. The kids—the Lost Children—floated through the woods like miniature zombies, trying not to get caught, trying to grab food on the run and getting grabbed themselves. The sound of bottles breaking and the occasional scream, the occasional laugh, came from the main house. Around midnight Friday Dan appeared on the porch and took a few pot shots into the woods, yelling something unintelligible. Albert came out to piss about three in the morning and found his fourteen-year-old brother Jack in a tree, like some ragged, rabid bat. Scared him so bad he'd pissed on his own foot.

"You're a fucking asshole, you know that?" Jack called to him from a branch above his head.

"What the fuck are you doing up there?"

A stupid question, since he knew the answer. He'd spent more than a few nights in the trees himself, back when.

The Uncles, it seemed, had stopped making shine altogether, and were concentrating their efforts on meth. They'd found a market. Albert counted eighteen cars coming and going over the course of three days, one of them Dr. Hawthorne's. The good doctor handed out oranges and put antibiotic cream on the children's cuts and bruises. Albert saw Jill around dawn, Saturday, kneeling beside a tree. She jumped a mile these days when anybody so much as touched her arm. Her nose had been broken some months back and even though Hawthorne had put a metal splint on it, it didn't look right.

"You hurt?" Albert asked.

She looked up. Her lip was split, her teeth stained with blood. "How the fuck do you think I am?"

There had been a time, when he'd first moved into the cabin—she was fourteen, maybe—when he'd brought her into the shack with him for a night or two, thinking he could protect her. It didn't work out. Having her in the cabin overnight made him too uneasy. She was too female, with her musky smells and her breasts, round and high and full, even at that age, straining against her sweatshirt, swinging free and loose. She was too careless with the way she sat, in that short little denim miniskirt she always wore, and too careless with what showed from the top of her shirt when she bent over. At least he thought she was careless. If she wasn't that was worse. If she'd stayed . . . well. He told her she'd have to find her own way. She'd spit on him. Scratched him, and then tried to rub up against him, until he pushed her out the door to land on her ass in the mud. Man, how she cursed him. But she got the message and didn't come back. She was too old now to hide in the little places the kids found all over the woods and too small to fight back, like he had done when the time came. She'd slip over to their side any time, pick a man to latch onto and begin some games of her own, or else she'd go find some sturdy tree limb and hang herself. Wouldn't be the first one. They called that old oak by the marsh the Judas tree.

Albert stayed in his cabin all day Saturday and Saturday night. It was the first time in a while he'd spent that much time up there—usually he stayed out as long as he could, often just getting some booze and some pot and sitting out in his truck in the woods until things died down in the wee hours. But he'd heard from Jack and Jill that things were shifting around from bad to horrible and he wanted to see for himself. And see he did. Where before The Others had been cruel and selfish and violent, now they were fucking psycho. Paranoid and picking fights even with each other. Still, the customers kept coming. All those cars of townies coming and going. And some of those good people would be at church in the morning, listening to the Reverend Hickland strutting his stuff and calling out about the war on God's people.

If Friday and Saturday were hellish, Sunday was plain weird. The place collectively crashed. After a week of using, The Others, both men and women, slept like they were in comas. The kids wandered about, scrounging food in the eerie silence. Only Fat Felicity, Harold and Sonny kept watch on the commerce.

Albert wasn't sure how much more he could take. He told himself the only reason he stayed was a vague hope Jack might grow up fast enough. At least then there'd be two of them, unless Jack slipped over, too, which is why Albert didn't confide in his little brother. It might happen. It had to happen, generation to generation, sins of the fathers on the heads of the sons and daughters. Even The Others must have been children once.

It was as though they could read his thoughts. Every time they got within speaking distance they had something to say. "You better watch yourself, boy," said Old Harold. "Don't go getting any ideas, Bert. Don't forget we all of us got a past together. Gonna have a future together, too," said Lloyd. "What do you think you are, better than the rest of us? In your little bachelor pad. Bringing little girls in there, are you?" said Dan, scratching his armpit and then smelling his fingers. Thinking you were better than the rest was the worst thing there was up on the mountain. Punishable in any number of unpleasant ways. His mother and the rest of the women spoke to him less and less, but Old Felicity shot him death eyes and spit every time she saw him. He hated her eyes, with their drooping lower lids, their watery, red rims.

On Monday, everybody was irritable and depressed. Gray clouds dangled like old dishrags in a murky sky. It was late morning—a time when school kids (other than Bobby Evans who was ditching) were in class, and upstanding citizens were at their jobs, but before the mail truck came around at just past one and the UPS men got round to this neighborhood. Albert and Bobby drove to Prattsville, twenty miles away. The air inside the cab smelled of coffee mixed with the sharp tang of adrenaline. On the side of the truck a stick-on vinyl sign read: *Garcia's*

Economical Landscaping. Back at the compound, hidden in a metal box under a bunch of scrap metal, were signs that said, *Rodriquez Lawn Care, Szniak Plumbing, L.E.D. Electrical,* and *Hidden View Nursery.*

"Good day for it," said Albert.

"You think so?" said Bobby.

"You're not such great company, you know that?" Albert reached over and punched him lightly on the shoulder. "Come on, cheer up. I know it's hard, but who needs her, huh? You think I wouldn't stand up and fucking cheer if my old lady and all the rest of those shits took off? You're goddamn right I would. Fuck 'em. I'm never having any kids, you know that? Never. You ever met anybody didn't have trouble, and I mean real trouble, with their families? They are there to fuck you up. That's it. They are there to see if you're strong enough to survive and if you're not, you're not. It's like Darwin right? Survival of the fittest. Throw the baby bird out of the nest and see if it can fly and if it can't then feed it to the cat. They tell you it's all about love and that shit, but it's not. It's about biology. Survival of the species. It's a badge of honor, is the way I look at it."

"What is?" asked Bobby.

Albert chuckled. Bobby was like every other kid—looking to make sense of crap that was never going to make sense. Life, as Albert saw it, was just a load of steaming horseshit and that was that. But if you were weak, like young Bobby was weak, you needed a reason. You needed meaning. "Look, you got abandoned, right?"

"She might be back."

"Maybe. But let's say she doesn't come back. You're motherless, pal. Motherless. That means you got to be a man. No more kid shit. You think some guy in Africa or China or someplace, somewhere where they leave their weak out to be eaten by lions, like the Eskimos, tossing their old people out on the ice to die, you think they don't have to grow up fast and strong? Sure, that's why blacks are such good athletes, right? Because in olden days their parents ran off and left them out in the jungles and they had to survive. They had to fight for themselves. Fend off tigers and snakes and shit. And if they did, then they were stronger, tougher, more likely to survive. You got to think of it as a kind of gift from the natural order. You know?"

"You think?"

"I know. Trust me."

141

Bobby fidgeted in his seat and cracked his knuckles. "You still live near your folks," he said in a hesitant voice. "Maybe you should show me."

"Goddamn it, Bobby. You know, I should do it." It had started a few days ago—the kid pestering him to take him up to the compound. "I should take you up on the mountain one day and show you what tough really is."

"Don't get mad, Albert. I'm just saying . . ."

"Well, stop saying. You don't have a clue. I don't get you sometimes. What do you want to hang out on the mountain for? Just drop that shit and keep your mind on the job at hand, okay? You think you can handle that? Good. Then focus. No rain yet, so there'll be no footprints if we move fast enough. That's what you have to watch out for in winter, if there's snow. But the cold's good. Keeps people inside minding their own business like they ought to. You got your gloves, right?"

"Sure." Bobby pulled a black leather pair out of his pocket.

"Good boy," said Albert, as Bobby smiled and went a little pink.

Albert had scoped out the house six times over the past month. You had to be thorough. You had to be professional. No drugs. No booze. No crazy knife-wielding, psycho bullshit. He'd made that very clear to Bobby. This wasn't some jacked-up ghetto shit. This was clean. Mostly, he'd told Bobby, it was about seeing what you were made of. Seeing what kind of blood ran through your veins. It was also about seeing how far Bobby was willing to go, how far he was willing to push his limits on Albert's say so.

Albert liked having Bobby around. It felt good to have a friend, someone who looked up to him. It was a clean thing, something he could be proud of. Not a trace of mountain on it. Some people might say Bobby was too young to be Albert's friend, but that wasn't so. Six or seven years wasn't much. And Albert believed he was doing Bobby good. Who else did the kid have to turn to these days? Having Bobby around was like having a protégé. But today would be a one-time thing. Albert was clear—he wasn't going to initiate the kid into a life of crime. This robbery was merely about gauging willingness and nerve, seeing if the kid could keep a secret, which Albert thought of as the measure of a man's integrity. It was also about . . . well, Albert couldn't think of a good word to describe it—*sharing* was too faggy. It was about the power of secrets. Things just between two people. Call it a rite of manhood. Maybe he'd take the kid up to the compound some time. Just to show him how a man could live independent from all assholes, or nearly so, if he put his mind to it.

Albert glanced at Bobby. He was smoking, but then Bobby was always smoking these days. His eyes gazed fixedly at the road ahead. A muscle in his jaw tensed. Well, that was all right. It was natural. First time out. Albert reached over and gave Bobby's bony knee a squeeze. Not much muscle under that skin. Maybe he should abort the mission.

"You're all right, aren't you, sport? Still time to turn around, you know?" Leave it up to fate, maybe. Leave it up to the kid. He was old enough. A damn sight older than Albert was when he'd taken responsibility for himself. "It's up to you. I'm okay either way. I won't lose no respect for you, if you want to go on home. What do you want to do, young Bobby?" And he smiled, to show the kid he meant it, the way a brother would.

There was only a moment's hesitation. "No. I'm good. Like you said, it's just an insurance thing, right? It's not like we're taking anything sentimental, right?"

"No personal things. Except maybe some jewelry, but even that, I take only replaceable stuff, like gold chains and single stone rings. Nothing that looks like Grandma passed it down. And no religious stuff like crosses. Bad karma. I knew a guy who threw a bar of soap into a kid's aquarium. Laughed when he imagined the kid's face when he came home to a tank full of dead fish." There was no reason for Bobby to know the guy was Albert's uncle, Lloyd. Bastard. "No cause for that shit. You have to have ethics."

"Right."

"So? What's it gonna be? You wanna skip it? Go for a pizza?"

"I'm good."

"Your call, Bobby." And Albert kept on driving.

"Tell me about the house again," said Bobby, as if it was a bedtime story.

"It's a nice house, but not too nice, so there's no alarm. Backs onto a wildlife preserve, so no backyard neighbors watching us go through the window, not that there's likely to be anyone home this time of day. Working neighborhood, but not blue-collar. Those guys get laid off too much, or the job site's shut for one reason or another. Stick to office worker types. No kids, which means a better class of jewelry, most of the time, and a little more cash lying around, and maybe some cameras and silver and iPods and laptops and whatever other crap yuppies can't live without."

Bobby lit a cigarette off the butt of the previous one. He jiggled his leg and drummed his fingers on the dashboard while Gregg Allman sang out about the midnight rider. It was one of the songs Albert listened to when he was on the prowl. Not gonna let them catch old Albert, no sir. The road goes on forever. As they turned off and got closer to the prey house, he switched the music over to *Dead or Alive* by Bon Jovi. Kick it up a notch or two, but not too much, not so much some passing motorist heard the bass pumping and took a long enough look to remember who they were. Not so much young Bobby would flip out into psycho mode.

They pulled into the quiet development. Houses nice and far apart. Two acre zoning here. Albert parked the car in between two houses.

"You all right?"

Bobby looked at him, a little pale and wide eyed, but solid. "Yup."

"Let's do this, then."

The inside of the house was dim, even though it was morning. Lots of trees around the house. This was good—less visibility from outside. The sliding glass doors had been a cinch to jimmy. People would never learn the power of a few well-drilled holes with screws through them. Not that that would have stopped Albert. Glass broke easily. They walked into the family room. Albert stepped over the threshold with a sense of entering sacred space. There was something about the sweet violation that was not unlike seduction. His breath quickened.

They were in what he was sure the homeowners must call 'The TV Room' since a huge flat-screen hung over the fireplace dominated the space. The air smelled of coffee and air freshener. He ran his finger along the mantle and checked the finger of his glove for dust.

"Tidy people," he said, in a quiet voice, the voice he always used on a job. It was what he thought of as his Holy Voice. And then, to Bobby, "Stay here."

While Bobby stayed by the door, Albert poked his head around the corner to get a lay of the land. He had an idea from the outside, but it was often hard to tell until you were inside a place. Kitchen to the left, some room beyond that—dining room probably—office to the right of the family room. A hallway led from the kitchen to what he presumed was the formal living room and the stairs to the second floor. That would be their first stop. Bedroom for camera, jewelry, cash in the back of drawer, and then work their way out. A scratching noise brought him up short.

He laid a hand on Bobby's chest, stopping him from moving forward. The boy's heart thumped under his sharp breastbone.

"What?"

"Shush." Albert listened, ears straining, skin at the back of neck crawling.

And then . . . *peep*.

Huh?

Peep, peep.

"Fucking birds," Albert smiled. The scratch of claws on paper and seed. *Peep.*

Albert scanned the room, making an inventory, estimating space in the two canvas lawn-mower bags he'd brought to carry out the take. Ah, that enormous, expensive television. Such a shame since it was too big to grab, although the DVD and game console fit into the bag nicely. Couple of nice silver candlesticks and three picture frames. Leave the photos of Romeo-and-Juliet on their vacations and their wedding day. He never took photos. Frames were generic, people's faces in them, specific. No evidence, thanks very much.

"They got a lot of CDs" said Bobbie, who had opened a lacquered cabinet.

"Fuck the CDs. No resale. Upstairs."

Along the hallway, they passed photos of fields and churches and lakes and in each of them the back of the same woman's head. She didn't like her photo being taken, apparently.

"What is that?" Bobby said.

On the wall hung three objects—a small enamel dish; a Celtic cross made out of stone; and, on an iron plaque, a little statue of a man with a raised lance standing over a dragon, with a little bowl attached beneath the dragon's legs. It was at this latter item Bobby stared, his face mere inches from the statue.

"Looks like a holy water thing. You know, from a church," said Albert.

"Cool. Can I have it?"

"What do you think this is, a shopping trip? Mommy, can I have a bag of cookies? Jesus."

"I'll take it then." Bobby moved to take it off the wall.

"Leave it," said Albert, grabbing his wrist.

"Why?"

"I told you, I don't take nothing religious." He held the boy's wrist.

"Fine. Okay, okay. Let go."

Upstairs the rooms were as tidy as newly cleaned hotel rooms, and as easy to find things in. Some nice jewelry in a wooden box on the dresser. Diamond studs, gold chains, a few pins and a couple of watches. Camera in the closet. Wad of cash, which Albert didn't bother to count, in a sock at the back of the bedside table drawer, behind the nasal spray, the condoms, the personal lubricant and old copies of Time magazine.

It was all so sweet and simple. He looked at the perfect queen-sized bed, the cream-colored comforter, the pale green pillows. So sweet, so clean, so pure. He felt the old urge to defile, to damage, to deface. Knowing the occupants would feel violated by his mere presence wasn't quite enough, but it would do because he was a professional; he was better now. He could resist certain urges. But once upon a time . . . memory filled him with shame, even now. It was his third job. A big house. Bed like a pale blue cloudless sky. They'd been drunk, high. The Uncles and him. Somebody had pissed in the drawer where the woman kept her panties. He'd pulled his jeans down, squatted in the center of the bed . . . He'd been a kid. Nothing but a stupid, fucked-up kid. He had an excuse, unlike The Uncles. Besides, they used DNA evidence now. He shook his head.

"Here," he said to Bobby and handed him the cash, watching the kid's eyes grow wide at the heft of it. "You hold it. I trust you," he said. "Okay, that's enough. Downstairs."

Bobby followed Albert's lead. He moved through the house quietly, taking no chances. Move like a dancer, like a ghost, like a shadow.

He was halfway across the living room, going for a nice little gold dish, when he heard the cough.

Birds did not cough.

His head snapped around to Bobby, frozen, his mouth open, his face white.

Albert became instantly ice-calm, his blood slowed, his stomach clamped, his breath stilled. The world focused precisely, with meticulous accuracy, on the next second. *Cough*. Phlegmy cough. And a squeak. Coming from the room on the far side of the kitchen. A rattle of china.

Fuck.

He put his finger to his lips. Bobby nodded, but looked as though he might start blubbering. Albert would have to do whatever it was he was going to do quickly. He leaned forward, craned his neck without taking another step. He could just make out something in that room. The edge of a bed. A wheel. Part of a . . . yes, a wheelchair. A slippered foot. A bandage on the ankle. A sore showing above the bandage on a liver-spotted leg with skin so wrinkled it looked like it needed ironing. Then the chair backed up, repositioned itself, Albert saw an old woman—no, a female relic—in profile. Soft tufts of white hair. Eyes in pouches of skin so slack it was amazing she could see anything. A hearing aid in a big fleshy ear. She clacked her false teeth and looked up at something.

"Who's a pretty bird? Is that you? Of course it is. That's a pretty Rudy."

How had he missed this? *Because she lives in the back of the house, asshole, probably never leaves that fucking room except to use the john right next to it, and you didn't do a full walk-round, did you, jerkoff? Amateur!* Why hadn't she heard them come in? Or had she? Had she already called the police? The hearing aid. Deaf? He prayed she was deaf. There was no way he was killing an old lady. No fucking way.

They couldn't go out the way they'd come. From where she sat now she'd see them pass through the kitchen. They'd have to risk it. Go out the front door, brazen as brass.

So be it.

He turned to Bobby, put his finger back up against his lips with one hand, and with the other gestured for him to go out the front door. They had the bag of jewelry, the camera, the trinkets from upstairs. Then he remembered the other bag. It was in the family room. He considered leaving it, but no, he couldn't. His fingerprints were probably on it somewhere. No more fuck-ups.

He grabbed Bobby's trembling upper arm.

"Take the bag," he whispered. "Meet me at the truck." He squeezed hard. "Go slow. Like you have every right to be here. Got it?"

Bobby nodded and moved, a little too quickly for Albert's taste, to the door. Turned the latch with a click that sounded like a hammer blow. Stepped out. Was gone.

Albert took a breath and moved to the kitchen door. From the other room the woman cooed to her bird. "Sing for me, sweetie. Sing for Gracie." *Peep. Peep.* Albert peeked around the kitchen wall. The stupid old bitch, who should by all rights be dead by now, was smack dab in his sight line. He smelled, or fancied he smelled, the powdery scent of her. It hid something sharper, urine, perhaps, or something sweeter, like decay. It flashed through his mind that he could go back the way he'd come through the living room, slip around behind her, and snap her brittle old pullet neck before she even knew what was happening. Perhaps it would even be kinder, save her a slow death from whatever it was old ladies in wheelchairs died of. Save her children the burden of her unwashed ass. He imagined the feeling of her jaw beneath his hands. The fragility of it. The loose skin slipping around over the bones. Bones like old ivory. The flutter of heartbeat. He couldn't help it: birds came to mind.

And so, no. Not if he could avoid it. Not if she'd let him out.

He stepped into the path where anything might happen next, where anything was possible. Their eyes met. The thrill of that. For, no matter what happened, he was powerful and she was nothing but string and flaps of flesh.

Amber.

Time is an ant trapped in amber.

Her eyes are the color of amber.

Her mouth opened. She might scream, he thought, not that it would matter, for how much air could there be in those withered, dried out lungs?

And then she shut her mouth.

Her eyes did not blink. Still as translucent stones.

A prickle ran up his arms. She surprised him. Her eyes were fearless. He imagined, in that sharp shard of a second, that her eyes had become dark mirrors, sending back his fear (fear he hadn't known he had) to him. Bouncing it into him so his cheek paled with ice and his chest burned with fire.

"Who are you?" she said, with the intonation at the end, who are you? as though she might even be pleased to see him, whoever he was, and her voice was disturbingly even.

"Just reading the meter, Ma'am," he said with a smile he hoped was winning.

"Are you now?"

Another decision. Would she allow the deceit? Her eyes sparkled; jumped for a moment to a corner of the room he couldn't see. A phone, perhaps. Obviously no time for such a thing. Not even if she'd been lithe and twenty. (Which, if such had been the case, other things might now be happening, things involving tight, hot slippery skin and smells other than old coffee and urine and the acrid whiff of desiccated flesh.) The canary peeped and even that sounded like a question.

Why wasn't she scared? Why wasn't she pissing herself? Panic was better. A panicked brain wouldn't remember much, but this calm, this composure, he didn't get it. He hated her then. Hated her vulnerability, which made him yearn to hurt her, but no, something else, because in that twitch of time he saw something, something stronger than it should be. Her, sitting there, a bag of sticks in a pale blue housedress, ulcerated sores on her purplish ankles. Her, with something like understanding in her eyes.

Did she have the fucking nerve to forgive him? He'd kill her if she did.

Perhaps she saw something change in him, shift from nerves to nerve ends, because she blinked once, and then, unsmiling, yet still infuriatingly calm, she nodded. Curtly. Just once. Where was fucking Alzheimer's when you needed it? What was the old sack of skin noticing? Would she see enough to give a description? The question, the decision, was his again.

Albert put his finger up to his lips and let his smile shift into something not winning at all. His smile was canine and sharp with cunning and bloodlust and a promise that he knew she understood. *Shall I be faceless then? And you too senile to notice me? Or will I come on back some night, some sweet dark night when your child's at home?* He raised an eyebrow, lobbing the unspoken question back to her side of the kitchen floor's great divide.

Granny nodded.

"Good girl," he said.

Bobby had the engine going, smart boy. Albert pointed to the bag of loot sitting on the seat between them.

"Put that on the fucking floor at least. Get it out of sight."

Bobby, his hands still trembling, did as he was told.

Albert pulled off down the street without a backward glance, going the speed limit, hanging loose. "Give me a cigarette," he said. When Bobby had lit him a smoke, handed it to him, and taken one for himself Albert said, "You did all right back there, kid. That was unforeseen. You didn't freak out. You did all right."

Bobby tapped his thumbnail against his lip nervously. "What happened?"

"My bad. I have to admit it. I didn't quite do my homework, now did I? You'd think I was a fucking amateur."

"No, I mean. Back there. With her. What did you do?" His voice was nearly a whisper.

"With her? What the fuck do you think happened?" Bobby looked as if he was about to cry. Perfect. Now the danger was over the kid fell apart. "Answer me," Albert said, because the adrenaline still buzzed and he was pissed at himself and needed to let it out. But Bobby was silent, his lower lip quivering. Albert reached over and flicked his index finger against the boy's ear, making him yelp and jump. "I said, answer me. What do you think I did?"

"I don't know," said Bobby.

"Shit. I didn't do fucking anything, you little whiner. You think I'd hurt an old lady? Is that the way professionals behave? Is it? Is that what you think I am, an amateur, some cranked-up gangsta gang-banging little old ladies?"

"No. I don't think that."

"Well then, what the fuck *do* you think?"

"I don't know."

"You intimated I hurt the old bitch, didn't you intimate that?"

"No, man. I didn't intimate anything, whatever that means."

"It means *allude*, dummy. It means *imply*. You should read. I read."

"It's just that she saw you, right, and you told me to leave. I don't know . . . I know you wouldn't hurt anybody . . ." His voice trailed off.

"You watch too much television." Albert chuckled, pleased at the way Bobby fidgeted, squirmed, tried even now to win approval. "You got to be like ice, see. You come in, you do what needs to be done, you don't lose your fucking head. Got that?"

"Sure. Absolutely." He looked over at Albert, his eyes dry, his lip firmed up. "I'm sorry, Albert. Really. I'm sorry, man. I just . . . you know."

"You were scared, right?" Albert punched him lightly, affectionately, on the shoulder. "No shame in that."

"Yeah, I guess."

"Listen, young Bobby, it's not about not being afraid, it's about keeping cool anyway, you got that? Keeping your head even when you think you might piss your pants, right?"

"I wasn't going to—"

"'Course you weren't, course not. You were all right back there. I said that, didn't I? You handled yourself all right." A sharp squeeze to the knee, made Bobby jump, but then the kid laughed. "When I fence this shit," Albert said, "you'll get your cut. Just like I promised. I keep my promises, right? Right?"

"Right." Bobby sat back, put his feet up on the dashboard.

"Don't leave fucking marks on my dash," said Albert.

That night, when Albert lay in bed trying to sleep, he thought about that old lady. It bothered him, he had to admit, how calm she'd been. He doubted she would say much of anything the cops could use. He'd left no evidence behind and the family was always good for an alibi, if not for much else. No matter what happened, what tensions there were up on the mountain, the clan kept their ranks tight against the law. It would be just another unsolved break-in and everyone would sit around the roast beef at Sunday dinner and give thanks the crazy drug addict hadn't hurt granny. He wondered if they knew what a tough old turkey granny was.

How did that happen, that absence of fear? Was it an old people's thing? Was it something you got when you neared your own death? He didn't think so. He'd seen people die. Two people. An uncle and an aunt. He'd seen more dead than that, of course, but dying was different. The moment of process. He'd seen the terror in their eyes as they struggled like smothering animals, clawing for their last breaths. No, it wasn't nearness of death that took away fear. It was something else. Like the worst had already happened, maybe, and there was nothing left to worry about.

But that wasn't the only thing keeping him awake. It was the feeling he couldn't shake that she'd *seen* him, not just his face, not in a description-to-the-cops sort of way, but *seen* him. What had that expression been on her face? That near-forgiveness that had made him *want* to strangle her?

Albert got up and pulled a bottle of whiskey from the trunk. He didn't bother with a glass. Just down, down, down, and down, until he drowned the old bitch and finally fell asleep.

CHAPTER EIGHTEEN

As Tom drove down Quaker Road on his way home from his new job at Kroeler's Paint, he noticed Carl Whitford, the sheriff, and Rita Kruppman standing on the sidewalk in front of the library. Carl waved and Tom did the same but then realized he was being asked to pull over.

He thanked God he hadn't been drinking.

Rita waved and ducked into the library, pointing at the books she carried. Tom pulled over and rolled down the passenger window. "Hey Carl. What's up?"

Carl tilted his hat back, took off his sunglasses, and checked for smudges before putting them back on. Although Carl Whitford was still in pretty good shape—firm, if a bit tightly packed around the middle—his face was developing jowls. In a few years they'd be puffing up over his collar, giving him the look of a huge strangling chipmunk.

"I've been meaning to call," said Carl. "How are you?"

"I'm all right. You?"

"Oh, good. I'm good." Carl leaned into the window. "I thought maybe you'd drop by the station."

"Why would I do that?"

"Well, sometimes people do if a family member goes missing."

"I guess they do, sometimes."

"Been what, a few weeks now. Technically, I should have had a talk with you before this."

"But you didn't want to intrude."

"Not if I didn't have to."

"You don't have to."

"Still, I have to ask."

"So ask."

"Is Patty missing?"

"That depends on what you mean by missing."

"Look, Tom. I know you're going through one hell of a time. You know this town."

"Yup, I do."

"Well, I just want to make sure there's nothing I need to know. You tell me you have reason to believe she's all right, that's good enough for me."

Tom hung his head. He had known Carl his whole life. They'd gone to school together. Their fathers played poker together and now *they* played poker together, although Tom hadn't been part of the game for a while. The truth probably was Carl knew everything there was to know, including who Patty was with right this minute.

Tom lifted his gaze to meet Carl's. "Anybody else filed a missing persons?"

"Can't say as they have."

"So, I guess that's the kind of missing they are."

"Interesting way of putting it." Carl looked down the street and seemed to be considering what else to say. Then he looked back at Tom. "Kids all right?"

"We're working things out."

The Sheriff knocked the door of the truck with his knuckle. "You should come out for a poker game some night. Not good to sit around, Tom."

"Yup."

"And, by the way, Rita said you should call her if you need anything."

"She did, huh?"

Carl shrugged. "People care about you. That's all I'm saying."

The next day, by mid-afternoon, Tom's arms ached. The muscles in his neck bunched and his shoulders cramped. He had thought tossing pallets of bread around took strength, but here, loading five-gallon buckets of paint into boxes and then hefting the boxes onto pallets waiting for the forklift to take them to the loading dock, he understood the insidious power of ceaseless, repetitive motion. It was hot on the assembly line. The machines clacked and rattled and pounded and even the earplugs didn't help much. The plant and attached warehouse were cavernous and the aluminum and steel walls amplified and echoed the cacophony of forklifts and assembly belts and the endless thwack and whack of rubber mallets on paint lids. Tom had a headache halfway through each shift and was nauseous by quitting time.

Since he was new man in, the foreman moved him around the plant, using him where he was needed, sizing him up for some final destination. Loading the boxes was better than some of the other duties he was called upon to perform. The one he hated most was when they asked him to climb into the huge vats and scrape paint from the inside. If it was ninety degrees on the factory floor, it was a hundred and ten in the vats, and not even the industrial masks stopped the fumes from getting through. The stench permeated every corner and crevice of the place, and the inside of his nose felt singed. At night, at home in bed, he fancied the vapors had pickled his skin, tainted his clothes, his furniture, his bed sheets—making him dream of death by chemical burn, death by incineration, death by nerve gas. The old timers said you got used to it; he remained unconvinced.

When he worked on the line, hammering lids onto the cans, he stood next to a guy named Hank Corkum who had been released from prison after serving three years for assault. Corkum's joy was to put paint scrapers, gloves, rubber mallets and anything else he could get his hands on into the can before he sealed the lid. Tom saw him do it the first day they worked side by side and Corkum knew he'd been seen. That day at lunch break Corkum had followed Tom into the men's room and stood with a mallet in his fist and stared at Tom until Tom shrugged his shoulders and said, "I need this job, friend. You won't get trouble from me." And Corkum grunted and turned and left Tom to his business.

Tom did need the job. As hard as the physical conditions and the monotony were and as much as he missed the early morning road, the solitude and the friendly banter with the customers, the pay at Koehler's was better than he'd earned driving the bread truck and, most importantly, it was a regular shift—eight in the morning until four in the afternoon. He'd been lucky to find any job at all in these times, and with his lack of education. He wasn't good for much, was he? That seemed to be the consensus. At least he was home when the kids came in. Ivy went to Dorothy's some afternoons, and when Ivy was home, she seemed determined to replace her mother. Nervously tidying and sweeping, dusting and polishing. Tom would send her up to her room to do her homework, and when he went to check on her, he'd find her scrubbing the bathroom. It was as though by keeping order and cleanliness in the house, she could somehow banish their grief. Maybe she saw dust as a layer of gray, silt-like, torpor-inducing sorrow, endlessly floating down to infect them. Tom worried she would become obsessed with the house, with him,

154

and forget she was just a little girl. But Bobby was another story. He wasn't home much these days. Tom didn't know what was up with his son, didn't know whom he was with, or what he was doing, only that the boy had turned even more silent, sullen and contemptuous since Patty walked out.

Patty.

In his mind, he could say 'walked out' now. That was something of an improvement, he supposed, but still, even thinking her name sent a knife through his gut. Over the weeks, shock and despair had turned to anger. With every bucket of paint he dropped into the box, he named another anger. Anger for their children. Anger at her selfishness. Anger at her cruelty. Anger at his blindness over all those years. Anger at himself for loving her still.

He caught his finger between two paint cans. The metal edge cut into his cuticle and blood pooled and then ran down to his knuckle. He cursed and wiped the blood off on his overalls.

It was three o'clock in the afternoon, and the shift was winding down. Eyes darted to the clock behind the metal cage high on the wall and work slowed. Lips could already taste beer. Fifty minutes to the bell. Aching muscles could already feel hot water. Forty minutes. Thirty. Aching feet could already feel shoeless freedom. Fifteen.

Greg Atkins, the foreman, tapped him on the shoulder. Sweat beaded on Atkins' meaty face and his expression was one of embarrassment. Tom wondered, with a twinge of panic, if he were about to be laid off.

"Tom, there's a guy waiting outside on the dock. Says he needs to talk to you."

"Who is he?"

"He seems pretty upset." Atkins' thick fingers fiddled with his belt buckle and he avoided Tom's eyes. "You maybe want to go talk to him."

"Is it my kids?" Tom pushed the button on his line that would re-route the paint cans to another belt. "Something happen to them?"

"No, it's not your kids, Tom."

"What is it, then?"

"You best go see. Knock off for the day." And with that Atkins walked away.

Tom grabbed his lunch pail and headed for the loading dock. As he neared, he saw five men standing in a cluster talking. Laughing. When one of them saw Tom he pulled at his mouth, erasing a grin, and nudged the man nearest him. The second man glanced over his shoulder, saw Tom and stepped away. With that the group dispersed, although they didn't go far. The sun was blinding, creating a huge blank eye of whiteness at the dock opening. Tom squinted into the brilliant day, seeing no one there, only a few trucks waiting for tomorrow's loading, and a battered brown Chevy parked just outside the steel mesh gates. The inside of his stomach felt raw, as though it were being scraped with a wire brush. He gazed around, puzzled, and was just about to ask one of the men if somebody had been looking for him, when the door of the Chevy opened and a man got out. The man hesitated, put his hands in the pockets of his jeans, and stepped forward, haltingly, a little unsteady. He was a short man, although powerfully built and a little bow-legged. The tee shirt he wore flashed too brightly white. Tom was sure he didn't know the man. He couldn't make out his features since the sun was behind him. The man came forward, to about halfway across the lot, and stopped. He stood looking at Tom, weaving slightly.

"You looking for me?" Tom said.

"Can I talk to you?" the man said. He swiped his index finger under his nose.

"I know you?"

"No. Kinda. I mean, no."

Tom's body knew who it was first, the same way you suddenly knew, with a gut-clenching, spiraling certainty that it wasn't a vein you'd cut, it was a spouting artery and all your blood was going to flow onto the kitchen tile before you even had a chance to dial 911.

His first thought was that something had happened to Patty and this man had come to bring news of her death. His stomach dropped and rolled and the sky and earth exchanged places. He reached for something to hang onto, caught the foam dock seal. How would he tell the children? Their faces swam before him. Patty's face hung in the air.

The man took a couple of steps forward into a patch of shade and Tom saw him more clearly. A nose that told of bar fights, high cheekbones, milky brown eyes, a wide mouth, now loose with emotion. It was a face marked by hard living, but traces of the handsome man he must have been once were still apparent.

"I'm Larry. I didn't have no one else who'd understand," the man said. "I'm Larry Corkum."

156

With an effort, Tom began to breathe. He squatted, and then jumped off the dock, felt a pain in his knee where his lunch pail knocked into bone. He came close to the man, smelled alcohol. Saw that his skin was bad, bumps where his beard had ingrown, a couple of sores it looked as though he'd been picking at. *What had Patty seen in this man?* "Tell me," he said.

"I, I, I want to know . . . I want to know if you heard from her."

"Heard from her? What do you mean? Is she all right?" Tom wanted to lay hands on this man, this *Larry*, but sensed if he came too close, the man would bolt.

"She left me, man, she left me in *Albany*," he wailed, saying the word Albany as though the particular site of the abandonment increased the injury, the insult.

The news hit Tom in the center of his chest. She'll come home now, he thought. She'll come home. Everything in him leaped, soared, and then, in nearly the same instant, crashed down, because maybe she wouldn't, or maybe Larry was lying and had harmed her, maybe she had never left him at all, but maybe she had been taken away. But look at this *Larry*—he was a mess, crying even now, snot bubbles and all. Not a murderer, just a loser, just a guy left in *Albany*. Tom's thoughts were dust devils, whirlwinds sucking up dirt from below and shooting it up in a fierce scatter of possibilities. Larry was still speaking through the blubber of his tears.

"I can't believe she left me, man. I thought she'd go home to you, maybe? Or maybe she'd changed her mind and then I thought, you know, I know it's crazy but I had to talk to you, I had to say how sorry I was, tell you how I'd like to rip out my own eyes!" Larry put his hands, claw-like, up to his face.

"Hey, now," said Tom. "Hey, now!"

Larry dropped his hands and held them out to Tom, as though about to embrace him. "I didn't know, you get it, man? I didn't know!"

Tom stepped back. Larry Corkum was high as a kite.

"But now I do know. I know what it feels like. I didn't want that for you. I didn't know she was a fucking witch! She put something on me, and I bet she did on you, too. Some fucking hoodoo shit. I can't shake her, you know?" His voice trailed off.

"When did you see her last?"

"I don't know. A week maybe. Took me a while to get back here. She took my wallet, took the fucking car."

157

"She stole your car?"

"She stole my soul, man. Stole my soul." He hung his head, tears dripping from the end of his nose.

Tom could not take this in. That she stole. That she took money, a car, left another man. Who the fuck was she, this woman he had lived with for so long? Disgust for the self-pitying, melodramatic wreck before him hit Tom with such force he stepped back. Then, the image of his own sorry state arose, of how he sat for days in front of the television, not bathing, drinking scotch, crying, ignoring his children. "Shit," he said.

"She didn't come here? She didn't come back here?" Larry said, arms wrapped around his chest, shivering slightly.

"No."

"Oh, Jesus, Jesus. What am I going to do?"

"I have no idea."

"I'm out of money and all."

Tom knew that if Larry asked him for money he would kill him. He would put his hands around his throat and squeeze until his eyes popped out of his head and lay on his bloated cheeks. His hands flexed. He realized he must have dropped his lunch pail at some point. His body was working on some primal level not connected to his brain. It might do anything. Anything at all.

"Larry! *Larry*! What the fuck are you doing, man?"

Tom turned as Hank Corkum hopped down from the loading dock, nimble as a cat, light on his feet and quick for a man his size.

"Hey, Hank," said Larry. "I just needed, you know."

"No, I don't fucking know. I told you to stay the hell away from here. Why don't you listen to nobody, man?" Hank kept his eyes on Larry, crossing the asphalt in a few long strides, his hands out to either side, palms up, in query or supplication.

And Tom thought: *So again, everyone knew but me.* It was very hard to keep his hands at his side, not to hit something, break or tear or crack something.

"I wanted to say I'm sorry. Like in that program, right, where you make amends and shit."

"You have to be fucking sober for that, Larry. You hear me? Doesn't mean shit if you're high, you asshole. You took my fucking car? And you're drinking?" Hank looked at Tom for the first time. "You want to pop my idiot cousin, I'm not going to interfere."

Tom considered the offer. It would be easy. He didn't know what it felt like to snap someone's jaw under his fist, had never hit anyone that hard before, although he had no doubt he could do it with a single punch. Faced with the invitation to crush the man he held responsible for his present agony, he could not deny the allure of bloodshed. Larry Corkum stood before him, eyes ragged and roaming under the weight of his own pain, skin blotched and pocked with the effects of whatever drug he was taking, cheeks hollowed by a variety of hungers, hands quivering slightly, not even preparing to defend himself. His mouth was slack and open, his breath a funk of beer fumes. He swayed on unsteady legs.

"Yeah," Larry said. "You go ahead. You hit me. I deserve it."

"No, thanks," said Tom.

Larry began to crumple in earnest then. His lower lip trembled and his eyes dripped large, oily tears.

"Come on, Larry. Get you out of here." Hank stepped forward and pushed his cousin's shoulder to move him toward the car. "I'm driving."

"Wait, wait." Larry looked at Tom and then, slowly, extended his hand. It hung there in the sticky air, shaking, the color of ham. "I'm sorry. I'm really, really sorry. I didn't know. Just didn't get it."

Tom did not want to shake Larry's hand. He wanted to turn and get as far away from this man, from this place, as was possible. He looked down at Larry's hand, and saw it as an already-dead thing, simply unaware of its own mortality. "Let's just leave it, okay?" he said.

Before he could stop him, Larry reached out and took his hand, grabbed it and pulled Tom into an awkward and surprisingly fierce embrace.

"You're all right, you know that?" Larry blubbered into his neck. "She don't deserve you."

Tom was so stunned he just stood there, his eyes meeting Hank's whose wide-eyed shock probably mirrored his own. Larry punched him lightly on the back with his fist all the while clutching his hand up against his chest.

"Shit," said Hank.

"I love you, man. I'd fucking cut off my arm. My fucking arm," Larry mumbled.

And without really knowing why, except perhaps it was the only way Tom could see to end this grotesque waltz, he reached up with his free hand and slapped Larry a couple of times on the back. "Pull yourself together, Larry. For fuck sake. Come on now. Come on."

159

Hank tugged at Larry's arm. "Quit acting crazy and get in the fucking car."

Larry let Hank lead him away, muttering all the time he was sorry, really sorry.

Tom stood in the sharp, unforgiving light and felt as though a strip of his flesh had been pulled away. It was hard to breath and for a moment he was rooted, still sensing the weight of the other man hanging in his arms. At last, he turned to go round the building and find his car in the employee parking lot.

In the mouth of the loading dock stood a small group of men. He knew their names. Ed, Bob, Clint, Austin, Wooly and Huck. Had known most of them his entire life, knew the names of their kids and where they lived and in at least three cases, to whom they'd lost their virginity. But he hadn't known this about them: hadn't known they could stand at that coward's distance and watch a man's humiliation and anguish and smile about it. Hadn't known they could stand in the shade of a rubber and brick overhang and smile and snigger behind their thick, paint-spattered fingers. It did something to him; all that knowledge piled up inside him like stones. It filled him somehow, and protected him. His bent shoulders straightened. His head realigned from its bowed position to sit at ease and his eyes grew calm. Tom regarded these men with an unfaltering gaze and it seemed as though the distance, both temporal and spatial, was very great. It was a sort of detachment, an objectivity from which he imagined himself on a smoldering pyre, strapped to the post of his agony, waiting for the flames to begin, the smoke to rise, and while he accepted that soon he would be consumed by the loneliness all around him, just for this moment there was a kind of pride in his position. His naked pain glowed with a kind of grace.

One by one, in silence, the men stopped sniggering and without looking at one another, they turned and disappeared into the factory shadows, until Tom was left alone. The factory clanged and clattered and voices, some of them gruff with embarrassment, skidded and scattered along the heat ripples rising from the asphalt.

It was a long walk to his truck and Tom was less than half way there before his cheeks were wet and he was half-blind. Inside the cab, the air was hot as a crematorium oven. He thought he might dissolve to nothing but a puddle of bubbling fat and charcoaled bone.

CHAPTER NINETEEN

The apostle Paul wrote **'Children, obey your parents in the Lord, for this is right,'** *Ephesians 6, verse 1. The original command to honor father and mother applies to all of us throughout our lives. But in this place children, specifically, are told to obey their parents 'in the Lord.' Because of his total lack of experience and judgment, it is absolutely necessary that a child be taught to OBEY his parents INSTANTLY and WITHOUT QUESTION. Explanations and reasons for this may and should be given to the child from time to time. But, at the moment a parental command is given, THERE MAY NOT BE TIME OR OPPORTUNITY TO GIVE THE REASON WHY! Therefore, it is imperative that a child be taught the HABIT of unquestioning OBEDIANCE to his parents. For, until the young child develops, his parents stand to him in the place of God. And God holds them RESPONSIBLE for teaching and directing the child properly.* **'He that spareth his rod hateth his son: but he that loveth him chasteneth him betimes."** *Proverbs 13:24.* **'Chasten thy son while there is hope, and let not thy soul spare for his crying.'** *Proverbs 19:18* – **Reverend Wilson Carothers, Church of Christ Returning, 1956**

The unseasonable, dry-fever heat thickened the night air with insects. The hard clay earth cracked into a crazy quilt and the fragile new leaves on the trees drooped. They needed rain and everyone said when it came it would come in a great thunderous clap of wind and fury. But for now, the air was a sultry hot breath on the face, fragrant with resin and tar.

Albert drove the truck by steering the wheel with his left wrist, the fingers dangling and loose. With his other hand he probed his teeth with a wooden pick. He and Bobby had shared a meat-lover's pizza at the Italian Garden and were now on their way to visit Gladys Corkum.

"She's good people, for mountain," Albert said. "Although this isn't real mountain, you understand. That's not for you. Not yet anyway. This is like mountain-light."

Everything was a question of degrees and Albert had been trying to teach this to Bobby. In town, you had the fat cats who lived on Washington, in the big houses, like Pataki, looking out on the river. Then folks like Mrs. Carlisle, who had a real nice house, but no mansion, and then people like Bobby's family, doing all right for themselves, working class, and finally, people like Stan Mertus who were scrambling pretty close to the 'mountain line.' The mountain was like that too, only in reverse. Erskines at the top, which meant exactly the opposite of what it would in town. People like Gladys and the other Corkums, close to the bottom, living in houses on a web of roads just off the highway, neither here nor there.

"I'm cool," Bobby had said.

"I'm counting on it." Albert glanced over at the younger boy. He had pulled the hood of his sweatshirt up over his head. Bobby never wanted to go home, kept asking if he could hang out up at Albert's cabin. Albert thought it must be rough, thinking you had a normal family, and then finding out it was just as fucked up as anybody else's. He wasn't ready to bring Bobby up to the mountain, although he was eager to see how he'd handle himself at Gladys's.

"You know where that guy lives?" Bobby said.

"What guy?"

"*The* guy, Albert. The one my mother took off with." Bobby kept his face turned to the window.

The houses here were not like the houses in town. The houses here were more or less just shacks on little pieces of land, yards scattered with car parts, broken furniture, and tires filled with the dried out skeletons of geraniums and snap dragons. Some of the shacks were wooden, painted bright colors: pinks and blues, and one purple. Most were unpainted, and one or two were tarpaper over ragged insulation and wood frame. One was burned out, just a couple of walls and some black earth. Every year, in the deep freeze of a dark winter night, a shack or two burned down and people died—the culprit generally being a short-circuited and untended electric heater, or a wood stove with a faulty chimney. The bright colors made Albert think of the three pigs and the big bad wolf. They looked like they'd blow down with even the mildest of huffs, the most inconsequential of puffs. At least trees surrounded his place. Even if it was a lie, they offered the illusion of protection.

Albert knew where the Corkums lived. Knew Larry Corkum, Patty's lover, to see, anyway. Larry was younger than Bobby's mother, a nice enough guy, but not too bright. The kind of guy who could be talked into things. Albert had sold him a lid once or twice and over-charged him. Larry didn't seem to mind. "Yeah, I know where he lives. You want to go by and see it?"

"No."

"Good choice. Won't do no good, young Bobby and I can guarantee that his people aren't any happier than yours."

"What's that supposed to mean?" He turned to Albert, a slight flush of emotion on each cheek.

"Still protective of Mom, huh?"

He turned away again. "No."

A scrawny deer hobbled out into the road, one leg dragging uselessly. Albert swerved around it and then looked back in the rearview mirror. "I should have hit that thing, put it out of its misery. Would have busted up the truck, though."

"If you'll take me here, how come not up to your place?"

Albert looked over at Bobby. "So, what's the big attraction at my place?"

"I don't know. Curious, I guess. And—"

"And what?"

"Well, you're up there. You've got your own place. I hate being at my place. All that silence and moping around. Ivy thinks she's my fucking mother now, trying to bake cookies and shit. What's that about?" He shook his head and picked at a hangnail. "Anyway, I just thought it might be kinda cool, you know, I could come up there sometime. Maybe get a bottle of brandy or something from my old man's cabinet."

"Jesus. What am I going to do with you? We're here," said Albert, and they pulled up in front of a tiny tar-paper-and-board house. Plastic covered the windows and parts of the outer walls. Scraps flapped in the wind like thin shavings of dead skin, ragged and frayed.

"Come on," said Albert.

Bobby's hand went to the door handle and then hesitated.

"Nervous?" Albert grinned at him.

"Maybe. A little." Bobby blushed under his hood.

He looks about twelve, thought Albert. "Don't be. Gladys'll like you." He reached over and punched Bobby lightly on the shoulder, then got out of the cab and waved at Bobby to follow. The younger boy got out of the truck and shuffled across the dirt.

Albert knocked and walked in, calling out "Hey, Gladys, how you doing?"

Along the left wall was a kitchen of sorts. A stainless steel sink with a piece of yellow cloth stuck around it with double-sided tape, drooping, only half-hiding the cleaning products below. A battered stove, a small refrigerator painted a streaky pink. An assortment of milk crates, upended to form boxes, stacked one on top of the other, acted as shelving. Several boxes of macaroni and cheese, a box of cereal, a glass jar of rice, another of dried peas, and five or six tins of soup. There was a green-topped chrome table and four chairs. A brown plastic door, folded back like an accordion, divided the main room from a small back room in which stood a crib, a cot and a set of drawers. The air smelled of cigarettes and diapers.

Against the wall opposite the kitchen a thin woman reclined on a legless, spring-shot, and stained blue sofa. A cluttered white plastic coffee table stood in front of the couch and a small television in the corner was tuned to a game show. An electric fan was plugged into the same extension cord as the television and a lamp, the wires a threatening snarl. A large square of brown speckled linoleum served as a rug. The woman on the couch twisted her neck towards the door. "Close the fucking door, Albert! You wanna let all the bugs in or what? Who's that?"

"Hey, Gladys," said Albert. "This is Bobby."

Gladys was in her thirties. Her hair was unevenly dyed blonde, frizzy, and flat at the back where her head had rested against the arm of the couch. She had pouches under her pale eyes and her lips were thin, her teeth small and gray. She was still pretty, though, in a washed-out and worn sort of way. She wore jeans, an oversized man's cardigan (even though the evening was warm enough to warrant the fan) over a black tee shirt and large grayish-pink fuzzy slippers.

"Bobby who?"

"Evans," said Albert. "And yeah, he's Tom Evans's kid, so don't go there."

"Huh," said Gladys, looking at Bobby without smiling. "What brings you boys here?"

"Been a while since you left an order at Maverick's. Thought maybe you might need a delivery."

"I wanted a delivery I would have left word. I'm busted. You giving it away?"

"Have I ever given it away?"

Gladys snorted. "Well, then. You want a beer?"

"Yeah, all right," Albert answered. "Maybe we'll do a little something-for-something."

"You know where they are." She turned back to the game show. Celebrities sat in cubicles built to form a large X's and O's board. They answered questions posed by the game's host and the contestants had to guess whether the celebrities were lying or not. "They got Whoopie Goldberg in the center square now," said Gladys. "I heard that woman owns the show."

"You only got two beers," said Albert, his head in the refrigerator.

"Yeah? So split one with your friend. You sitting down, honey, or what?"

"Thanks." Bobby pulled a chair around so he sat on the other side of the coffee table.

Albert opened a cupboard and reached for a glass. "Fuck, Gladys, you got mice turds in here."

"I don't bother them, they don't bother me. No roaches though. I can't stand those little fuckers." She shivered without taking her eyes off the screen.

Albert handed Gladys a beer bottle and poured some into a glass he then handed to Bobby. "So, what you been up to?" He took another chair and straddled it, his arms on the back. He peeled the corner of the label off his beer and then smoothed it back down again.

"Playing Florence Nightingale. Jake's sick again. That kid is always sick. I wasn't never sick when I was little, but he gets every cold, every barfy bug that goes around. He been puking all day. Only been asleep the past hour."

"That's too bad," said Bobby. "How old is he?"

"Jake's four."

"Gladys's got a boy my age, too," said Albert.

"Really? Wow," said Bobby.

"What's that supposed to mean?"

"You don't look old enough," said Bobby, shifting on his chair.

Gladys laughed, swung her legs off the couch and looked at him. "How old do you have to be?"

"You just look so young."

"Aren't you the sweetest thing? Hell, I was fourteen when I had Ricky. That's how I met this sorry sack of skin," she said, waving her beer bottle at Albert. "They ran together for a while." Gladys leaned forward and slapped Albert's thigh. "You remember how you used to come sniffing round?"

Albert grinned but said nothing.

"Yessir, little big man he thought he was. So I said one day, 'Bertie, darling, you want to come over and park your car in my garage?' And this fool looks at me all innocent and sweet and says, 'Gee, Gladys, I don't got no car. I ain't even got a bicycle!'" Gladys threw back her head and laughed. Albert laughed, too.

"Yeah, well, maybe it wasn't me sniffing round. You were only too happy to see me later when I came back looking for parking space—once I'd learned how to drive."

"Nice try. I was your first driving teacher."

"You wish," said Albert.

Gladys leaned back on the couch and drank from her beer, then lit up a cigarette from a green and white menthol pack. "Yeah, Ricky's in the Navy now. Has to support that baby-mama of his. He's a better man than his father; I'll say that for him. So Bobby, it's Bobby, right? How are things at your place?"

"Gladys," Albert growled.

"I'm just asking."

"All right," said Bobby.

"Well," said Gladys, "don't let it get you down, kid. More assholes in the world than angels. Might just as well get used to it."

"That's what I been telling him." Albert pulled a plastic bag out of his pocket then and rolled a joint and they smoked it, laughing at the game show for a while, until Jake began to cry in the back room, calling for his mother. "Shit," said Gladys and went off to tend to her son, who'd begun retching.

"Let's go," said Albert.

"Shouldn't we stay and help?" Bobby said. "I mean, she's pretty high, we all are."

"You think this is high? This ain't high. I've seen Gladys drive a truck down the highway doing ninety after drinking a case of beer and smoking enough dope to knock out five full-grown men. Believe me, she ain't high. Hey, Gladys, we're leaving," he called.

They heard a car pull up and moments later the door opened. Bill Corkum stepped in, wearing a 69'ers jersey and baggy shorts that fell to below his knees. He saw Albert and Bobby and stopped in his tracks. "What are you doing here?" He sniffed the air. "Right," he said.

Jayne Miller stepped in behind him. "Hi all," she said, and then, "Oh."

"This is pretty," said Albert, glaring at Jayne as though there had been something between them she just wouldn't admit.

"You on your way?" said Bill.

"Maybe. Maybe not," said Albert. Just looking at Jayne, standing there with her hand on Bill's back, made him want to break something. She looked good. Hair all black and shiny. Her fingernails painted a pale pink. She wore a white mini skirt and a tee shirt that showed her belly button. She had a little silver chain around her ankle.

Gladys walked back into the room, a little boy clinging limply to her neck, perched on her bony hip. He had stains on his pajamas and he gazed dully from caked and swollen eyes. "Hey, Bill. Don't you ever call first?"

"I would have, but your phone's out again."

"What?" Gladys grabbed the phone off the wall and held it to her ear. "Fuck!" she said and slammed it back into the cradle. "I paid that fucking bill. I know I did."

And with that, the little boy vomited weakly, spilling a yellowish trail of bile down the front of his mother's cardigan. "Jesus Christ!" she yelled, and held the boy at arms length, his stomach still twitching, his cheeks puffing up with the effort not to vomit on his mother again. Gladys bent him over the sink, his legs dangling in mid-air, the stainless steel digging into his belly. He retched. She slapped him on the back of the head. "You gonna puke you say something first, you little shit. Don't be puking on me, you hear!" The child whined something unintelligible. She held him there with one hand on his back, the other swiping at her clothes with a tea towel.

"For fuck sake, Gladys, it's not his fault," said Bill.

"Fuck off," said Gladys.

Jayne stepped around the men. "Give him to me," she said, her hands reaching out. "Why don't you get yourself cleaned up? I'll deal with him." She grabbed another towel which lay balled up on the counter and plucked the child from the edge of the sink, holding him on her hip. She wiped his mouth with the towel.

"Thanks, honey. Goddamn stink," said Gladys and she disappeared into the back where the bathroom was, muttering under her breath.

The three young men stood, shuffling uneasily from foot to foot, jingling coins in their pockets, looking at Jayne and Jake, not meeting each other's eyes. Jake began to cry. It was as though, with his mother out of the room, all the tears he'd kept in leaked out of him—large glossy tears fell without sound, dripping from his chin. His eyes were huge and glistening, looking out on the world with an expression that said he expected no pity and no help. He turned his face to Jayne and gazed at her as if he didn't know what kind of a creature she might be. And still, the tears kept falling. Then he turned and looked at Albert.

The sick child and Albert locked eyes. The kid just stared, soul-dead and hopeless and horribly patient; utterly undefended by any normal survival instinct to hide something of himself. It was all just there, the kid's entire sorry soul, sliding out of his eyes. Albert imagined the child's body transforming into a desiccated husk, as though he was constructed of nothing but tears and now that they had begun to leak away they wouldn't stop and there would be nothing to hold him together. He'd just leak and leak until he began to implode, crumpling inward in a crinkled mass. Albert wanted to break away and couldn't. He wanted Jayne to wipe those tears off the kid's face and tell him to cut it out. Crying wasn't going to get you anywhere. But the tears just kept coming. Albert's fingertips tingled, and his vision speckled as his breath grew thin.

Jayne reached up and, using her thumb, gently wiped the tears away and the child turned to look at her again. She shifted Jake on her hip. The weight of him had pulled down the neckline of Jayne's tee shirt and her small white breast lay squashed against him. She wore a bright pink lacy bra. She ran water and dampened the towel, trying to clean his vomit-spattered face. Jake laid his head against Jayne's neck and began to suck his thumb.

"Poor little kid," said Jayne. She touched his forehead and then said, "He's really hot, Bill. I think he needs a doctor."

"Gladys don't have health insurance."

"Gladys," Jayne called, stepping into the doorway that led to the back of the shack. "Do you have any baby aspirin? Jake's got a fever."

"I know what he's got. You don't have to tell me," Gladys called back. "And no, I don't have any fucking aspirin. He'll be fine. He always gets better."

"Well, I still say he needs a doctor," Jayne said, turning to the men again. She looked from one face to another.

"Here," said Bobby. He reached in his pocket and pulled out three crumpled ten-dollar bills. "Take this."

"Where'd you get that?" said Albert.

Bobby shrugged. "My old man."

Bill looked at him like he'd never seen him before. "Yeah, all right, then." He, too, reached in his pocket and pulled out some bills. "I got a bit." He looked at Albert. "What about you, man?"

"Not my kid."

"Oh, it's like that, huh?" said Bill.

Jayne stepped forward and took the money from Bobby. "You're a sweetheart, Bobby. A real sweetheart." She gave him a peck on the cheek and color mottled his skin.

"He's just a little kid," said the boy.

"Shit," said Albert. "Here." He pulled some bills out of his pocket and gave them to Jayne. "At least get him some fucking aspirin. I'm out of here." He tossed a small bag of marijuana on the counter. "Tell her she don't owe me anything."

"Mr. Big Man, huh?" Bill smiled at Albert and, seeing the look on his face, "Hey, I'm kidding, man. Just yanking your chain."

"Try and do the right thing and see?" Albert said to Bobby. He turned and headed for the door, looking as though he'd walk right through Bill.

Bill moved out of the way as Albert stepped into the night, with Bobby following.

"Come on, Albert. Just trying to lighten the mood, you know," Bill said.

Albert ignored him.

"Thank you," Jayne called. "Thanks, both of you."

The little boy retched again.

"Not your kid, either Miss Nightingale," Albert tossed over his shoulder and heard Jayne ask Bill who Miss Nightingale was.

Albert stalked back to the truck and got in, slamming the door. Bobby scrambled in after him. A mosquito buzzed in Albert's ear and he swatted at it, leaving a smear of blood on his neck.

Bobby said, "That was weird."

"What was?" Albert lit a cigarette.

"She always like that?"

"Who?" His mind was still on Jayne, standing there with the baby in her arms, her breast exposed. It was a stupid color for a bra. It was a hooker's color.

"Gladys."

"Like what?"

"Well, she was kinda rough on her kid, wasn't she? I mean, slamming him up on the sink like that. He's only four. Can't weigh more than thirty pounds."

"What do you think's gonna happen to that money?"

"Take the kid to emergency I guess."

"That money's going to go on more beer and a pizza and maybe a bottle of fucking Thunderbird and whatever else Gladys can get for herself. That kid's not going to any hospital. Jesus, you're such a fucking innocent." Albert started the engine and pulled out into the street. There were no streetlights and beyond the headlights, the shacks looked sinister.

Bobby huffed and pulled out a cigarette of his own. "So why'd you give them money, then?"

This was a good question. And one to which Albert had no answer. Why had he given the money? Because he wanted to look good to Jayne? No, she wasn't worth it, sleeping with a Corkum and wearing clothes like that. She was never the class he thought she might have been. She was just like Bobby's mother. In his mind, Jake's eyes appeared, staring into his, and filling up like some sort of darkly enchanted pool that would never empty. "I don't know. Must have been the grass."

"Naw, I don't think so," said Bobby.

Albert looked at Bobby, who smiled as though he'd just proved some point. "Gladys does what she can. You don't know shit about bad mothers," he said.

"I don't know shit?" Bobby pulled his chin back in disbelief. "You can't say that to me. Not now."

"Get over it. One day I just might show you what bad mothers can do."

"Like yours?" Bobby asked in a quiet voice. "That's whacked, man. Whacked."

"You have no fucking idea," said Albert. He was angry then, and took the curve too fast, making the tires squeal. It occurred to him he really could take Bobby up the mountain one day, like a sort of field trip to the nightmare zoo. Give him an education so complete he'd run back home and study hard, go to college, and be a fucking doctor himself so he could take care of all the little Jakes in the world to his heart's content. Albert could do that, and maybe he would. Might be the best thing.

CHAPTER TWENTY

Dorothy muttered as she drove to the Evans' house. She was doing something so against her nature that her underarms would doubtless bare the dark evidence of her nervousness. The rich, sweetish aroma of the chicken and prune casserole resting on the back seat perfumed the car. The casserole dish sat next to a cardboard box packed with a salad, a loaf of crusty bread and some strawberries. It was nearly 6:30 and the light shone in long blinding slats near the horizon, which made Dorothy squint as she turned onto Joshua Road. She remembered when Bob Evans, Tom's father, had built the first house out here when it was still all farmland. Now there were other houses, small houses constructed with care by people who usually built things for other people and who had obviously delighted in bringing their artisanship home for the ones they loved. However, they had been mostly sold and sometimes sold again. They were on large lots, all of them, and one day someone was going to come along and buy these houses, bulldoze them and put up behemoths of dubious taste and inferior workmanship. It was happening all over, these nouveau developments full of people who believed they couldn't have a baby unless they provided little junior with a bathroom of his own and fed him in a kitchen the size of half the original house—as though the size of a house was an indicator of how much happiness it could hold.

It was easy to tell which two houses, other than Tom's, retained the original owners: a pair of neat cape-cods next to each other. The Doyles and the Millers, if Dorothy remembered correctly. The paint on each house was fresh, one bright yellow, the other white with green shutters, the flower beds tended, the walkways weed-free, the porch steps straight and true. The rest were at various stages of slow decline. Renters occupied at least two, she knew from town gossip, and they were the easiest to identify—a broken pane of glass replaced with plywood, a sheet tacked over a window rather than curtains, dandelions gone to seed everywhere, cheap plastic toys strewn about the lawn: a bright blue pail, a doll with only one leg, a tricycle, a leaky plastic pool. You just couldn't count on

172

people to have pride anymore, she thought. Had no one taught them decay sets in before you knew it and if you didn't hold it off with a firm hand it would overtake you? You had to keep your back straight and your stride brisk.

Which brought her back to Tom Evans. Tom was slouching, slipping into a posture from which it was quite possible he would not recover. Dorothy frowned. If it was just Tom, well, she'd leave him to it. Like most everything, it was really none of her business. But it was not just Tom. It was Ivy and Bobby as well. Something needed to be done and alas, it appeared Tom was not up to doing it. It was all both vexing and somewhat embarrassing. She had come home just after five, ready for a little gardening, a glass of wine even, a salmon dinner, and a book by Vita-Sackville West she had not read before. And there it was: the blinking light on her answering machine.

Dorothy did not get many messages on her machine—an antiquated contraption that depended on overused cassettes—and the ones she did were generally requests to either donate money to a cause she did not support, or Mabel, inviting her to church again. Apparently, Dorothy was now on a prayer list.

She was, she had to admit, terribly worried when she heard Ivy's voice on the phone. The girl rarely called, preferring, sensibly, to drop by the store if she wanted to visit. *Hello, Mrs. Carlisle. It's Ivy. I'm okay. I just wanted to say hello, I guess. Bye.* Simple enough words, but the tone was alarming. The child sounded on the verge of tears, the tremble and crack in her voice unmistakable. Dorothy had sat down for a few seconds, trying to determine if there was any way she might avoid calling her. Then, shamed, she slapped the back of her own hand and picked up the phone.

Ivy answered on the first ring.

"Hello?"

"Ivy, dear, it's Mrs. Carlisle."

"Hi."

"What's the matter?"

"Nothing."

"Ivy, do not be coy. It's clear something is wrong and you want to tell me what it is or you wouldn't have called me."

"Dad's in his room."

"Can you ask him to come to the phone, please?"

"I don't think so."

"Is he sick?"

There was a pause of significant length.

"No," said Ivy, but the meaning was unclear.

It was impossible not to wonder if Tom Evans was drunk. Dorothy seemed to speak into a great black stretch of space, a sheer sided, pitch-shadowed crevasse between the phone she held and the one in Ivy's hand.

"Is Bobby there?"

"No. He was here, but he's gone."

"I see," she said. "Have you had dinner?"

Again, the pause was significant.

"Mrs. Carlisle?"

"Yes, dear?"

"I was going to make grilled cheese, but we don't have any bread." The words came out in a rush, and Dorothy sensed the obstacle of guilt Ivy had had to overcome to speak them. Saying something like this was like telling a secret, wasn't it? A family secret. Dorothy's chest constricted and her lips compressed. She thought how satisfying it would be to throw a bucket of cold water in Tom Evan's face.

"Ivy," she said, rather slowly, for she had no idea what she might be about to say, "I'm so happy you called me. Really, dear, it's such a coincidence." Luckily, she was one of those women who always made double the recipe of everything and froze meals so she didn't have to cook every night. "I'm sitting here, surrounded by—" she mentally scanned what she had in her freezer "—chicken and prunes. I know that sounds like an odd combination, but it's actually very good, and there are olives in it. Do you like olives?"

"I like green ones."

"Perfect, then, because these are green olives, and I've made far too much, as I always do, and I wonder if you would mind if I popped in with it? I can't think what got into me, making all this. Do you think you would like that? You'd be doing me such a great favor. Isn't it wonderful the way these things work out sometimes? What do you say?" There was another silence on the phone during which Dorothy imagined Ivy's puckered brow, imagined her tapping her front tooth with her thumb as she did when trying to figure something out. "Really, dear, just say yes and you would make me very happy."

"Okay," Ivy said, her voice soft as feathers.

And so here she was, driving up Joshua Street, turning into the Evan's driveway, with enough food to feed six people. Thank God for microwaves. The headlights scanned the small house. Ivy stood at the living room window, her hand on the head of the dog whose paws rested on the sill. A moment later the front door opened and the dog bounded out, Ivy following. Her hair was pulled into a braid from which tendrils escaped, and she wore a white dress with pink flowers on it, which was slightly too small. Ivy pulled at the armholes with her thumbs. Dorothy could not help but wonder if she had put it on after she had called, dressing up for a dinner guest.

"Rascal, come on," Ivy said to the dog, "Don't jump. Don't jump."

Dorothy stepped out of the car and petted the dog, which did not jump, but wiggled and whined and seemed to be smiling at her. "Good boy," she said, and then she hugged Ivy. The child clung to her for a moment and then stiffened, stepping away.

"I didn't tell Dad you were coming," she said. She glanced over her shoulder at the dark window above the front door, which Dorothy presumed was her father's bedroom.

"That's perfect, dear! It will be a surprise then, won't it? And I wonder, well, I know it was your idea to call me, but do you think we could say I just took it upon myself to come by? I so rarely get the opportunity to do anything so spontaneous, and I'm rather sorry I didn't think of it myself, truthfully. Would you mind very much if I took the credit?"

"I'm not sure Dad's going to be, well, he won't be mad at you, but . . ."

"Oh, he won't be mad at me!" said Dorothy, and she noted Ivy rubbed the Boy Scout whistle hanging around her neck, as though it were an amulet. Frankly, she didn't care very much if Tom was angry or not. No bread, indeed! "No one can be angry at someone who comes bearing gifts of chicken and prunes! Now, take that salad bowl, dear, and I'll get the rest, and then we'll see to your father."

Rascal was already at the door, looking over his shoulder encouragingly, as if he were leading some sort of doggy version of the assault on Bunker Hill.

"Come on, then. It seems Rascal's hungry, too." Dorothy shut the car door with her foot and marched up the steps.

In the kitchen, she set the stove to 350 degrees and took the foil off the chicken so it would heat quicker. She made no effort to be quiet, hoping the noise would rouse Tom out of his belfry. She rattled knives and fork, and dropped two on purpose. Ivy ducked her head and looked at the ceiling.

"Why don't you turn on the radio, Ivy? I could use some music, couldn't you? All this quiet isn't good for a festive dinner."

"I don't know," she said.

"Well, I do," said Dorothy. She turned the radio on and the sudden, ear-shattering blare of screaming guitars shocked her so that she stepped back as though from an exploding bomb, her hand in front of her, the fingers splayed.

Ivy laughed and dove for the volume button. "That's Bobby," she said, still laughing. "He likes it loud."

"Good grief," said Dorothy. "That can't be good for your ears." Approaching the machine with due caution, she fiddled with the dial until she found a classical station. "Excellent. Bach's concerto for oboe and violin in C minor. Precisely the correct music for chicken, don't you think?"

"It's pretty," said Ivy.

Movement from upstairs. Something thudding, and then footsteps.

"The bear arises from hibernation," said Dorothy.

"Grumpy bear," said Ivy.

"Not to worry, we have food." Dorothy gave Ivy a quick hug and then told her to get the plates.

Tom appeared a moment later in the doorway. He had been sleeping, apparently. His face looked as rumpled as his clothes and there were marks along his cheek where he'd slept on a fold in the pillowcase. They looked like scars. He rubbed his eyes, and wiped whatever he'd cleared from them onto the seat of his jeans. There were little flakes of white matter in the corners of his mouth and he moved his tongue around as if it was dry. He seemed not entirely sure where he was, or who these people in his kitchen were.

"Mrs. Carlisle?"

"I see sleep has not addled your powers of perception, Tom. Now, do sit down. You're staring. You look as though you could use something to drink." Dorothy caught the glimmer in his eye. "Ivy, do you have any orange juice? I didn't bring anything to drink, I'm afraid."

Ivy opened the fridge and stared into it. Dorothy looked over her shoulder. There was something that might once have been a tomato, a half-full plastic jug of milk, something green (broccoli, she prayed), and a single egg resting in a notch in the door.

"I don't think so," said Ivy, who kept her head in the appliance far longer than was necessary, given the lack of items therein.

"Tea, then. I'm sure you have tea. Tom, where do you keep the tea? And didn't I tell you to sit, dear?"

"What's going on?" said Tom. He pulled one of the metal padded chairs toward him and sat heavily.

"Well, I wanted it to be a surprise and apparently that's worked beautifully," said Dorothy. She found the bread knife and, noting spots, rinsed it under the tap before cutting the crusty loaf. "I got on a bit of a cooking jag and it all rather got away from me, I'm afraid. I made far too much food and couldn't think of anyone who would eat it for me. And then Ivy called to say hello—Ivy, do get your head out of the fridge, you're letting all the cold air out. Why don't you put some water on for tea? Thank you, dear. Where was I? Oh, yes, I do make far too much food for just me, and I've been meaning to invite you all over for dinner one evening anyway, but then the forces of the universe conspired and here I am. It seemed the right thing to do." She knew she was prattling and vowed to stop. No wonder Tom had that baffled look on his face.

"What did?" Tom's eyes tracked first Ivy, then Dorothy, then back to Ivy.

"Why, come over with dinner, of course," said Dorothy.

Tom regarded her with an expression only slightly less baffled than before. Dorothy thought, not for the first time, what a truly handsome man Tom was, in the old fashioned, manly way. His features were roughly shaped, without anything pretty or childlike in them, nothing of the boy. They were also, just now, bound and shadowed by pain. Deep ruts along his mouth. Muscles twitching in his clenched jaw. Blue swaths under his eyes, which were red and inflamed from tears, or from the effort required not to shed them. His lips pressed together as if he were afraid, should they part, something inhuman would escape, or find purchase. Dorothy concentrated on evenly slicing the bread. It was embarrassing, to see a big strong man so exposed. It was unseemly, somewhat shameful. It was like looking at a newly amputated limb, something pink and unprocessed, something that should be kept bandaged.

177

Dorothy knew from personal experience what it felt like to lose someone you loved. Death, not abandonment in her case, but she recognized death came in many forms. Tom faced several deaths—death of his marriage, death of the future he had believed in, death of trust, death of the possibility of loving and being loved. Perhaps the worst of all, that. It wasn't true, of course, Tom was young and vital, he could find love again, but it probably didn't feel possible to him. It was normal in the midst of such mourning, to feel love was over. It occurred to Dorothy Tom was a man made for a woman, incomplete and purposeless without one. It was so obvious she was surprised it hadn't occurred to her before. It was a tragedy, not that Patty had left him, for Dorothy believed that was inevitable, sooner or later, but rather that Tom had picked the wrong woman to begin with.

Men were unschooled in loss. Women were told from birth, practically, that love was painful, that hearts were broken and some things were simply unfixable. Women, in other words, were prepared for pain. Men were not. Men were taught they could overcome all obstacles through sheer dint of will, concentration, perseverance, strength of body and of character. Dorothy remembered the images from her girlhood of those tragic heroines: Camille, Tess of the d'Urbervilles, Anna Karenina, Evangeline, Mary Queen of Scots. All those drooping, wistful, tear-wilted beauties. In Dorothy's teenage bedroom, there had hung a black-framed print of John Everett Millais's Ophelia floating down the brown-tinged river, pale and lovely, her right hand clutching, even in death, a small cluster of wildflowers—red for blood, white for purity. The model was Lizzie Siddell, who almost died from the illness brought about by laying in a cold bath for hours while Millais got her beautiful, doomed expression just right. In Dorothy's day, girls were taught a certain lovely nobility bloomed in sorrow, in being impaled on the sword of grief. It got into a girl's idea of life in such a way that when heartbreak did come upon her she was, if not actually able to see the dramatic romance in it, at least not so utterly blindsided as men. Poor Tom, like most men, he was as vulnerable as a porcupine flipped on his back when he was in love, and just as nearsighted.

He should have married Rita Kruppman, Dorothy thought, which brought all sorts of possibilities to mind. Rita was so good with children. She had born up so well in the face of her husband's, well . . . life change.

The affection Rita still held for Tom was no secret. It was a horrifying fantasy—Dorothy as matchmaker. She could feel hives breaking out on her skin at the mere idea. But still.

The teakettle whistled in a strident, reproving way and Ivy lifted it from the gas burner. She poured it into a warmed pot with two teabags, a recipe Dorothy had taught her for decent tea. She stirred it once and then covered it with a rose-patterned cozy. The consoling scent of roast chicken wafted from the oven, seasoned with the salty pinch of olives as a tangy under-note. The dog barked twice and they turned to see him standing by the side door near his empty bowl, tail wagging hopefully.

Tom said, "I'll feed Rascal," and stood, somewhat slowly. As soon as he did, the dog began to wriggle and whine and dance, his toenails tapping on the linoleum, his jowls pulled back in a doggy smile. Tom took a can of dog food from below the counter, and emptied it into the dish. Rascal plunged his muzzle into the mess and ate with such a gulping frenzy that Dorothy wondered when he'd been last fed.

The look of distaste must have showed on her face, because Ivy said, "He has really bad manners. Doesn't matter how often you feed him."

"Dogs are like that," said Tom.

The chicken was warmed, the salad tossed and the tea poured. "Shall I set a place for Bobby?" Dorothy asked.

"Probably not," said Tom.

"Well, there will be plenty of leftovers," said Dorothy.

The three sat around the kitchen table. The last twilight was gone and the starkly unforgiving overhead fixture reminded Dorothy of institutional lighting. The linoleum needed mopping. A brown stain in the corner of the ceiling indicated there had been a leak. Bits of dried dog food had hardened to rough brownish gray nuggets on the floor around the dish. Stubble showed on Tom's cheeks, there was a fine black line of grime under his nails and Ivy's hair was in need of a wash. On the radio, a Beethoven piano concerto filled in the conversational gaps and muffled the sound of teeth and jaws working.

"It's good," Tom said, more than once.

And Dorothy said things such as, *I'm glad you like it, and Oh, it's a simple recipe, and It's lovely to cook for someone who appreciates it.* She watched his face and was gratified a little color crept back in and his eyes brightened. "You have to keep your strength up," she said.

179

"True," he said.

Ivy was quiet during the meal and kept her eyes on her plate. Dorothy suspected she was still a little afraid she might get in trouble although, looking at Tom, she didn't think he was paying enough attention to anything to get angry.

"How is your rock collection coming, Ivy?" she asked.

"I haven't done much lately."

"I thought you and your Dad were going to go, what do you call it? Rockhounding? Is that it?"

"We will," said Tom.

Ivy put her fork down. "When?"

"Soon."

Later, when the food was finished and they had done the dishes and Ivy—exhausted by food and anxiety—had gone to bed, Dorothy sat at the table with Tom.

"Now, tell me, how are you, really," she said, stirring honey into her chamomile tea.

"Coping."

"Coping."

"I'm all right."

"After William died, I fully expected the grief to suffocate me. I was so tired all the time."

"Nobody died."

"Oh, I think they did."

"She's not dead."

"In a way, she is exactly that."

"She's not dead," Tom repeated. His eyes sparked red. "She didn't die. I wish she had."

"Do you? Why?"

"Because at least then I'd be able to believe she loved me once, I'd be able to go on thinking she gave a damn about me, about her own kids, that she had one single ounce of human feeling. I wouldn't ever have to have found out what a lying bitch she was." His voice had not risen in volume, but the tone had darkened, grown raspy and choked.

"Tom . . ."

"And what a goddamn stooge I've been all these years. I knew, I knew,

180

you see, and I didn't let myself know, all at the same time." He glanced at the doorway. "I mean, I always knew about Bobby. She never lied about that. I didn't care. But now I'm wondering about Ivy."

"Tom! You mustn't let yourself think these things. There's no good in it!"

The veins stood out in his neck, his cheeks were mottled. "If she was here now I'd put my hands around her neck—" He held his hands before him, large enough to encompass a person's skull and still have the fingers meet.

Just as quickly as the rage came, it vanished. Where there had been thunder and fury, there was only a face full of rain. "It's like I'm under the ice," Tom said. "Like I'm trapped under the ice, looking up."

The vision of Tom, mouth open, hands scrambling to find a breathing hole, was hideous. "Oh, Tom," said Dorothy for really, she could think of nothing else. What was she supposed to do with this? What could she possibly say that did not drip with cliché and platitude?

"How can I ever trust myself again?" he said.

And there was the crux of it, really. Once you had been betrayed, not only by the woman you loved, but by your own perceptions, how could you trust yourself to make any decisions at all, about anything? It was paralysis—physical, emotional, spiritual.

The dog's barking and the sound of someone coming in the front door saved Dorothy from having to say something inadequate.

"Hey, dog," came Bobby's voice.

A moment later, the boy stood in the kitchen doorway. He'd shaved his head since Dorothy had seen him last. Why was it African-American men looked so handsome with their heads shaved and white men always looked like they'd just chopped up their families with an axe? His pants hung low on his hips below the elastic of his underwear and his tee shirt, which sported a graphically designed cannabis leaf, was torn at the shoulder.

"Oh. Hey, Mrs. Carlisle. What's up?" he said.

"Where have you been?" said Tom, rubbing his hand over his face.

"Just hanging with friends."

"What friends?"

"You don't know them."

Tom turned in his chair to face his son. "What are their names?"

181

"Bob. David. Pete."

"Last names."

"I don't fucking know. Jesus. What is this shit?"

Tom stood. "Apologize to Mrs. Carlisle. You don't use that language, understand?"

"Sorry," Bobby mumbled.

"Are you hungry, dear? There's some chicken and some salad and strawberries."

"No, thanks," said Bobby and he disappeared up the stairs so quickly he might never have been there at all.

"What do you do with that?" said Tom.

"I think the best thing to do would be to go grocery shopping tomorrow, don't you?" said Dorothy.

He looked at her as though he wasn't sure what she meant. "Groceries?"

"Yes, Tom. You know, those items that include edibles. Things you feed people, things you feed children. Eggs. Milk. Spinach."

Tom lifted one corner of his mouth, attempting a smile. "I got it."

"Shall I make you a list?"

"Not necessary."

"Well, I'll be off then," said Dorothy, and she gathered up her pans and bowls, avoiding Tom's face, fearing she had been too blunt. She walked to the door and Tom followed her. She stopped just short of the front door. She hung her head for a moment, puffing out her cheeks with held breath. It was all so unsatisfying. Although she would have preferred to walk out the door without any further conversation, she knew if she did the night would be spent tossing and turning. The pillow would lump up under her head and the bed sheets would twist around her feet. Her thoughts would loop and echo with all the things she ought to have said but hadn't. Damn. Standing so, she noticed a dent in the wall, as if someone had slammed the door open with such force the knob had smashed through the dry wall. Under this, near the molding, was another hole. Someone had kicked the wall with considerable force. She exhaled. "Tom . . ."

He was right behind her, nearly stepping on her heels. "Where'd that come from?" he said, looking at the shin-level hole.

She put her hand on his arm and was gratified to see he didn't pull away. "I'm not going to give you some nonsense about being a lonely old lady looking for a family, since you and I both know I am not a lonely old lady, in the same way we both know I didn't just happen to cook dinner for six tonight. No, Tom, please let me finish. For some inexplicable reason I find myself drawn to this family—to Ivy in particular, truth be told—and I believe for her sake it would be best if you permitted me to take the reins here—for only a little while—until you are ready to take over again."

"Thanks, Mrs. C., but we'll manage."

"You're drinking too much. Wallowing—" Tom began to say something but Dorothy raised her hand. "—in self pity. It's not good for you, and it's not good for the children."

The hangdog look was gone now. Tom's mouth was firm, his eyes steadily on hers. "Mrs. C., I know you mean well, and I appreciate everything you've done here. But I can take care of my own damn family. What's left of it."

"I've offended you." Heat rose up her neck in a telltale rash of mortification. "I don't know what's come over me."

"No offense. And I appreciate the dinner. Let's just leave it at that, okay?"

CHAPTER TWENTY-ONE

You think Satan isn't at work here? Right here, right now? You think all this rock and roll music, with its roots in voodoo Africa, this free love, which is anything but free, these drugs the kids are using, isn't the work of Beelzebub himself? These kids are going on trips, all right, trips straight to hell. Well, you tell Satan he isn't welcome here. In Jesus' name, say it. It may not be fashionable, it may not be groovy, like the hippies are saying, but I'll tell you one thing: Heaven's always cool. And evil's always hot as hell. Tell Satan to go back from where he came. We know where he's welcome, don't we? We know the Devil's high roost. You see those witches' lights up high, some nights, don't you? Hear those foul songs coming down from the mountain. Oh, Satan's here, all right, and we know who's giving him succor. — **Reverend Daniel Hickland, Church of Christ Returning, 1967**

Bobby and Albert lay stretched out on the sun-heated slab of rock near the old stone bridge deep in the woods where they'd first met. The air was soft on their bare chests, warm as a hand and aromatic with the sharp incense of moss and algae. The breeze whispered in the leaves, chickadees and finches twittered and a woodpecker occasionally rat-a-tat-tatted. Water burbled over stones and dragonflies hovered while in a nearby black locust tree a bright-eyed kingfisher watched a deep pool by the riverbank for silver fish-flash. Now and then he dove, breaking the water's surface with his lethal beak.

Albert blew smoke toward the clouds and looked at Bobby. Like Albert, he had balled up his shirt to form a pillow under his head. The boy's chest was narrow, the ribs clearly visible, and hairless. One hand was stretched out on the warm stone, the other rested on his stomach. His nipples were the color of almonds and his belly was concave. A faint shadow of fuzz ran in a thin line to somewhere below the band of the underwear showing a couple of inches above his jeans. His expression was self-satisfied and content: his lips curled slightly, his eyes closed, his brow unlined. It was not an expression he wore often.

"Pretty good out here, huh?" Albert said, and Bobby murmured his agreement, half-asleep. The boy's pale skin was turning pink. It would hurt later, be sensitive even to touch. "You're getting burned; you should put your shirt back on."

"Albert," Bobby said, sleepily. "Why don't you ever let me come up by you?"

"I told you. It's not the place for you."

"Seems like no place is."

"Come on."

"I mean it," Bobby said, his eyes open now. "Give me a cigarette, will you? This town's sure not for me, not after everything that's happened."

Albert handed the boy a smoke and held the Bic lighter for him, cupping his hand around the flame. Although he might have tried to argue with Bobby a month or two ago, there wasn't much he could say these days. The kid wasn't going to be able to live down the talk and, being Bobby, he wasn't likely to fight through it either.

"So, you'll get out, leave town one day," Albert said.

"We could both get out."

"Yeah, maybe."

Bobby leaned on one elbow, his face earnest. "I'm serious."

Albert ground his cigarette out and flicked the butt into the river. He watched the current carry it away. "So, you're serious."

"What's keeping you here?"

"I got responsibilities."

"Your brothers and sisters?"

"And the rest." Jill, and Jack, and Little Joe, Kenny, Toots and Ruby, Griff and Frank, the baby—Cathy, and little clubfoot Brenda. The whole sorry pack of them. Ever since Jill had had the last, botched, abortion she'd been sickly and even more withdrawn than usual. She dragged her hair in front of her eyes, hiding no matter how close she stood to anybody. She said she was glad there'd never be any more babies, said it over and over again, until he snapped at her, said he believed her, for fuck sake. Little Ruby had come running at him last week, saying Jack had taken a

185

switch to her, and she had the welts on the back of her skinny little legs to prove it.

As though reading his mind, Bobby said, "If it's so bad, like I said before, I don't know why you don't go to somebody—child welfare department or something."

"And I told *you* before. Don't work like that. Social workers? Not on the mountain."

"So how does it work?"

"We take care of our shit." What he didn't tell Bobby was that if he contacted Family Services he'd be signing his own death warrant. Plenty of accidents happened on the mountain. Trees fell. Axes slipped. Footing was treacherous. Fires started. People disappeared and graves were dug deep enough to return the slopes to silence. There had been these two women walkers years back. Come from off in New York State somewhere, hikers with fancy boots and packs and topographical maps. They got lost with night falling and stumbled out of the woods near his grandmother Sybil's cabin, where Albert lived with his mother, Gloria, and his uncles Ray and Lloyd. Both women hikers with their hair cut like men and no makeup and it was clear what they were. They asked stupid questions nobody ever asked, like how were they all related, with their noses so high up in the air you'd think they were hound dogs, and everything about them leaking disapproval and righteousness. Sybil was so pissed off at the questions Albert thought for a minute she was actually going to answer them. Albert, who was only nine, was fascinated to hear what the answer might be, which must have showed on his face, because Lloyd smacked him so hard he fell off the stoop. He took off running then, into the woods. He knew where to hide so he could still watch. He was too far to hear what Lloyd and Ray said to the women, but whatever it was, they said it close up, with the women backed into the wall. Not even the tall one with the mole on her cheek looked so self-righteous then. Lloyd piled them into the truck and drove off down the mountain and came back a while later. Said he left them on the highway and they could fucking get a lift to town from there, old dykes, and they wouldn't be saying shit to anybody about anything. Which Albert guessed must have been about right, since nobody ever showed up, although he had waited for a couple of weeks after thinking now, surely now, somebody would come.

186

Bobby was saying something. Begging again.

"Come on, Albert. I won't get in the way. Maybe I could help out, you know?"

"How are you going to help? And help what?" Albert stared up at the endless sky. He liked the vertigo it gave him, liked the idea he could fall up, just keep on falling and drift off into the blue, smaller and smaller until he was nothing, nothing at all. He didn't want to look at Bobby. It bothered Albert, the sort of conclusions the kid drew. You'd think Albert had been spilling his guts, and he hadn't been. Maybe just a hint or two, here and there, just to see how the boy would react, but nothing else. He kept the code. He kept his mouth shut. Erskine's don't talk.

Bobby sat up and crossed his legs Indian-style. He was close to Albert, one of his knees touching Albert's thigh. "You've helped me a lot, you know. Don't know what I would have done without you. I just feel . . . shit, I don't know. Kind of left out, you know? Like you know everything about my life and I don't know anything at all, not really, about yours."

"Nothing to know."

"Yeah, right."

"What are you going to do? Pout? Jesus Christ, does that work on your old man?"

"I'm not pouting." But he was.

"What the hell's so important about being on the mountain? Why don't you want to stay in your own tidy little bed, home with Daddy and the nice big television and fridge full of food and little sister in the next room and even a fucking dog? You've got it made, kid. Jesus, sometimes I could fucking knock your teeth out."

Then Bobby was crying. Tears drifted slow and thick down his cheeks.

"Cut that out," said Albert. Astonished and horrified at what he was feeling, Albert wanted to reach out and wipe away those tears. He wanted to put his arms around the kid, hold him to his chest. It made him clench his fists, made him strain against the two tethers of rage and . . . what? He refused to name it. "I'm warning you," he said. If Bobby didn't stop crying, he wouldn't be held responsible. "Stop it! You are not coming up to the mountain, is that clear?"

"Okay, Albert. It's clear."

"Fine. So what are you sniveling about?"

He wiped his eyes. "I don't belong anywhere. Nobody wants me."

If he had said it with self-pity, if he had said it with even the slightest hint of a whine in his voice, Albert might have blacked his eye, might have picked up a rock and concussed him with it. However, there was no self pity, nothing maudlin in his voice—only a flat, accepting resignation. He was stating a simple truth, an immutable fact.

"Sorry," Bobby said. "Sorry."

Albert saw the younger boy as if from a long way off. As though Bobby was as alone as Albert felt: an isolated, skinny, sad boy, sitting on a rock in the middle of a swirling river. It was as though he was a younger version of Albert himself, and Albert realized perhaps this was what he had seen in Bobby all along. Not really himself, maybe, but a variant. Not as tough, sure, and not as smart, but a boy at a turning point, little boy lost, and maybe, just maybe, with a slim hope of being found. Albert would always be sitting on the rock in the middle of the river, he knew that, sure as he knew water was wet and rock was hard. Nobody was going to find him. He had no one but himself to depend on. But, fucked up as Bobby's family was, his father was still there. Bobby didn't have any idea how good he had it. Maybe the only way to teach him was to show him how bad it could be. His gut tweaked. If he showed Bobby the truth of life on the mountain, he'd probably never see the kid again, and Albert was surprised to find out how much that possibility disturbed him, but maybe it was time for some self-sacrifice here. Some nobility. Yes, that was it.

"All right, you win," said Albert. "I've reconsidered. I'll take you."

"Where?" said Bobby, his face still blank.

"Up to the old homestead, young Bobby. I'll take you up to the fucking mountain."

"You will? You're not fooling?"

"I'm not fooling. But you better take me up on it quick before I change my mind."

"Really?" Bobby said. "Tonight?"

"No, Saturday." There would be lots of people around on Saturday night, lots of cars coming and going. It would be easier to slip the kid in unnoticed. "All right? All right then." Albert looked at the flush of pleasure spreading on the boy's skin, on his cheeks, his chest, mixing with the first tinges of sunburn. He looked away.

"Really? Wow. That's fucking fantastic, Albert. I really appreciate it, man. I won't be no trouble at all. And I'll get a bottle of something from my old man's cabinet. I'm not coming empty handed, you know?" He grinned from ear to ear. "That's really great!" He clapped his hands and rubbed them together. He kept nodding his head, saying, "All right, then. All right."

"Listen, Bobby, what would you tell your old man? You can't exactly tell him you're hanging out with me up on the mountain."

"No problem, I've thought all this out, right? I can like, say you're a friend not from here but from Pemberton," he said, naming a nearby town, "somebody from school he doesn't know, and then you can call and pretend to be the father, right? And say it's all right and I'll be fine and all that shit. He won't give a shit. He's a fucking zombie these days."

"I'm not sure. It sounds complicated."

"No, no it's not. It's simple. Isn't that what you're always saying? Simple plans are the best, right? No complications. Like the houses—nobody home, no dogs, no alarms, all that, right?"

"It's rough on the mountain. I live rough, Bobby. It's not like your comfortable little suburban life."

"Hey, I don't mind. What, you think I can't handle rough? I can. I can handle rough."

"I'm not talking about no indoor plumbing, although there ain't no goddamn hot tub, I'm talking about other stuff." He felt exposed and it made him squirmy.

"Albert? You wouldn't change your mind now, would you?"

"Look, kid. You just don't know." Albert sat up and grabbed his shirt, jerking his arms into the sleeves so violently he tore a seam. "Fuck! There's a lot of drinking and drugs, all right? Sometimes things get out of hand. It can be dangerous."

"Like fights?"

"Yeah, that's it. Fights."

"You got your own place, though, right? We'd be in there, right?"

"It's a fucking cabin, Bobby, it ain't a hotel!"

Bobby considered for a moment and then said, "You don't have to worry about me, Albert. I can take care of myself." He cracked his knuckles, popping them one after another. He nodded his head quickly, in little bounces. "And we'll be together, right? I mean it would be the two of us if anything happens, and, well," he hesitated, looked at Albert and then looked away again, "I'd have your back, you know, if anything happened."

Maybe it was the dumb defiance, the pride in the jut of the kid's chin, maybe it was his unbelievable ignorance, or maybe all three, but part of Albert wanted to laugh out loud. Part of him wanted to slap the kid upside the head for his idiocy, part of him was kind of proud of the sentiment, even if the kid wouldn't last thirty seconds in a fight with his knife-happy mother, let alone with The Uncles. Then there was that other part of Albert who found the back of his eyelids prickly with something revoltingly like tears. It was laughable, the kid having his back. A joke.

But all right then, let him come, let him come. Let him see what it was like at the bottom of the well. "I'll call your old man. If it goes without a hitch, all right then. It's your ass."

CHAPTER TWENTY-TWO

Three days after her visit to the Evans', Dorothy sat under the dryer at Julia's Hair Salon. The chairs were pink leather, the mirrors framed in gold and the air smelled of hairspray and shampoo. Clive Hawthorne's wife, Francine, and Doris Heaney, who owned the *Pretty-as-a-Picture Dress Shop*, were getting manicures across the room. Dorothy couldn't help but notice them watching her. The whoosh of hot air afforded her a certain amount of privacy, thank heaven. She kept her eyes firmly on a copy of *The New Yorker*. After some minutes, Eva, a young woman with luxurious red curls and the sort of green eyes produced by vanity contact lenses, escorted her to a seat in front of the mirror, ready to brush out her hair. Shortly thereafter, Francine and Doris came over, waving their hands to dry their bright pink nails.

The usual pleasantries and smiles and then Francine, a thick-waisted woman approximately Dorothy's age, with hair dyed resolutely auburn, and three very large rings on her fingers, said, "We just wanted to tell you, Dorothy, how wonderful we think it is that you're taking such an interest in the Evans family."

"I'm not *taking an interest*, Francine. I'm a friend of the family. I've known Tom all his life, as have you, and you, Doris. You were great friends with Tom's mother, weren't you?"

"Well, yes, but the family's certainly changed since those days." Doris's slightly bulging eyes meant her thyroid condition was probably acting up again. "Such a pity."

"None of us are spared misfortune, Doris. It visits every house." It would be, Dorothy decided, unkind to mention Doris's husband, Melvin, who was known to have led a rather, shall she say, *gregarious* life himself before he and Doris found salvation with Reverend Hickland.

"You do realize she ran off with a Corkum?" said Doris.

"I don't pay attention to gossip, which takes some effort in this town."

Eva laughed a rather snortish laugh. "Sorry," she said. "I need to get another brush. I'll be right back." The girl disappeared into the back room and as Dorothy watched her flit off, she wished the girl wasn't quite so tactful.

Francine plopped down in the chair next to Dorothy's. She glanced at Doris and then back to Dorothy again. "We wanted to talk to you about all this."

"All what?"

"Don't be difficult. You know very well what we mean. Between Patty Evans running off with a Corkum and Tom drinking and those poor children, well, things are clearly escalating. Mabel even told us Bobby has been seen with one of those Erskines. Steps have to be taken."

Dorothy frowned. "You've lost me."

"*Lost* is an interesting choice of words. *Saved* is another word," said Doris. She clasped her hands lightly at the level of her heart.

"We've been discussing the situation in our Bible class and we feel it's pretty clear, Dorothy. The influence of the mountain is creeping down toward us. This is a war we can't afford to lose. Reverend Hickland says—"

"Oh, for heaven's sake!" Were all Church of Christ Returning parishioners going to start spouting Hickland's pompous nonsense?

"Exactly, Dorothy, for heaven's sake," Doris continued. "Reverend Hickland says if we don't band together against Satan, who apparently already has a foothold among us, the evil will spread. You must cut out the evil root! You must—"

Dorothy stood and picked up her purse.

"—exorcise the demons. Drive them into the swine and drive the swine off the cliffs."

"You've all lost your minds!" Dorothy said. She'd brush out her own damn hair. She quickly paid Eva, who stood discreetly at the cash register.

Francine called to her as she stepped through the door, "We're trying to save you, Dorothy Carlisle! And the Evans family! You'll all be left behind."

"I certainly hope so!" said Dorothy.

That evening, at her kitchen table, Dorothy finished up her asparagus omelet and salad. Still fuming and restless from this afternoon's unpleasantness, she stabbed at the last piece of radish with her fork. A single candle graced the table, next to a yellow and burgundy-speckled orchid. The table was one of her prized possessions: an arts and crafts piece designed by Charles and Henry Greene. It was an odd shape, almost a circle, but with subtle, shallow arcs in the edges, giving the table the slightest impression of a cross. On the seven o'clock NPR news, she listened to a story about the overturning of a Nigerian woman's sentence to be stoned to death for having sex outside of marriage. A bit of good news from halfway around the world. Dorothy was rather surprised they didn't bring stoning back to Gideon.

She wiped her mouth with her napkin, blew out the candle, and brought the dishes to the farmer's sink in the kitchen, where she washed them and set them in the wooden rack to dry. She flipped off the radio. She was restless. Of course, she would not go to the Evans house. But something. She needed action or else she would sit not reading a book and fussing until it was time to go to bed.

She remembered the boxes she had put together the week before, waiting for her next trip up to the mountain. She looked at her watch. It was a Tuesday night, when she presumed the moonshine customers to the mountain would be few, if any at all, and the forecast was for clear weather. It wouldn't do to leave food and clothes and books out when they would get rained on.

Having made up her mind, she felt better and set about getting the boxes from the guest bedroom. She had never liked the guest room, a plain room with white walls and a matching blue bedspread and curtains. It always felt like a hotel room, and since she and William had had no children and his brother had long since moved to Denver, it had rarely been used. Over the years since William's death, the room had become a sort of storeroom for little things she picked up here and there for the Erskines. Dorothy did not want gossip about her nocturnal visits, and so she never bought anything in town, other than grocery items. All the rest—books and kids clothes and so forth—came from the big box stores out on the highway. With no children or grandchildren of her own, she didn't want to have to explain why she bought so many children's clothes.

Over the past weeks, she had divided the goods and clothes into three boxes so none would be too heavy to manage. Powdered milk, peanut butter, prepared macaroni and cheese, cans of baked beans, peas, corn, and carrots, tins of soup, tins of tuna and sardines. Protein was important. There were socks, underwear, and two pairs of running shoes for the children. She'd had to guess at sizes, of course, but she tried to bring up a couple of pairs in different sizes every few months. Children went through shoes so quickly. Tee shirts and diapers. Some crayons and coloring books. *The Secret Garden. The Five Children and It. Rumblefish.* There were also two books specifically for Albert, a collection of Raymond Carver stories, and *The Crossing*, by Cormac McCarthy. She hoped these manly, pared-down works would appeal to him and had written *To Albert* on the inside, although of course she had not signed it. She had questioned the value of books over food when she had first begun her deliveries, wondering if they would be tossed aside, if she were wasting money that might otherwise go to things of higher practical value. However, over the years, in casual conversation from time to time, Albert had mentioned, in a showing-off sort of way, that he had read this book or that, saying he liked Joseph Conrad but thought John Cheever was a wimp.

"You must keep the librarian very busy," Dorothy had said one day, surprised at how easy it was to keep up the deception.

"She says I'm advanced," fifteen-year-old Albert had said, surprising her not at all with his own talent for untruth.

"Perhaps you'll be a writer yourself one day," she'd replied, and he had grinned hugely.

Only once in all the years of going up to the mountain had she ever feared her anonymity might have been breached. It was three years back on a fragrant June evening. The moon had been full and the sound of crickets filled the night. She was coming down off the mountain when Albert's truck passed her. She hadn't been sure it was him at first, since the headlights blinded her, but as he passed she had been quite sure. She didn't think he recognized her, for her car was a nondescript Honda sedan and she always wore a hat pulled low over her face just in case. As the truck came alongside, she put her hand up over her face and turned away. She saw Albert a day or so later and he nodded at her and said hello and passed a few niceties as he always did, without in any way indicating anything out of the ordinary. Such a relief.

Still, she did wonder sometimes. What did they think of the magically appearing supplies? Initially, she had been concerned no one would find them by the side of the road where she'd left them, or they'd be considered garbage, even though she affixed a bright pink paper sign that read, "For the Erskines." The first few times, she and William had gone back the next day to see if they were still sitting there, but they were always gone. And then came the day when a carefully printed note appeared on a little stick. "Thank you," it said, "Albert Erskine." Printed very carefully.

Now, she carried the boxes one by one to the trunk, each one emboldened by a pink sign. Traditions should be maintained, Dorothy felt. She loaded the car and headed out for the mountain. It was a pretty night, with the scent of warm spring on the air like honey and peat, and the crescent moon just discernible now and then over the tops of the trees. Dorothy rolled the window down to breathe in the dark perfume and drove slowly. There was something enveloping and comforting about a star-filled sky seen through the black outlines of trees. One knew one's place in the world at such a moment. One knew how small one was in the great scheme of things. Dorothy found that reassuring somehow. She was, in the end, responsible for so little.

She rounded the last curve before the track led off into the deeper wood where the compound lay hidden. She cut her lights so as not to draw attention. She sat for a moment, listening. A slight breeze rustled the new leaves, and far off in the woods dogs barked. This didn't bother her. Dogs barked at all sorts of things in the woods at night and the Erskines were known for keeping several huge beasts of indeterminate breed chained near their shacks. They would settle down in a moment. Someone shouted something, but it was too far off to make out the words. The dogs protested with another round of barking, and then petered out. Something small moved in the undergrowth, a fox, perhaps, or a raccoon. A soft mewling noise. She hoped it wasn't a mother skunk with an early litter of kits. She didn't much fancy a tomato juice bath. She waited, and when all was still again she began to unload the boxes. Her shoes sank a little ways into the muddy ground and made a slight sucking noise when she stepped. One, two, three, she piled the boxes in a neat stack on a large rock so the damp earth wouldn't creep up and so they might be more visible. She hoped if raccoons or other creatures prowled nearby they would find the scent from the garbage heap not far from the compound more appealing than the smell of freshly laundered overalls.

It was very dark, with the slim moon now behind a cloud, and she had to be careful of her footing. Lights—feeble and sickly—twinkled from unseen windows far off in the heart of the wood. A few early fireflies, their love life restricted by bad timing, flashed hopefully in the trees. The breeze shifted and carried a strange sweetish odor. She presumed it was from a still, but it was an odd smell for beer or liquor and she hoped it wasn't a bad batch, which might make people ill. Funny how the night brought scents to you that in the day you probably wouldn't notice at all, so busy were you with all the other impressions with which eyesight flooded the brain.

Her work done, she checked the stack of boxes was secure and, satisfied, turned back to the car. It was then the small curl of sound reached her ears and she stopped, her fingers on the door handle. It was a sort of cry, perhaps even the sound she had taken for an animal's mewling a few minutes before. However, this was not an animal. She froze, holding her breath. Part of her very much did not want to hear the sound again. A voice in her head told her to get back in the car as quickly as possible, and lock the doors. She was aware of her own heartbeat, and of the blood pulsing in her veins. Crickets. A mosquito near her ear, which she forced herself not to swat. And then . . .

"*Mmmuhuuh . . . mmmuhhaaaaa . . .*" Bestial, but not the sound of an animal. Human. "*Uuuhhhuhhh.*" Human made inhuman. A sort of low keening—bereft even of the hope anyone might hear. Dorothy's skin prickled and tightened. The sound held no threat, but seemed to echo from an abyss of despair. Her horror was not of something red in tooth and claw, or even fist and blade. Rather, she recoiled from understanding. She feared for her soul if it peered into that abyss. As though under some hideous enchantment, Dorothy stared at her own trembling hand, unable to move. *Oh God, oh God, oh God. Protect us.*

The sound, the cry, came again then. Mourning made manifest. Such grief was surely as isolating, as solitary as any cell of stone or steel, as any nail and cross. Left to its own devices it would suck the entire world into the center of its tarry core. It was alone out there. No, thought Dorothy, not *it*. God would not forgive her thinking of whoever it was as an *it*. She listened harder, forced herself to see a person behind the cry, and envisioned someone stuffing their mouth with leaves or dirt or their own fist, trying to muffle that sound. Then, certainty rushed like an unexpected gust through an open window, and she understood the sound-maker was a child, so occupied with grief he or she probably wasn't aware of Dorothy's presence. If asked, she could not explain why she knew this. Perhaps something in the timber of the voice. She pulled her hand away from the car. It was creased from the pressure of her grip. She faced the forest.

"Hello," she said, swallowing the tremor in her voice. "Who's there? Are you hurt? Hello?"

It was as though she had fired a shot. The response was a small, piercing shriek, like a rabbit pinned to earth by owl's talons. Dorothy's hands flew involuntarily to her ears. Even the crickets went silent. "I won't hurt you," she said. "Can I help? Tell me where you are." She took a step forward and as she did, a rock sailed past her head. She jerked and it hit the side of the car, bouncing off with a crack and a bang. It was not a powerful throw, but it left a mark, a small dent and scratch she could see even in the murky night. Something told her the stone had not been intended to hurt her, but how could she know what rage lay under the surface of such sorrow? She scanned the woods, trying in feeble moonlight to catch a glimpse of the child. She stepped forward. The gluey mud beneath her feet smelled of rot.

"Child," she called. "Stop that and come out." She sounded braver than she felt.

A movement to her left and then a rain of small pebbles, some of them landing on her shoulder, one on her cheek. "Stop that!" she cried, more in shock than pain. She jumped back in horror at a new cry, one a thousand times more effective than pebbles or stones. The child, whoever it was, screamed. A wordless howl of bestial fury and survival fear.

Without thinking, Dorothy scrambled back inside her car, fumbling with the handle, slammed and locked the door, her fingers trembling with the keys. Through the trees, a flash of something pale and thin and fast and—was it possible?—naked. Running and zigzagging. Visible for only a second. Not long enough to make out sex or age. Under ten? Under fifteen surely? Dorothy started the car and the headlights made everything outside their beams invisible. The car jumped forward. Dorothy forced herself to let up on the gas. She would crash into a tree if she didn't calm down. Her hands were slippery on the wheel. She breathed so shallowly she was afraid she'd hyperventilate. She kept looking in the rear view mirror; her imagination filled with images of ghostly children running after her car, of tiny naked bodies jumping in front of her headlights. She feared she was going to cry. Slowly, she told herself. *Slowly. It was just a child. A child, a child.* The curves of the road seemed endless. Far longer to go down than to come up. The trees looked as though they might suddenly rip a root out of the ground and grab the car. She imagined she was lost forever in enchanted nightmare woods. What had she seen? What had she done? What had she not done? *Oh God, we confess we have sinned against thee in thought, word, and deed, by what we have done, and by what we have left undone.*

The lights from the main road began to flicker through the trees ahead. As safety neared, Dorothy's breathing began to normalize, and as it did a pitchy bile of self-loathing rose in her throat. She had run in fear from a child, a despairing child. She turned onto the main road, her wheels skidding ever so slightly on the curve. In a few minutes, she would be back in her own house. She looked in the rear view mirror one last time, half-expecting to see a truck of angry Erskines coming after her. She did begin to cry then, the tears stinging and bitter, full of self-contempt.

At eight-thirty the next morning she stood at the scuffed counter in the Sheriff's office, facing down Carl Whitford, her arms folded across her chest and her face red with indignation.

"I'm telling you, Carl, something's going on up there."

"And I'm asking what you were doing up there, Mrs. Carlisle." Carl stood behind the counter, his arms folded over his chest as well, as though he was mocking her. Behind him, on the imitation wood paneling, hung a photo of smirky George Bush. She unfolded her arms, entwined her fingers. She would not be laughed at.

"I was dropping something off, but that's not the point, now is it?"

Elliott Blanders, the deputy, sat with elbows on his desk, nursing a cup of coffee in a paper cup, regarding her with more annoyance than interest. She knew how she must look, a more-than-middle-aged woman puffed up with righteousness. She probably sounded like Mabel, like Francine and Doris. She didn't care.

"It just might be the point. You know as well as I do why people go up to the mountain."

"You're not implying, surely, that I was there to purchase illegal alcohol?"

"Can't think of any good reason for you to be up there, honestly. They're not exactly your kind of people, now are they?"

"My kind of people? Your kind of people? What does that mean, exactly?"

"You know what I mean."

"Yes, and that's precisely the problem, isn't it?"

"I'm not going to argue sociology with you. But believe me, you don't have all the facts about what it's like up there."

"Carl, *everyone* in this town knows what it's like up there and I am ashamed of us. We've done nothing about it year after year, decade after decade. I admit I glossed over things, didn't want to look too closely. I am guilty of that, and more, probably. Nevertheless, I can't ignore it any longer. Not with what I saw last night. And neither can you." She thrust her chin out and widened her stance.

Carl inflated his cheeks and made a squeaking noise through his lips, the kind of noise with which adults amuse children, pretending to be elephants. Dorothy was not amused.

"Stay out of it. It's not safe up there," Carl said.

"That's what I'm telling you, Carl! If you know it's not safe for me, then how can you imagine it's safe for those children? Answer me that."

He ran his hand over his face and turned to look at Elliot, who just shrugged. Carl studied the floor for a few minutes. "All right, I know you think we're not doing anything, but that's just not true. We know more about what's going on up there than you might think and all I can say is you have to trust us."

"Trust you."

"Yes. And stay out of it."

"I beg your pardon."

"I don't mean to be rude, but you heard me."

"There is no time, Carl. You must do something immediately. Today."

"What I must do, Mrs. Carlisle, is my job in the best way I see fit. I'm telling you, politely, to let those of us who are qualified handle things in the right way, at the right time." He put his hands up. "No more. That's final. And I don't want to hear any more about you going up there for any reason."

It was useless. She could see that. Damn this town. She turned and opened the glass door to the street. "You do what you see fit, Carl. We must all do what we see fit."

CHAPTER TWENTY-THREE

I don't understand where people get the idea that The Tribulation is a time when people will be able to blissfully wait for Jesus to come and rescue them. The tribulation is going to make the firebombing of Dresden look like a day at the beach. Few people realize that right now we have a window of opportunity. It won't be open long. When the rapture comes, you don't want to be left behind. Can you imagine the horror of the tribulation before Jesus' glorious return? **"For then shall be great tribulation, such as was not since the beginning of the world to this time, nor ever shall be"** *(Mat. 24:21). There is only one reason why the tribulation is going to be so horrific. God will be trying as hard as He can to get man's attention. Every time we read in Scripture that God has poured out His wrath on the earth, we also read that man had refused to repent for his evil deeds.* **"Neither repented they of their murders, nor of their sorceries, nor of their fornication, nor of their thefts"** *(Rev. 9:20-21).* — **Reverend Ken Hickland, Church of Christ Returning, 1998**

It had gone without a hitch, just as Bobby said it would. When Albert called the house earlier that morning Tom Evans sounded so downright pleased his kid had a friend to spend the night with that he pissed Albert off. *Well, that'll be real nice for Bobby. I sure appreciate the interest you and your family are taking in him, Mr. Gardner. Sure appreciate it.* What an idiot, Albert thought. Fine then—Evans wasn't going to take care of his kid, Albert would. And now here they were, Saturday afternoon, with Bobby beside him in the truck cab, as keen as a dog on the way to a grouse hunt. Albert had picked him up at the high school, where Bobby told his father he was meeting the fictional Ernie Gardner for a pick-up game before they went to his house. They'd snagged a pizza on the way and the air smelled of pepperoni and tomato sauce. It wasn't until they were out of town and turned off the highway that Albert noticed how Bobby popped his knuckles and bounced his knee.

"So, what do you know about us, anyway?" asked Albert.

"Nothing," Bobby answered, too quickly.

"Come on. Go ahead and tell me what you've heard. You won't hurt my feelings. Believe me, there's nothing I don't know about my own family."

"Well, I heard some stuff maybe."

"Of course you did. Town leaks gossip like a rusty bucket. We've known each other for what? Four, five months? You wanting all the time to come up and hang with me on the mountain. But you've never said what you know, and what you don't know. Never asked too many questions at all for that matter, so I have to figure you have some ideas. Have to conclude you think you already know some things. So why don't you tell me, young Bobby, what you think you know."

Bobby looked at Albert quickly, then away. "Well, you run some businesses up there. Like you're bootleggers."

"True. What else?"

"I don't know. Nothing."

"So you ain't heard anything else about what might be for sale up there?"

"No. Honest. I haven't heard anything like that."

"Like what?"

"Nothing."

The road was rough, and steep. Bobby held on to the strap above the window, his other hand braced against his knee. There was nearly as much sky in the windshield as land. He gunned the engine. "Scared?"

"No," said Bobby, and then, "Kinda steep, isn't it?"

"You think?"

The mountain slopes were a mass of hickory, chestnut, beech, cedar, spruce, and pitch pine, but now and again they passed through clear-cut openings. Stubbled and broken earth, these gaps looked as though a cunning, specifically-targeted tornado had roared through. Distant stands of trees bore silent witness to their fallen brothers. Chasms of red-clay earth were wounds where the run-off, with no tree roots to absorb it, had formed channels, deep and ever-changing, as though dragons had dug their great claws through the ground.

201

Then, at last, they came upon the compound, near the peak of North Mountain, where the view of the valley might have been wonderful if anyone had thought to trim the trees. The rutted, debris-strewn drive led into the woods, and was the only overt evidence of habitation. "Duck down," said Albert.

"Huh?" Bobby looked at Albert, puzzled.

"I said, duck the fuck down. The family ain't exactly social."

Bobby unbuckled his seatbelt and crouched on the floor under the dash. As they passed the main house, Albert waved at Sonny and Old Felicity. Felicity smoked a hand-rolled cigarette while Sonny picked his nose and carefully examined the results before flicking them into the garden. When Sonny saw Albert's truck, he stood up and grinned, waving frantically, excited as though he hadn't seen Albert in months when in fact he'd seen him not three hours ago.

"Hey, Albert!" he called. "Hey, Albert!"

Albert waved back. "Hey, Sonny."

Sonny's T-shirt was too small and a wide band of white fat drooped over the top of his jeans. Felicity sat with her legs wide apart, her stretch pants straining against her thighs. She wore a baseball cap printed with the words "Thinking Hurts" in pink. Her gray hair hung greasy and lank over her ears. She raised her chin and spit into the dirt by way of greeting.

Albert steered the truck farther into the woods, until the track was nothing but a bouncing rut. Bobby cried out as he hit his head on the underside of the dash. Albert pulled up on the far side of his cabin, where he figured, even if they were watching, nobody would see Bobby getting out of the truck. He cut the engine.

"Stay here," he said. He walked around the cabin. He stood in front of the cabin and took a piss in the direction of the main house, scanning the tree line to make sure none of the kids were hanging around. He didn't put it past them to go telling tales, using information as bargaining chips if need be. He'd done the same before he learned other ways of defending himself. His blood popped and fizzed with adrenaline. He told himself again what an idiot he was to risk bringing Bobby up here. The kid was a civilian. If anything happened to him, there'd be hell to pay. Still, there was the break-in. Albert could always hang that over the kid if things went south and he wanted to tell his old man or the cops, which would be pretty much the same thing. The kid was a fucking virgin, in more ways than one, and he was in Albert's truck. The image of Bobby's thin pale chest floated past. His jeans hanging low off his skinny hips. Albert wondered if it was too late to take him back and be done with it.

"Albert?" Bobby stood there, out of the truck, bold as fucking brass, his backpack in one hand, his sleeping bag in the other.

"Jesus Christ!" Albert dashed to the door and, using the key he kept round his neck, opened the padlock. He swung the door open and pushed Bobby inside.

"Hey! What are you pushing for?"

"I just don't want the whole goddamn place coming to see who I've got in here, is all. And you don't want that either."

"Why not?"

"I'm an asshole for bringing you up here." Albert slapped himself on the forehead. "What the fuck was I thinking? Get back in the truck. Go on!" He held the door open again.

"Ah, come on, Albert. I'm sorry. I get it. Nobody gets along with their family. Don't make me go back there, Albert. Not tonight. I won't be any trouble, and look," he fumbled in his backpack and produced a bottle of brandy, "I brought this. We can drink it, like, you know," and his face broke into a grin, and he waggled his fingers beside his mouth like Groucho Marx with a cigar, "you know, like gentlemen."

The idea of the two of them sipping brandy like gentlemen struck Albert momentarily speechless, and then he laughed, laughed so hard he had to bend over to catch his breath. Bobby laughed too, and they hung onto each other's shoulders and laughed until they had tears in their eyes. The kid was all right.

A couple of hours later they sat smoking cigarettes and drinking beer. So far, three cars had appeared, the occupants conducting business and disappearing quickly. Each time, Albert rose and watched from the window before relaxing again.

"I like your place," Bobby said.

"Oh, you do, huh?"

"Yeah, it's got character." Bobby lounged on a malodorous yellow beanbag chair. He'd had three beers and a couple of brandy shots. His voice was low and loose. "You sure got a lot of books. You read all them?"

"Every single one," said Albert from where he lay on the pullout couch. There were no sheets, just an old sleeping bag over the stains. The metal from the frame had worn through the material and created ulcerous-looking gaps.

"Wow. Where'd you get 'em all?"

"You want to know a secret?" Albert smiled and his face shone in the glow of the fire from the open door of the woodstove. "Mrs. Carlisle. She's been coming up here for years, leaving shit. Clothes for the kids, cans of beans and evaporated milk and crap like that. She left a few books, like *Robinson Caruso* and *Treasure Island*, in a box marked especially for me."

"Really? Why?"

"I have no fucking idea. I was pissed off at first. I mean, I didn't want her goddamn charity, right? But then, I don't know, one night I was going out in the woods and I knew how boring—"

"What were you doing out in the woods at night?"

"Camping. Shit. I was camping. Anyway, I knew I'd be bored out there for hours so I took a flashlight and this book with me. *Huckleberry Finn*. This story about a kid with a drunk old man. You read it?"

"Naw. I'm not much for books."

"You should read, Bobby. You don't want to grow up to be an uneducated fool, do you?"

"No."

"Well, then. Anyway, I liked it. I really liked it. So I watched and waited and figured out her schedule—she and her old man came up about every few months or so. She used to leave stuff at the compound entrance. I watched for her lights way down the road and then I stuck a thank you note on a stick in the spot. Said I'd like some more. And that was that. Every few months I got books, and you can bet your ass I got out there before anybody else did. Those books were for me. Only lost out a couple of times."

"Lost them, like somebody else took them? Why didn't you just share them?"

"They don't care about the fucking books, just about pissing me off."

"So you and Mrs. Carlisle have, like, a relationship, then."

"She doesn't know I know it's her. At least I don't think she does. She'd never said anything. Neither have I."

"Why not?"

"What the fuck for? So I could be her little charity pet? She can do what she wants, or not do it; I don't care. I can buy my own books now, if I want to. And I don't have to worry about saying 'Thank you Mizz Carlisle,' every time I pass her on the street, you know?"

"I guess. Huh. She left you food, too?"

"You tell anybody and I'll knock your fucking teeth out. You're a suburban kid, really, aren't you? Through and through. I don't think you'll ever get out of that."

"Yeah, I will," said Bobby.

"Not that I blame you. It's not your fault, but, man, what you don't know about life."

"Like what?" Bobby peeled the label off his beer and squirmed on the beanbag.

"You had a girl yet, Bobby?" Albert leaned back on an elbow.

"A girl?" He rolled the label into a little tube.

"Or maybe you like boys?"

"I'm no fag. I like girls."

"So, you fucked anybody yet?"

"No. Almost though." The boy's skin was fire-lit and pink with both embarrassment and liquor. There was a slight sheen on his upper lip.

"Oh, almost. Almost. What does that mean—you touched somebody's titties? You do that, Bobby? With some little girl from school?"

Bobby shifted, uncomfortably. "Yeah."

"Tell me about it."

"Naw."

"I bet it never happened. I remember when I popped my first cherry; I couldn't wait to tell everyone."

This was not true. There had been no 'first time' for Albert, not one he could point to as an event that separated what came before from everything that came after. No rite of manhood in the way of other boys. There was the first time he had had sex away from the compound, with Gladys. Teacher and tender tutor. He'd bumped into her one night in Mavericks when he snuck in for a little underage drinking and she was plying a trade as old as time itself. She'd been shaking her stuff, with her boobs all pushed out of the top of the scarf she'd tied around her chest like a kind of blouse. He must have looked a fool with his mouth hanging open. She'd taken pity on him and brought him home with her. She had been sweaty and musky and eager for him, surprised only when he flipped her over and insisted on taking her from behind. Said she couldn't imagine where a boy his age could learn such things and he never told her. She was the only woman he'd ever had sex with who was still a sort of friend. But it sure as hell hadn't felt like the first time for anything. Just a different time, in a different place, with a different person in charge.

The light was beginning to fade—purple and orange through the trees. Albert got up from the bed and went to the small rickety table by the window to the right of the door. He took the glass off an oil lamp and lit the flame. A willow dream-catcher hung from a nail stuck in the wooden bar bisecting the window. This Indian girl had given it to him last summer. They'd hung out for a few weeks and then she'd said she was going away and couldn't see him anymore. She gave him the dream catcher because, she said, the bad dreams would get caught in the sinew-woven web, in the center of which was suspended a tiny quartz crystal, like a drop of dew. She said the magic was very old and powerful. He'd almost thrown it away, but then didn't; he'd nailed it up as she told him, but he didn't notice any difference in his dreams. The crystal glinted in the lamp light. As he replaced the glass on the lamp, the room took on a softer glow. The shadows weren't banished, certainly not defeated, but they knew their place. A spider, the size of a half-dollar, sat dead center of a web it had spun in the corner of the window. He considered killing it, and then didn't. Live and let live.

He looked out the window. In a moment of drunken sentimentality a couple of springs back, Albert had planted a forsythia bush outside this window. He'd pilfered the plant from a park in town. The flowers, a cheery yellow in early spring, were gone now and the bush was a green scraggle during the day and a flap of rags in the moonlight. He looked through the leaves to the main house. They called them parties, what went on up there. Figures roamed inside, flashing across the lighted windows. Big Sonny's shuffling retard gait, and it looked like Lloyd, and his wife Joanie were up there as well. In Albert's mind, he had a high power rifle with a long distance sight on the top. *Stay away from the windows*, isn't that what they always said in police movies? A country and western tune squalled from a portable CD player no one in the family could have come by honestly. *Ten feet tall and bulletproof*, the nasal-voiced singer bragged. The sounds ebbed and flowed and Albert preferred the noises. It was easier to judge what was going on if you heard voices.

A gaggle of kids hovered at the edge of the wood, Toots and Kenny, and Ruby, and it looked like a couple of Lloyd and Joanie's kids were there, too—Griff and little club foot Brenda. There was a bigger kid with them, looked like Jack. Albert hadn't really talked to his little brother in a while. From the way the other kids gathered round him, it looked like he was taking some sort of a leadership role. They circled round Jack. Jack pointed to one of them—to Toots. They were probably making plans for when things got bad. Toots looked toward Albert's cabin. She and Jack started in this direction; the other kids skittered off into the tree line.

"Fuck," said Albert.

"What's up?" Bobby put his beer on the floor and made a rocking motion like an old man to get up out of the sucking beanbag chair.

"Stay where you are. I think we're about to have visitors."

Toots and Jack crossed the muddy ground. Toots hung behind, and Jack took her hand, tugging her. She snatched her hand back and scowled. Albert stepped out of the cabin, closing the door behind him. The air smelled of earth, with the slight metallic whiff of trouble. This must be the way animals sensed things, he thought, smelling that sharp trace of adrenaline and fear they all gave off, for even the dogs had disappeared under the various structures. They'd stay down there, dug into the mud, nose to tail, until whatever was going to happen was over.

The kids were near now. "Hey," he said.

"Hey," said his little brother. "What are you doing?"

"What's up, Jack?"

"What do you think's up?" Jack stood a few feet in front of Albert, his arms crossed over his skinny chest, his hair standing up every which way. His eyes were deep set, like Albert's, and he was nearsighted. He didn't have any glasses though, and squinted badly. "We can't let the kids hang alone tonight. Others are all high."

"What do you want me to do?"

"Don't be an asshole, Albert. Let us in. It's not like it was, even. It's worse."

"Can't do it. Sorry."

"Albert," said Toots, wiping at the hair falling into her eyes. "Don't make me be with them tonight. It's been bad all afternoon. Meth bad." She wore rubber boots and leggings with holes in them.

207

"Fuck," said Albert. Ten year olds shouldn't even know about stuff like meth, but it was years too late for that.

"If you were paying any attention to what the hell's going on up here, you'd know that they've been on meth for months." Jack and Albert locked eyes.

"I know what's going on," said Albert.

Jack's jaw clenched with anger. He was going to snap one of these days. When the time came he was going to go off like Albert had done that night back when he'd been Jack's age. His little brother was going to have to make choices. He was going to have to lay somebody out, maybe more than once, and prove he was a man, crossing the floor to the adult side. And when he crossed, what would he do—build himself a cabin in the woods someplace like Albert had? Join the fun and games? Or maybe, Albert thought, little brother Jack would kill one of the uncles, or Old Harold. Or maybe he'd kill Albert himself, sneak up on him while he slept one night, full of revenge dreams for all the nights his big brother didn't protect him. Albert wouldn't blame him, either. He still had some killing dreams himself.

Somebody cried out from the main house.

"Where's Jill?" said Albert, for he recognized the pitch and waver in the voice. It got so you could tell that sort of thing, even from so far away.

"Exactly where you think she is. They called her in to cook," said Jack.

My sister, thought Albert. Wizened and pinched like an old woman already. Jill. My sister. For whom Old Harold bragged he'd been paid five hundred dollars when she was barely thirteen. Then, nine months later, had come Kenny—Kenny of the pale yellow hair nobody else on the mountain had.

She cried out again and a man's laughter followed the cry.

Albert heard a sound behind him and turned to see Bobby's face in the window. He looked gray in the fast-failing light. Albert's stomach flipped.

"Who's that?" said Toots, pointing.

"Nobody," said Albert.

"Is he yours now?" she said. "Are you keeping him?"

"We know you've got him here," said Jack, a smirk on his face. "Ruby saw you from the woods when you brought him in. You think you can hide shit up here?"

"They know?" Albert jerked his chin in the direction of the main house.

"Not yet. You're out of your mind, bringing an outsider up here like this—especially first of the month, when the checks are in."

They all turned as a sedan emerged from the woods, the tires crunching over gravel. Rock music ricocheted through the trees, the bass making the air vibrate. The music drowned out the noises from the house, or maybe they'd seen the car arrive, too, and piped down. It was packed with college kids, girls and boys, all of them giggling with the danger of being up on the mountain. Albert hated them. They had no fucking idea, just thrill seekers who'd shit themselves if they really knew.

Ray came out of the house, leaned into the car, and pocketed some money. A minute later he was back. He passed something to the driver through the car window. Albert focused on him, willing him not to look this way, but he did. Toots and Jack dashed around him into the cabin.

"Shit." Albert ducked inside and slammed the cabin door behind him, keeping one eye on the main house through the smeary window. Jack stood on the balls of his feet, as though ready for a fight. He was small, but he had an unpredictable streak. He was wired for the fast strangling jab to the throat, the bone-snapping kick to the side of the knee. His slightly slanted eyes were full of fury. His cheekbones were sharp, his reddish hair like an explosion above his head. "You're not throwing us out tonight," he said.

He was one of Peter Pan's lost boys. They all were.

Toots stood in the corner between the stove and the foldout bed, a hungry gremlin, all ragged and clutching at shadows. Bobby was rooted in the middle of the room looking around as if vampires had just invaded the place.

"You know the rules," Albert said. "I don't tell anybody where you are. I don't join in on nothing. I'm not part of them, but I don't fight anybody else's battles. You got to go."

Jack looked over at Bobby. "You sure you're not one of them? Got your own private party here?"

Albert took a step toward his brother. "I'd be very careful what you say right about now, Little Jack. Very careful."

"Hey, I—" Bobby started.

"Sit the fuck down and shut up," Albert said to him. He pointed at Bobby, but didn't take his eyes off Jack. "This doesn't concern you."

"Please, Albert," Toots said from the corner. "We ain't got anybody else. Jack can't stand up to them alone." She sounded like she was crying. "Jill's already got a split lip."

Albert heard a noise and looked out the window. The teenagers' car turned around while Ray watched, and headed off slowly down the mountain. If only it were that simple. Ray stood for a moment, scanning the woods. His eyes stopped on Albert's cabin. Then he turned and went back in the house.

"Who's Jill?" said Bobby.

"Our sister," said Jack. "Who the fuck are you?"

"Bobby Evans. I'm Albert's friend."

Jack laughed. "I didn't know Albert had friends."

"Jack, I swear I'll break your fucking arm if you don't shut up."

"Somebody hurt your sister?" Bobby leaned forward. "Who hurt her? Shouldn't we do something?"

"I thought I told you to shut up!" said Albert. "Jesus, you too, Toots! Stop that snuffling. I can't hear myself think." He put his hands up to the sides of his head. Sometimes it seemed all he ever heard were the sounds of somebody crying, somebody crying out. It was his nightmare nursery rhyme, his lullaby. Toots was just a little wraith in the dark spot behind the stove, trying to disappear, maybe once and for all.

It still wasn't too late to drive the kid back down the mountain. Drop him off in town and let him sleep in a fucking doorway for all Albert cared. Let the rest of the kids take care of themselves. Put the pedal to the metal, head out and see where the world would take him. And there was Bobby, looking at him like he was supposed to do something. Looking at him like he expected a superhero. The Avenger of North Mountain.

It occurred to Albert, just for a flashing moment, that maybe he'd known this was going to happen when he agreed to bring Bobby up here in the first place. Nobody in the world had ever looked up to Albert Erskine, and when he was brave enough to peek into the folded-up corner of his mind where he kept such knowledge, he knew he wasn't worth looking up to. That was the heart of it. He looked at Bobby, skinny little runt. Jack, like a little mongoose, ready to fight the cobra. Toots, broken little household imp, smelling of ash and unwashed clothes. His tribe of lost children. If he sent them away now, it would be over. He'd be alone again, and if you'd asked him a couple of months ago what he wanted more than anything else he would have said it was just that: to be alone. Now he wasn't so sure.

210

Jack said, in a low voice, "You have to take a stand, Albert. You can't always be on the fucking sidelines. There are no sidelines up here. You should know that. It's time."

"When did you grow up?" Albert said, when what he really wondered was when little Jack had become more of a man than he was. He locked eyes once again with this small and semi-feral boy who was most likely illiterate, although Albert had never taken the time to find out, and whose future was almost certainly, as Albert imagined his own to be, bleak and short. When he saw what was in those eyes—all the familiar corroding resentment and scalding sense of injustice—it felt as though he looked back in time, to his own not-so-distant past. In the unforgiving light that seemed to fill the cabin—the light of exposure, of being known—Albert imagined his life and his pride as rocks easily turned over, revealing all the wriggling, shameful things beneath. He imagined he heard small, soft-bodied things scuttling for the shadows, scratching at the corners with their claws. It was useless, he knew. Once known, shameful things are never unknown. He took a breath, dropped his eyes for a moment, and then said, "Fine, then. Bring 'em in."

Jack blinked, as though he really hadn't expected it to be this easy.

"I'll get them," said Toots and, before Albert could change his mind, she scurried across the floor and out into the night, making no more noise than any other small creature accustomed to avoiding predators.

It was a matter of a minute or two, during which time no one in the cabin spoke, and then the door opened and the small herd of dirty, bruised children bustled in, looking around as though they had just stepped into some foreign, potentially treacherous world. Kenny and Ruby made a dash for the foldout, and hunched up in a corner. Griff and Brenda, with her sloping, painful walk, held hands and took a spot in the corner next to the table. Next came chubby Little Joe. Eight-year-old Frank arrived last, carrying two year-old Cathy. Cathy sucked her thumb and had obviously been crying; her only garment the messy and malodorous diaper drooping around her hips. The air buzzed with anticipation and the murmur of high-pitched whispers. Eight little kids, and Jack and Bobby and Albert, crammed into a cabin built for one.

Albert scratched his head. "This is going to be one long fucking night."

"This is a lot of kids," Bobby said.

Cathy whimpered and Frank jiggled her, trying to calm her, his eyes wary and alert.

"You got another diaper for her?" said Jack.

"No," Frank said. Cathy turned her head and tried to hide in Frank's neck. "We can use my T-shirt," he said. He squatted on the floor and stripped off his shirt. There were old cigarette burn scars on his back. Eight of them in two perfect squares.

"Holy shit," said Bobby.

"Exactly." Albert held his nose as the noxious fumes filled the cabin. He'd never get that smell out, the smell he remembered all too well from his years in the trailer-shack with Gloria and his grandmother Sybil. That smell was one of the reasons he'd sworn he'd never have children.

Noises tumbled down through the pines from the house. Voices, shouts and the sound of breaking crockery or glass. Laughter.

"Are we going to try to get Jill?" said Jack. His jaw was set and Albert knew fantasies danced in his head, visions of storming the house and rescuing their sister, maybe taking out a few of the others at the same time.

"Nope." Albert looked out the window and watched the shadows and forms in the windows on the other side of what seemed an ocean of mud and garbage. "We wouldn't get her. Not now. They're too far into it."

"Next time, then," said Jack, who'd taken a seat on the floor. He sat on his jacket because the floor, wood laid straight on the earth, was damp in summer, in winter ice cold. His head slumped on his forearms, which rested on his bent knees.

Next time, huh? Yes, it was clear. There would be a next time now. There was no going back. Once given entrance, he'd never get rid of the kids. Not doing what The Others did was never again going to be enough. By letting the kids stay, he'd become the refuge, the stone at the mouth of the cave. The three headed dog. Whatever came after tonight, things were going to be different. He didn't know whether to laugh or cry, and feared he might do both.

"Bobby, come here," he said and when Bobby was close enough he grabbed his arm and put his mouth to the boy's ear. "You want me to get you out of here?"

"Naw, it's okay."

"I don't know what's going to happen."

212

"I said, it's okay."

"Your funeral," Albert said.

"Where do you want me to put this?" Frank said, holding the soiled diaper.

"Give it to me." Albert took it and, stepping outside, threw it far into the woods. He watched the house. Whatever was going on in there held their attention, for now.

He returned to the kids. "All right. Get into bed. All of you. And go to sleep."

"It's too early."

"Go to sleep anyway."

"We going to stay the whole night?" said Toots, and for the first time in as long as Albert could remember there was a hint of a smile on her face.

"Yeah, but don't get used to it," Albert said.

The kids moved about and arranged themselves like little piglets on the foldout. Albert told Bobby to put the sleeping bag over them, but when the younger boy came near them, they pulled away. He tossed it to them and they pulled it up to their chins, peeking out. Albert hoped they'd all gone to the bathroom first. It was his only sleeping bag. Jack roused himself long enough to move to the beanbag chair where he lay curled with his hands between his knees. Albert wondered when he'd last slept.

"I guess you and I are sleeping on the floor," said Albert.

"How old is he?" said Bobby, looking down at Jack.

"'Bout your age."

"That's what I thought."

Albert poured two large glasses of brandy and handed one to Bobby. They sat with their backs to the door, listening to the younger children breathe. Other than Cathy and Kenny, none seemed able to sleep, although they remained silent, their eyes only half-closed. Listening, Albert suspected. It's what he used to do at their age, what he still did most nights if he didn't drink enough. They were watching him, too.

It was quiet inside the cabin, and the air was hot and smelled of children in need of baths. The cabin was like a tree house, someplace where you needed a special password to gain admittance, but once admitted, it was yours and trespassers would be prosecuted. The only problem was, Albert thought, now everybody had the fucking password.

213

"Albert?" Bobby asked after a while.

"What?"

"Is this why you don't move off the mountain?"

Albert didn't answer and a while later Bobby said, "I think you're a great guy. Honest." His voice only slightly slurred with brandy. He patted Albert's shoulder and squeezed it. Albert surprised himself by permitting this.

Now and again, they heard noises outside and Albert got up to look out the window. Once it was Old Harold pissing and stumbling by the side of the house; twice it was more cars coming for dope or booze; once it was Dan and Ray in some sort of slow motion wrestling match, which ended when Carrie threw a pan of water on them. People moved in and out of the house and tossed bottles into the woods, spit into the night air, but no one came through the pines to the cabin. At some point Bobby slumped down on his sleeping bag, put his jacket under his head and fell asleep, and by then most of the kids were asleep as well. Jack snored on the beanbag chair, his head at an angle sure to cause him pain when he woke.

Albert should have been embarrassed to have Bobby see the way they lived, and mortified because Bobby would surely know the truth of what went on up at the house, and be able to deduce what had happened to Albert himself. He should have been embarrassed, and enraged because of it, but he wasn't. He felt tired, that was sure, and invaded. But something else. He felt clean, somehow. That was the word for it. Clean. As though something filthy that had stuck to his skin for years had finally soaked off and disappeared.

He imagined he floated in a cool pond of water. Silver water. A strange texture to the water, like mercury. It shimmered all around him, reflecting nothing, absorbed all the images floating just outside his line of vision and transformed them into an argent pool—opaque and formless. It was a seductive sea where nothing was expected of him, each separate action, and each single decision fused into the liquid surrounding him, blending it into a pearly mass where all things were acceptable and no judgment existed. Then, in the way of dreams, the quick flash of intuition, he realized the opalescent fluid was something toxic. His skin tingled. Deeper. It burned. The water burned his skin. He floundered, finding no bottom to stand on, no branch or rock to cling to, no bank to scramble onto. He screamed and . . .

214

He jerked awake, crying out, a mosquito stinging his neck, the buzz loud as a dentist's drill. He swatted it, found blood and the fragile crust of wing and thorax on his palm. Across the room, pairs of eyes stared and for a moment he thought they were ghosts. His flesh goose-pimpled. "Go back to sleep," he said to the eyes. Brenda and Griff and wolfish Jack. Something weighed him down. Bobby was next to him, his leg like a sack of sand over Albert's, dead to the world, his mouth open and a thin trail of glimmering drool hanging from his lip. Shouldn't have drunk that last brandy. Albert kicked Bobby's leg off his. He shook off sleep like a dog shakes off water. He edged away from Bobby and sat with his back leaning against the door. He watched the light from the newly risen moon slide across the bodies and the floorboards as it played hide and seek with the clouds. He watched it slip across the floor like some sort of enchantment, like a spell, like something searching with a bone-pale light.

Now that he was fully awake again, Albert's mind wouldn't quiet. It raced with scenarios of what might happen tomorrow. There hadn't been much sound from the main house for some time, although he couldn't be sure how long. He wanted to light a match and see what time it was, but didn't want to risk doing anything that might set the children to crying. It was as though the world had separated, had taken on the illusion of two dimensions—that which was inside the cabin and that which was outside. The one contained within the body of the other. The weight of outside, all that darkness in all its forms-- slouching and encroaching and dragging its desires with it—pressed down on the flimsy walls and roof, threatening to collapse the insubstantial structure into matchsticks. The air was thick with funk, nerves, and the smell of unbrushed teeth, stale brandy-breath, and yeasty bodies. Albert imagined the inside of his lungs as sticky with the stagnant, child-filtered air. He closed his eyes, tried to picture himself somewhere wild and lonely and windswept. Told himself to breathe regularly. Calm down. Inside his head was a space as inky as the presence he imagined outside the cabin. It rippled with waves of panic, like concussions, like a movie of slow motion explosions. With every breath, his insides billowed and roiled.

All the calm of a few moments before, when he'd fancied being washed clean, was gone. His life before this night seemed like some long ago delusion. Maybe he'd been dirty, he would admit that, but he'd also been damn near invisible. Now, he was all clean and shiny and as easy to spot as a mirror's flash along a rock face in the noonday sun.

Brenda moaned—in her sleep, Albert hoped. A small, humpbacked field mouse pattered along the wall behind the stove and disappeared through a crack in the wood. Keep going pal, he thought. And then he decided. Fuck it. He positioned himself next to Bobby and placed his palm on the boy's mouth. Softly. Felt the warm drool on his skin. He shook Bobby ever so gently. "Wake up," he whispered in his ear.

Bobby's eyes snapped wide and his body went rigid. He tried to slap at Albert, but Albert stretched out, leaned hard into him with his shoulder and his chest so the boy wouldn't struggle. No doubt at least some of the children were alerted, but to hell with them. He put his face close to Bobby's. "Keep fucking quiet," he said. "I'm warning you."

Bobby nodded once and although his eyes retained the look of a trapped bird, Albert took his hand away. Bobby gulped air. Albert looked at the boy closely, judging how this would go. Bobby's bony hip dug into his belly. The look in Bobby's eyes was unmistakable, and familiar. He knew exactly what Bobby was thinking. Maybe it was just as well, for that would certainly be the end of whatever this was.

"What are you doing?" Bobby whispered, more a mere movement of lips than sound. He lay still under the weight of Albert's strength and muscle.

Albert smiled a milky flash in the dark. "I'm getting you out of here," Albert said. "We're both getting out of here."

"What?" Confusion in the boy's face now.

"Get your stuff and follow me." Albert rolled off him.

Bobby rose to his knees. "What about them?" He gestured around the cabin where the children stirred and watched and waited.

Jack said, "Answer him, Albert. Go on."

Albert pulled a backpack off the top shelf over the couch and shoved things inside it. Jeans, T-shirts. He stumbled in the dark and cursed. He picked up a book, held it to the moonlight and then tossed it aside, picked up another and stuffed that in the bag.

Kenny began to cry and within seconds little Cathy snuffled and sniveled and then began to howl. Children shifted and moved in the shadows and to Albert it seemed sinister, as though they were zombies, getting ready to attack.

"Shut her up!" growled Albert.

Frank tried to shush her, bouncing her and patting her back and letting her bury her little head in his armpit and the howls died down to muted whimpers. The silence was thick in the corners of the room, crawling with accusation and childish fury.

"You're a cock-sucking motherfucker," said Jack, standing.

"Aren't we all," said Albert. He grabbed Bobby's shoulder, bunching up the fabric of his T-shirt. He pushed him roughly toward the door, and opened it. "The cabin's all yours, Jack. I'm gone. Consider it your inheritance."

A light switched on in the main house. A door slammed. They had fucking radar up there. There might not be much time.

"I don't want your fucking shack." Jack said. The boy took steps toward him, stumbling a little, rubbing his leg, as though it had gone to sleep and had pins and needles. "Albert, come on. Take us with you."

From the main house came the sound of something breaking. Something wood, not glass. A chair maybe. Albert turned toward the sound. High-pitched voices followed. The women, more than one, and shrill, Sybil maybe, cursing someone out, or maybe Gloria, or both. Fighting each other maybe. Darkness magnified the sounds, disassembled them around the tree trunks, the hummocks and litter piles, bounced and tossed them between the structures, the outhouse, the broken down cars. Something metal—metal against metal. Pots? Glass shattering. A voice, Dan's, swearing like a rabid wolverine. The curses scudded through the trees like ragged, startled crows. Albert and Bobby stood in the open doorway, Albert still with a clump of Bobby's tee shirt in his fist. He had to wait, see if they were coming out, or if he had time to slip through, put the truck in neutral, and let the grade roll him out past the house before he turned the engine on.

"Maybe we should take them," said Bobby, looking at the kids.

That was all it took. In an instant they started, all of them, grabbing at Albert, nipping at him, fingers around his legs, his belt loops, his arms. *Take us with you. Don't leave us. Don't leave us. Don't leave us.* Wheedling, demanding, crying. Louder. Louder still. He shook them off, his skin prickling, panic rising. He didn't want to hurt them, but more than that, he didn't want their hands on him. "Get the fuck off! I'll hit you if I have to! I'll do it, you little shits. Get *off*!"

"Fuck you," said Jack. "You get in that truck, we're getting in, too."

"I'd like to see you try," said Albert, dragging Bobby to the truck, praying the noise up in the house was enough to muffle the voices of the children.

Somebody from the house screamed. A child. A girl.

Albert stopped in his tracks. "Where the fuck is Toots?" he said.

CHAPTER TWENTY-FOUR

Dorothy knelt on the shop floor and swept up the shattered remains of a dropped plate. She was discombobulated, not herself at all. Since her trip to the mountain, she had slept poorly, her brain chattering like a demented monkey, and her utterly unsatisfactory meeting with Carl Whitford had not helped. She had no appetite. She found herself peeling her split nails, and scratching at mysteriously appearing bumps on her skin. Unaccustomed to indecision, her fretting, fussing, and paralytic confusion soured her stomach and only increased her self-recrimination. This was the second thing she had broken while dusting, the first being a pretty hand-painted glass vase. The fact the broken plate had brought her to the verge of tears, only testified to her state of mind.

She emptied the broken china into the wastebasket. How she wished William was here. Who else had she ever talked to, ever trusted to provide sage advice? She went to the window and looked out, unconsciously scratching the back of her hand, watching to see if Ivy might be coming down the street. But the street was quiet, just a couple of teenage girls giggling as they walked past, a truck coming down the street. The truck. Familiar. Albert Erskine's truck.

Dorothy's heartbeat quickened, pushed up into the base of her throat. Should she try and flag him down? Talk to him? They had always had a civil relationship. If she told him what she'd seen, would he confide in her? Could they go together to the Sheriff? The truck neared and she opened the door and stepped out. She was about to raise her hand when she saw he was not alone. Bobby Evans sat in the front seat, with something on his lap. A knapsack? They were engrossed in conversation and did not look at her as they passed. And then they were gone, leaving her there as witness on the sidewalk, but witness to what?

After spending a few hours pacing about the store, doing nothing useful, obsessing, and rehashing, Dorothy closed shop, went home and didn't hesitate to pour herself a decent-sized, medicinal shot of scotch whiskey.

She put her nose into the glass and inhaled. It smelled nutty, of peat and wood smoke. She downed it in one throat-searing gulp. The amber warmth spread along her throat into her belly and out into her arms and legs. The most beautiful lilac and pewter sunset exploded behind the trees. She watched it until it faded, and tried to persuade herself all was right with the world. *And all shall be well, and all shall be well and all manner of things shall be well.* Julian of Norwich's prayer. It didn't work. She poured herself an unheard of second drink, with a little water this time, and then ran a bath in which she soaked for half an hour. When she got out, she lay down across the bed, intending to get her thoughts in order and make some decisions. Perhaps it was the whiskey on an empty stomach, or the several nights of sleeplessness, but she dozed without realizing it, dreaming unsettled, fleeting dreams, and when she awoke, it was nearly ten.

She rolled to the side of the bed and sat up, blinking. In the clarity that sometimes occurs when one drops ones troubles into the arms of Morpheus, what she must do was now obvious—absurd she had not seen it before. In the bathroom, she quickly splashed cold water on her face, rinsing away the lingering whiskey-fugue. She pulled on some sweat pants and a sweatshirt and went down to the kitchen. She hesitated then, and stood looking at the phone. Since that night she'd so indiscreetly suggested that she 'step in' Tom had been cool toward her, although as polite as ever. She wanted very much not to have to make the call, for it was a boulder pushed off a cliff. Once rolling, she wouldn't be able to stop it. Nevertheless, she knew what she knew. She could not unknow it. With knowledge came responsibility, a responsibility she'd been shirking for a long time.

She picked up the phone and punched in the Evans' number.

"Hello?"

"Tom, I hope I'm not disturbing you."

"No, no. Just watching the boob tube. What can I do for you?"

"Well, this is probably just me being silly," Dorothy realized her hands were actually perspiring. She wiped then on her trousers. "But, is Bobby there?"

"Bobby? Why do you want to know if Bobby's here?"

"Is he there, Tom?"

"No. He's not. He's at a friend's house. Spending the night."

"I see."

"Mrs. Carlisle, what's this about, exactly? You're worrying me."

"Yes. I'm sorry. It's my fault entirely. I should have said something earlier. And I'm probably wrong; Bobby is doubtless precisely where you think he is."

"All right, what's going on?" His voice rose. "Why do you think he isn't at his friend's?"

"Because I saw Bobby this afternoon in Albert Erskine's truck. He seemed to have a backpack or something with him."

"What the hell are you talking about? Bobby doesn't even know Albert Erskine. I hardly know Albert Erskine! You've got it wrong."

"Tom, I'm very sorry. But this is not the first time I've seen Bobby with Albert. I think they've been friends for some time, which in itself may not be a problem—"

He cut her off. "I'm going to call the number of this boy's house, the house where he is. I'll call you back. You and I are going to have a little talk, Mrs. C."

With that, he hung up. She stood in the kitchen, her mouth open. She put the phone down and her fingertips flew to her mouth, one hand over the other.

She sat at the kitchen table and waited. He would phone back. Tell her that Bobby was safely at his friend's house, that she was a meddlesome old woman, which she was.

Ten minutes passed. It was as though dozens of bats, a whole colony of them, swooped and flittered through her head, unable to settle, seeking only to avoid. Fifteen minutes passed. She stared at the phone. At twenty she could stand it no longer and was willing to call back, willing to be told what a bothersome fool she was and she would have called, but the doorbell rang, followed by a loud knocking.

Tom stood under the porch light. His huge frame filled up the space, his hair looked as though he'd combed it with a wrench. Ivy held onto his hand, her eyes sparkling, cheeks flushed, wearing bedroom slippers and pajamas with rabbits on them. Dorothy opened the door.

"It's the number of a goddamn Chinese Restaurant! There's no such person as this Ernie Gardner character. How could I have been such an idiot?" He swept past her into the house, Ivy tripping along behind him. "Why the hell didn't you tell me?"

"I'm sorry, Tom. This is my fault entirely."

"I'll say it is!" He glared at her. "I'm going to get him. I need you to watch Ivy. Ivy, sit on the couch."

The little girl did as she was told. Dorothy put her hand on Tom's forearm as he made a move toward the door. The muscles rippled under his shirt, like a horse shaking off a fly. "Tom, there are some things you need to know before you go up there. Just hang on."

"More things I need to know? Wonderful! Tell me, but be goddamn quick about it."

"I'm sure Albert wouldn't do anything to put Bobby in harm's way. He's really a rather nice young man. He tries very—"

"Oh, for God's sake. Save it. You don't even believe that or you wouldn't have called me to begin with."

It could not be denied. "Still, he's not like his family, Tom. You must keep that in mind. And there is something else. Ivy, would you go into the kitchen and get yourself some cookies and milk, dear? The cookies are in the tin on the counter." The little girl did not move and it was only then Dorothy realized how frightened Ivy was. *She* was frightened—imagine what a ten-year-old might be feeling. She sat down and gave her a quick hug.

"Is Bobby okay?"

"Of course he is, dear. He's just on a silly adventure and your dad has to go get him because he's worried, but that's all. Now come on, off you go so I can have a chat with your father."

"All right. Sure. Go on, Ivy," Tom said, as though only just now remembering she was there. "It's okay. I promise."

When she'd gone, Dorothy stood and faced Tom. She felt lightheaded and sat down again. "I'll be as brief as I can." She kept her voice low. Without going into too many details, she told him of her trips to the mountain, and of what she'd seen the last time she was there. "I've told Carl, of course, but he seems to think he needs to wait for something to happen before he takes steps. I don't understand it."

"Jesus Christ," said Tom.

"You should call Carl. Have him go up with you. He'll pay attention to you."

"Oh, yeah. I really want everybody talking about how my son's an Erskine now. How that's what happens to Patty Evans' kid and what do you expect. No way, I'll handle this myself." He pointed a finger at her. "And you are not to call him, either. Is that clear?"

"I don't think that's wise, Tom."

"Is that clear?" His voice was barely controlled.

"It is, but you must be smart about this. We don't know what you're walking into."

"I know my goddamn kid's up there." He stalked toward the kitchen, picked up Ivy and held her for a moment, whispered something in her ear before putting her down. As he strode past Dorothy and out into the night he said, "Take care of my daughter."

Ivy came and stood next to Dorothy. She trembled and Dorothy led her to the couch where she spread a blanket over both of them.

"It's all right, pet. Really it is. You have a wonderful father – you know that, don't you? Everything's fine." She stroked the silent little girl's hair and when she could think of nothing else to say that made any sense she, too, fell quiet, and prayed.

CHAPTER TWENTY-FIVE

When the end times come they'll be no hiding, no escape.
Everything will be fire and no hand will there be to help
you. — **Reverend Ken Hickland, Church of Christ**
Returning, 2005

The scream floated in the air as though it had physical form, like a trapped ghost hanging in the branches of the trees.

Again, Albert demanded to know where Toots was.

"Where do you think?" said Jack.

"She slipped out to pee when you fell asleep," said Ruby. She picked at a scab on her index finger.

"I'd have heard her," said Albert.

"She's good at slipping out," said Ruby. "Mostly."

"Why didn't anybody watch her?" said Bobby.

It had gone quiet inside the house now. Figures moved by the windows.

"Thought you were going," said Jack, standing in the doorway, leaning against the jamb as though he owned the place, arms folded, kids huddling near him. Only the tightness of his mouth and the rigid set of his shoulders revealed his fear.

Albert kept his grip on Bobby, but didn't move. His head was filled with the inside of that house, filled with the smells of nicotine stained fingers, the taste of them in his mouth, the images of thick, hairy thighs and yeasty, shit-stained shorts. Salt and slime. Pain unimaginable. The impotence of it. The fury. He read a book once, about some kid who had it like he had it, but who disappeared when it happened, floated up to the ceiling, went into some other dimension, where they could do whatever they wanted to his body while his mind soared up in the stratosphere somewhere. Albert had thought, lucky little fucker, how'd he learn to do that? There'd never been anywhere to hide for Albert. Not outside. Not inside. Not really. Even a hole between the tree roots only hid your body.

The front door of the house opened. Lloyd and Dan stepped onto the porch, hanging off each other's arms. Laughing, the motherfuckers, they were laughing. Stuck together like conjoined twins, they turned in the direction of the cabin. *What had Toots told them?*

"Get back! Now!" Albert practically threw Bobby inside.

Bobby crashed into Jack and although Jack kept his feet, Bobby didn't. He fell hard, and cried out as he landed on his knees. Albert shoved Jack and Ruby out of the doorway, jumped inside, and slammed the door behind him. No door had ever felt as flimsy. It might as well be made of straw, of twigs. Bobby scrambled to his feet, rubbing his knees, his eyes glinting, but whether with tears or with fear was hard to tell. Albert knew by the look on his face that one thing at least had been accomplished tonight—at last, Bobby Evans wanted to go home.

"So, how do you like the life of a mountain man, now, young Bobby?" Albert grinned and Bobby dropped his eyes. If Albert got the kid out, their friendship was over. So be it. "Right," Albert said, and he turned to the window. He kept to the side so, with any luck, they wouldn't see him. All around him, children breathed—snuffly little sounds, wet and miserable.

"What are they doing?" Jack said, coming to the window's other side.

"They've gone back in," said Albert, and so they had. The house had gone quiet again, although someone was pacing inside, the shape going back and forth in front of the window like a duck in a shooting gallery.

"Not all of 'em," said Jack and he gestured with his chin to the side of the house. Sure enough, in the dark shadow of the house the red dot of a cigarette floated in the air, down to waist-height, up to face-height, a slow brightening of the glow, and a quick flash of face. Fat Felicity. Sitting watch. Ragged old bitch.

"Get the kids settled," Albert said to Frank, as though the eight-year-old wasn't a kid himself. Little Cathy was already lolling, thumb in her mouth, on the couch—more passed out than sleeping, felled from fatigue. One by one, the kids curled up and kept an eye on Albert in case he did another runner.

"Maybe we could go now," said Bobby. "Couldn't we?"

"No," said Albert. "Sit."

Jack and Albert watched Fat Felicity watching the cabin, smoking cigarette after cigarette. Maybe she was just keeping the mosquitoes at bay, but it felt like she wanted them to know she was out there. Half an hour later, the front door opened and Harold came out. He stuck his head around the corner of the house.

"Fel!" he yelled, and then said something Albert couldn't hear. The old woman tossed her cigarette to the ground and went back into the house.

"What do you think they're doing?" Jack said.

"No fucking clue." Albert said. "Nothing good." He pulled out a cigarette of his own and lit it.

"Can I have one?"

Albert handed one to his brother and said, "Keep it away from the window."

"Not like they don't know I'm here. Better they think somebody's alert."

"You want one?" Albert asked Bobby.

Bobby sat on the wooden chair, his arms crossed, his hands tucked under his armpits. "No, thanks."

"Milk and cookies after this, huh?" said Albert, not looking at him. "Milk and cookies."

He shifted position. His knee hurt. He didn't remember hitting it on anything but it ached. He wriggled his toes in his boots to keep the circulation going. Standing watch was hard on the body; keeping still sometimes took as much effort as running. All was still now—the house through the clearing, the children behind him. It might all be mistaken for something quaint, if you didn't know better, if you couldn't smell the stink and the urine. Then, the light changed up at the house. Someone at a back window. The window opened and someone climbed out.

"Fuck," said Jack.

It was Jill, Jill in a sleeveless dress and bare feet, her arms skeletal in the gray light. She reached out to someone else. Gestured urgently. A small face appeared and then disappeared. Jill looked around, found an old plastic pail, and stood on it, bending at the waist inside the window, hauling something, someone up. She dragged Toots out the window, put the child on the ground, and gently closed the window behind her.

"This is not good," said Jack. "Should we go out?"

"No," said Albert.

"What's happening?" Bobby came toward them. The children stirred.

Jill was hunkered down, talking to Toots, who lay curled up. Jill stood and jerked the younger girl roughly by the arm, drag-yanking her to her feet. She bent down, put her arms around Toots and started moving. She half carried her.

"They're coming this way," said Jack.

"I've got eyes," said Albert. "Shit."

He went to the door and slipped out, gesturing the rest should stay inside. He tried to wave them off into the woods but they came on, resolutely, determinedly. He would not help them, then. They'd have to make it alone. If The Others caught them first, so be it.

Something banged and crashed inside the main house. Jill swooped down and slung Toots over her shoulder. The child cried out and Albert winced, then rushed forward and took Toots from Jill. The child cried out again, squirmed, and then went still. Jill's face was battered, the lip split, one eye swollen. There was blood in her hair. Blood down the front of her dress.

"You hurt bad?" said Albert.

"Get her inside, for God's sake, Albert. Get her inside."

He looked down then, at the child in his arms. There was blood on her, too. She wore only a tee shirt and underpants. The underpants were wet, and they were stained red.

"What the fuck?" said Albert. His instinct was to drop her as though she was a bomb about to go off. Jill put her hand on his arm. Her mouth was firm, her brows drawn together and, even battered, she was resolute. He didn't drop Toots. He carried her inside, looking all the while over his shoulder, the hair on the back of his neck standing up, sure he would see The Others coming at him with knives, hatchets, clubs.

Inside, the children clustered round him. They murmured and cried, as though they were once voice, one soul. Jack pushed through. "Holy shit," he said. Toots was limp and still.

"Is she dead?" asked Little Joe.

Jill cried out and reached for the little girl. Albert shifted Toots so her head rested on his shoulder. "No, she's not dead."

"She's awful hurt, though," said Jill, and she started to talk, fast. "I couldn't do nothing. I didn't even see nothing at first. Dan caught her out in the woods when he went to take a piss. How'd she let herself get caught? She's the best of us at running. They were mad as hell, you know, because they'd been looking for the kids and knew something was going on down here. They know, Bert; I mean they know about him." She pointed at Bobby's pale face. "And they know about you having the kids here, too. They're all paranoid shits. Fuck that crystal—it makes 'em crazier than a sack of rabid weasels. They're talking about how weird you been lately and how you're gonna go to the cops about the lab they got—"

"What lab?" Bobby said.

"The fucking meth lab," Jack said.

Albert looked at Bobby who shivered.

"Oh, man, Albert," said Jill. "They sure as shit are watching you and when they are watching you it don't matter where you are or what you think you're doing down there at Maverick's and shit in town. They say they got somebody on you day and night and what an asshole you are thinking you're outside everything and it's about time somebody taught you a lesson and Lloyd, he said he'd like to be the one to knock you off your—"

"You high, Jill?" Albert said. She was talking a mile-a-minute and her eye, the one that wasn't closed, was wild. She picked at her elbows, first one, and then the other.

"No, I ain't high, but I sure as hell wish I was." She stopped picking.

Albert didn't believe her. The Others didn't like anyone around who didn't join in, and if they wanted you around, you best do as you were told. He just prayed she'd keep it together. He tried to figure out what to do. His arm, holding Toots, was warm and wet. He thought she was probably still bleeding. "I'm gonna put her down," he said. "Jill, I want you to take a look at her, figure out how bad she's hurt."

Jill stepped back. "I don't want to."

Albert laid the little girl on the table. She didn't cry out or move. Her eyes were open, tracking him, then again, he thought, maybe they were just rolling around in her head; he couldn't be sure. He touched her forehead. It was cold and clammy and her cheeks were mottled. "Too fucking bad if you don't want to. I need to know."

"I'll do it," said Jack.

"Jill will do it," said Albert.

Jill stepped forward and Albert turned his back. The rest of the kids followed his lead and looked away. Some stood, some looked down at the floor, even the smallest among them silent, as though it were a ritual, some spell designed to conjure up powerful things.

"Jesus," said Jill, bent over the child.

"How bad?" said Albert.

"She needs a doctor."

"Can she wait until morning?"

"How the hell should I know, Bert? I'm not a fucking nurse."

Albert reached into his duffle bag, pulled out a shirt and tossed it to Jill. "Wrap her up in this. I need to think." While Jill wrapped up Toots the little girl whimpered, and the sound pleased Albert—at least she hadn't gone catatonic, hadn't slipped into a coma or something. He figured she was in shock, maybe bleeding internally. "It's pretty quiet up there; you figure they've passed out?" Albert asked Jack.

"Not if they're methed up, you idiot."

"Right. Fuck." He had to pull his thoughts in line, had to pay attention. For better or worse, he was leader here and if he unraveled the kids would panic.

"Okay, here's what we're going to do. I'm gonna go out with Bobby and we're going to slip the truck into neutral and slide her down the hill a bit, away from the house. Give me about five minutes. Then I want Jill and Toots to come out and meet us."

"What about the rest of us?"

"If they don't know we've gone you'll be fine. Take off in the woods if you have to."

"I wanna go with Jill," said Ruby.

"Me, too," said Griff.

"I ain't staying with the babies," said Frank.

"Me neither," said Little Joe.

"You'll do what I fucking tell you," said Albert. "Come on, Bobby."

"Wait," said Jack. "They're moving."

"If you're shitting me—" said Albert.

"See for yourself."

They stood on the porch, looking at the cabin. It took a moment to make out who was who in the darkness. Dan, Lloyd, Ray, and Old Felicity. They talked. Dan shook his head. Lloyd hopped around from foot to foot like his boots were on fire. Sybil came to the doorway and said something, and Dan pushed her back inside. She cursed.

"What are they doing?" said Bobby in a whisper.

"I wish I fucking knew," said Albert. "But I don't like this."

Harold appeared, and pushed past the group on the porch.

"Fucking little bastard," he yelled, loud enough to be heard by the children in the cabin. "I'll huff and I'll fucking puff."

"Get ready," said Albert. "I think we're doing a runner."

"You're not fucking leaving us," Jill had picked Kenny up, balancing him on her hip. She grabbed Albert's arm. "You took sides when you let 'em in, Bert. You fucking know that."

Donna and Cindy came to the porch. Cindy tried to pull Lloyd inside. He slapped her, knocking her sideways, and both women disappeared back inside the house.

"Mama," said Ruby, peeking from the window.

Harold came back round the corner of the house. He carried something. He stood at the bottom of the steps, talking to the men on the porch.

"Holy shit," said Jack.

"What is it?" said Bobby, his hand on Albert's shoulder.

Albert shrugged him off. "It's a can of gasoline." He turned to the Jack. "Help me move that trunk."

"Why?"

"Do what I fucking tell you. Bobby, watch them. They make a move in this direction you tell me. Jill, get the kids ready."

Albert took one end of the trunk and Jack the other. They swung it into the middle of the room. Albert stepped behind it and pulled at a board, then another. They gave way with a crack and creak. He lifted out a section of the wall, a perfect square of wood and pink insulation.

"Huh," said Jack. "You think of everything."

"Hoped I'd never have to use it. You go out first. Take Toots. Can you carry her?"

Little Cathy started to cry and Kenny sniffled, hanging on to his mother's thigh. Jill rested her hand on her son's head and with the other tried to get Toots sitting up. The girl, still silent, reached weakly for her. "I'll take her."

"She's too heavy."

"She weighs nothing."

"Maybe not for a minute or two, but she's more or less deadweight. Don't argue with me, Christ! You got to help the others. Cathy's not going to be able to go for long. And you or Jack'll have to take turns carrying Brenda I guess. Joe, you, too. I'll take Toots as soon as we get out."

"Where are we going?" Jill said, handing Toots over to Jack.

"I don't know. Into the woods for now."

"They're moving around up there," said Bobby, his voice like a tightly pulled wire. "Arguing."

"Good. Keep them busy." Albert pushed Jack and Toots out the escape hatch. "The three still up on the porch?"

"No. They came down. They're just kinda standing there now. No, I think they're moving. Albert, I think they're coming this way."

"Hurry up! Get out, get out, come on, all of you." Little legs and bums and backs under his hands, pushing them, shoving them. Griff cried out as he barked his shin. "Run deep into the woods. Stick together! Stick together!" The last thing he wanted was to lose another kid to The Others. The realization he would go down fighting for these little ones struck him like a board.

"Albert," Bobby was next to him, on all fours. "You ready?"

"Go, go!" said Albert, and shoved him, then scrambled through after him. The hole was small, and it was a tight squeeze. He scraped his cheek on a nail. Now his head was out he heard voices from the front of the cabin.

"I'll huff and I'll puff and I'll burn your house down," said Harold, and there was laughter.

Maybe it was just Albert's imagination, but he smelled gasoline and sulfur. He scrambled to his feet, wiping at the blood on his cheek. The wound was deep; a rivulet trickled on his neck. Quickly, he pulled the wooden square back into place. If the others saw it, they'd know which direction to follow and seconds counted. As he wrestled with the board, he tore his fingernail. He turned, crouched low and took off. He stumbled on a tree root, caught himself and ran, blind and fast, following small figures in the pine-scented night. His fear snapped and snarled like a dog at his heels. If it got its teeth into his tendon he was done for. He could smell it—feral, acrid, and pungent. From the corner of his eye, Jack beckoned from a hollow. Albert clambered into it. The air was thick with the buzzing of mosquitoes and the sound of children panting.

"Anyone missing?" he said. His heart pounded like a maniac on the door of his sternum.

"No, all here," said Jack.

They were a pack of baby foxes in the den of rotting leaves and mud and insects, hounds on their trail. Eyes popped and blinked, the dirty faces pale and streaked. Bobby breathed hard, near panic. Albert reached out and squeezed his knee. "You got my back, right? You and me, right?"

Bobby swallowed. "Right. I'm okay."

Albert peeked over the top of the earth mound. The Others were creeping around the cabin. They must think Albert and the kids were still in there. Good. He was afraid they'd known about his 'back-door.' Harold came round the corner, pouring gasoline at the baseline. Lloyd said something to Harold and he stood up, walked back around to the front of the cabin. The sound that followed was unmistakable. He'd kicked in the door. More voices, louder, the words garbled. Then a brighter light. Orange and flickering.

No point in staying to watch his house burn down.

"They'll be looking for us. Come on."

"Sorry about the cabin," said Jill.

Bobby pointed. "Who's that?" he asked.

Something else, coming through the trees. Lights. A car.

CHAPTER TWENTY-SIX

Tom's mouth was set and his hands gripped the wheel. He forced himself to take the steep mountain road slowly. If he went off into the ditch, it was all over. As he got closer to the compound, he smelled smoke. At first he assumed it was simply one of the wood stoves, but then realized it was too strong for that. His foot pressed down on the accelerator slightly. He scanned the forest. Red-tinged light. His heart skipped and a jolt like electricity ran into his fingertips.

The truck pulled into the rutted path that served as a driveway to the main house. Fire crackled from a structure a way back in the wood, an outbuilding of some sort, he thought. Women, three of them, stood on the porch of the main house, watching him approach. A group of men—how many?—loitered by the burning building, backlit against the flames. They didn't seem to be trying to put it out. One of them tossed something in the underbrush. No sign of either Bobby or Albert. Tom cursed himself for not having a cell phone, but then doubted there was a signal up here anyway.

Tom put the truck in park and reached under the front seat, making sure the crowbar he'd stashed there was within easy reach. One of the women—the thin one—took a couple of steps in his direction. The fat one pulled her back into the house and closed the door. The fat one's face appeared at the window a moment later. Tom stepped out of the truck, leaving the door open, and faced the approaching men. Instinct told him it was important to act as if nothing was out of the ordinary here. *A building on fire? Happens all the time.* No point even commenting. It was like approaching a pack of semi-feral dogs. Calm authority. Show no fear. There were four of them. He recognized Harold Erskine—baggy old elephant—and Ray Erskine, looking ten years older than when he'd last seen him. Basset hound pouches drooped under his eyes; his jeans and stained tee shirt hung off him. It flashed through Tom's head that maybe he was sick—cancer? He had the look. Tom wasn't sure about the remaining two, who looked as unhealthy as Ray. He thought the one with those same baggy eyes was Lloyd. His cheeks, like Ray's, were sunken and all the men except for Harold had sores on their faces. Some kind of skin disease?

The men were silent, which was unnerving. They stopped their advance, but didn't stop moving. It was like they couldn't stay still, twitching like puppets. Only Harold Erskine was reasonably still—maybe he was pulling the strings.

Tom stuck his hands in his pockets, casual as anything. "I'm Tom Evans," he said.

Harold spoke up. "What do you want, Tom Evans?"

"I think my son's up here."

"Only us Erskine's up here."

"He's visiting Albert."

"I said no."

Ray—Tom was sure the man's name was Ray—ducked into the house. The other men fanned out just a little, but enough. The door to the house opened again and a plump, youngish man stepped out.

"Hi there, hi you. Who are you? I'm Sonny!" the plump man said.

"Get back in the fucking house, Sonny," said Harold.

"Do I—,"

"Get in the fucking house!"

"You don't have to yell at me," the man said as he slinked back inside.

"And you, too, Tom Evans. Say goodnight, now."

"Where's Albert?" Tom inched back toward the truck cab.

"Not here," said Harold.

"He's fucking deaf," said Lloyd. "You too old? You going deaf, Tom?"

"Maybe he's a fucking retard like Sonny," said the other man.

The burning building collapsed with a whoosh, sending a spark-storm into the night air. "You better hose down those trees," said Tom. "And I think you better tell me where my kid is."

"I don't think that's why this guy's up here at all," said Lloyd. He picked at one of the sores on his jaw line.

"Me, neither," said the one whose name he didn't know.

"I just want to get my son. No trouble." Tom reached back into the truck and pulled out the crowbar. "Not unless there has to be."

The door of the house opened and out stepped Ray. He leveled a rifle at Tom. "He's Whitford's friend. Aren't you Whitford's friend?"

Tom turned to face the gun. His stomach cramped. "I'm just here for my son."

"That's my dad," said Bobby, starting to stand and slipping in the mud. Albert grabbed him and pulled him back down. "Motherfucker! What the hell's he doing up here? He's going to get himself killed. Idiot. Idiot!"

"That's my father!"

"We're getting out of here," said Jack.

"Stop, everybody! Bobby, you are not going up there. It'll only make it worse. And the rest of you—you're not going anywhere. They'll come after you, pick you off, now or later. If not tonight, tomorrow. We've got to stay together and get out of here once and for all. Let me think. Let me fucking think!"

"He's right, and I can't take care of Toots alone," said Jill.

His cabin collapsed. *Foosh.* Gone. Ray came out onto the porch. He had a rifle.

"Oh, shit," said Albert.

"Now what, genius?" said Jack.

Bobby's father put his hands up in the air. He dropped the crowbar he'd been holding. Maybe he'd just get back in the truck and start down the mountain. Maybe if Jack ran down that way he could catch up with him, have him wait for them and drive them all the fuck out of here.

Lloyd walked over to Tom Evans and punched him in the stomach. The big man doubled over and Lloyd brought his knee up into Tom's face. Tom staggered back and then stood, roared, and threw himself into Lloyd's middle, slamming him into the side of the truck. Albert couldn't make out everything they were shouting at this distance, just "Take him out!" and "Fuck him up!" Bobby struggled to rise and Albert grabbed him again. "I will knock *you* the fuck out if you don't chill. You go up there and they'll kill you both, understand? *Understand?!*" The boy was crying, but he nodded. The other children began to cry as well, with Jack and Jill shushing them as best they could.

Tom Evans and Lloyd rolled around in the dirt for several minutes, and then Tom Evans broke away and turned toward the house. Ray sighted the gun and fired. The shot's sharp crack bounced through the trees and Bobby shrieked, holding his hands over his ears. But Tom Evans didn't fall down. The truck lurched to one side as the tire flattened. Ray fired again and sparks flew up from the engine. Tom hunched down, covering his head, while Harold yelled and waved at Ray.

"What the fuck!" Harold said, and then something they couldn't hear. "—get out now? Idiot!" Harold marched up the steps and ripped the gun from Ray's hands. He slapped him across the face. Then he turned to Tom. Lloyd and Dan stepped back.

"Ah, fuck," said Albert.

"What, *what*?" Bobby clawed at him.

"Listen. Fast. I'm going to draw them away." He was not saying this. "They'll come after me. The rest of you—get Evans's attention if you can. Get him with you." He could not possibly be saying these words. Could not possibly be thinking about doing what he was thinking about doing. There was some arguing at the house. The women had come out. But Albert knew it wouldn't make any difference.

Jill pulled his arm. "You can't be serious. Who are you, the lone fucking ranger?"

He shook her off. "But if you can't get Evans, get the fuck off the mountain anyway. Bobby, you too, you can't help him up here. I'll meet you down at the marsh, but if I'm not there, keep going. Jack, do not let Bobby get near that house! It's up to you, little brother. You and Jill."

Without another word, he took off running, scrambling up the hollow. His chest burned, his stomach burned and the voice inside his head told him he was clearly having a breakdown. *Turn right you moron*, it said, *run into the woods*, it said, *keep going*, it said. Albert skirted past the still burning wreckage of his house, moving fast now, because there was almost no time. He would get his truck, drive it right into the midst of the bastards, and hope Evans got out of the way in time. The hood of his truck was up. Wires hanging. Battery gone. *Fuck! Fuck! Fuck!*

His mind raced. Seconds mattered. Run, Spot, Run. And stop when? Then, everything slowed, as though he were watching a film of people running underwater. Bobby's face back there in the cabin, looking up at him like he was worth something just for letting those kids in. Like he was a hero or something. Stop running when? Now? Probably not, but still ...

He came out on the far side of the clearing, just back of the house. They couldn't help but see him there. "Hey, you fucktards!" He waved his arms. Picked up a rock and chucked it, hitting Lloyd in the middle of the back. "Hey, you motherfucking cocksuckers!" They spotted him. Albert turned his back, waggled his ass at them. "I'm going to burn your fucking house down, you assholes! You hear me?" He took off into the woods, glancing over his shoulder to make sure they'd heard him. They had. And here they came—Lloyd and Ray and Dan.

Past the garbage dump, past the old outhouse, and into the deep woods. Behind him they lumbered and hooted, but he was faster than they were and smarter. He'd always been smarter. His left knee hurt, but it didn't matter. All that mattered was that he kept on running, zigzagging. Branches slapped his face; brambles stuck to his hair and sleeves; thorns tore his skin. But it was only the three uncles. Old Harold had stayed behind, and Old Harold had guns of his own. There was only one thing that would get Old Harold away from Tom Evans: disruption of commerce.

Albert came into the clearing where Ray's trailer and shack stood, or leaned. Dark as a husk. Albert wanted to burn it, but how? He had nothing and he didn't want to take the time to look around inside. Voices in the brush, and barking. Fuck, they'd turned the dogs loose. That was bad, bad, bad. Grunter snapping, biting, back in time, he was back there—at the mailbox races he and the other kids had been forced to run. Run, you kids, Harold would say, while Fat Felicity stood beside him with a hickory stick in one hand and snarling, snapping Grunter's chain in the other. Grunter the wolf-dog, the kids called him. *Run to the mailbox and back. You better win, too.* Albert ran. And so did his sister and brother, Jack and Jill. His cousins ran. His half-brothers and half-sisters ran. They all ran, while the dog went lunatic with excitement, drooling and snapping, and they scratched and fought and tripped each other when they could; they climbed over each other and pushed each other's faces in the mud. Because so much was at stake. For what did you win? A day when the drunken uncles didn't come after you. A day when you didn't have to bend over and take it. When you didn't have to open your mouth and gag. When you didn't have to. You just didn't have to.

Run, you kids . . . Albert dashed, and nearly tripped on a vine. He slapped other vines out of his way, going deep, making it harder for them to follow. It had been easier when he was little. Monsters behind him. Breathing, thundering, slavering, beasts in the forest behind him. He was ten years old again, his back throbbing from the belt, his mouth full of the taste of Harold, his eyes salt-stung and fury-blind. His breath was ragged. His own sweat acrid in his nostrils. He had to calm down, not let the nightmares take over. The dogs were stupid, untrained. They'd run off after every scent, confused by all the excitement . . .

Barking. *Run, you little fucker, we're gonna find you!* Rational mind flew away like a startled owl. He was sobbing, now. But he was almost there, passing the generator they kept at a safe distance from the lab, and then he was there. The area around the trailer was littered with red-stained coffee filters, gas cans, old batteries, iodine bottles, cold remedy packets—too many to count—Prestone containers, matchbooks. He wiped tears from his eyes. He wasn't sure what he was going to do, but whatever it was, it had to make a big bang. Meth labs were notoriously flammable. There had to be matches in there, or else a gas burner or something. He'd go in, get a match, and blow the place up. They'd come running, and he'd be off down the mountain to anywhere but here. He looked behind him; saw a flashlight way off in the trees. The dogs were snarling at something, high pitched yelping—he hoped they were fighting each other or tearing the uncles to shreds, but he doubted it. He had only minutes, maybe less. A cinderblock served as a step. The door was padlocked, of course, but no troubles. He picked up the cinderblock, considered the hazards of sparks, and struck the lock anyway. The lock broke and nothing blew up. A good sign. He opened the thin door and stepped in. Jesus the smell. Like the piss of a thousand cats. Something sickly sweet. He'd never find anything, it was pitch black, the windows covered in tin foil so that not even moonlight got in. The square of gloomy light coming in the door revealed a counter covered with filth, candy wrappers, cola cans, beakers, Tupperware, more coffee filters, rubber gloves . . . he couldn't make out anything he wanted. Where were all the goddamn matches? Where was the heat source? They'd be on him in seconds and then . . . The fumes were so potent he held his T-shirt hem over his mouth and nose. He'd have to risk turning on a light. What did it matter? They knew where he was headed. He felt along the sticky wall for the switch, looking upward to see if there was a fixture. A bulb, there was a bare bulb. His fingers found the switch and as he flipped it it occurred to him it might not be wise, for there was something wrong with that bulb—there was something in it—and in the time it took for the current to travel along the wall into the strange bulb, Albert Erskine knew he'd made a dreadful mistake.

The bulb blew apart and as it did, a combination of buckshot and gasoline vapor struck Albert in the face and neck. A single spark. That's all. The trailer was already filled with gases—hydrogen chloride, phosphine, methanol, anhydrous ammonia. And then the entire trailer was filled with fire.

Albert had just long enough to register fury and terror in equal measure before his nose and mouth filled with flame, and his lungs sucked in flame, and there was no word for the pain for it was instantly beyond pain the way water is beyond wet and ice is beyond cold and nothing mattered but the pain beyond pain and then the universe was black and red and there was a moment's whirling and turning and falling into a strange dark whiteness and no way to scream for there was nothing left to scream with and then nothing to scream about nothing left at all no monsters in the forest and no more pain and nothing to fear and Albert's last thought was how different it all might have been the things he might have done and then somehow even that was all right and none of it mattered the things he'd done and he'd not done perfectly underst...

CHAPTER TWENTY-SEVEN

Harold had Tom sitting up against the side of the main house. Felicity and Meg had persuaded him not to do anything until the men got back with Albert. They didn't want whatever was going to happen to happen at the house. Too easy to trace, they said, and Harold allowed they were possibly right. What difference did a little while make, anyway?

Tom tried to talk sense to Harold, until the old man told him that if he said one more word he'd blow his balls off. And so Tom waited, his mind crackling with fear for Bobby, picturing him in any number of horrible ways—slung up to a tree, face down in the mud, in a shallow grave, cut or shot or burned. If Tom got out of this, he vowed he would kill someone. If Bobby wasn't in this house, where the hell was he? How many cabins were scattered through the woods? He wondered how long Dorothy Carlisle would obey his order not to call Carl. Wouldn't someone see smoke coming from the mountain and call the fire department? Wouldn't they come? He watched Harold Erskine adjust his testicles and spit into the dirt. Tom tried to determine if he really believed the old man would shoot him.

Then—**Boom!**—the explosion. A puff of orange and smoke over the trees.

"What the fuck?" said Harold and he looked away. It was all Tom needed. He launched himself upward and his fist connected with the old man's chin, snapping his head back, making him stumble. Tom jerked the gun out of his hands.

"Where is my son?! Where is he? You got three seconds you sack of shit." He was shaking. Shaking so hard he didn't know where the shot would end up if he fired it. He didn't care.

"Dad! Dad! Over here!"

"Bobby! Where are you?" Without taking his eyes off Harold, Tom stepped backwards until he was a good distance from the old man, and then turned to see Bobby standing at the forest's edge waving both arms. Someone else was with him.

Tom looked at the truck. Flat tire, shot through the engine. "Stay!" he called to Bobby and ran to the cab, turned the key. Nothing. Again. Nothing. All right then. All right. What now? They'd walk down. He looked to Harold. Gone. *Fuck!* Into the house? The woods? Where? There would be other guns.

"Dad! Come on, come here, quick! Hurry!"

Tom ran to his son, carrying the gun. He threw his arms around Bobby, who held on to him tightly for an instant and then pushed him away. "I'm sorry, Dad, I'm so sorry."

"Never mind. You're all right. We've got to get out of here."

"There are kids, Dad. We have to take them. One of them's hurt. Albert's gonna meet us."

"What are you talking about?"

And then he saw them. They looked up at him like small animals in a burrow—muddy and feral and battered. He imagined them baring their teeth, digging into the earth, or his flesh.

A boy of about Bobby's age stood. "There's no time. They'll come looking for us now—especially with you. We have to move. Can you carry her?" He indicated a little girl, clearly injured, in the arms of a battered teenager. "Well, can you? Don't just fucking stand there!"

"Give her to me," Tom said, and then realized he still held the gun.

"Give that to me," said the boy. "I know how to handle a fucking gun."

Tom looked at the boy, and then nodded. "Point it at the ground and keep the safety on." He held out his arms for the little girl.

"Her name's Toots," said the girl. "Be careful with her."

They stumbled and crept, trudged and dragged themselves and each other. The dark protective woods engulfed them, soothed them, made them jittery and startled them by turns. They were beset by biting insects and by shadows and all the while they went down, down, down, circling the top of the mountain and then switching back, in hairpin loops, along deer tracks and through patches of bramble and vine, following Jack's lead. At one point they heard an engine. "All terrain," said Jack. Thorns and twigs scratched their faces, arms, and hands. Their aim was to move away from the sound of voices, from the sound of ever-more distant engines, from the smell of smoke and from the glow of burning things. They were afraid of shifting winds and the possibility of wildfire.

They were small creatures sniffing the air, trying to bury themselves in the caliginous forest. Animals snuffled and grumbled and skittered past and around them, roused and unsettled by the smell of smoke, the distant crackle of burning and the unnatural nighttime herd of humans. The children did their best not to cry out when they were startled, when fingers seemed to reach up from the ground to snag their feet, or from the branches to yank their hair.

Toots, in Tom's arms, urinated in her sleep or in her unconsciousness and the warm trickle of it wet his shirtfront and his jeans and mixed with sweat and grime. Near Ivy's age, Tom thought, and the idea of it pierced him.

If Tom or Jack or Jill heard something they could not explain as animal or wind, they threw an arm out and dropped to the ground and the children, as though by prearranged signal, did the same and stayed that way until it felt safe again to move on. Once or twice they thought they saw a car climbing the mountain, but couldn't be sure, and couldn't risk coming out for fear it was The Others. They drifted and swayed around the mountain, slipped and crawled, drooping with fatigue. Little Cathy cried silently in Jill's arms. Ruby snuffled. Jill's face shone like steel when the moonlight caught it. Bobby's eyes were as wild and resigned as a weasel in a leg trap. They slithered in the mulch of old leaves and mushrooms and once an owl swept in front of them on silent wings, so ghostly and pale none of them were even sure they'd seen it.

They arrived at the marsh in due course, eyes expectant and hopeful. They waited for Albert until they could wait no more, the mosquitoes feasting on them, the children crying, and Toots's condition urgent and prodding.

"He'll find his way to town," said Jack.

They went on. Tom's jaws ached from clenching and now and then he willed himself to relax, afraid he'd crack a tooth with the force of his anxiety. His arms ached from carrying Toots, his legs ached from the pound and thud of downward walking, a slice of pain ran through his left ankle, his feet were blistered, and his skin was afire with bug bites. Vigilance burned his eyes. And then he began to sense the land leveling out and felt, more than saw, a hesitant shift in the darkness, more charcoal now than black and then more pewter than charcoal and then silver and gold, like treasure seen through the trees.

242

"We'll be on the road in a minute," he said, his voice still a harsh whisper from the night's habit.

"I'm hungry," said Rudy.

"Me, too," said Brenda, lurching along, stoically insisting on walking.

The sound of their high-pitched voices was startling. He had thought them mute with shock from whatever it was they'd been through, as was Toots, he suspected. Toots who stared at him like he was an alien thing about which she cared not at all—a new sort of moving thing, like a conveyor belt with no useful destination. She was utterly without sound, not even her breath registered.

"We're near the road. Someone will stop, won't they?" said Bobby. "A car or something?"

"Sure," said Tom.

"The family'd never think we'd dare," said Jill. "Never in a million years."

Sometime later, they came to the patch of ground that delineated mountain from not-mountain. The trees thinned. There was a patch of wetland, not too wide. They would get their feet wet, but wouldn't have to wade. After that lay a straggly swath of gravel and weeds and then, asphalt.

Tom handed Toots over to Jill. "Hold her and stay here for a minute. I just want to go look around. Give me the gun, Jack."

He began by stepping on rocks, picking his way through the wetland, but at last there were no rocks, no path, and no choice but wading into the fetid mire. His boots squelched and mushed in the bog, which smelled of rot and algae. A frog jumped from a rock and dove, panicked, in a pool of mucky water. As he stepped, Tom's feet made sucking noises, as though the very ooze was trying to hold him back, just as he was getting so close to open, two-lane refuge.

On the highway, he looked this way and then the other, squinting, trying to see if anyone was out there scouting for them. It seemed not. It was barely dawn. The world was a great still wasteland beyond the mountain. Nothing and no one as far as the curve in the road would let him see.

He gestured for the others and waited while they picked their way through the bog. They would stay along the roadside, heading south, toward town. Someone was sure to come along. They would stop for children. A car would stop. A woman, probably, a woman would stop for children. He would send Jill and Toots and the younger ones, Cathy, Brenda, Ruby, Kenny, and Griff, if there was room along ahead in the first car, to the hospital. Someone in a car would have a cell phone. There would be cell reception here. They'd call Carl. Then this would be over.

He plucked Toots from Jill's sagging arms, noted that the older girl's face was pale as aspen bark. "You've done great, Jill," he said, and she looked at him with an expression that might be taken for astonishment had it not been buried by her exhaustion.

"There's no cars," said Frank. "Where are the cars?" He scratched bug bites on his cheek and smeared dirt, making him look like he was in camouflage.

Outside the softening effect of the forest's gloaming, they looked like refugees from some catastrophe, some vanquished children's army—their clothes filthy, ripped and stained. Their faces grim far beyond their years. Pinched and pale, underfed and over-exposed kids, all of them. Tom assumed he looked as bad. His eye was blackened and he'd been blowing blood out of his nose.

"It's early," said Tom. "They'll be along. Let's keep walking."

Brenda sat down, rubbing her misshapen foot. "I don't want to," she said, her voice stubborn and flat.

At that, the rest sat down as well. Tears were close, hovering there just waiting for the slimmest invitation to settle. They had nothing to eat. No water.

"You can't stop here," said Jack. "Look," he turned to Tom, his hands out, "if we stop here, that's the end, get it? They will be coming. Don't you think they won't. You don't fucking know them. You don't know shit."

"All right, son. I don't think anyone's coming after us."

"Don't you fucking 'son' me. And if you don't think they're coming, you're out of your fucking mind."

"Mister. They are coming. They are," said Jill.

He looked into her eyes and believed her.

"I'm not going anyplace more," said Kenny. "I want to go home."

There was a small chorus of *me, too,* and *I'm hungry* and the wet and whiney sounds of a number of tantrums in the making. Tom shifted Toot's weight. Looked down the long, curving, and empty road.

"Piggy backs," said Bobby.

"What?" said Jack.

"You never had piggy backs?"

"Maybe," said Brenda, suspicious.

"It's like riding horses. You ever done that?"

"No."

"Well, come on, then. You hop on your noble steed." He crouched with his back to her and gestured to her to climb on. She moved hesitantly, as though afraid he was about to trick her. "Mount up now, on the horses. Jack and Jill, you're horses. Little Joe, you're one of the horses. Dad?"

"Good thinking, son."

"Take Cathy, Joe, she's light," said Jack.

Brenda still looked doubtful.

"Good girl," said Jill. And she urged Brenda onto Bobby's back, then lifted Cathy onto Little Joe's back and hunkered down as Kenny climbed on her own, his arms tight around her neck.

"How are we going to do the rest?" said Jack. He looked at the two remaining boys, Frank and Griff. "Who's it gonna be?"

"We're not babies," said Frank. "We can walk."

"Come on," said Jack. He blew his lips out and pawed the ground. "I'm a horse."

"I can walk with Frank," said Griff, looking at the ground, shuffling his holey sneakers in the dirt.

"Suit yourself," said Jack.

"Maybe we could switch. You go first," said Frank to Griff. "You're younger."

And so Griff climbed on Jack and they set off walking. They trudged and kept looking behind them for cars. They kicked up little puffs of gray dust from the gravel. It would be all right, Tom reasoned. They weren't even that far from town, he figured, judging from where they'd come off the mountain. Maybe three miles, maybe a little more. It was a long walk, but he was sure they wouldn't have to make it all the way. Somebody would stop.

They had been walking maybe ten minutes when a low drone behind them signaled an approaching vehicle. They stopped and turned. "Get ready to run," Jack said, "just in case."

It was a car, pulling a trailer behind it. Tourists. Camping. Out to see America with the wife and kids. Room for all of them in that trailer. Bet there'd be water, too, in little green bottles all the way from a spring in France. Tom wondered if he should step out into the middle of the road, but then pictured himself as a hood ornament. "Jack, hide that gun in the ditch! Get off to the side a bit," he shifted Toots so he could hold her with one arm, her head resting on his shoulder, and stepped out, not into the center of the road, but enough so his intention couldn't be mistaken. The sun, just rising, was to his left, and behind him, which was good. Mr. and Mrs. Middle America wouldn't be able to tell what kind of condition he was in until they'd stopped. He put a big smile on his face, and waved his hand in what he hoped was a friendly wave. "Wave, kids. Wave at them." He pointed at Toots, held his hand up like a traffic cop, telling the car to slow down, to halt, willing it to stop.

The car slowed, his heart raced and one of the kids said, "Yea!" and then the car moved out into the other lane, putting distance between them. Tom took another step out into the road, gesturing frantically. "Stop!" he called out, "Please, stop!"

The car kept moving. As it went by Tom saw a woman driving, a man next to her, and a boy in the back seat. The woman wore big sunglasses, covering half her face, and she was so fat the lenses cut into her cheeks. The little boy was fat, too, a fat white face with wide eyes and a mop of black curls. All Tom caught of the man was a glimpse, his mouth, open, lips moving.

"You said they'd stop," said Ruby in his ear as they all watched the car disappear. Her tone was accusatory and disappointed.

"The next one will," he said, although he felt he'd been punched in the stomach. They didn't stop? For kids? *What was wrong with people?*

"Welcome to the mountain," said Jack.

Tom stared at him. He'd heard it all his life.

It's the mountain. What can you do?

What can you do?

Nothing.

What can you expect of people who live like that?

Nothing.

People like that? Those people.

Them.

Us.

Fifteen minutes later, they heard the sirens. A police car rounded the bend, coming from the direction of the mountain; it slowed to a stop and the siren went silent. Carl Whitford and Elliott Blanders stepped out. Seeing the police, some of the children wanted to run into the woods again, and Tom and Bobby had their hands full convincing them the police were there to help. When they settled them down Carl persuaded Jill to sit with Toots in the back of the Sheriff's car until the ambulance got there. Then, Carl turned to Tom.

"Glad to see you're all right. We've been up on the mountain most of the night poking around. Dorothy Carlisle, God bless the nosy old biddy, called about midnight and told me what was going on."

"I didn't hear any sirens," said Tom. He stood with his arm around Bobby, loathe to let the boy out of his reach ever again.

"You never want to tip off an Erskine," said Carl. "Only makes things worse. Good thing Dorothy called, although maybe if she'd called earlier some things might have been different."

"Meaning?" said Tom, watching the deputy hand out water to the kids.

Carl glanced at Bobby. "Albert Erskine's not with you, huh?"

"He was supposed to meet us at the marsh. He never showed up."

"Uh-huh."

"He'll turn up," said Bobby. "He probably just missed us. He'll turn up."

Tom gave the boy's shoulder a squeeze. "Of course he will."

Carl just raised his eyebrows. "There's a whole herd of Troopers and DEA on the way. Fairly pissed off, too, since they had this big raid planned for next week." He shrugged. "Just can't plan for what goes on up there, I guess."

He made a call on his cell and passed the phone to Tom. "Talk to your daughter," he said.

"Ivy? Yeah, sweetie, I'm fine, fine." It was hard to say more. His throat was all closed up, his vision blurred. "Bobby, too. Sure. Bobby, too. Tell Mrs. Carlisle we're on our way."

Moments later the ambulance arrived. As the medics tended to Toots, Jill and Jack hovered nearby. Jack's face held thunder, one shoulder was cocked up, and his fists were loose but boxer-ready.

"Hey," Tom said, "it's all right, Jack. The doctors will take care of her. You go with them if you want.

Jack glared with such dark fury that Tom's jaw dropped.

"Not Hawthorne. He can't come near her. If he comes near her, I swear to God I'll kill him myself. You hear me?"

"Clive Hawthorne? Why not Dr. Hawthorne?" said Tom.

Carl took Jack by the shoulders and looked into his face. "No, not Dr. Hawthorne. I'll see to that, all right? I say so, it's so."

Jack considered for a moment, and then nodded. Tom's head spun, and when Carl Whitford's eyes met his he saw all the knowledge of the entire town piled up in his pale irises.

"Ah, Jesus Christ," he said.

CHAPTER TWENTY-EIGHT

"Be strong in the Lord and in the strength of his power. Put on the whole armor of God, so that you may be able to stand against the wiles of the devil." Ephesians 6. We fight against the cosmic powers of this present darkness, against the spiritual forces of evil. I'm calling on you here, today, right now, to take up the whole armor of God. We're winning, people, in this great battle. Lock and load for Jesus. We're winning now; the evil will be rooted out of our midst, once and for all. Yessir. It's a great shame on us, no doubt about it, all this peering in on us from the outside, but maybe we deserve it. Maybe it's God's judgment on us for not cutting out the cancer sooner. We've been talking about evil for a long, long time, people. And now we see the fruits. Right in our midst. I read to you from Mark 7, versus 21-23: "For from within, out of the heart of men, proceed evil thoughts, adulteries, fornications, murders, thefts, covetousness, wickedness, deceit, lasciviousness, an evil eye, blasphemy, pride, foolishness: All these things come from within, and defile the man." Defile our good town, people. But we're onto you now, Satan, and we say, be gone, in Jesus name! — Reverend Kenneth Hickland, Church of Christ Returning, 2009

"I believe it was the Austrian writer, Robert Musil, who said, "There is no truth which stupidity can't make use of." — **Dorothy Carlisle, 2009**

And so began Gideon's Year of Shame. It started with the raid up on the mountain, and a very sophisticated operation it was, too, with Drug Enforcement Officers and Hazmat and the Bureau of Alcohol, Tobacco and Firearms. Swat teams surrounded the compound, heavily body-armored agents broke down doors and swarmed into every cabin like fire ants. The Erskines, drug-addled and exhausted from extended methamphetamine use, never stood a chance. Fat Felicity managed to hurl a frying pan at the first agents through the door, which earned her a black eye and a badly wrenched shoulder. Sonny came out of the woods, slouched up to one of the feds and asked if anyone had a chocolate bar. Other than those two, the entire compound was sleeping when the feds arrived, bludgeoned by exhaustion and depression from the extended methamphetamine use. Erskines were as easy to round up as smoke-tranquilized, albeit still aggressive, bees. Someone had leaked word of the raid to the media, and the seven television crews who showed up shuffled around looking disappointed there hadn't been a standoff of Waco proportions. The burned out trailer was left to the people from Hazmat. Sonny Erskine led them to Albert Erskine's remains, which were buried in a shallow grave out in the woods. They were removed and cremated, the expenses covered by Mrs. Dorothy Carlisle, who took possession of the ashes when it was determined no one else wanted them.

Dr. Clive Hawthorne was far more trouble to arrest than the Erskines, screaming about his civil rights and his credentials and generally making an enormous spectacle of himself, the highpoint of which was when he vomited on the foot of a cameraman who got a little too close. The media crews, sniffing at the salacious details about to unfold, settled in for a long stay.

It was exciting for a while, lots of scandalous talk about child molestation and dead babies buried all over the mountainside and drug fiends and how homosexuals were probably at the root of it all. The churches were fuller than usual, and there was much beating of chests and vows to keep Satan in his pit where he belonged. Reverend Hickland adopted the cry, "Ever vigilant, ever vigilant against the devil!" The journalists took copious notes.

When the trials began, the children were paraded one by one onto the witness stand and one by one they told their tales. Some people even said surely they must be making some of it up for it really was too horrible, wasn't it? Children as young as twelve having babies? Babies born deformed and murdered by Dr. Hawthorne, buried in shoeboxes? Children forced to commit unspeakable acts?

Jack Erskine was the first up, being the eldest boy left alive, now that

Albert was dead, and the day he took the stand the courtroom was packed, for rumor had it he was going to reveal shocking details. In fits and starts, Jack described how his mother sucked his 'junior' and inserted her finger into his bum. Gloria, who weighed well over two hundred pounds, liked to lie on top of her little son, forcing him to kiss and caress her.

"She wetted her pussy—sorry—her vagina and wetted my rear end and started going back and forth with her fingers."

When Jack was five or six, Gloria began practicing fellatio on him, trying to give him an erection sufficient to enter her. He was too small then. Later it wasn't a problem.   Why didn't he tell anyone? The prosecutor, a brightly blonde woman from the state capital asked.

"Who was I gonna tell? They were all doing it. When she wasn't at me, the uncles were."

"The defense has questioned why you didn't try and get help for yourself and the other children," the prosecutor said. "You could have told someone at school, couldn't you? A teacher, or guidance counselor?"

Jack took a moment before answering. He looked around the packed courtroom, going face to face. Those who met his eyes dropped their gaze almost immediately. There was something in the look of the boy, implying he recognized them or something. But none of them had ever been to the Erskine compound, for heaven's sake, they'd never taken advantage of a child. Not a single one of them.

Finally Jack spoke. "We're mountain, right? We been mountain for—like—as long as anyone can remember. Hundreds of years, you know? Nobody gives a shit—sorry—nobody cares what happens to us."

The blonde prosecutor, her back as straight as a brick wall, asked the boy, "What did your grandfather say would happen if you did tell someone what was going on?"

Jack's voice was coolly matter of fact. "Said they'd kill us. I figure that's what they tried to do when Albert brought Bobby Evans up. Set fire to the cabin, thinking we was in there. Tried to kill us all. Killed Albert, didn't they?"

At which point the defense made an objection.

Many people thought the devil was surely loose on North Mountain and the testimony of Harold Erskine seemed only to confirm this. The old man sat proudly on the stand and boasted how he had screwed all the kids, male or female, whatever their age. "Up their bums or in their cunts, it didn't matter to me." Several women left and chose not to return after that.

When Tom Evans took the stand, one day in late autumn when the trees were bare and the wind was wet and chill and people were thinking about Thanksgiving just a couple of weeks away, the crowd overflowed onto the steps. Tom Evans! Saving those children—who could have anticipated that? No one had seen much of Tom Evans in the months preceding the trial and some were surprised at how drawn he was, how somber. While he testified, he held on to a silver Boy Scout whistle he wore on a thick string around his neck.

Dorothy Carlisle sat in the front row for every day of the trial, and when Tom Evans testified, she sat with his children, Bobby and Ivy. Tom's voice was low and several times he had to be asked to speak up. A rim of sweat dampened his upper lip and dark stains spread under his arms.

Toots Erskine's testimony was given in a closed courtroom.

In the end the Erskines—Harold, Felicity, Carrie, Gloria, Sybil, Ray, Lloyd, Dan, and Meg, as well as Dr. Hawthorne and several other adults who were not Erskines but were part of the extended, impossible to untangle, skein of compound dwellers—were sentenced to prison terms on a variety of charges ranging from gross indecency to rape of a minor. The sentences ranged from two years to eight years. The drug trials, held separately, would keep many of them in jail for considerably longer periods.

The county prosecutor was still trying to determine what precise charges would be laid against whom in the matter of Albert Erskine's death. The good doctor's wife, Francine Hawthorne, moved away—no forwarding address.

Everyone was exhausted when it was over and happy to see the back end of the journalists, who complained they couldn't get decent coffee and wanted high speed internet WiFi in the bed-and-breakfasts. They talked as if nobody could hear them, and seemed to be of the opinion something was intrinsically wrong with Gideon, that what happened there couldn't happen anywhere else.

It was a relief, although no one admitted it, that the Erskine children were fostered out of the county. It was best all round, wasn't it? The children wouldn't want to be reminded, surely, and well, now it was all over, better to put it in the past. Dorothy Carlisle petitioned the court to be allowed to act as a foster mother, but was refused on the grounds of her age (which made her go very red in the face indeed), and because she had no experience with even normal children, let alone these psychologically damaged little people. It was odd, Mrs. Carlisle wanting to be so involved with the Erskine children, but then she was always a little off, wasn't she? Apparently, she'd gone to New England somewhere, or at least that was all anyone could get out of Tom Evans.

Shortly thereafter a pastor in Michigan was arrested for keeping four underage Korean girls in cages in his basement. Sex slaves, apparently. The devil was everywhere, and luckily for Gideon, he had a roaming eye.

By the time people sat around their Thanksgiving turkeys, they saw no reason to keep going on about it. There was no reason to keep rehashing it. It was all around them. Guilt settled over the town like a fog, in which was heard the whispers of children.

It is the middle of a rainy December now and at the Evans house, Bobby and Ivy are in the kitchen, doing the dinner dishes. Tom lets Rascal out. The street is slick and shiny. A car sits parked in front of the house and at first, Tom thinks nothing of it. Rascal barks four times. Rabbits, maybe. When he lets Rascal back in the dog shakes off a spray of icy water and Tom, warding off the water with his hands, glances up at the car again. Rascal runs into the kitchen to be with the children. The light over the car's front seat is on. Odd, Tom thinks and he wonders if it's some goddamn journalist wanting one last statement. Only as he closes the front door does he realize who is in the car. He stares down at his hand, gripping the handle so tightly his knuckles whiten. His heart thuds against his ribs and his mouth is sawdust. He turns the handle, and then lets go of the door knob.

No, he thinks. Nope. Uh-uh.

He goes to the dark living room and stands at the window. He closes his eyes. He will not look, not yet. She can see him, if she's looking. He opens his eyes and there she is, standing by the passenger side, wearing a beige coat. She is smoking. He wonders if someone else waits in the car, but no, she is alone. Even though it is dark, he sees her quite clearly in the light from the street lamp. Her skin looks blotchy and older, the lines running from nose to mouth deep and shadowed. She has circles under her eyes and her hair is pulled back. For the first time, he sees her not as she was that day so long ago in New York City—a young girl with an air of erotic mysticism about her—but as a tired woman, disenchanted and frightened by the future. A part of him wishes he loved her less for this lack of enchantment, this failure of glamour. Tom's heart trembles, cracks, becomes as transparent as a soap bubble and as fractured and sharp as the inside of a prism. Forgiveness is hard, perhaps impossible. The desire for revenge is effervescent. The desire to feel her in his arms is molten.

He won't go to her. She has to take the walk. She has to come in the door without any help from him. He will not make it easy on her. He watches her. But she does not move. Why could she never, not even now, take responsibility for what she wants? She tosses the cigarette onto the ground, and annoyance flashes through him. She was always careless. She grinds it under her booted heel.

Tom goes back to the front door. He can do that much. She's come this far, after all. He opens the door and stands, backlit. Her hands go to her mouth, as though she is stopping herself from speaking, or from begging, perhaps, or from screaming. Tom does not want her to beg or scream. He wants her to stand in that unforgiving light and say whatever is true. Could it be so complicated, just the truth of where her home is and where it is not? But perhaps, like some bird confused by the sharp and sparkling lies of skyscraper lights, she has become confused.

They stand like that. And then she walks round the car, gets in and starts the engine. As the car moves away, he wonders if he is going to run after her and is slightly surprised when he goes no farther. Within seconds, she is nothing but red taillights on a rain-sparkled street. He goes back in the house and closes the door. He leans his head against the cold wood. There is a clatter and shriek in the kitchen and then Ivy laughs.

"Bobby, you're splashing me! Stop it! Dad! Ooh, I'm gonna get you! Dad! Help!"

Bobby dashes past him, thundering upstairs, and Ivy runs after him, a wet sponge in her hands. Rascal scampers up the stairs, barking. Ivy and Bobby are laughing. Tom inhales, holds it, and exhales. He turns the brass switch on the door, locking it.

"Watch out, you two, I'm gonna get you!" he says, and runs up the stairs after them.

Nantucket suits Dorothy. She lives in a gray shingle bungalow in Cliff, where it is an easy walk to the Hinkley Lane Beach. She has a rose garden. The inside walls are white. There is a view of the sea from the kitchen, her bedroom, and the living room. Her furniture is blue and white. She has a fireplace and a radio, but no television. The many shelves are filled with many books. She chose Nantucket because of the sea, and the idea of freshness, and the fact it is a small island, and she thinks it would be hard to lose anyone there. She has made a few friends, among them the fabulously named James Coffin Starbuck, a sixty-five year old Nantucket native from an old whaling family. He has just the sort of leathery, bleach-eyed face you would expect from someone with that name and history. James owns a whale-watching boat for tourists, but today Dorothy is his only passenger. She carries with her a bronze urn of ashes. The air is rich with salt and sea and the breeze is icy and clean on her face. When the time comes, she uncaps the urn and shakes it, releasing Albert's ashes to the wind. They ascend and twirl, spinning as if confused, unsure of where they are, and then the wind catches them and flings them into the salty, sun-sparkling air as though it were all so easy, as though flying away takes no effort at all.

ACKNOWLEDGEMENTS

Writing is a solitary pursuit; nonetheless, there are many people to thank for this novel's birth. My thanks to DEA Agent Eric Brown of Camden, New Jersey, for his insights into methamphetamine production and the sorts of booby traps agents find in meth labs. My thanks to Lily Krauss for encouragement and for turning my scribbled map of Gideon into something that felt real for me; to Susan Applewhaite, Barry Callaghan, Michael Crummey and Holly Hogan, Cecilia Davis, Lynne and Van Davis, Larry and Miranda Hill, Isabel Huggan, Holly Johnson, Krystal Knapp, Lisa Pasold, Michael Rowe, Harriet Stewart, Sister Rita Woehlcke, and others who shone a light into the darkness. Thanks also go to my agents, Kim Witherspoon and David Forrer at Inkwell Management, who helped shape the manuscript. My unending gratitude goes to Duff Brenna; without him this novel would have remained in my desk drawer; and to David Memmott, for being such a wonderful publisher and for continuing his support of literary fiction.

Although a work of fiction, this book was inspired by events surrounding Nova Scotia's Goler Clan. Some of the dialogue during the trial in the final chapter is taken from transcripts I found in *On South Mountain – The Dark Secrets of the Goler Clan*, by David Cruise and Alison Griffiths. I want to acknowledge my appreciation to Cruise and Griffiths for their book.

The sermons at the beginning of various chapters came, in some cases, solely from my imagination. Others are direct quotes. The sermon quote by Rev. Charles G. Finney is taken from an article published in *The Oberlin Evangelist*, September 29, 1852, entitled "The Salvation of Sinners Impossible," and the one at the beginning of Chapter Ten (although attributed in the text to the fictional Rev. Joshua Cotton), is excerpted from another Finney article in the same publication, entitled, "The Wrath of God Against Those Who Withstand His Truth," December 9, 1857. The quote at the beginning of Chapter Seven comes from a sermon delivered by Rev. Sam P. Jones on August 2, 1885 at a camp-meeting near Cincinnati, Ohio. The poem quoted at the beginning of Chapter Fourteen is excerpted from "Tom Gray's Dream," written by Illinois poet Retta M. Brown. The quote at the beginning of Chapter Nineteen is excerpted from a pamphlet first published in 1960 by Herbert W. Armstrong, *The Ten Commandments*.

Lastly, I thank my husband, Ron, because every time I get lost in the dark woods he finds me and leads me home.

Photo by Helen Tansey

ABOUT THE AUTHOR

Lauren B. Davis is the author of the bestselling and critically acclaimed novels, *THE RADIANT CITY*, a finalist for the Rogers Writers Trust Fiction Prize; and *THE STUBBORN SEASON*, chosen for the Robert Adams Lecture Series; as well as two collections of short stories, *AN UNREHEARSED DESIRE* and *RAT MEDICINE & OTHER UNLIKELY CURATIVES*. Her short fiction has been shortlisted for the CBC Literary Awards and she is the recipient of two Mid-Career Writer Sustaining grants from the Canadian Council for the Arts. Lauren reviews books for *THE GLOBE & MAIL* and *THE LITERARY REVIEW OF CANADA*, leads monthly *SHARPENING THE QUILL* writing workshops in Princeton, New Jersey. For more information, please visit her website at: www. laurenbdavis.com

For information on
other Wordcraft of Oregon titles,
please visit our website at:
http://www.wordcraftoforegon.com

CPSIA information can be obtained at www.ICGtesting.com
261356BV00002B/1/P